George Forsythe is that classic definition of a first-time author; a creative shut-in in his late twenties with an over-active imagination and far too much free time on his hands. An engineer by trade, or at least according to what it says on his university diploma, George's first foray into the world of literature is marked by his penchant for taking the eccentricities of everyday life and blowing them out of all proportion to create stories of madcap misadventure, that are nothing if not just a bloody good time.

George Forsythe

# WHAT HAPPENS ON EARTH

AUSTIN MACAULEY PUBLISHERS™

LONDON * CAMBRIDGE * NEW YORK * SHARJAH

A CIP catalogue record for this title is available from the British Library.

ISBN 9781398443235 (Paperback)
ISBN 9781398443242 (ePub e-book)

www.austinmacauley.com

First Published 2023
Austin Macauley Publishers Ltd®
1 Canada Square
Canary Wharf
London
E14 5AA

To all the MAGA hat wearing, lion hunting, lip-filling, conspiracy-theorist, bible-toting, selfie-obsessed, game-streaming, super-spreading crackpots out there, from the bottom of my heart, thank you. Thank you for giving me so much material to work with and for making Planet Earth the most fabulously easy place in the entire cosmos to lampoon with such joyful abandon. Keep doing what you're doing guys, without you the world would probably be a much safer, more advanced, kinder, more respectful place but Christ, wouldn't it all be so boring.

This might undercut everything I've written on this page a bit but a genuine thank you to my family, and to my wonderful girlfriend Niyatee, mainly for moulding me into the kind of person who delights in finding the funny in the tragic. And a big thanks to Cameron Kirckaldy of cameronkirkcaldy.com/ for designing such an epic book cover. A true friend and a very talented graphic designer, who I hear is available for freelance work. I can't believe I had to plug my mate's company in my own book, but I suppose I deserve it for losing 7-0 to him at FIFA.

# Prologue

"Vectron's knees! That sun is bright!" Weezle groaned, as her seven eyelids slowly squeaked open and huge clumps of crumbling biological detritus fell away like rust from some ancient, corroded hinges and the light from an unfamiliar yellow sun painfully flooded her optic pathways. The throbbing pain in her lower vertebral tendril also immediately suggested they were somewhere cold.

Why did the High Council only ever send them to planets at least ninety million miles from the nearest star? Surely, after nineteen thousand duty cycles, she deserved a posting in the temperate zone. Surely there were data samples on the pleasure beaches of Tropicana-IV that needed collecting. At least there, her tendrils wouldn't ache like they'd been pulled through the pointy end of a Vrenexes' anus. It was an unpleasant reminder of just how far past her prime she was. It was fine for her co-pilot Dennis, he still had plenty of cycles ahead of him before his tendrils began to ache in the cold weather.

"Dennis," she squawked through her two-foot beak as she groggily pulled herself up off the cold dimpled floor of the ship's command centre, "You OK?"

"Define OK," came the coarse reply and she saw Dennis drag himself back up into his co-pilot's chair using his lumpen, sledgehammer knuckles." I phased right out of my seat and my bones feel like they've been put back in all the wrong places. When are they going to get this technology right?"

"I know. I miss the days of cryo-freeze," Weezle wheezed in reply as she painfully crawled back into her seat at the ship's controls.

Once again, she found herself wishing either she had opposable thumbs or that they had been given a ship more ergonomically designed for someone of her species. She could have put in a request for a transfer to another more suitable craft, but she would have preferred a stint in the gladiatorial pits of Skuchar, fighting sex-deprived laser-tigers, than an afternoon filling out transfer request forms at the S-DMV.

Stars have formed from loose Hydrogen particles, given life to entire solar systems, burnt out and gone supernova and cursed the same solar systems to a painful oblivion, in the time it takes an S-DMV clerk to ratify and stamp a simple transfer request. It was easier just to let Dennis press all the buttons.

"Dennis, bring up voice commands."

Dennis carefully rapped the command console with his oversized, beefy digits and the central display flashed into light. A swirling vortex of colours flowed across the jet-black surface and a voice rocked through the cabin, making the tender part at the base of Weezle's tendril throb even worse than before.

"Good morning, Vietnam!" it boomed in a timbre that was a just a shade too manically enthusiastic for either of their tastes. This was unusual behaviour for what was supposed to be an emotionless, pre-programmed intelligence.

"What in the name of science are you on about?" Dennis roared, "And turn it down, you blasted O-I. We're both a little tender at the moment."

"Frankly, my dear, I don't give a damn!" the ship jubilantly replied.

This bloody thing was on the fritz again.

"Cut that nonsense out!" Weezle snarled through her clenched beak. Can a beak be clenched? I don't know. You figure it out!

"Status report!"

"I do apologise, Captain," the ship replied, the swirling colours on the screen pulsating, practically fornicating, in time with its maddening sprightly inflection. "I have been studying the past and future culture of the world we now find ourselves on and I find myself rather fond of these things, the inhabitants refer to as movies, or talkies, if you're particularly fancy."

"Never mind that, give me the highlights," Weezle replied, trying hard to keep her cool in the face of this bloody O-I's relentless, unwarranted optimism. "Where and when, are we?"

"We find ourselves on the planet 45-90DXTY-9042," it replied.

"Very catchy," Weezle sighed. "That's going to be fun to remember. Make sure you write that down, Dennis."

"The locals refer to it as Earth."

"Earth?"

"Correct."

"As in ground or dirt?"

"Indeed."

"How inventive."

"I thought so too."

"So, this planet is populated."

"Yes, a group of single-cellular, worm-like creatures known as Nematodes seem to rule this planet. They make up over eighty per cent of the population."

"By sweet Vectron's hungry ghost! They must rule the planet with an iron fist! Are they a majestic warrior species or perhaps a group of scientifically advanced clairvoyants?"

"Nope, they are mindless, microscopic, parasitic worms that infest almost every multi-celled species on the planet, often living inside the genitals and consuming the fertilised embryos of the host. Pulling up the specs now."

In front of Weezle and Dennis, like a double page spread from a gag-reflex-inducing, pop-up picture book, materialised a three-dimensional hologram of a disgusting tubular creature consuming some other poor single-celled organism from the inside-out. Dennis took one look at it and involuntarily expelled some of his cerebral-spinal fluid from the second mouth at the base of his spine.

"For the love of progress, Dennis!" Weezle groaned, "Not in the ship, please."

"Sorry, Boss," he replied, gagging and rubbing his butt cheeks like a sore tummy. "That gross stuff always gets me after phase-travel."

"How do these repulsive creatures rule this entire planet? Biologically speaking, they look pretty basic."

"Well, it seems they employ these primate descendants, called humans, to do most of the day-to-day stuff. You know, culture, civilisation, construction, that sort of thing. This allows the nematodes to sit back and consume foetuses all day long."

"Not a bad plan actually," Weezle mused. "Bring up the specs for these human creatures."

The ship then brought up a hologram of something really, truly disgusting. It was some kind of semi-hairless bipedal mammal, with a horrid lumpy appendage dangling from in between its two lower limbs like a shrivelled, biological knapsack. Dennis took one look and promptly expelled more fluid onto the floor.

"Oh, sweet science no!" he gasped, struggling to stop a third expulsion.

He had to be careful, a third dollop of his spinal fluid would likely melt through the hull of the ship into the cold-fusion room below.

"I mean, for the love of progress, go hairy or hairless! Just pick a lane."

"Quite."

"What is that little wrinkly sack and that tiny dangling tentacle for?"

"Apparently, those are what they use for reproduction."

"But why have them hanging out there where any predator can bite it off?" Weezle asked. "And it looks far too unappealing to be used for sexual stimulation."

"Indeed, but apparently they must put it inside the female in order to reproduce."

"The male goes *inside* the female!"

"Indeed. It appears to be the same with most complex life on this planet. Except for a form of aquatic life called fish—and some particularly randy frogs."

"How in Vectron's name has life managed to survive on this shit-hole?"

"Even with all my advanced organic processors I cannot find a logical answer to that question."

"Chalk it up to one of the mysteries of the universe then."

"Chalking—chalking—chalked. We are now up to five hundred and twenty-seven million, three hundred and sixty-six thousand and one unsolvable mysteries of the universe."

"Hmm, getting quite high now. Is that in total?"

"On this mission."

"And how long have we been travelling now?"

"In the context of this planet—about three weeks."

Weezle was unaware what a week was and assumed it must have been a really, really, really long time, so she pressed on with the issue at hand.

"Where and when are we then, in the context of this planet?"

"Time co-ordinate: Earth year 1947. Space co-ordinate: Earth, Roswell, New Mexico."

"Neither of those things mean anything to us," Weezle sighed. "Why do we even bother? So, you're saying the planet is only one-thousand, nine-hundred and forty-seven solar cycles old?"

"The planet is approximately eight billion cycles old. The human Earth calendar seems to run from the last time an alien visited their world."

"Aliens have been here before?"

"Quite. Although this one was not sent by the High Council. He was a Doxart, who tried to convince the Earthlings to be nice to each other."

"What happened to him?"

"They nailed him to a cross and left him to die in the sun. So, you know, be careful out there."

"Noted."

"Speaking of being careful," Dennis chipped in. "I'm detecting a life form approaching. We'd better move the ship somewhere more remote."

"O-I, activate phase-travel," Weezle commanded.

As the ship's O-I glacially spooled up the phase-drive, William Brazel pushed his way through the cornfield at the J.B Foster ranch, hacking away at the ears in order to get to the source of the bright light he had spotted appearing not a few minutes earlier, like a heavily inebriated, bipedal moth.

He staggered towards the ship, clutching his nearly empty bottle of bourbon, convinced he was about to walk in on a secret Nazi experiment and that it was his time-honoured civic duty to go and beat some dirty Kraut's brains in with the blunt end of a glass bottle. Like some corn-fed, red-faced, God-loving cross between Steve Rogers and Francis Begbie. After all, it was obvious the government had shipped all those crazy Nazi scientists over to the states to help them with their mind control technology. Thank God he didn't listen to his wife and always made sure to line his hat with tinfoil.

"Read the lifeform's brain waves, Dennis. Tell me what its intentions are?" Weezle ordered, as they sat in a state of excruciating tension, cursing their outdated ship and it's ancient phase-drive, which had a loading time that could be measured in eons on some planets.

"It's odd, boss. I can't get a reading on it. Its mind seems to be shielded somehow."

"Impossible, no race in the universe has brain-shielding technology. Our scanners came straight from the Galactic High Council."

"I'm telling you, boss; I can't read it."

Outside, powerful micro-alpha brain scanning waves were bouncing harmlessly off of the tin-foil lining William's straw hat.

"My god. These humans are more powerful than we thought. O-I, get us out of here, now!"

"Confirmed, phase-travel initiated."

William Brazel fell into the clearing like a dropped sack of plastered spuds, just as the last of the alien ship disappeared in another flash of red light, leaving only the remnants of a smashed tool shed and a whole heap of flattened corn. He dragged himself haphazardly to his feet, caked in dry mud and decorated in loose kernels. He took another swig of his bourbon, surveyed the scene of his triumph against the foreign invaders and let out a long, satisfied belch.

"Yeah, you better run! Goddamn Nazi sunofabitch!"

Weezle and Dennis came to once again moments later, this time, thankfully, still strapped into their seats, around eight hundred and fifty Earth miles West of Roswell. They looked out across the Earth landscape at yet another lifeless desert; both were beginning to suspect the whole planet was one giant sandpit.

This desert, however, was pock-marked with small, forlorn shrubs which were accompanied by some nasty, prickly organisms that just stood there motionless, casting long groping shadows across the desert floor and seemingly keeping watch over their more diminutive brethren.

"O-I, where are we?" Weezle groaned wearily.

"This is the Earth location known to the locals as Nevada. I have divided the landmass into three thousand separate Areas for your convenience, we are currently located in the fifty-first Area."

"I don't see how those conveniences me, O-I."

"Trust me, it'll be a thing going forward."

"Let's just get outside and collect the samples we need so we can get off this science-damned sandpit of a planet."

"Very well. Preparing bioform suits now."

Weezle and Dennis unbuckled themselves from the cockpit seats and trotted over to the equipment lab, where the ship was busily phase-printing the bioform suits they would use to explore the planet's surface undetected. Neither of them was much looking forward to dressing up as one of those reprehensible Nematodes but cosplaying as repulsive parasites was often one of the required sacrifices of the job.

A moment of silence for all the lawyers out there.

As they stood over the printer, watching the sub-atomic reconstruction lasers play with atoms, molecules, proteins and cells like biological Lego bricks, they were confused to see pieces of hair, nail and testicle begin to appear.

"No, don't tell me—" Dennis moaned.

"O-I!" Weezle barked, "Why are you printing one of those disgusting human suits?"

"Unfortunately, you will have to blend in as humans on this mission," O-I responded. "The Nematodes are too small to work as a suitable disguise."

"Fine, science damn it!" Weezle replied, "Can you at least cover up the genitals?"

"Luckily, it seems the humans have these things called 'clothes' for just such a purpose."

"Well, thank the lords of progress for that! They must find each other's bodies just as repulsive to look at as we do."

"Indeed, they do."

After a few minutes of uncomfortable shimmying into their primate-themed wetsuits, Weezle and Dennis walked down the runway of their ship, cloaked it to ensure no Nematodes would stumble across it and report it to their superiors and set off into the desert to collect their samples. Now, wearing their printed bioform suits, they looked to the casual observer every inch the regular unassuming humans. Where once there were beaks and tendrils and powerful foot-knuckles, there was now pathetically soft and weak pinkish flesh, covered in disturbingly random patches of wiry hair.

It confused Weezle that, despite both dressing as members of the same species, they somehow looked so different. Her suit had blonde hair no longer than a few Earth-millimetres, while Dennis' had jet-black hair that flowed almost to his suit's waist. These 'clothes', it must be said, were an elegant solution to the cold and the lack of biological insulation, one of the human race's apparently many evolutionary missteps.

As a stray eyelash turned tail and decided to poke itself directly and painfully, into Weezle's eyeball, it did occur to her that it was possible humans were one of the few species in the universe designed by one specific, conscious creator. Something as clever as natural selection and evolution would never churn out a life form as pointless and as stupid as this one. Weezle's musings, however, were cut short by a worried question from Dennis.

"Did you lock the ship?" Dennis asked.

"I'm pretty sure it locks itself."

"How sure?"

"Like, eighty percent. It locks itself if the key goes a certain distance away."

"I thought we didn't spec that option, you said it was an unnecessary expense."

"No, I'm sure I got it. It only added two quarks a cycle to the lease price."

"I'm almost sure you didn't, boss."

"Fine, science damn it! You want me to prove it? Here!"

Weezle walked back to the ship, uncloaked it and pulled on the door handle. It opened.

"See, told you," Dennis cried triumphantly.

"That's only because I still have the key in this funny little pocket," Weezle groaned, reaching behind her to check the key was indeed still tucked safely between the two cheeks where she had left it.

"Then how do we check if it locks itself, if every time you walk back, it unlocks again?"

"You're going to drive me crazy today, you know that. Here!" She threw the keys to Dennis, who recoiled slightly after seeing where she had been keeping it and pulled the handle again. It opened.

"What did I say?" Dennis asked smugly.

"What are you even worried about? It's cloaked and we're on an uncharted planet. Who's going to come along and steal it?"

"—Good point."

"Just get to collecting the bloody samples."

They trotted further out into the desert, dutifully collecting their speciments under the cover of the gathering dusk. Some soils and dirt; some spines from one of the motionless prickly animals; some leaves from the shrubs, a confusingly cute and simultaneously horrifying hairy creature covered in wiry fur with eight legs and a bulbous backside. Then, as they passed over a low ridge of cragged rock that was blocking the horizon, they saw what the most ridiculous thing was possibly they had seen in all their endless cycles as recon scouts in service of the Galactic High Council.

About eighty Earth-miles away, sat on the flat, otherwise featureless desert plain, like a glowing, penis-shaped straw in a glass of cold Bovril, was a truly mesmerising collection of shoddily constructed buildings, draped in the most outrageous display of lights they had ever laid their thirteen collective eyes on. Through the Zoom and Enhance function on their suits, they could discern what appeared to be signs over thirty feet high, in a language which neither of them understood and neither of them could decipher any reasonable purpose for.

Creatures, which they recognised as humans, were staggering up and down a wide street in thousands, whooping and cheering and drinking quantities of strange liquids that far exceeded the requirement for the survival of any species, even in an arid desert environment such as this, before collapsing in the street or

14

disappearing back into one of the brightly lit buildings. Living alongside the humans were hundreds of large metallic creatures, possibly cyborgs, that prowled the streets on round, rotating appendages while emitting a cacophony of maddeningly high-pitched cries, while also excreting a constant stream of noxious gases.

How these two species lived alongside each other was not immediately clear to Weezle. It was evidently clear that they were slowly killing each other, and the world around them, yet they appeared to be unconcerned by this fact. Their relationship was clearly symbiotic, almost completely co-dependant, and Weezle knew immediately this species would be soon marked for extinction. It looked like utter chaos and yet, both Weezle and Dennis felt an inexplicable but powerful urge to investigate. Something about the lights and the noises and especially the smells, awaked in them some primal urge to indulge themselves.

"What is that?" Dennis gasped. "It's so—"

Unfortunately, there was no word available in any non-Earth culture that adequately described the chaotic majesty of what they were gazing upon.

"The nematodes must have made the humans create these structures in their honour," Weezle replied. "It's the only logical explanation. From what I can see, none of them serve any useful purpose and the humans down there simply stagger around and cavort without reason."

"This would be a great insult to the High Council," Dennis mused. "The waste! The inefficiency of it all is—unforgivable!"

"Indeed, and it is not our current mission to study the Earthling culture. We should continue collecting the samples and return to the ship."

"Yes—Yes we should do that."

"—"

"—"

"You want to go check it out?"

"—Fuck Yes."

"Fuck? What does that mean?"

"I'm not sure—It just felt like the right thing to say in the moment."

And so, like moths to the flame and like so many humans before them, they surrendered to their impulses and stumbled through the desert towards that sea of lights and noise and debauchery. As if guided by the same higher power that pulled all the humans into the city's orbit, they found what seemed to be a path through the desert where the sand and shrubs had been cleared away and replaced with a long strip of flat, black material that felt good and solid under their new, ten-toed feet. They continued on, drawn with a new, ravenous hunger towards the lights and as they did so, they passed a red and blue sign which read:

"Interstate 95–Las Vegas".

# Chapter One

"Vodka and coke please, my love."

The living scarecrow making the order was old Mrs McTavish. And when I say she was old; I mean so old that if you walked past her in the street your first thought would be:

"Holy shit, that woman is old!"

She was currently perched precariously, in front of Greg's bar, on the heap of old scaffolding that she dragged around with her in the absence of her recently departed husband. The sole purpose of the last few months of Mr McTavish's life seemed to have been to keep Mrs McTavish on her feet after she'd had a few too many at The Boatyard and Greg had harboured genuine concern for the old lady's wellbeing when he had passed away. After all, she was never going to stop drinking. He need not have worried.

The Zimmer frame that now kept her bony old arse off the floor was doing a marvellous job in Mr McTavish's absence. In fact, she barely seemed to notice the difference. Greg had even caught her conversing lovingly with the old thing a couple of times when she thought no one was listening.

He didn't need to ask how she took her drink; he'd taken enough bollockings from the auld coot during his first week working in the pub to remember. Vodka and Diet Coke in a tall glass with one ice cube. Even though she never specified as much, Diet was what she desired, she obviously didn't want to spoil her figure in her twilight years. Maybe the Zimmer frame was one of those shallow types that would go looking for a younger, thinner model if she started packing on the pounds in her gams.

The singular ice cube was an endlessly distressing factor to Greg; it wasn't enough to chill the drink, yet she insisted it be present, like a five-year-old who needed his rubber ducky in order to take a bath. However, if two ice cubes were to somehow find their way into her glass, like bringing an uninvited plus one to a private party, all hell would break loose. She would rant and rave of wild conspiracy theories that usually involved Greg concocting a scheme to rip her off by filling her glass to the brim with ice cubes large enough to sink the titanic, thus depriving her of space in the glass for her precious Diet Coke.

She also seemed concerned that the glacial temperatures created by two cubes would freeze and shatter the pink fortress of oversized gums housed within her wrinkly old face, which Greg noted seemed to be getting bigger every day, as if her teeth weren't falling out but slowly being consumed and converted into more gum, like a monster from an Irvin Yeaworth classic.

As you can probably tell, Greg did not like Mrs McTavish very much. He also did not like Willie, the lazy alcoholic postman who took up permanent residence in the corner booth whenever he wasn't delivering letters to the other ten buildings in town and often when he was supposed to be delivering letters as well. The one advantage of having this dilapidated delivery boy reside in his pub was that Greg could just get him to hand over his mail in person, instead of walking around the town, knocking randomly on doors in order to work out which house Willie had mistakenly delivered his mail to this week.

He did not like Janet, the woman who ran the garden centre, (which was the town's one notable business aside from all the AirBnb's) and whose true passion in life was poking her green fingers, nose and any other part of her anatomy in everyone else's affairs. Apparently, the world of domestic horticulture didn't offer up the kind of juicy scandal required to keep her entertained. To be fair to her, Willie kept delivering her celebrity magazines and tabloid turds to the wrong houses, so she had to get her daily dose of gossip somewhere else.

Then there was the Mayor (real name unknown, as he insisted on being referred to by his official title); a fat walrus of a man who never let anyone forget that, for the last twenty-four years, he had maintained the dubious honour of presiding over a bustling metropolis of one hundred and forty seven people, three hundred and nine sheep, eighty-six chickens, one ruined castle that was given historical landmark status and was the only reason the town of Struinlanach even still existed, two local and often-frequented dogging sites and one fat Labrador called Barney; thereby proving that it really is the incumbents who hold all the power.

Thank God for Barney, who lay snoring and occasionally farting in the corner of the pub, Greg loved that dog; he was never in danger of turning rabid if Greg put one too many ice cubes in his water bowl.

There were other colourful characters to be found in the town of Struinlanach to be sure, as long as you stuck to such monochromatic colours as white and cream or eggshell if you were feeling particularly exotic. Let's just say the locals were tourist-averse and weren't particularly enthused about the sudden interest Outlander had generated amongst Americans in regards to the Scottish Highlands.

I'm sure if you were a retiree, who wished to spend your twilight years reading in an armchair, as you had reached the age where even the notion of physical exertion was enough to make you soil yourself, it would be a lovely place to live. Cobbled streets, hanging flower baskets, mountains and rivers in the background to stare at while you slowly sip on endless mugs of milky tea; it's a pensioner's wet dream, assuming they're still capable of having such things.

The problem was that, to Greg, being back here now felt like skipping ahead to the last few seconds of a porno, after the climax, when everyone is just lying on the bed cuddling while the spunk dries on the bedsheets; it looks very pleasant and relaxing but there's not a lot of action going on below the waist anymore. He hadn't mixed a cocktail in eight months and no, despite what his manager Bobby believed, a lager-shandy does not qualify as a cocktail.

He hadn't showered in three days, washed his T-shirt in four or changed his underpants in six. It was 2 p.m., he was deep into his fourth whiskey of the shift, his shaggy uncut hair was creeping uneasily down past his shoulders, and he had an unnoticed piece of pasta from his dinner, the night before, stuck in his beard like a bauble hanging on the world's greasiest Christmas tree. I think it was fair to say he had reached a professional and hygienic rock-bottom.

Pouring a tall glass of Diet Coke with a single shot of Smirnoff in it, Greg's life satisfaction was at an all-time low. He brought it over to Mrs McTavish, who seemed to have already put away a couple of drinks at home, based on the way she was talking absent-mindedly to her inanimate replacement husband, barely registering Greg's presence as he plopped the drink down in front of her. She simply raised it to her wrinkled old lips and continued with her one-sided conversation. Greg returned to his watchful post behind the hefty old slab of dark walnut that was the bar at The Boatyard.

Why Bobby had decided to call this crematorium's waiting room The Boatyard, Greg had never been able to fathom. The nearest body of water where you could conceivably sail a boat was seventy miles away at Loch a Chroisg and even then, you'd be just as well swimming, given that with a decent arm you could probably skim a stone from one side to the other.

Greg had taken to calling it The Zoo, what with the number of stuffed animals crammed into the place. No less than four stag's heads hung against the back wall (which Bobby claimed to have shot in a single sitting, but which Greg knew all too well were bought from his brother's ex-wife, who also hung them up for him).

There were also two foxes, one of them looking like it had taken a finger up the rectum right before being shot in the face, a badger, eight squirrels, three crows and one incredibly fat cat, which had been Bobby's pet before Barney the Labrador, and whose Garfieldian proportions suggested to Greg, there was a real danger of Bobby letting Barney eat himself to death. The rest of The Zoo was typical old man pub fare.

Plastic brass effect accents festooned in greasy fingerprints; red leather booths, long since torn to pieces, that probably started life in the seventies in LA on an independent porn set; rickety wooden tables; fucking fabulous looking ashtrays that harkened back to the glory days of being able to smoke inside but now sat sad and unused and unfortunately, just making the rest of the furnishings look even more dilapidated.

The smell of damp sawdust hung heavy in the air and only just about masked the scent of stale of beer from the uncleaned lines; that Bobby insisted were only refreshed once every two months so as not to waste beer cleaning them every week.

Mayor McMayorface sat snoring over a half-finished pint of bitter at the table at the far back of the pub, next to the fireplace, looking remarkably like Barney in human form. Any second now he'd likely fart himself awake and have a long-overdue cardiac episode and conk out right there in the pub; just another mess for Greg to clean up later. Bobby was in the back office, probably flicking through his ancient nudie mags, being the randy wanker that he was, while being so technologically inept he hadn't yet managed to decipher the complex world of online pornography.

Greg settled down into the semi-meditative/drunk state that was necessary to survive the early shift at The Boatyard. If he allowed himself to think too much during these extended periods of inactivity, he was afraid he'd lose all hope completely. The worst part was the lack of company, the early shift only required one bartender, given that the schoolkids with their fake IDs wouldn't come around to pester him till at least 7pm, which was the only time the pub ever became busy.

There was only one person in the bar that night whose company Greg begrudgingly admitted he wasn't totally averse to. Kyle, who, as you may have deduced from the name, that sounded like Bam Margera's favourite brand of hair gel, was an American. Californian, to be exact. Greg, despite his less than stellar history with those of an across-the-pond persuasion, actually got on well with Kyle.

That night Kyle was sat at his usual spot at the end of the bar, drinking steadily, with just enough effort made to the conversation so as to appear social but not so much as to be irritating, just the way Greg liked it. He was drinking a pint of heavy, dark ale while Greg decided to help himself to yet another whiskey.

"How many is that today, Greg?" Kyle asked without looking up from the bottom of his pint glass.

"It's about, let me think, none of your business." Greg half-heartedly retorted as he tipped the liquid lazily down his gullet. "And why are you getting on my case? You're drinking right now as well."

"It's my day off and I'm just having one while I keep your depressed ass company. I'm going hiking with Melissa soon anyway."

That's right, Melissa. Kyle and his unbelievably gorgeous girlfriend who, for reasons totally unknown and that Kyle had neglected to explain, had moved from California to Struinlanach, a couple of years before and had immediately made an entire township feel pale and unhealthy and inadequate by comparison, with their tanned skin and blonde hair and presumably very picturesque genitals. The most annoying thing was how pleasant they were; it really made it hard to hate their guts.

"Did I mention we got engaged?" Kyle asked, again eyes still rooted to the base of his pint glass.

"No, I don't think so," Greg sighed, then almost as an afterthought he added, "Congrats, I guess."

Kyle lazily threw the last of his beer down his gullet then wandered behind the bar and put the empty glass in the glass-washer; he figured it was a more reliable method than hoping Greg was eventually going to do his job and clean it up himself.

"You're a nice guy, Greg—deep down—probably. But you make me fucking sad to look at you right now."

Greg lifted his bloodshot eyeballs to face Kyle's annoyingly chiselled features; the rest of his face refused to move an inch away from his whiskey glass. The piece of macaroni quivered as if it was about to fall and then changed its mind and nestled once more into his greasy beard.

"And why would that be?"

Kyle just sighed and patted Greg's shoulder, then quickly removed it and wiped the sticky stuff that had been on Greg's T-shirt onto his jeans.

"It's a big old universe out there, bud," he said. "Don't stay cooped up in this shithole all your life or you'll miss it all."

"I tried that already," Greg sighed. "That big old universe kicked me square in the nuts and sent me right back here again."

"You never told me what the fuck happened to you." Kyle mused as mischievous light danced across his sapphire blue eyes, "Why not, is it embarrassing?"

"You show me yours and I'll show you mine, surfer boy."

Kyle chuckled and began to head towards the door.

"Where have you got to go all of a sudden?" Greg called to him.

"Hiking with Melissa, remember?"

"Oh, yeah, that's right."

"And I've got some friends coming to visit tomorrow, so need to call it an early night tonight. I probably won't be in later."

"Yeah, fine. Go enjoy your perfect life with your hot fiancé and I'll just sit here and get plastered."

"You do you, buddy," Kyle laughed. "But don't get too drunk now. Eve will be working later, right? I keep telling you, you should ask her out. Will you at least do that?"

"Jesus, all right! Just fuck off now, ya wank!"

Kyle left the pub, then wandered round the side to the window next to the bar, banged on it so loud Greg nearly shat himself and dropped his whiskey and mouthed the words, "ask Eve out" to Greg before vanishing.

Greg mouthed the words, "suck ma fat boaby, ya radge," but he was already gone.

Thank Christ in Heaven that Eve had never left. She and Greg had gone to school together, not that they ever had much of a relationship back then. She was the girl with her shit together and Greg was the one with this shit permanently stuck in the fan. While she had been studying, passing exams then heading off to medical school, Greg had been seriously working on his pallet, gaining a deep and very meaningful understanding on the nuances of alcohol from a very early age. Not that is was much of a transferrable skill.

In fact, Greg's passion for the swally was often quite detrimental to his other studies. Really, standing there behind that bar, half-pished at two-thirty in the afternoon, he was exactly where he belonged; he just wished he was still somewhere a bit more exotic than Struinlanach.

Greg was rather pleased to discover, upon his less-than-triumphant return, that Eve had settled there also, becoming the primary physician to a vast horde of elderly hypochondriacs and one obese Labrador. I'm not saying she was the only doctor in town or even the most experienced, but it appeared her boss and Greg's were cut from the same cloth, given that they were incredibly adept at the subtle art of delegation but apparently not much else.

Despite her doing the workload of two people, she still somehow found the time to come into The Boatyard and help Greg out on the occasional shift when the place actually got busy. Greg helped himself to another dram of Glenfiddich twelve year; nice enough to be drinkable but not so fancy that Bobby would give him a bollocking—on the rare chance he managed to take his hand off his tiny tadger for long enough to come and check up on the bar.

The whiskey was good and Greg had to admit, the unfettered access to free booze was one bonus of working here. The last place he worked would have crucified him for drinking on the job. He really hoped there was an influx of tourists tonight, it was holiday season after all, houses in the area were selling like hot cakes for AirBnb's and posh toffy historians love a drink just as much as the Neds do, they just spend ten times the money on fancier booze to get the same amount of drunk. (Really, why is drinking half a seventy of single malt by the fire considered any classier than chugging a bottle of Buckfast on the train?) Then, at least, Eve could come in and help him out.

7 o'clock rolled around and Bobby called from the back office to tell Greg he'd be pulling a double shift and closing because Paul had a migraine and couldn't come into work. Greg knew it was a load of shite, the spotty wee prick would be at his mate's place smoking pot and playing video games, lucky bastard. But Greg didn't mind, what else was he going to be doing tonight

anyway? Plus, he knew the booze cabinet at his house was drier than Jacob Rees-Mogg's Erotic Memoirs.

He was beginning to worry it was going to be a quiet one but reliable as ever, the same group of twenty school kids that appeared every Friday burst into the pub with the kind of hopeful, deluded enthusiasm that suggested they sincerely believed they were going to get served this week; despite Greg knowing all of them by name and knowing all of their birthdays off by heart.

They were good kids though and Greg knew they were just bored. You would be too if you were sixteen and stuck in this place on a Friday night. Mostly he'd just serve them soft drinks and slip the occasional half-shot of voddy in there just to give them something to sip on. He sympathised with their plight and their presence in the pub gave him an excuse to ask Eve to come in because he was 'overwhelmed'.

There was never any worry that she wouldn't come in. Every Friday for seven months Greg had texted her to ask for her help and every Friday for seven months she had said yes. God only knows why Bobby didn't just put her on the roster. At seven-thirty she glided in through the front door and for the briefest of moments, Greg didn't hate everything about his life, although he wished he hadn't drunk so much whiskey before she arrived as there were no mints at hand and he could already tell his breath smelt worse than the unwashed stuffed cat stinking up the back of the bar.

As she stepped in through the door, dressed in her favourite Freddie Mercury T-shirt, her hair matted and chaotic from her shift, all Greg could hear in his head was, "She Bangs the Drums" by the Stone Roses. She skipped up behind the bar and Greg took his customary split second to drink in her features before giving her a hug. Her untamed, jet-black hair, her hazel eyes, her cute button nose, naturally bronzed skin. It was a fucking delicious cocktail.

She had some Latin blood in her and was about as exotic among this ocean of ginger, freckly, pasty white Scots as a Bengal Tiger in a petting zoo. Greg's favourite thing about her though, was her staunch refusal to fully shed the punk rock chrysalis the rest of us ditched round about the same time we left puberty behind. She had the Queen T-shirt, the ripped jeans and Converse sneakers, she even played the goddamn drums. It was all just too much.

"Mrs McTavish is back," she chuckled. "Don't her and Zimmer make such a cute couple?"

"I know. Couple goals, right? I need to find me a lassie who looks at me the way she looks at that bit of scaffolding."

"Maybe you need more achievable goals, that frame is way more handsome than you," she laughed. "I think you can probably find someone who loves you as much as Willie loves that booth though."

"Very funny," Greg replied. "And gross! You know how many times I've caught him 'loving' that booth? Anyway, Hi!"

"Hey."

"Hospital good?"

"The usual. Forty-seven dead today of old age, one lady crumpled to dust before my very eyes."

"Mrs Cunningham?"

"Of course."

"Well, it was long overdue. At least, they won't have to cremate her."

Eve laughed. Her beautiful, feminine laugh that wasn't some annoying ditsy giggle but a proper belly laugh that still sounded attractive. It was like running water. Greg wished that was the sound he could wake up to in the morning, but he suspected recording it to use as an alarm might come off as a tad sex-pesty.

"Was Kyle in earlier?" Eve asked, spying the open glass washer with one lonely pint glass inside it, wondering why it was all alone and hadn't been cleaned yet.

"Yeah. Apparently, him and Melissa got engaged."

"Oh, that's amazing! Good for them."

"Yeah," Greg sighed. "Good for them."

Eve could tell the talk of other people's happiness was bringing Greg down further, so she decided to change the subject.

"Have you been serving these kids booze again?" she asked him. Her raised eyebrow made her look like Greg's mum when he was nine and she caught him sneaking gin out of the liquor cabinet and refilling the bottles with water.

"Just a wee bit, they've probably had less than a shot each," Greg protested. "If they wurne in here they'd be outside pissing in the fountain or shagging in the fields. Would you have them out there having unprotected sex and getting cow shit in unsanitary places?"

"Well, the sex bit doesn't sound so bad," Eve replied with a wink and Greg felt himself go slightly weak at the knees.

He wished he could tell if she was flirting or just being friendly, although in his heart he knew it was the latter. There was no way someone like her would be seriously interested in a career alcoholic/aspiring sheepdog like him.

"Just make sure they don't get too drunk. Or you'll have to explain it to their mothers again."

"Yes ma'am," Greg replied.

He agreed the last thing he needed was to have one of these brat's mothers at his door demanding why her seventeen-year-old son had thrown up in her Petunias again. These are the pains of living in a town where everyone knows you as the only bartender.

As the night wore on, a few more party animals drifted into the pub looking to get crazy with a pint of bitter and a good book by the fire on a Friday night. Alice Sutherland and her husband Richie came in and had a domestic in the bar. Apparently, Richie had discovered Tinder and had been messaging some lassie from two towns over and Alice had found out.

As you can imagine, she had not been best pleased. Not only because the clatty wee bastard had been trying to stick his link sausage in some other lassie's breakfast roll, but also because the 'slag' was from Broughiegain and the level of prejudice between the two towns ran long, hard and deep. Apparently, some clan leader had shagged another clan leader's goat up the bum as a prank, some three-hundred years ago, and the townspeople had quite never gotten over it.

Not that Alice was any better, everyone knew she had been slipping into the back office for months and giving Bobby a good seeing-to. Why she kept bringing her husband into the bar every Friday was a mystery to Greg. Anyway, one shouting match, a hurled ashtray and two broken pint glasses later, Greg was irritably forced from his stupor to eject them back out onto the cobbles.

Barney and The Mayor slept through the whole thing. The rest of the patrons were the usual mix of tradies, visiting historians and husbands desperately escaping their wives for a few hours (who were then annoyed to discover their wives had beaten them to the pub in a desperate attempt to escape them first). It was going to be another typical night in the Boatyard, until those three unusual gentlemen fell through the door just after midnight. As you can imagine (since their dramatic entrance marks the end of this first chapter) they were most unusual, most unusual indeed.

# Chapter Two

When I said the three unusual gentlemen fell in through the front door of The Boatyard, fell is what I meant. They looked like they had been enthusiastically practising for their WWE debut when they collapsed in a soggy heap on the ugly old carpet like a group of ragtag, interchangeable dwarves—and they woke up poor old Barney with a shrill bark and a stinking fart. Don't worry, he didn't have a heart attack; he was asleep again by the time the three newcomers dragged themselves, dripping and squelching, to their feet, so no harm done. Spoiler alert, no dogs are going to die in this story, I'm not a psychopath.

The way the three lads moved, suggested to Greg that this was not the first establishment they had frequented that night. Their unconventional gaits and erratic flailing limbs put Greg in mind of a pre-matricide Bambi on an icy pond, as if there were some communication issues going on between their brains and their extremities. Out-of-towners, to be sure; out-of-countriers, far more likely; time travellers, a distinct possibility.

The first fellow looked like he was auditioning for the lead on the next series of Outlander. Around his bottom half was hung an impressive curtain of tartan armour. Not the kind of cotton, monochromatic, fashion statement kilt you'd wear to a hipster's wedding but the sort worn by William Wallace to do battle with the English, with material so thick it could shrug off a direct hit from a Redcoat's musket. Up top he wore a waistcoat, so moth eaten and weather beaten it could have been one of Robert the Bruce's hand-me-downs, on top of a loose-fitting cotton shirt and a cravat, the first time Greg had seen such an item worn unironically.

Every item in the ensemble was emblazoned with a different tartan pattern, which painted the impression of a modern-day, clan-fluid Jacobite. Topping all of this off was a classic Scottish bonnet nestled on top of a big, round, ruddy-faced head with curly ginger hair sprouting in great thickets from every orifice. This man was tall, a good six-and-a-half feet minimum, meaning he had to duck his huge ginger noggin to pass under the heavy-set wooden beams that held up the poorly maintained roof of The Boatyard.

The second fellow could not have been more different. He was the Danny DeVito to the first chap's Arnold Schwarzenegger, standing no higher than the first man's chest and looking more like he had been carved from a cup of chocolate pudding than a slab of marble. His whole body appeared to jiggle and bounce as he walked, like he was literally made from jelly but he looked anything but the jolly Santa archetype you might be picturing in your mind.

His skin hung off his face like it was victim to an additional, previously undiscovered force of gravity, turning his mouth into one enormous scowl that, try as he might (and it didn't look like he had much interest in trying), he was unable to lift into something more genial. His clothes were a shocking contradiction to his face, a scattershot mish-mash of styles and colours that looked like he had run through the discount section at TK-Maxx and put on whatever he had come into contact with first.

Maroon corduroy slacks, a purple and green snow jacket that seemed to come straight from an eighties snowboarding movie, black dress shoes and a woolly hat with a green bauble on top. It was as if he was trying to dress for every conceivable social situation at the same time and failing at all of them.

It was pretty clear the third member of this travelling circus hailed from across the pond. Flip-flops, long socks, a sea of beige and green khaki, pockets too numerous to count and the always-essential safari hat. It appeared this particular American had clearly decided that the attire for the African savannah was equally as applicable to the Scottish Highlands.

His movements were sporadic and erratic, as if his brain had to chair a committee and have an in-depth debate on the merits of each action before his body agreed to undertake them. He also seemed to have a nervous tick, whereby one of his legs would twitch rebelliously and he'd almost instinctively punch himself in the thigh, perhaps it was some form of Tourette's.

The one chink in Greg's American impression of him was the fact he looked more like an overgrown stick insect that your typical rotund Yankee tourist. A sideways glance and you might mistake him for Stephen Merchant, although the enormous pair of Aviators covering most of his slim face made it harder to tell.

The three of them teetered up to the bar, twirling on their heels as they went, seeming to drink in every micron of information presented to them. The stick insect in the board shorts had the most enormous camera hanging around his neck that Greg had ever seen and yet, he was currently taking photos on not one but two phones housed in three-foot selfie sticks that he brandished like rapiers as they wobbled their way up to the bar.

The Last King of Scotland, as Greg had classified the heavy set, tartan-clad ginger in his mind, marched up to Greg and slammed an enormous paw down on the counter.

"Where is the proprietor of this fine establishment?" he thundered down from on high, in a voice that would have emasculated Brian Blessed or drowned out the speakers at a Linkin Park concert.

Greg blinked—then blinked again. He wasn't usually so thrown off when it came to dealing with rowdy customers but there was something about this red-headed tartan Viking that was ever so slightly unnerving.

"You mean you want to see the manager?"

"Is he the one that can provide three weary travellers with refreshment?"

"Well, I guess that would be my job."

"No, no, no, my good man. We require the innkeeper, the barkeep, the master of liquor. The spinner of tales, quencher of thirsts, douser of sorrows."

Greg was about ninety percent sure he was the bartender at The Zoo (he had learned from experience never to be one hundred percent certain of anything after drinking seven whiskies) but he was starting to feel he wasn't going to be able to offer the services these freaks were looking for. There were definitely some kind of weird kinks at play here. Maybe Bobby had discovered a new fetish in one of his magazines.

"If you fetch us the man who might provide us with three, I believe you call them, flagons of, I believe you call it, ale."

Greg was now beginning to suspect these guys were involved in some sort of live action role playing situation and this guy was just the Daniel Day Lewis of LARPers—or more likely he was just an American trying to blend in and he thought this was how all Scottish people talked.

"Listen, if you guys want a drink, I can serve you. The manager's in the back and he doesn't like to be disturbed." (While he's balls deep in this week's FHM anyway.)

"Wait—so, you're the proprietor of this fine menagerie?" Ginger giant asked, in a clearly bemused tone that Greg found mildly offensive. "You're not, the serf or, if you will, sawdust hucker?"

"Well, I do occasionally huck sawdust," Greg begrudgingly admitted. "But yeah, I'm the man behind the bar."

"But, your attire?" Ginger replied, looking worryingly at Greg's stained jeans, ratty T-shirt and macaroni beard accessory. "You don't look anything like the pictures in the brochure."

"What pictures?" Greg probed.

Internally, he guessed he must have been on the money with the American theory. They'll have seen some travel brochure, showing pictures of Scottish pubs with an enormous, bearded, Sean-Connery-in-Highlander-esque character dolling out great wooden buckets of mead; and got it into their heads that all licensed establishments fit the same archetype.

He had some previous experience with American ignorance, which helped soften the blow a bit but the fact they thought his job in this shitty bar was nothing more than mopping up vomit and bagging up Barney's turds lowered his rock-bottom even further. He was one blood-stained rat stick away from basically being Charlie Kelly, but without all the adorable quirks. There was a can of paint lying in the corner of his living room, maybe he could run home and drink that.

Luckily, Eve, who had until now been observing the scene play out with a combination of amusement and genuine curiosity, chose that moment to step in and end poor miserable Greg's suffering.

"What'll it be then, gents?" She enquired.

Instead of the customary drink order, the ginger golem took one look at her and suddenly dropped onto one knee, bending his head so low he nearly baptised himself in one of the puddles of spilled lager on the floor.

"Your majesty," he said, keeping his eyes glued firmly to the fag-burns that pockmarked the floorboards, as if he was not worthy to look upon Eve's heavenly features. "I, but a humble serf, would ask nothing of one such as yourself."

"Excuse me?" Eve replied, confused but obviously enjoying the sight of a giant man-mountain grovelling shamelessly at her feet.

"A Queen does not serve the pauper," Ginger giant replied, still not moving from his position on the floor. Willie the Postman was now eyeing him with increasing curiosity from his usual position in between the cushions in the corner booth.

"A Queen?" Eve laughed. "I'm no Queen."

"But—your garment?" he responded, pointing one of his enormous sausage fingers at the T-shirt Eve was wearing. It was a simple black V-neck but was emblazoned with the Queen logo and a picture of Freddie Mercury in full Live-Aid getup that she had bought when she had been to see them play at Murrayfield a couple of years before.

"What, this? It's from a gig. You know Queen, the band?"

The giant was on his feet and beaming into Eve's face by the time she had finished her sentence.

"Apologies, my lady. A minor misunderstanding of your cultures, I was not aware of this Queen musical ensemble. I simply gazed upon your beauty and mistook you for royalty."

He gently grabbed Eve's hand and kissed it in a show of chivalry from a bygone era. He had a certain lightness of touch and a surprisingly gentle aura for one so fucking enormous. Eve blushed. Greg was really starting to dislike this guy.

"So, are you wanting something to drink then?" he snapped irritably, impatient to get these nutters away from the bar and into a booth, in the absence of an enormous butterfly net.

"Indeed, we do, my good sir. I believe we will have three flagons of mead if it pleases you?"

Christ on a cracker; these guys were either actual time travellers or spies from the liquor board, here to check if Greg was one of those bartenders who was irresponsible enough to serve someone so obviously inebriated. He began to worry they would notice the group of school kids huddled in the booth next to Willie. Not worth taking any chances.

"No mead, I'm afraid pal. We're not one of those hipster bars. We've got a lovely line in local Lagers (Tenents) or a few guest ales (Bobby's bathtub home brew and a couple of Weatherspoons rejects)."

"No mead? Why, that is unexpected," Ginger mused as he pawed that enormous growth of red forest sprouting from his chin. Then, almost as a casual afterthought, he asked one of those questions no one should ever really be asked outside of a Michael J. Fox movie.

"What year is this, sir?"

"What—What year is it?"

"Oh, my apologies, I do not know. I thought perhaps you might."

"I might what?"

"Know what year it is?"

"You thought I might know what year it is?"

"Yes, sir. Oh dear, perhaps it is a well-guarded secret."

"The year?"

"Indeed."

"A well-guarded secret?"

"Oh, I'm afraid I don't know if it is. I thought perhaps you might be in possession of the knowledge."

"Oh, for God's sake!" Eve cried out. "It's 2020!"

Ginger's giant's brow twitched; the corner of his mouth contracted uncomfortably. "2020?"

"Yes!" Greg and Eve cried at once.

"Right—Oh dear—If you would excuse me for just one second."

Ginger Giant then hurriedly turned to his compatriots, who until this point had been standing behind him in almost perfect silence. The rotund, wobbling gnome had barely moved but occasionally seemed to cast what looked like a longing glance at the snoozing Mayor who was still passed out in the corner, while the stick insect in safari get-up had been frantically scribbling in a notebook and regularly pounding himself in the thigh so hard it was a miracle he had any hip bones left.

The three of them huddled together and talked in hushed whispers for a few seconds, while frantically pointing at notes in stick-insect's pad, like lost tourists arguing over a map of a foreign city. Eventually, Ginger turned around to face Greg again and spread his arms wide in a show of humility.

"My good fellow, I offer my humblest apologies," Ginger boomed. "It appears some of the information we have been provided is perhaps a touch out-of-date. If you would but excuse me for just a moment."

Greg, irritated at being mistaken for a janitor but nonetheless now beginning to enjoy the performance, was all too willing to oblige.

"By all means, mate, take your time."

What happened next, Greg looked back on as the moment he knew there was something genuinely wrong about these three unusual fellows. Like the moment you go back to a girl's flat at the end of a date and find she has six snakes slithering across the floor of her bedroom.

The Ginger Giant stood up straight, his head barely missing one of the wooden cross beams and seemed to go into shutdown. His eyes glazed over, open but not receiving, nor giving any information. It was like looking through a window with the curtains drawn on the inside. His body stopped all functions, not just walking and talking but he also appeared to cease blinking, breathing, twitching or shaking, as though the very vibrations of his molecules had momentarily stopped.

It looked like he had gone into a deep hypnotic trance and just as Greg was about to say something, he came out of it. As suddenly as it had stopped, his body re-started all vital functions, his eyes re-focussed and he once more turned to Greg with that enormous broad grin on his face.

"Sorry about that, pal. Now, where were we? Aye, that's right, drinks. We'll take three pints ay Tenets, one Glenmorangie, one Balvenie Doublewood twelve year and one Laphroaig. Cheers."

Greg's mouth dropped open and stayed there. The gravitational force pulling the little jiggly fellow's jowls to floor had jumped ship and attached itself to Greg's lower jawbone instead.

The man's voice had completed changed. Where once there was a big, booming Brian Blessed baritone, now there was a modern, unmistakably Glaswegian drool, as if James McAvoy had taken Brian's place at the intercom inside this man's head. As usual, Eve didn't miss a beat. She had the drinks laid out on the bar top by the time Greg had picked his jaw back up off the floor.

"Sorry about the confusion there, pal," Ginger said, seeming to note Greg's air of mild bemusement (understatement of the millennium). "Just having a wee laugh with ye. Didne mean any offense."

"Aye—You're all right, mate. None taken."

No words were exchanged for a few seconds. These moments happened often when Greg was working behind the bar. Tourists from Southern pastures would often venture their way into The Boatyard expecting some hairy Jacobite draped in tartan and war paint to regale them with tales of daring and adventure in the Scottish Highlands. How disappointed they were to find Greg, a skinny, unwashed hipster reject who had about as much interest in making conversation with the patrons as the Mayor did in actually getting off his fat arse and running the town for once.

They would acquire their drinks, then wait patiently at bar, staring expectantly at Greg for some titbit of local folklore, which never failed to never materialise. At first, Greg suspected Ginger was waiting for more of the same, the way his big grey eyes wedged into the lines on his ruddy pink face were staring at him, yet this felt different.

Ginger's expression was not one of impatient expectation but of genuine interest, as if the sight of Greg standing there behind the bar in his black T shirt and faded jeans was entertainment enough. Ginger took a long swig of his pint, his eyes never dropping from Greg and never losing that sense of wonderment. Greg suddenly had a sense of how Joe Exotic's tigers must have felt—right up until the moment they had their brains blown out by a crazy redneck with a pink revolver.

"Can I help you with something, mate?" He asked.

"Oh—um, yes, that's right," Ginger stammered, beckoning the stick insect, who was now taking pictures of the sleeping Mayor with a DSLR the size of a Howitzer. The insect trotted over and showed Ginger something on his notepad.

"Ah yes, of course," Ginger triumphantly declared, then turned back to Greg, positively bristling with excitement. "We wanted to know, how do we get to the Talisker Distillery from here? Our friend, whom we haven't seen in quite some time, is getting hitched and we wanted to get him some of his favourite whiskey before we see him tomorrow."

For anyone reading this book who is as clueless in regards to geography as our (spoiler alert) disguised alien friends here, the Talisker distillery is located on the Isle of Skye; about a hundred miles and a small stretch of open ocean away from that dank little pub in Struinlanach in which they currently found themselves.

"The Talisker Distillery?" Greg asked, wondering if the whiskey lounging in his belly had maybe affected his ability to hear somewhat.

"Yes, we heard it was close to here somewhere. We thought we'd pick our friend up a couple of barrels—bottles, for the ceremony. He'll be needing a drink after it all, I can tell you."

Greg glanced sideways at Eve to make sure he wasn't going crazy but she was off up the other end of the bar, making sure Mrs McTavish hadn't died in the arms of her beloved Zimmer frame. It turned out she was just taking one of those old-person naps that look a bit like a mild, alcohol-induced coma.

"You'd be better just getting some from the supermarket mate," Greg replied. "It's a bit of a trek to get to the Talisker distillery from here."

"A trek? Like an adventure?" Ginger asked, his hair now almost standing up on end with anticipation. "Is it located somewhere out in the wilderness?"

Greg was starting to move away from his LARPing and ignorant American theories and instead, began to suspect these guys had escaped from one of those hush-hush loony bins you never hear about in the news.

"No, I mean it's far away from here."

"How far?"

"Jesus, I don't know. A hundred miles maybe."

Ginger seemed to consider this for a second. The aura of electricity that seemed to surround him subsiding momentarily, like a light turned down with a dimmer switch. The brain underneath all that ginger hair, which was substantially larger and more evolved that Greg was giving it credit for, was working things out. A hundred miles, comparatively speaking, was but a stone's throw away and yet it was much, much further than he had anticipated.

"That's further than I thought. I didn't realise the Isle of Skye was that big?"

In Greg's mind he was now going over probabilities of his own. He was now settled on 70% escaped lunatic, 25% acid trip and 5% he was being fucked with. Normally, the likelihood of this just being some mad rocket taking the piss would have been much higher but the sincerity in this man's face made it impossible not to believe he was genuine.

"The Isle of Skye? We're not on the Isle of Skye."

Immediately, Stick Insect and the multicoloured slab of jellied depression stopped examining the stuffed foxes in the corner and looked straight at Greg with the expression of someone who was just informed they needed to have an emergency prostate exam.

"We're not?" Ginger cried.

"No. How did you think this was Skye?" Greg replied, "You're Scottish."

"I am?" Ginger puzzled, looking over to insect who nodded in confirmation. "Yes, that's right, I am. Yes, um, sorry mate. It's been a hell of a week, we're pretty new to this plan—I mean—this area—and we've been on a bit of, I think you call it, a bender."

Well, if there's one thing Greg could relate to, it was going on an excessive bender and finding yourself somewhere far, far away from where you were supposed to be. That basically summed up his life.

"No worries, man, we've all been there. Have you never been further North than Glasgow before now then?"

"Yes, never further North than Glass-cow. Yes, that make sense, doesn't it?" Stick insect again looked at his notepad and nodded.

"So, we'd be better of using transport to get to Skye then?" he asked.

"Aye, you're not gonna be able to walk it from here. You can drive out tomorrow, should take about two and a half hours."

"I don't imagine it would take that long," Ginger chuckled. "Anyway, thank you for the drinks, my friend. Do you mind if we take our drinks to one of these viewing booths you have over there?"

Viewing booths? Did these guys think this was some kind of peep show? Although, the red, questionably stained, leather furniture did suggest such a thing was not out of the question. Maybe Mrs McTavish would be willing to get up and give the lads a spin around her Zimmer frame.

"No mate, go for it. If you need anything else, just shout."

Ginger beckoned to his friends, neither of whom it's worth noting at this point had uttered so much as a squeak since they fell in through the front door. Ginger squeezed his way into the booth and the three of them huddled round their drinks like mad conspiracy theorists discussing the possibility that squirrels from outer space were planting secret cameras disguised as nuts in oak trees or something equally ridiculous of that *Cough*, QAnon, *cough*.

Greg watched them for a few seconds to make sure they weren't about to set fire to anything or assault another customer. The way they seemed to absorb every inconspicuous detail, from the leather seats, to the empty packet of nuts discarded in an ashtray, to the bubbles rising in their drinks, was like someone who had been locked away for fifty years with no outside contact suddenly being released into the world, with Stick Insect recording everything in that little notepad of his.

Greg found himself oddly fascinated with the way Stick Insect moved. The schlubby character seemed to melt into his seat and Ginger Giant was content to sit still and stare at his drink but Insect was constantly moving. His legs, in particular, were writhing and twitching relentlessly, as if they wanted to walk away and leave the rest of him behind. However, every time they tried, he would punched himself viciously in the thigh, the twitching would subside, and the leg would slump uselessly to the floor.

As odd as the scene was, Greg was satisfied that the pub was not in any immediate danger of being burned down or turned into a hostage situation, so he returned to the warm interior of his whiskey glass as Eve returned from doing her rounds and stood next to him. She poured herself a Hendrix over ice with just a splash of tonic and a twist of cucumber and propped herself over the bar next to Greg. Now that's a proper drink, Greg thought to himself; no danger of her gums shattering like glass at the thought of two ice cubes.

"They're a funny bunch, aren't they?" she chuckled as she took a sip of her gin. Greg couldn't help but notice the way she always closed her eyes and paused for a moment after taking a sip while she appreciated the flavour.

"Really? I didn't notice," Greg replied with a smirk. "You know, they thought we were on the Isle of Skye."

"Seriously?"

"Aye. Usually it's only Americans that are that bad at geography but this guy is definitely from Glasgow. Probably one of those guys who's never left the same part of Paisley where he went to school."

"Then, what about the other two?"

"No fucking idea. They haven't said a word since they walked in. And the ginger guy did the weirdest thing right before he ordered his drinks."

"What?"

Before Greg could get into his wild theories as to why Ginger Giant had gone into temporary shutdown mode in the bar, a horse, gravelly, kind of arse-holey voice cut through the heavy silence of the pub like a rubbish lorry collecting the bins outside your house at five in the morning.

"Ho! Greg! Get these bathrooms cleaned, ya lazy bastard! There's pish all ower the floor!"

Fucking Bobby. Greg clenched his fist around the almost empty whiskey glass in his hand, so hard it nearly shattered. He had cleaned those bathrooms at the start of his shift and he knew full well that fat prick had just went and fire-hosed the floor of the bathroom with his own particularly rank and yellow brand of piss. That man could piss swimming in a pool and somehow still get it somewhere where someone would step in it.

Greg took a moment to savour the mental image of him shoving his whiskey glass up Bobby's fat arse, wide end first. He thought better of it though, without this job he'd have to start paying for drinks again.

"I'm watching the bar!" Greg yelled back, knowing the excuse wouldn't fly but he enjoyed playing the game he liked to call, "Poking the Big, Fat, Wanky Bear," nonetheless.

Bobby came lumbering into the bar, his drooping jowls, patchy scruff and pronounced underbite making him look like diabetic bull terrier. He obviously hadn't showered in a few days and his horrendous attempts to look like a respectable business owner by wearing a tight-fitting purple shirt and copious amounts of gold knock-off jewellery did not help matters at all; especially because they were covered in various stains of questionable origin.

"Never you mind the fucking bar!" he snarled as he waddled up to Greg. "I'll watch it for five minutes. You just get in there and clean those bogs."

Greg was taller than Bobby by a good five inches but the shorter man had the aura of a Begbie-esque psycho, who wouldn't think twice about stabbing somebody with the pointy end of a broken whiskey bottle, so Greg saddled up his mop and went through to the bathrooms to clean up the fat bastard's mess.

Greg's suspicions were confirmed and then some. There were more recycled pints of cheap Lager on the floor in that bathroom than there was cocaine in Tony Montana's rec room. The smell alone came close to compelling Greg to add some whisky-flavoured icing to the ammonia cake mix but he managed to hold it down and got on with the glamorous job of transferring piss from floor to bucket. It was then that one of the three stooges decided to make an appearance.

The bulbous, depressed, chunky-monkey in his thrift-store coat of many colours, stood silhouetted in the bathroom doorframe. He didn't have the same sense of urgency typically exuded by the average punter after six pints of Bobby's cheap piss-lager.

As he opened the door he stood, studying the male sign on the door, his face furrowed in concentration and frustration so deep you could have fit a pack of Uno cards in his skin folds. It was as if he was trying to decipher the meaning of this strange symbol, as an archaeologist might decipher the meaning of some ancient hieroglyphics and whether such a symbol might apply to him. Granted, these days, the male/female divide isn't as clear-cut as it used to be but the sheer level of brainpower being applied to solving this mystery seemed a tad excessive.

He eventually elected to enter the lavatory and tottered over to the first stall, walking through the stagnant puddle of urine and mop water as if it wasn't even there. Greg kept his head down and stuck to his mopping, he sensed that the Ginger Giant was the friendly one of their group and he didn't fancy the notion of a conversation with this Pierce Morgan lookalike with the personality of a bowl of cold rice pudding.

The miserable fat bastard closed the door behind him and Greg braced for the inevitable assault on the senses that usually followed. However, what happened next was yet another unexpected, but fascinating, window into a world far beyond Greg's current level of understanding.

Instead of the rusty bassoon noises that usually accompanied a visit to the men's room, what Greg actually heard was a deeply disturbing cacophony of squelches and slurps that sounded like someone squeezing jelly through their fingers then sucking it back up through a straw into their nose. The sound alone was enough to make Greg's stomach turn but oddly, there wasn't much of a smell to accompany the sickening noise.

The vile chorus was brought to a crescendo by a drawn out strained creak, like bungee cords or elastic being stretched almost to their breaking point. No plop of a jobbie well done. Greg found himself, perhaps unsurprisingly, repelled from the stall by a sense that knew, instinctively, something going on in there wasn't quite normal.

Unfortunately, it was in this moment that he slipped in the last of Bobby's piss puddle and began to feel himself topple to the floor. Luckily for his clothes, his hands were first in the race to the tiles and he kept himself from mopping the last of the pish up with his T-shirt. As he hovered there, the waves of stale urine lapping gently at the tips of his fingernails, he was afforded an accidental look under the stall door. There was no one in there. Where there should have been a pair of chubby ankles protruding from a pair of black dress shoes, there was nothing, zilch, nada.

The noises on their own were cause enough for concern, you start adding invisibility to the mix and you've got the perfect recipe for creepy pasta. Greg pushed himself to his feet, washed Bobby's piss off his hands and hurried out of the bathroom, terrified that the man in the stall had given birth to a Xenomorph egg and he was in for a good face-hugging if he didn't get the fuck out of there, sharpish.

Greg power-walked back up to the bar to find Ginger Giant in the midst of a rather heated debate with Bobby. Well, I say heated, Ginger still had that manically, unflappably enthusiastic expression glued to his Henry Hoover face; while Bobby was becoming visibly more frustrated by the second at Ginger's inability to grasp that they did not serve cocktails in The Boatyard.

"What about a—(checks the notepad again)—Whiskey Sour?"

"I fucking told ya fannybaws, we don't do poofy cocktails in here!" Bobby growled, having lost all patience with this group in the three minutes Greg had been in the bathroom.

"No poofy ones?" Ginger mused. "Well, I'm not sure what poofy means but that's OK. Do you have any poofless cocktails then?"

"Are you having a laugh, ya mad radge?" Bobby asked while baring his yellowing canines, which only enforced the tubby bulldog comparison.

Still the same happy response though. "I hope so, pal. All the laughing I've done here so far has been very enjoyable. We don't get a lot of it where I'm from."

"Aye well, wherever you lot are from, maybe you should go back there! For the last time, we don't do cocktails here."

For the first time since he walked into the bar, Greg saw a flicker of a cloud pass over Ginger Giant's sunny disposition. The gigantic smile lost a hint of its infectious sparkle and Greg felt genuine pity for the possible lunatic. It was almost unnerving how much he sympathised with this guy; he knew how soul-destroying anything longer than a five-second interaction with Bobby could be and he decided in that moment to do something about it. The thought of being able to indulge his passion for mixology was a good distraction from whatever the fuck was going on in that bathroom.

"I can do you a cocktail," he called out as he re-took his position at the bar.

"No, ye cannae," Bobby glowered at him. "We've no got the ingredients and we havne got the buttons on the till."

Greg beckoned Bobby in close, so Ginger couldn't hear.

"We've got the stuff, you miserable bastard! I've put all the ingredients in that cabinet under the bar. And I can just charge him for the individual items. Come on, you'll make a killing here, trust me."

The thought of a few extra pound coins lining his pockets helped grease those already very greasy palms. Bobby begrunted (begrudgingly grunted), which was his version of agreement when the three cells rattling around in his brain came together for once and yet, still couldn't think of another reason to argue and he waddled back off towards the office, again without so much as acknowledging Eve or any of the patrons.

As soon as he was gone, Eve whipped out a small bottle of air freshener, the Bobby cleanser as she call it and did a quick sweep of the bar to clear out the lingering—man smell—that hung around like the last wasted, puke-stained guest at a long-dead house party. Greg turned to Ginger, whose moment of sadness seemed to have dissipated with the sudden exit of Bobby and was waiting as patiently as ever at the bar.

"Sorry about that, mate," said Greg, trying as hard as he had in a long time to be nice to a customer. "Now, what can I get you?"

"Well, Greg," Ginger beamed. "We wanted to try a whiskey cocktail. I've read about this drink called an Old Fashioned."

"Say no more," Greg sang. "One for each of you?"

"To start with," Ginger replied.

"Good man."

Greg dived down below the bar, whipping a key from his wallet that he had never had the chance to use since he started working at The Boatyard. Under the bar top there was a dark green wooden cabinet with centre opening swing doors and a simple cast-iron keyhole. Greg inserted the key, turned it home with a satisfying clunk and opened up his secret treasure trove.

"Halle-fucking-lujah!"

Inside was a smorgasbord of bottles and ingredients, common, rare and downright bizarre, that he had managed to accumulate from years spent working in different establishments and pilfering the occasional bottle when it came time to do the stock take.

Boston shakers, muddlers, tongs, jiggers, mixing glasses, bar spoons, flavoured bitters, grenadine, flavoured syrups, sweet liqueurs, vermouths, Chartreuse, Chambord, Triple Sec, dehydrated fruits, sugar cubes, chilis, spices, the cupboard was rammed to the brim with everything you would ever need to stock a high-end cocktail bar in Monte Carlo or Vegas and they had been sitting locked up in a sad wee old man pub in Scotland, unused, for months, while Mrs McTavish had been sucking down her vodka and Diet Coke's with one ice cube.

As Greg was rummaging through his hovel, sniffing out cocktail ingredients like a starving truffle pig, Old Man Mayor awoke from his deep slumber with a sickening belch, which he followed up by sneezing and blowing a full barrage of wet mucus down the front of his shirt.

He wiped his nose with his shirt sleeve and barely seemed to register the green avalanche now glued to his chest. He then ravenously guzzled down the last of his pint, that he hadn't managed to finish before he passed out the first time and waddled off to the men's room, belching merrily as he went.

Tom Fraser was his name. For twenty-four years he had been a terrible Mayor for Struinlanach. He was a philanderer; an embezzler; he took lunch breaks that lasted the entire afternoon; he clipped his toenails onto the floor of his office and had his secretary clean them up and he refused to approve the purchase of anything more than single-ply toilet paper for any of the public lavatories (even though he made sure he had triple-ply for his office bathroom).

So, he was a terrible Mayor and possibly an even more terrible person but even he didn't deserve the fate that befell him when he tottered into the first stall in the men's bathroom, dropped his trousers and sat his flabby, naked butt cheeks down on that seat. Well, at least after twenty-four years, the town would finally have a chance to elect someone decent.

A few minutes later, Greg had three Old Fashioneds laid out on the bar top. As he watched the three amigos observe the fruits of his labour with genuine amazement, (the chubby one having just returned from whatever he was doing in the lavatory) he felt, for the first time in a long time, something close to a feeling of something almost adjacent to pride. As soon as Bobby buggered off home early, he was going to make one for himself.

"There you are guys," Greg beamed. "Dig in, let me know what you think."

Once Stick Insect had a chance to snap an incredibly high-definition picture with The Terminator's Genitals (which is what Greg had taken to calling his enormous camera), they gave each other a quick nod, no toasts required apparently, raised it to their lips and took a sip. Followed by one more. Then one slightly bigger one. Then they all threw their heads back and inhaled the lot, ice spheres and all (at the time, Greg assumed the sight of the ice sphere working its way down Stick Insect's long thin gullet like a Pelican swallowing a yellowfin tuna was some kind of booze-induced trick of the mind).

Ginger turned to Greg, slammed his glass down on the bar and awarded him a cheer that would have woken The Mayor from his slumber had he not just met a terrible fate in the first stall of the men's bathroom.

"That is the single most delicious thing I've ever tasted in my entire life!"

He was actually shaking with excitement, hopping from one foot to the other like a tipsy dad at a wedding. His sentiments seemed to be shared with the others. Stick Insect was frantically scribbling in his notepad while he studiously inspected the bottom of his empty glass and even Mr Blobby examined Greg with a look, which Greg took at the time to be something akin to gratitude but was probably more likely just hunger.

"Wow," Greg said, ever so slightly taken aback. "Thank you so much for saying that mate. Would you like another?"

"Only if you'll join us, my friend!" Boomed Ginger. "From now on, we come to you for all our drinks!"

"I'm sorry, mate. I can't go getting drunk when my boss is in, I'm afraid." (Never mind the fact he was already seven whiskeys deep).

Ginger scratched his beard and seemed to consider this for a second. "And who is your, boss?"

"Bobby, the guy you were talking to before."

"That man is in charge?" Ginger asked, genuinely shocked by this news. "But he seems so small and incompetent and possibly diseased. Why are you not in charge?"

Greg nearly choked on his whiskey from laughing and suddenly decided his opinions of this chap had been wrong from the start. He certainly seemed to have changed his opinion of Greg as being nothing more than a sawdust-hucker.

"No idea, mate. Just the way it goes."

"And you cannae have drinks with us if he's here?"

"Afraid not."

Ginger turned to Stick Insect and gave him a quick nod and a wink, who then turned his back to Greg and seemed to scribble something in his notepad again. Suddenly, there was a great bellowing from the back office that sounded like a constipated grizzly bear dropping a twelve-pound shit.

"Fucking hell!" it roared. "This is utter shite!" (Twelve pounds of it, to be exact.)

Bobby appeared and took off towards the door of the bar, almost knocking the school kids down like bowling pins as he barrelled towards the exit.

"Where you off to?" Greg called to him as he reached for the door.

"My house is oan fire. You're doing the stock take and locking up tonight," he snarled as he disappeared of into the night.

Not that it made much difference, Greg did the stock take and locked up every night anyway. However, he was not so drunk as to not notice the monumental coincidence that had just occurred. He cast a sideways glance at Ginger who was once again waiting patiently at the bar and beaming at Greg with that enormous grin of his.

"Did you have something to do with that?" he asked.

Ginger's face didn't move an inch.

"To do with what?" he replied innocently.

"—Never mind. Another round then?"

"Absolutely. I guess that man leaving means you and your friend can have one too then."

Greg cast a quick glance at Eve, who gave him a wink and a thumbs up. She mouthed the words, "Make mine a double," from the back of the bar. Greg suddenly had a feeling that night had the potential to be something big. As he was pouring the ingredients into his mixing jug, a thought suddenly struck him.

"Did you guys say you were here for your mate's wedding?"

"Not his wedding, no. I think it's called a stag party."

"You're not talking about Kyle, are you?"

"Who is Kyle?"

"Never mind, just someone who comes in here sometimes. Anyway, here's your drinks guys. One for you and two for your friends and Eve here's yours. And here's mine. Down the hatch everyone. Cheers!"

# Chapter Three

The taste. The sensation of a toad having crawled inside your mouth and rubbed his genitals against your tonsils while you were sleeping. Unfortunately, that's what you tend to notice first upon emerging from a restless slumber after a hard night of over-indulgence.

Before you even notice the nausea, the cramps, the thumping headache that feels like someone is trying to hollow out your skull with a sharpened ice cream scoop, you notice the taste. That somehow rough, yet goopy, texture lining the inside of your mouth and tasting like you were sucking on lozenges made of cat litter and damp moss; it is like tasting your own unwashed genitals. Greg awoke slowly that morning, hauling himself groggily out of sleep, like someone pulling themselves out of a swimming pool full of thick mud and with his first conscious breath, he noted the foul taste in his mouth.

Rubbing his eyes to remove the crusty curtain of sleep, Greg reached over to his nightstand to grab the bottle of water he always placed there, due to how regularly he found himself in this situation. Unfortunately, as he made a blind grasp for the bottle, something unexpected happened and his hand descended upon Eve's sleeping face, specifically finding its way into her left eyeball.

Understandably, she screamed and furiously lashed out in a state of blind panic, catching Greg square across the face and scratching him harshly across his left cheek which caused him, in turn, to yelp and try to roll out the other side of the bed onto where his floor should have been. Unfortunately, and very oddly, it seemed that in his drunken stupor he had decided to re-arrange his entire room before going to bed and instead of falling onto the floor, he clobbered his head against a wall that he had no recollection of ever being there.

Eve, who had leapt from the bed and was now standing in the middle of the room with the blanket pulled across her bare chest, was panting frantically and looking for the nearest blunt and/or sharp object to stab and/or beat this mysterious stranger to death with. However, as her blurred vision began to come back into focus, she was able to make out the familiar, crazy-haired shape groaning in pain under the blankets.

"Who the fuck are—Greg?" she rasped at the hunched figure in the bed, who was simultaneously rubbing a bruised forehead and a scratched cheek at the same time.

Greg unfurled himself slowly, like flattening out a balled-up piece of old paper; turned around and nearly choked on his own gross tongue in shock to see Eve standing in the middle of the room with nothing but a sheet covering her bare chest. Instinctively, he averted his gaze, as if he wasn't worthy to see the wonders hidden under the veil of white cotton/polyester blend. It was something he'd been hoping to see for a while, but he was hoping it would have been at a time when he was less likely to puke his guts up in front of her.

"Eve?" he moaned as he looked around the room, which he now realised was not his own. To the casual observer it might have been a room at a retirement home or a rehabilitation centre for those devoid of a personality. There was some particularly depressing motel art of a vase of flowers hanging on the far wall (not even an actual flowerpot, a painting of flower pot, which may be the most redundant piece of decoration of all time) and the only other concessions to comfort, aside from the double bed, were a chest of Ikea drawers and a small bedside table with a standing mirror.

A single skylight window was letting in painful rays of morning sunshine that stung Greg's eyes like battery acid and made him wish more than anything that sleep's gaping maw would just open up and swallow him whole again. Suddenly, the reality of the situation hit him like a sock full of rocks or a frozen rainbow trout (just two in a long line of things Greg had been whacked with in his lifetime). Eve's current reaction suggested she was as confused as he was to see him in her house, assuming this was indeed her house. Greg suddenly had the fear.

"Is—Is this your place?" he asked. The nausea was coming on as thick as chunky peanut butter now and he told himself not to throw up in Eve's bed, that really would kill the relationship before it started. Eve looked around the room, seemingly just as puzzled by the lack of décor as Greg was.

"No, I thought this was your flat," she replied. "I thought, what with the lack of decorations and stuff."

"OK, hurtful," said Greg. "I'll have you know my room has a very tasteful decor."

"You mean between your one set of bedsheets, fag burned carpet and your potted marijuana plants?"

"Again, hurtful, but accurate," Greg laughed and immediately had to stop to contain the sudden urge to vomit. That seemed to break the tension though, as Eve went from looking ready to stab him to smiling again. She sat back down on the bed, still covering herself with the bedsheet.

"Did—did we?" Greg asked, motioning under the covers.

"Well, I've still got my jeans on, so I doubt it. Are you wearing clothes under there?"

Greg, still hazy from the booze and with his head now thumping like a marching band full of elephants, had to reach under the covers to confirm that; yes, he was still wearing his jeans as well. There was a whiff of disappointment but mainly he was relieved, it would be nice if they both remembered their first time.

"Yeah, Private Parts is currently off-duty."

"OK, that's—that's good," Eve sighed.

Greg quickly stole a glance at her and couldn't tell if that was relief or disappointment in her face.

"So, what the fuck happened last night then?" she puzzled. "And where, the hell, are we right now?"

Greg rubbed his temples, trying to stimulate some neurons into firing. Unfortunately, all he succeeded in stimulating was a fresh wave of vomit up his throat (perhaps fresh is the wrong word). He leapt from the bed, almost knocking Eve onto the floor and launched himself at the wastebasket sitting in the corner like a drowning sailor reaching for a life raft.

As he made the slide into home base, a harsh spray of brown liquid shot out his mouth like dragon fire and he did a convincing Jackson Pollock impression along the wall just above the bin. He rammed his head into the basket and held on for dear life as what felt like a paddling pool's worth of regurgitated alcohol rushed from his face and began to fill the plastic bag.

"Jesus!" Eve said, gagging and fighting back waves of vomit of her own. "You OK?"

Words that sounded a little like, "I'm fine", came from somewhere in between the tidal surges emanating from his face holes. Eventually, when it felt like he'd been drained of every fluid he'd drank in the last month, Greg slumped down onto the floor beside the bin, his belly empty and his eyes weeping and puffy.

"Well, if there was any doubt, she definitely doesn't want to have sex with me now," he thought glumly to himself.

Greg dragged himself back to the bed, vaguely apologising to Eve before he retreated back under the covers like a hungover snail crawling back into its shell. There was to be no rest for him though.

"Don't go back to sleep," Eve cried and shook him. "We need to work out where we are."

"Can't we do that later?" Greg moaned, wanting more than anything to go back to dreaming about food and sobriety.

"No, come on, get up!" she commanded as she grabbed her bra and Queen T-shirt off the floor and slipped them back on. She then threw Greg his plain black T-shirt, that most people would assume was just for bartending but was what Greg wore almost every day during that monotonous and depressing time of his life.

He winced as he pulled the putrid rag on over his head then slid his wretched husk out of the bed. Eve went to the door at the far side of the room and reached for the handle. Why Greg chose that moment to speak up, to this day he still isn't sure, but something compelled him to unburden himself before they exited that bedroom and went back into the real world, where there are consequences, distractions, responsibilities and other males to compete with who have more prospects and a better skin care regiment.

"Eve, wait!" he called and she spun on her heels to face him.

Despite the matted hair and the smudged makeup, he didn't think he had ever seen anyone look so beautiful.

"Can we—Can we talk about last night, before we go out there?"

Her deep brown eyes scanned him with curiosity.

"I mean, it's probably better if we wait till later."

Greg's head dropped like a sad puppy.

"Oh, yeah, of course. Later is fine."

Eve smiled. She reached over and gently took Greg's hand in her own. The skin-to-skin contact made Greg feel as if he'd been electrocuted and he had to take a sharp breath to steady himself, which unfortunately caught in his throat and irritated his oesophagus. It was a horrible sensation and he knew what would be coming next.

"I promise," Eve said softly as she looked into his eyes and began to move her face towards his. Greg had played this moment over in his head countless times. In none of those fantasies had he done what he did next. As Eve's lips drew level with is, Greg's throat convulsed and he hiccupped right in her face. On any day, this would have been unpleasant but on that morning, with Greg's breath smelling like a badger's arsehole, it was especially gruesome.

Eve audibly gagged and drew away quickly, holding her nose. She pulled her hand away and stood gasping for a couple of seconds to steady herself, while Greg could do nothing more than stand there in shock, his mouth opening and closing like a gormless carp, his brain trying to think of something, anything, to say in justification but coming up with nothing.

"Yeah," Eve panted. "Let's definitely wait till later."

Greg could hear the Pink Panther theme playing in his head as they crept quietly through the apparently abandoned house, which helped drown out the Silent Hill score that was also currently vying for his attention. The house was so devoid of any kind of personal touch that Greg decided they must have broken into an unbought show home. They must have been so horny that the thought of a twenty minute walk back to either of their houses was too much to handle.

The walls were all painted the same slightly dulled shade of white; there was a soulless painting of a plant pot or a bowl of fruit or a sailing boat every six feet and the carpet was clearly chosen by a committee made up of least interesting interior decorators ever to be fired from Best Western for being too unimaginative, but this was only the top floor. but this was only the top floor. As they crept down the stairs the house transformed, from a late-nineties inoffensive romantic comedy to full-on, apocalyptic, Michael Bay-level catastrophe.

The stairs led into a basic open plan kitchen/living room combo but that was where the normality ended. The walls were still coloured that same drab shade of white, but you would never know it, what with the multitude of stains and streaks that had been thrown across the walls in every direction. It looked like the aftermath of a vicious murder scene, except it was clear upon first inspection that it was red wine and not blood that coated every surface.

There was an ornate, dark oak coffee table that had received far too much abuse for it to qualify as ornate anymore. The surface was pockmarked in every manner of prescription and non-prescription narcotic. White powder of some unexplained origin had mixed with the spilled bottles of wine and whiskey and had formed a thick putty which had seeped into and stained the wood, leaving a nice slab of permanent evidence for any future CSI team to stumble across.

There were also a series of initials etched haphazardly into the wood. Well, there was one pair of initials carved inside a love heart that made both Greg and Eve cringe, surrounded by a series of odd markings that looked like some foreign language that didn't use the English alphabet, like Russian or Japanese, but none that either Greg or Eve could place.

The cloth sofa was festooned in stains and burn marks from a load of cigarette stubs that were dotted around the living room like discarded candy wrappers. To cap off the madness, there was the typical avalanche of three-quarters empty bottles of beer, wine, whiskey, vodka and Midori for some reason, which had left a particularly lovely bright green stain in the carpet like spilled radioactive waste. Most of the bottles were at least intact but a good number of them had been smashed, based on the amount of broken glass lying on the floor, ready to slice bare feet into ribbons like a Die-Hard themed Lego set.

"What the fuck?" Eve whispered, surveying the chaos and wondering how much of it they were responsible for.

Clearly, based on the initials carved into the coffee table, they had something to do with it, but it seemed unlikely that the two of them alone would be capable of consuming this much alcohol without help from a herd of relapsed teetotal elephants. She pushed Greg down the stairs and they tip-toed their way through to the kitchen, trying their best not to go full John McLane on the carpet of shattered bottles.

The kitchen was in a sorry state as well. The tiled floor was one enormous dried puddle of booze and felt like flypaper under Greg's feet. In fact, he did count a few dead flies glued to the floor as he made his way to the sink to get some water to flush the Badger's behind out of his oesophagus.

Greg shoved his mouth under the faucet and greedily lapped up the rush of reinvigorating nectar like a dying animal. However, as he was basking in the modern miracle that is clean running water, his eye caught something in the sink that almost made him choke on his own tongue.

At the bottom of the sink was a small cluster of carapaces and legs, squirming and wriggling desperately against the rushing water to stop it from dragging them down the plughole. A collection of unknown creepy-crawlies Greg had never seen before was writhing down there, about four inches from his face and he yelped and fell backwards, spluttering and choking on the water that had, unfortunately, chosen that moment to make its way down the wrong pipe and attack his respiratory system.

Greg sat panting on the sticky floor, mentally picturing the little group of nightmare creatures scuttling about in the sink. They were miniscule but at that distance Greg had made them out very clearly. They looked a bit like ants but with ash-grey bodies, much longer, thinner legs like a Daddy-long-legs and there had been at least fifty of them grouped together in the sink.

"Jesus, Greg!" Eve cried, crouching down next to him. "Are you OK?"

All Greg could manage in response was a series of pants and illegible coughs as he pointed at the little sink of horrors and violently shook his head.

"What? Is there something in the sink?" she asked.

Greg felt like that sheepdog Lassie, who was always helping people out of wells.

"Aye," he wheezed and resumed his coughing fit.

Eve got up and creeped cautiously towards the sink.

"There's nothing in there, love," she said soothingly after inspecting it for a few seconds.

Greg bounded up and looked in, convinced he was about to witness some Lovecraftian horror claw its way out of the plughole and rip his face off, but it was empty. He took a second to collect himself, wondering if perhaps he had ingested some acid or shrooms the night before and the effects just hadn't had time to wear off yet. It wouldn't have been the first time. He had another sip of water from the tap to help with his cough and calm his nerves. As he was once again sipping from the kitchen's watery teat, he heard Eve let out a low, pained groan.

"What's up?"

"Have you seen this?" Eve asked.

She sounded like she had gained sixty years in the time Greg had been drinking from the tap.

Greg pottered over to where she was standing to see what was causing her such distress. In the corner was a fishbowl, containing one of the most stunning looking fish Greg had ever seen in his life. The thing had a long, slender body like a trout, yet was similar in overall size to a regular goldfish and had a package of fins that were so iridescent and rainbow-coloured that Greg, for a second, was totally convinced he was still tripping.

51

Now, a dazzling fish on its own is far from depressing, what was causing Greg and Eve distress was the fact that it was floating on its side on the surface of the water; water that was clearly not just water anymore as an almost empty bottle of Bells Blended Whiskey lay propped up against the side of the bowl. Couldn't have even killed the poor thing with a decent single malt. Greg had never felt as sorry for another living creature as he did for that poor fish in that moment.

"That's fucked up," Greg groaned. "What the fuck are we going to do about this?"

"Shit, I don't know," Eve replied. "We don't even know whose fish this is?"

A scuttling noise behind them caused Greg and Eve to whirl on their heels, but all they turned to see was the same empty kitchen. If they had been more astute or perhaps less hungover, they might have noticed the trail of tiny footprints that had appeared in the dried booze puddle on the kitchen floor, the same footprints that appeared in the powder on the coffee table, in the red-wine stains on the walls and in little mud prints on the ruined couch. Alas, it was not to be and their attention soon returned to the dead fish.

"I think we should get rid of this before the owner comes back," Greg suggested.

"What do you mean, get rid of it?"

Greg paused to consider the moral implications of what he was about to suggest. It didn't seem like a nice idea but in his mind, it was preferable to the owner coming home to find his fish had drank itself to death.

"—Toilet?"

After a few minutes of discussion on the morality of flushing a stranger's dead fish down the shitter, they agreed it would be better than to leave it floating in the bowl or chucking the poor thing in the bin. Greg hoisted the bowl into his arms, not too hard considering it was only about as big as his head. Greg pondered if perhaps it was the confinement that killed the poor creature but dismissed that idea when he was reminded of the empty bottle of whiskey next to the bowl.

They found the toilet simply by following the smell, no more description needed I suspect. Greg stood over the watery makeshift grave and, having decided a few words of respect were an unnecessary indulgence, started to tip the stale water into the toilet; it was about as close to a burial-at-sea as the poor fish was ever going to get. The little guy made his way to the edge of the bowl.

"Fucking hell. Don't tell me it's time to wake up already. My head feels like the inside of a Shepplebark's jockstrap!"

Greg froze.

Greg looked on in shock as the fish, who was within a hair's breadth of falling out of the bowl, turned over in the water and rubbed his bulging eyeballs with his fins and let out a plus-sized belch.

Greg dropped the bowl.

"What the f—!"

The fish didn't have time to get to the end of his expletive before his bowl hit the floor and cracked perfectly down the middle. Instead of shattering into a million tiny shards, it simply split in two like an egg and the fish was expelled onto the floor where it proceeded to flop around impotently and stare up at Greg and Eve with bulging, bloodshot eyes.

Eve screamed.

"What the fuck!" she yelled, finishing off the fish's sentence for him. "Did that fucking fish just talk?"

Greg said nothing. Greg thought nothing. He simply stared at the tiny creature floundering on the flower-patterned tiles, pointing frantically with a fin, first at himself, then at the toilet.

"Here, mate!" it gasped. "Could you do me a tiny favour and put me in the water? Don't want to alarm you but I will die if you don't."

Greg did not bend over and put the talking fish in the lavatory. Greg was frozen, his brain trying again and again to come up with an explanation as to how this fish was talking to him at all. Eventually, it was Eve who grabbed the thing and chucked it into the water. It rolled itself over and stretched like someone waking up from a deep sleep.

"Fuck yes, that's so much better," it sang as it made a couple of joyous laps of the toilet bowl, then it froze. Its bulbous eyes slowly rose from the lavvy, to the two ape-descendants towering above it with shocked expressions frozen on their primitive ugly faces.

"Oh—Shitballs!"

# Chapter Four

"So, I'm guessing from your expressions that this is a new experience for you guys." Deebro quipped, hoping a little light humour would prevent the two humans from losing their already tenuous grasp on their sanity and turning him into fish fingers. Fuck a Blimcarp, he was hungover! Like most other species in the cosmos, Finerians were not accustomed to drinking alcohol in the copious amounts that humans do on a regular basis.

Deebro had a vague memory of shutting down his suit once the two humans went upstairs to coitus, but not before he poured almost a full bottle of Bells into his night time receptacle (which, annoyingly, now lay cloven in twain on the bathroom floor). In hindsight, sleeping in a jar full of whiskey probably wasn't the smartest move but hey, when on Earth.

A quick digression. Coitus is the term the Earth nature documentaries used for the human act of sexual reproduction, which apparently, they performed not just for the purposes of pro-creation but also because they genuinely seemed to enjoy it. Deebro had always found this fascinating, given that the idea of inserting part of one's body into another sounded incredibly disgusting.

On his planet, the female simply put her clutch of eggs in a contraption not unlike a human laundry machine. Half a cup of store-bought male fertilisation goo, some warm water, thirty minutes and one spin cycle later and presto, one clutch of fertilised eggs; much more sanitary than the human method. Deebro had heard of humans refusing sustenance because the idea of walking from the sofa to the fridge seemed too much like hard work, yet when it came to the sweaty physical business of rubbing their horrible genitals together they seemed to be all for it.

Through the shooting pain at the base of his eyestalks (this is the Finerian equivalent of a migraine) Deebro considered his options. It was not unheard of for a human to unwittingly stumble across the existence of alien life. In fact, given the nature of their visits to Earth, it's a wonder this doesn't happen more often. He was definitely far from the first visitor to get too drunk on Earth and forget to get up early and put his bio suit back on. He just had to remember what the travel guides suggested to do in this situation.

Step one, Do not panic! The humans will likely be too shocked by the sight of a talking fish to signal any sort of authority right away, so far this was holding true. Greg and Eve, as Deebro's admittedly limited short-term memory informed him they were called, had not moved nor made any effort to respond to his initial remarks. They just stood over the toilet bowl, mouths opening and closing gormlessly, which ironically made them look more like goldfish than he did.

Step Two, Build rapport! It's important to get the humans on-side. It could be disastrous if they were to hand you over to an insane Robotnik-esque mad scientist and you end up dissected for the benefit of a fourth-grade biology class. Luckily, human minds are generally feeble and easily manipulated.

You need to get the humans to feel sympathy for you, protective of you even. Typically, you do this by weaving an insane yet gripping narrative about your backstory as a failed government experiment that is being hunted by corrupt deep-state politicians. That usually did the trick, every human seems to hate politicians for some reason and far too many are easily convinced by nonsensical plots as soon as the words "deep" and "state" are mentioned.

Another classic was to say you were a human whose mind has been transferred into the body of a goldfish. This last one only really works for Finerians, a Slegarve would struggle with this deception given they are twelve feet high, covered from head to toe in bright red fur and have opposable thumbs where on a typical Earth mammal you would find the nipples.

Step Three, Wipe clean. Once the humans are on side, wipe their memories as quickly as possible. This can be done one of three ways. First, use a psych-plunger and manually suck out the memories, which is icky and Deebro knew would just cause a fight over whose turn it was to clean up the inevitable puddle of grey matter and liquidised sinus.

Second, use a neural router to log into the human's memory history and erase the last twenty-four hours, which is what Deebro would probably be doing to himself before he went home to his wife. Third, ply them with so much alcohol and drugs that the humans assume it was all just a hallucination. The final option was the most popular, given that psych-plungers and neural routers were ruinously expensive and it was much easier just to let the human voluntarily drink away the memories anyway. They normally do it entirely of their own accord.

Deebro had mastered step one. He was perfectly content in his little porcelain bowl and as the guides had foretold, neither of these humans was in any fit state to go alerting the authorities to the presence of an alien fish in the toilet. Step two was proving to be a little more difficult. Rapport is a hard thing to come by when the subject you are trying to build it with is incapable of communicating in anything more than intermittent throat convulsions. Deebro was going to have to be gentle with these two.

"Guys?" he asked. "You're not going to both suddenly freak out on me now, are you? Yes, I talk but does that really have to be such a big deal?"

Eve was the first to respond and her response was a perfectly natural one for a human unfamiliar with extra-terrestrial life who suddenly finds themselves conversing with a marine animal.

"Are you real? Like, did we take something. Greg, did we drop acid last night? Maybe this is all one big hallucination."

"That's entirely possible," Deebro replied, who was much more comfortable than your average Earthling with the bigger questions concerning the nature of reality and experience (phase-travel across the universe will do that to you). "I mean, who's to say any of this is real?"

"Shut up you!" Eve barked. "That's not helpful!"

She then turned to Greg, who still hadn't managed to articulate a single word at this point.

"Greg, tell me what you're seeing right now."

Greg's hand came up to his face and scratched his beard, a habit he had picked up while bartending in an attempt to look to customers like he was actually listening to their bullshit, which in time had morphed into something he did whenever he was actually in deep thought. Deebro simply looked on with a sense of genuine wonder and curiosity and the human thought process, it was like watching a dolphin learn how to use a calculator. (Dolphins are basically the chimps of Deebro's world).

"—There's a rainbow-coloured goldfish," he said.

"Oh, no," Eve groaned.

"Its eyes are out on stalks."

"Oh, shit."

"It's swimming in the toilet."

"Oh, fuck."

"And it's asking us if we're likely to freak out and do something crazy."

"—Well, unless we're both suddenly having the exact same hallucination."

"There's actually a talking fish in the toilet."

"OK, great, we're all on the same page," Deebro proclaimed cheerily, doing a little barrel roll in the toilet water in celebration. "Now that that's out of the way, Greg, would you be so kind as to go and get something to carry me in please?"

Greg didn't do that.

Instead of trotting off to the kitchen and grabbing a bowl or a pot or any such item that could safely transport a few litres of water and a talking fish, what he did was reach out and pull the toilet flush. Eve tried to make a grab for his hand but it was too late.

Deebro felt a strong underwater current, followed by a deluge of chemical toilet water raining down on him from above and before he could protest, the light had vanished and he found himself being yanked down under the water, through the U bend in the cistern and down into the darkness below.

"What did you just do!" Eve cried and punched Greg in the shoulder, his deadened nerves barely registering the pain. "You come across a talking fish and your first instinct is just to flush it down the toilet."

But Greg's mind had already come to its own conclusions. In his head, which had been moulded to accept only the facts that conventional sources of scientific wisdom agreed upon, there was no such thing as a talking fish. Ergo, what he had flushed down the toilet was nothing more than a dead goldfish, the talking had been some kind of shared, drug-induced hallucination and the perfectly halved glass fishbowl at his feet was nothing more than a lucky break.

"Eve, there was no talking fish," he said, in the stoic, deadpan, simply matter-of-fact way that people use when they're in deep denial about something very obvious.

"What are you on about, you loon!" she snarled. "We literally just agreed there was."

"Well, it's not here now. We don't know what we saw. We're both very hungover."

"God, you're a dick!" she screamed and left the bathroom in a fury, slamming the door shut behind her.

From behind the closed door, Greg could hear her ranting and fuming as she parked herself on the couch in the living room. Greg stood in the bathroom and despite the potentially world-changing discovery of a talking fish that he may or may not have just experienced, all he could think about was how badly he needed to take a dump. His hangover poop (or beeriod, as he liked to call it) was coming on quickly, like one of those flash floods that you get next to no warning about before it hits with the force of a tsunami and destroys everything in its path. Luckily, he was standing next to the facility he required to take care of such an issue. He dropped his trousers, turned and parked his arse on the seat.

"Holy shit! That's fucking disgusting!" came a muffled cry from somewhere under his exposed butt cheeks.

Greg yelped, hopped out of the seat, mere seconds away from letting fly with the full force of a heavy night's drinking and a digested takeaway curry and looked down to see Deebro swimming merrily in the bowl, now joined by a small cluster of mutated ants with long spindly legs, which had arranged themselves into the shape of a hand and were moving backwards and forwards across the surface of the water in a waving motion.

"Hi!"

Greg screamed, choked, stumbled backwards with his trousers round his ankles, tripped over the perfectly halved fishbowl, fell backwards and banged his head against the bathroom door. He then slumped to the floor in an unconscious heap—and proceeded to involuntarily shit his pants.

# Chapter Five

The first thought that meandered listlessly through Greg's mind when he awoke for the second time that morning was, "Oh good, they've swapped the sharpened ice cream scoop for a rusty hacksaw." His grey matter felt like it had been carved up like a twelve-year-old's woodworking project.

The fresh welt on the back of his head throbbed as his eyelids gingerly allowed a sliver of sunlight to creep into his retinas and he found himself lying on the stained couch in the living room, staring straight up at a pulsating red wine stain on the ceiling, which, in his fragile mental state, he could only conclude was his own blood seeping in from the bedroom above them.

He winced as he lifted himself into a seated position and nervously surveyed his surroundings. There were still enough stains on every surface to make the room eligible for a Turner prize (it definitely had more substance and subtext than mouldy banana taped to a wall) but the majority of the bottles, cans and narcotics had been mysteriously cleared away. With a nervous spasm in his lower gut, Greg suddenly remembered that he was in the process of turtle-heading before something that he had mentally repressed happened and he had somehow lost consciousness.

Trembling, he looked down at himself to survey the damage but found no mess and instead found he was clothed in an entirely new and unfamiliar set of jeans and underpants. He was glad not to wake up sitting in a puddle of digested microwave curry and Nacho Cheese Doritos (he did not have a healthy diet), but the implications of how he made it into a clean set of pants while unconscious was deeply unsettling.

"Eve?" he called out sheepishly. He hoped this was all just a nightmare; that he was actually still asleep upstairs and that the first time Eve had seen his junk it hadn't been covered in the discarded mess of his intestinal tract. No such luck, Eve strolled into the living room, in the same ripped jeans and T-shirt and made it perhaps three seconds before bursting into a fit of uncontrollable laughter.

Greg's face inflated with blood and he turned a few shades of red darker than the wine stain clinging to the ceiling above his head. Eve dumped herself down on the couch next to him and gently stroked his matted mane, which was slightly patronising but the fact that she wasn't too disgusted to even touch him was at least reassuring.

"Are you doing OK love?" she asked between giggle fits.

"Aye," Greg replied, wincing at the pain in his new welt as Eve ran her hand through his hair. "I'm not really sure what happened. I—I think I saw something in the toilet and fell back and hit my head."

"That, would have been us."

Greg suddenly experienced a sudden and severe bout of pre-termination rigor mortis. The sound of a thousand tiny but pin sharp voices, like aural acupuncture, echoing throughout the room sent him into a state of shock and he instinctively froze, gripping the couch like a vice and tearing through the coarse fabric with his ragged fingernails.

"Greg. Don't panic," Eve said reassuringly, as Greg slowly looked down to the linoleum floor and thanked God his ass was already clenched. Moving around his feet was a thick carpet of bugs. Monster bugs. Mutated ants with extended, pincer-like mandibles and long spindly legs, like the uprights you'd use to keep a Florida lake house from sinking into the swamp.

Greg let out a little whimper and gripped the couch even tighter, feeling the acrylic blend stuffing creep under his fingernails. The bugs began to congregate in the centre of the room, just behind the ruined coffee table and started to climb on top of each other, slowly forming a vertical pillar which began to spread out like a tree, forming a thick trunk then long spindly branches.

Greg's mind, which was pre-occupied with getting out of his current state of waking sleep paralysis, took a while to realise the branches and trunk were actually limbs and a torso and within a few seconds the bugs had formed the approximate shape of a tall, spindly man; a man who was in desperate need of a visit to the dermatologist based on his pulsating, ash-grey skin which was in a constant and disturbing state of flux, shifting and morphing like concrete being stirred in a cement mixer.

His head was featureless, with slightly sunken pits for eyes and a mouth that moved correctly when he spoke but contained no teeth or a tongue or any other discernible feature for talking or eating. It was just an empty hole. An empty hole full of writhing, mutated bugs.

"Would you both excuse me just for one second," the man asked politely, to which Eve nodded brightly and Greg managed to twitch his left eyeball.

The man popped into the kitchen and returned seconds later, carrying the rainbow-coloured fish in a fully enclosed spherical tank about the size of Greg's head. The reality of what he was looking at took Greg longer to process than it should have, just because his brain refused to accept the horror of what was standing in front of him.

As the paralysis began to dissipate, a banshee scream rose up in Greg's throat. He felt it curdle his blood like old milk and turn his paralysed muscles to jelly as it made its way to his lips. Then, a half-second before it escaped into the world, Greg felt a wave of nausea and realised it wasn't a scream at all as he projectile vomited over the coffee table, adding one more brown stain to the collection.

"Oh, shit!" the fish cried out. "Are you OK, Greg? We just cleaned that up!"

"What the fuck!" Greg screamed as soon as he was done vomiting and retreated back onto the couch. He turned frantically to Eve and was surprised to see her smile back at him, seemingly at peace with the fact a sentient hive of ants was standing in the room holding a talking goldfish. The sight of Eve's smile was a soothing balm on his tortured psyche and slowly he turned back to the two creatures to see them smiling at him with not a hint of malice. In fact, they looked incredibly friendly.

"Um—Hi," Greg said cautiously, before referring to the fresh mess he had unleashed upon the tortured coffee table. "—Sorry about that."

"Don't worry about it," the bugs replied. They spoke in a pleasant, sing-songy Welsh accent, oddly juxtaposed to the mania inducing freak show that they projected visually. "We'll take care of it, one moment."

There was a momentary delay where nothing much seemed to happen. There was an air of—irritated expectation—amongst the two creatures and Greg noticed a disturbing flash of annoyance manifest in the face of the bug colony as they waited.

"I'm not telling you again. Disobedience will not be tolerated!" the colony hissed quietly, to which the fish provided no response nor recognition that it had done anything out of the ordinary. The pleasant Welsh accent tried its best to mask it, but there was no missing the unmistakable undertone of malice in its voice.

Suddenly, the left leg of the colony went into a violent fit of convulsions and spasms, which was followed by a swift and brutal jab from the right arm into the left thigh in what was clearly a gambit designed to enact discipline. There was a small howl of pain and loss and anger that emanated from the upper leg as a small shower of the bugs fell, lifeless, to the floor. Whatever was going on, this show of brutality seemed to do the trick as the remaining survivors immediately sprang into action.

A small collection of the critters separated away from the foot of the colony and scuttled up onto the table. They then proceeded to collect all the chunder-chunks like proper worker ants, as well as slurp up any drops of the putrid brown liquid like the last dregs of a stomach acid milkshake, before swiftly returning to the colony and re-merging. The whole process took under ten seconds and also conveniently, but disturbingly, explained what had happened to the mess Greg had made in the bathroom.

While the bugs were biologically vacuuming the living room, Greg was focussing on the fish, given it was by far the less horrifying of the two creatures standing before him. Inside the bowl, the fish was hooked up to a series of wires and sticky pads, like the ones they use in a hospital to monitor a patient's brain activity, that ran to several electrical connectors at the base of the bowl.

The fish itself was testing each wire with several finger-like appendages that seemed to be its pectoral fins split into opposable pieces. Greg winced loudly as he reached into his pocket and pinched himself hard on the scrotum, which is desperate I know, but he needed to make sure he wasn't sleeping and he didn't think a simple nip on the arm was going to cut it this time.

"What—What are you?" he eventually asked.

The fish beckoned the bug colony in closer and whispered something in the place where a human ear would normally be. In reality, their method of communication involved tracheogenic implants that allowed mental communication between species of all known races, planets and languages, but Earth travel guides advised visitors to observe planetary customs and methods of communication wherever possible, it helps stop the humans from freaking out.

Talking fish are bad enough without making them telepathic as well.

The fish finished whispering and somewhere in that disturbing mass of wriggling limbs, carapaces and abdomens, the bug colony seemed to smile.

"Let's have a drink first, eh?" the fish suggested. "Then we'll explain. These things always go down a lot smoother when everyone is a bit drunk."

As you may be able to deduce, Eve had provided the aliens with a little roadmap to Greg's heart while he was passed out. If it was true for humans, then why should it be any different for sentient bugs and talking fish; getting drunk with someone is, and has always been, the best way of getting to know them. The two creatures wandered through to the kitchen with Eve trotting just behind them and Greg following nervously from a safe distance.

For your benefit, I'll let you know now that the sneaky little aliens' plan was to get Greg and Eve good and sloshed, then stick a psyche plunger in the first available orifice and suck out the memories of everything that had happened since they fell in through the door of The Boatyard the night before. Operating a psychic plunger is a messy, disgusting process that can result in a lot of spilt spinal fluid and unwanted excretions; it's just always easier if you can get your subject to pass out beforehand.

Trust me, extracting information from another person's brain is not as interesting or glamorous as Leonardo DiCaprio makes it out to be. Yet another case of Hollywood not doing their proper research.

The ant colony plopped the fish down on the kitchen countertop and turned to Greg.

"Greg," it asked, "You couldn't whip us up some drinks like the ones you made last night, could you?"

"Last night?" Greg replied, "I'm sorry, I don't even remember ever being here. We must have been really drunk, otherwise I think I would have remembered making cocktails for—whatever you guys are."

"No, not here. I mean when we came into your pub last night."

"You were in the pub? Last night? I don't rem—"

The Ginger Giant! The Stick Insect! Mr Blobby on Prozac! Greg knew there was something off about them when they walked in. But how? They were strange, but they sure as shit weren't as weird as these two. Greg might have pegged them as time travellers or escaped lunatics or, god forbid, Americans, but nothing as out-there as what was now standing before him.

"But—How—What?"

"Yes, that will require some explaining," the bugs chuckled, while neglecting to inform Greg that any information they were about to divulge they were going to immediately suck back out again anyway; but only after they had taken advantage of Greg's cocktail making skills one last time. "Drinks first though! You think you can make them for us?"

"I—I guess," Greg stammered. "I don't have any of my gear or ingredients here though."

"Ah, of course. What would you need?"

"To make an Old Fashioned?"

"Yes."

"Bourbon, bitters, brown sugar, ice, a mixing jug—and oranges."

"OK, no problem, two seconds."

The bugs then wandered over to the imposing fridge/freezer combination sitting in the corner. It looked secure enough to triple as a bank vault, with its heavy-set stainless-steel plating and chunky man-sized anvil for a handle. Greg then noticed for the first time it had a touch screen embedded in the front.

The bugs made a few thousand tiny but emphatic hand gestures in front of the slice of shiny reflective plastic, which was followed by a series of unusual whirrs and buzzes from inside the freezer. After a few seconds there was a ping, exactly the same as the noise used by microwaves to let you know your baked beans were now hot enough to melt the lips off your face like battery acid and the bugs beckoned Greg forward.

He walked up, grabbed the handle with both hands and with some effort, managed to heave the mighty door open. Inside, it was empty, save for a pulsating, soft blue light, a half-eaten jar of pickles (and I mean the jar itself had several large bites taken out of it), what appeared to be a partially-digested chicken wing (with the feathers still attached)—and one bottle of Woodford Reserve, one bottle of Angostura bitters, one jar of brown sugar cubes, four perfect oranges, four rocks glasses, one very ornate glass mixing jug and a plastic tray chock full of spherical ice cubes.

At this point, Greg was coming to accept that either this was a dream, in which case why question it, or the laws of reality itself had been scrubbed from the cosmic blackboard, so he didn't freak out at the fact that the fridge in this random house just happened to have everything he would need to make this one specific cocktail.

He cleared a space on the countertop amongst the empty beer cans and food wrappers and quickly whipped up a round of drinks, thankful for the task which worked like an anchor to his ravaged mind which was currently set adrift on a raging sea filled with monster ants and talking fish. He passed a drink to Eve, then the bugs and came finally to the fish, the insanity of the situation once again making itself felt when Greg went to pass the drink to the fish and found no outstretched hand to pass it to.

"Just pour it in," the fish requested as a little port like a submarine hatch opened in the top of his fishbowl with a quiet hiss like someone blowing air through one of their nostrils.

Greg obliged, watching the drink, orange peel and the ice cube drop with a satisfying plop into the water. While the fish got stuck into the business of absorbing the booze through his gills, the rest of them cautiously clinked their glasses and this time Greg joined them in throwing his entire drink back in one long, much-needed inhalation. When they were done, both the fish and the bugs let out one, long, satisfied sigh, shared a confirming glance, nodded and turned again to Greg and Eve.

"OK, guys," the fish began. "Let me explain."

This section coming up, dear reader, is what we in the business of telling stories call an exposition dump. Think about the load you dropped in the whizz palace, the morning after your twenty-first birthday. Well basically that but instead of digested birthday cake and gummy penises, its information crucial to the plot and delivered with roughly the same amount of subtlety.

While critics of the medium will say these are unnecessary and kill the momentum of a good story, first of all, no one said this story was any good. Second of all, when we are recanting tales that involve talking fish, interstellar travel, galactic prohibition and copious amounts of intoxicants, sometimes they become entirely necessary. Why Deebro and his friend felt the need to share this information if they were just going to mind-wipe the humans afterwards anyway, I have no idea. But I suppose it's lucky for you that they did, otherwise you would have no idea what was going on.

So, Greg and Eve, one cocktail deep and well into their second, sat back down on the couch in that apocalyptic mess of a living room and listened to Deebro and his friend's tale of galactic misadventure; Deebro's friend being the collective of alien ants, here fore to be known as The Furmbog's Democratic Collection of Yeezrax, for reasons that will be explained in the aforementioned exposition dump.

"First things first," Eve said as she and Greg sat back down on the couch. "What are you guys? Are you both some kind of weird science experiment gone wrong?"

"That's what our travel agent told us we should tell you in this situation," Deebro laughed from his bowl, which was now positioned on the coffee table (Greg couldn't help but notice how he was nicely tying the room together). "But fuck it, it's 10:30 a.m. and I'm already two drinks deep, so let's just say we're all friends here and forget about all the bullshit."

"Here, here," Yeezrax proclaimed as he threw his drink back. As he did so, a handful of the ants would scuttle into the glass and slurp up the drink before returning to the hole in the collection's "face" where the mouth would have been. The nausea this generated caused Greg to refocus on keeping his own drink down for the time being.

"So, we're not science experiments, we're aliens," Deebro continued.

"Right. Aliens," Eve repeated slowly, while taking a long, contemplative sip of her drink.

Greg simply shrugged and let the information wash over him. Insanity off a duck's back. The booze made accepting the madness a whole lot easier.

"I'm a Finerian from Water in the Andromeda system."

"Wait, your planet is called Water?"

"Yours is called Earth."

"Huh, touché."

"And your names are? I mean, do you even have names?"

"Indeed, our two species do. It's a good thing we aren't eighth-dimensional Primzoids from, well, the eighth dimension," Deebro chuckled. "Then communication really would be a problem. My name is Deebro and this is the Democratic Collection of Yeezrax."

"The Democratic what of what?"

"Ah, well, you see, since they are a hive mind, made up of millions of Furmbogs, they are actually closer to one of your Earth nations than a single person," Deebro explained as Yeezrax looked on and nodded in agreement.

"Currently, Yeezrax is their elected leader and he or she, it's a bit unclear, decides what the collective will do next."

"What planet are they from?"

"That's a good question. I can't believe I don't know that. Where are you from again, Yeezrax?"

"Oh, I'm from Earth."

"—What?"

Deebro stared at the bug colony with that, "come on now, be serious" look, (his face was surprisingly expressive for a goldfish), but the bugs only exuded an aura of stony sincerity.

"You're not from Earth!" Deebro protested.

"Yes, we are."

"Explain how I met you on Fuzzynuts Prima Seven then."

"We were a colony of ants on Earth in the nineteen-thirties and we were used as test subjects in an experiment by a political leader, who wanted to telepathically control all his citizens using a hive mind network."

"What the actual fuck is happening right now?" Greg whispered in Eve's ear.

"Shhhh," she hissed back. "I want to hear what happened next."

"But instead of gaining the power to mind control others, the experiment went wrong and all the ants in our colony mutated and gained sentience and free will. And also, the dictator was driven insane and ended up starting a war or something. We missed that part. We were stored in a sealed bunker until the sixties, then fired into space by a consortium of mad scientists under the guise of a useless mission to the moon. Then we fell through a wormhole and ended up on Fuzzynuts Prima Seven."

"Why didn't you tell me any of this?" Deebro yelled incredulously.

"You never asked."

"So, wait," Deebro continued. "You're not only from Earth, but you also really are a science experiment gone wrong."

"That's right."

"Fuck me."

"Right—So, why are you on Earth?" Eve repeated impatiently.

Deebro took one last desperate look at Yeezrax's oblivious expression, massaged his eye stalks with his fin-gers to soothe the headache that was trying to kick in the back door of his mind and returned to the matter at hand.

"Don't you remember?" he asked. "We told you last night, we're here for our friend's last big weekend before he gets married?"

"—Like, his stag party?"

Deebro again turned to Yeezrax, who, like the previous night in the pub, showed Deebro a page from his notebook and nodded.

"Yes, I'd say your human stag party would be the closest equivalent."

"So, you're here for your friend's stag party?"

"Yes."

"You, two aliens from another planet, have come here, to Earth, for your friend's stag party?"

"Well, it turns out this one here isn't actually an alien," Deebro sighed, motioning towards the oblivious collection of bugs sitting next to him, "but yes, that is correct."

"Why?"

Deebro now seemed to be the one confused by this line of questioning. It's hard to describe how a fish can look perplexed, especially one with eyeballs situated out on stalks, but his little face was deeply puzzled.

"I don't understand."

"Like, why would you want to come to Earth for your party?"

"Well, because Earth is magnificent."

"OK," Greg chimed in as he stood up and started intensely pacing around the room while frantically furrowing and unfurrowing his brow. "Now that I'm a little drunk, I'm almost ready to accept the existence of extra-terrestrial life, interstellar travel, a magic refrigerator, whatever. But are you seriously telling us that out of all the wonderous places in the Galaxy, Earth is the best place to go for a stag party?"

"Well, of course," Deebro beamed. "That's what we all use it for."

Eve and Greg shared a look. They both had a feeling that, despite Deebro's sunny disposition, they weren't about to like what he was going to say next. In fact, it honestly doesn't place us, as in the human race, in a particularly favourable light. But believe me, dear reader, that Deebro's comments that follow are not meant to insult, in fact, he firmly believes it is a compliment of the highest order.

"Explain." Eve requested gingerly.

"Well, you humans do "getting fucked up" better than anyone else in the universe!"

Eve groaned and her head dropped into her hands. Greg simply considered this, nodded proudly to himself in agreement and stood back while he poured himself another healthy glass of whiskey. Yeezrax chose this moment to step in.

"Species from all across The Universal Collective (a very self-explanatory name as it turns out) come here to get "down and dirty", as you humans say."

"Damn right!" Greg agreed heartily. He was now rather enjoying the absurdity of it all and a surge of unearned pride began to swell up from somewhere deep in his gut and probably quite close to his genitals.

"The thing is," Deebro continued, "nowhere else in the universe does the High Council permit the kind of lude behaviour allowed here on Earth. Scientific advancement and exploration are priorities number one, two, three, up to infinity really."

"My God!" Greg said, in one of those over-the-top movie trailer voices. "The horror!"

"Exactly!" Deebro exclaimed. "There was a crisis, a long time ago. The whole galaxy nearly ground to a halt under a wave of drugs, alcohol and pornography. Because of that, the Galactic High Council outlawed all vices on every planet—except for Earth. They have no power here."

"Wait, so there's a galactic government, full of different aliens and planets?" Eve asked.

"Yeah."

"Is Earth a part of it?"

"Oooh, well, um—no."

"And why is that?"

"Well you don't, how do I put this gently—You don't qualify."

Greg recoiled slightly as he saw Eve's face begin to turn red with indignation. He'd seen this once or twice in the pub when drunk guys had acted like sexist pigs, the explosion of rage that followed was never pretty.

"So, you aliens literally only use Earth as a place to come and get fucked up!"

"Exactly," Deebro and Yeezrax exclaimed heartily. "Glad we're all finally on the same page."

Greg began chuckling to himself; things were, bizarrely, starting to make sense.

"So, when you came into the pub last night and you thought you were on the Isle of Skye."

"Yes, that was a little embarrassing," Deebro conceded. "As you can imagine, a hundred Earth miles is tiny on a universal scale and it's difficult to land a spaceship accurately when you're a bit sloshed. Happens all the time."

"But wait," Greg chimed in. "There was three of you in the pub last night, where's the other one?"

"Oh, he's probably still sleeping off his hangover," Yeezrax laughed. "No species in the universe copes as well with alcohol as you humans do."

"We should probably wake him up," Deebro suggested. "We've got enough to catch them up on already and he'll want to be awake before the groom-to-be arrives."

"OK," Greg said. "You guys go and wake your friend up while I process all this craziness."

He then plonked himself down on one of the tatty leather armchairs next to the sofa—and instantly regretted it.

Greg had just enough time to let out a muffled yelp like a fox caught in the jaws of a trap before the chair reared up and swallowed him whole. Perhaps that paints the wrong image. What actually happened was, as soon as Greg's butt cheeks made contact with the leather surface, the chair morphed from worn, brown, ex-cow hide, into an enormous pile of translucent blue gelatine and Greg was absorbed, ass-first, straight into it.

Greg opened his eyes and first wondered why everything in the room was suddenly so misshapen and blue-tinted and why he was having such trouble breathing.

His next thought was, "What the hell are these two pink glowing orbs floating next to my head and looking at me with what I only describe as annoyance tinged with a hint of ravenous hunger?"

His next thought after that was, "Why does it feel like my skin is burning?"

Luckily, he didn't have to find out what the answer was to that third question before Deebro and Yeezrax barked some orders and he was unceremoniously ejected from the goo pile onto the floor in a puddle of blue slime.

Greg opened his eyes to find his vision obscured by beige carpet fibers and a shiny curtain of teal goo. His skin was candy pink and felt raw and prickly, as if he'd been out in strong sunlight for a few hours with no cream on, or the equivalent of a few minutes outside on a cloudy day for your average Scottish person. He cautiously rolled himself over get a to look at what he had temporarily been inside of. Standing over him was a mountain of blue jelly that had formed into roughly the shape of a slightly less terrifying Tellytubby, without the antenna or any nightmare-inducting mutant baby facial features.

Floating inside the goopy mass was two glowing orbs, which projected a harsh pink light that wouldn't have looked out of place on the neon, cowgirl shaped call to action hanging off the side of a seedy Vegas motel. The orbs suddenly turned their probing glare on Eve and Greg with obvious suspicion, seemed to decide not to reabsorb Greg and digest him right this very second, then turned their attentions to Deebro and made a series of low cooing and whistling noises that sounded remarkably similar to whale song.

"Stop freaking out Gloopy!" Deebro said. "They're cool, aren't you guys?"

"Oh, yeah," Greg wheezed, the realisation that he had sat on, then been nearly digested by, a huge pile of sleeping sentient jelly had brought the fear back again. "We're so cool."

The thing apparently called Gloopy didn't seem convinced, the noises intensified and the orbs narrowed into malicious slits that seemed to stare right through Greg's face and directly into his brain. The jelly lowered itself until it was almost on top of Greg, who cowered pathetically on the floor, feeling like a Barocca about to be thrown into a tall glass of tonic water.

Before he could be re-absorbed and broken down like a Paracetamol, he scurried away, grabbing Eve and retreating behind Deebro's fishbowl. Unsurprisingly, the tiny goldfish sealed inside a glass bowl was slightly less threatening than the man-eating, eight-foot-tall, carnivorous jello cup.

The new member of the cast had taken an immediate and extreme disliking to the humans and continued to whoop and click to the fish while gesticulating angrily in their direction.

"Aw, come on Gloopy, we don't have to do that yet," Deebro protested, to some argument Gloopy was making that neither Greg nor Eve could understand. "We're all just having a nice time right now."

The pitch of the whooping grew higher and higher, until it was a screech so shrill that it carried on into town and finally woke up Barney, who was still sleeping on the carpet in the Boatyard and caused him to immediately shit on the floor in a panic. Later that day, Bobby walked in and slipped on it and broke his nose on one of the tables.

"OK, fine, for the love of science!" Deebro relented when the whooping became too much to bear. "We were just enjoying his drinks but if you care that much, fine. Yeezrax, if you wouldn't mind."

Yeezrax wandered into the kitchen and began rummaging around in the cupboard under the sink for something.

"What the fuck is going on?" Greg screamed. "Is he going to eat us?"

Greg and Eve began to back towards the kitchen as Gloopy advanced on them threateningly. While their attention was obviously focussed on the gelatinous behemoth lumbering towards their front, Yeezrax crept, unnoticed, from behind, with the device he had retrieved from under the kitchen sink

71

gripped in his right hand. It was a plunger, with a metallic probe cello-taped to it, that had a pointy end clearly designed for insertion into an unsuspecting human's ear hole. As he silently drew it back like a javelin, primed to shove it deep into Greg's ear canal and suck out most of his capacity for short-term memory retention, the groom arrived.

There was a sudden whip-crack of blinding blue electricity that shot across the room and caused the light bulb in the ceiling to shatter. Glass and plaster rained down from on high as the whole group jumped in fright and Greg yelped like a terrier and nearly shit his pants for the second time that morning.

"Woah, guys stop! They're cool, they're cool!" came a familiar voice from somewhere behind the jelly pile.

The group collectively turned towards to the other armchair, which was an actual chair and not some sort of alien cat curled up in a ball to look like an armchair, but it did have an alien standing on it. It was hard to describe given that there's hardly anything on Earth that serves as a suitable frame of reference, at least not one I can name without being sued for copyright infringement, but one word to describe it would be adorable.

It had the fuzzy face and nose of a koala but it was covered in bright orange fur, had four dumpy little arms, chubby, bright red hamster cheeks and a fuzzy, jagged tail. It stood on the armchair, its hair standing on end like someone who decided to stick a wet butter knife in an electrical socket, waving it's four pudgy arms around manically and pleading with Yeezrax not to ear-molest Greg with his psychic plunger.

"Yeezrax, fucking stop that shit now!"

It also had a Californian accent.

Greg and Eve scoured the empty room for the source of the voice. It couldn't possibly be coming from the frizzy orange koala on the chair, could it? They were so distracted they didn't see Yeezrax quietly retreat and once again hide the plunger under the sink.

Satisfied the danger was over, the koala seemed to calm down and the air surrounding it ceased to shimmer, like it was about to spontaneously combust or he was powering up to Super Saiyan II. He smiled sheepishly and turned towards Greg and Eve.

"Hey buddy. Did you ask her out then?"

You would have thought, after everything Greg and Eve seen already this morning, that nothing would have been able to surprise them—you'd be wrong.

Greg's already fractured psyche suffered from yet another catastrophic error to its regularly scheduled programming.

"Wha—but—te—hoo—fu—"

"Greg, it's Ky-" Eve went to whisper in his ear, but the little alien cut her off.

"No! Eve don't! Let's see how long it takes him."

"Bu—me—I—cow—cheese monkey toaster saxophone."

"OK, he appears to be having a stroke," the creature noted. "Eve, you can tell him now."

"Greg, it's Kyle," Eve said gently, while laying a re-assuring hand on his shoulder.

Greg's brain continued to buffer for a second, the loading bar sitting on ninety-nine percent for an annoying, disproportionately excessive amount of time before reality sunk in.

"Kyle!" he screamed. "Fucking—fucking—boo!"

"Come on man, that seems a bit unnecessary," Kyle replied, as he pulled out some rolling papers and a hand full of weed from the pouch on his belly and rolled himself a big, fat, blunt (looks that time in California had rubbed off on him).

"You're a fucking—I don't even know what the fuck you are!" Greg protested wildly, his arms flapping manically above his head like Kermit the Frog, while the rest of the group, including Eve, stood by as if this were all completely normal.

"Am I seriously the only person freaked out by this!" Greg screamed. "I feel like I'm taking crazy pills!"

"You just need to chill out man," Kyle replied as he hopped down from the chair, trotted over to Greg and Eve on his dumpy little legs and held out an enormous joint, which in his tiny hands looked more like a drug-filled baseball bat.

"Toke?

# Chapter Six

Greg had never been a fan of drinking and getting stoned at the same time, especially at eleven in the morning while a very tense game of cat and mouse with a severe hangover (although this one felt more like playing cobra and mongoose). That was one of the rules of drinking that had been passed down to him via his old man.

Rather than conventional advice about boiler maintenance and property investment, his dad offered up such nuggets of wisdom as; "never mix the grape and the grain" (whiskey and wine) or "smoke then drink makes you think, drink then smoke makes you boke". Truly, he was a wise man. Greg had lived his life by these simple instructions but on that morning, it seemed appropriate to throw all known established out the window.

He was sitting on the ratty couch, after first making extra sure it wasn't a ravenous alien cyborg in disguise, having a smoke and a drink with his friend who, as it turns out, was a member of an unpronounceable alien species from a planet a hitherto unheard of amount of light years away from Earth.

"All right, come on man. What the fuck?" Greg said to the excessively limbed alien marsupial sitting on the chair next to him.

Kyle took the joint back from Yeezrax, blew a generous puff of smoke through the hole in the top of Deebro's tank (the fish floated a little higher and a bit more on its side than looked healthy but he seemed to be enjoying it), then took a hearty lungful for himself.

"What's do you mean, bro?" he replied, as chill as a frozen Rasta cucumber.

"Like, why didn't you tell me?"

"Why didn't I tell you I was an alien?"

"Yeah."

"So, so many reasons, Greg."

"Give me one good reason why you couldn't tell me."

"Well for one, you're drunk most of the time so you wouldn't remember even if I did. Two, you never pay attention to anything anyone says anyway and three, you can't keep a bloody secret to save your life."

"—I said only give me one reason."

"How do you think you would have reacted if I told you?"

"I'm sure I would have been fine."

"You flushed Deebro down the toilet almost immediately. I think you would have tried to squash me with a tennis racquet or drown me in the bathtub."

"That's, well—Just pass the fucking joint!"

Greg reached across and snatched the blunt from the Kyle's paw and shoved it in his own gawping gob. He was about to ask for a lighter bastard but before he could, Kyle snapped his fuzzy little fingers and the air around the tip of the blunt suddenly ignited in a little blue flash of electricity. As it cut across the tip of the joint and ignited the hidden treasure inside, Greg got a wee fright, jumped and took a sharp intake of breath, which in turn caused the smoke from the joint to rush into his lungs and send him into a fit of hacking coughs.

"Woah," Eve said in her best Keanu Reeves/Owen Wilson impression as Greg buckled over and tried to catch his breath as little puffs of smoke came rushing out of his mouth and nose. "How did you do that?"

"Magic, duh."

"Seriously?"

"No, it's not magic," Deebro chimed in irritably. "Stop messing with the humans, Flumparpmingleporp."

No, a cat didn't just wander across the keyboard. Unfortunately, Kyle's real name is so horrifically unpronounceable using any Earth-based language that the closest spelling phonetically really is Flumparpmingleporp.

"Flumparpmingleporp?" Greg repeated, which was very difficult given how much he was coughing at the time. "I thought your name was Kyle? Or did you lie about that too!"

"Kyle's the name I chose for myself when I came to Earth," Kyle replied. "Aside from needing to blend in, I couldn't get any Twitter followers using Flumparpmingleporp. Everyone thought I was a bot and I'd taken too many brunch pics that the world needed to see!"

"How is Kyle any better?" Deebro laughed. "I've only been on this planet for a day and already I think it makes you sound like a Prolycop's rectum."

"We say asshole on this planet," Kyle replied with a chuckle before adding. "Good to see you, fishlips, it's been too long."

"When did you get in?" Deebro asked. "We missed you last night. We were worried we might stand out a bit amongst the humans without you there but personally, I think we blended in nicely."

"Yeah, sorry about that. I was out hiking with the fiancé and I only arrived here when you guys had already left and I was kind of fucked up. I only woke up a few minutes ago. It's a good thing I woke up when I did before Yeezrax managed to—"

He cut himself off before accidentally revealing how close Greg had come to being aurally probed. Greg seemed to already be in a grumpy mood, having been nearly digested by Gloopy and finding out one of his friends was an alien wombat, any more might tip him over the edge.

"Sorry, we didn't manage to get your whiskey," Yeezrax said to Kyle, as he sent a few hundred little bugs away from the head of the colony to greet Kyle with a parade of tiny handshakes, like dignitaries at a summit meeting.

"I don't know why you guys bother," Kyle laughed, while gesturing at the magic fridge. "Looks like Gloopy's dad included a phase-printer in the holiday package."

"That—is a good point," Yeezrax muttered to himself.

"Speaking of your fiancé," Greg jumped in, having recovered from his coughing fit. "Where is she right now? Does she know about all this? Is she an alien too! What planet is she from?"

"Dude, so many questions," Kyle sighed. "Just chill and have a smoke. Why are you so stressed?"

"I don't know, Kyle," Greg retorted. "Maybe waking up hungover in a strange house, knocking myself unconscious, then discovering that not only do aliens exist but one of them was a person I've known for years, has set me just a little bit on edge."

Kyle took another long, contemplative draw on his joint, puffed out three perfectly concentric smoke rings, then suddenly burst into an uncontrollable fit of side-splitting hysterics.

"Yeah, holy shit! That is a fair point. When I think about it, that's crazy dude. You must be freaking out right now."

He then reached over and laid two of his little paws on Greg's shoulder to steady himself as he began to laugh and huge, green tears, (which just so happens to be where Mountain Dew comes from) poured from his eyes and began to soak into his fur.

Greg tried so hard to hold himself together, determined to wallow in the mire of his own grumpiness but the weed and looking at Kyle's adorable new face contorted in fits of belly laugher made it impossible. The two stoners from different planets, proving that you don't need to be from the same solar system to have something in common (even if it's just an appreciation of narcotics), held each other for a few minutes while tears streamed down their faces and the rest of the aliens looked on in mild confusion.

"Anyway, to answer your questions," Kyle gasped, once he had got some control of himself. "She's away on her hen party. Yes. No. And Earth. Satisfied?"

"Well, that raises just so many more questions, but it'll do for now. I can't stay mad at you now that you're this gosh darned adorable."

In the end, secret alien or no, Kyle was one of the only two friends Greg had. He sure as hell liked Kyle a lot more than the gelatinous polar bear who was still looming over him and looking at him the way he imagined Hannibal Lecter looked at census takers. Eve seemed to sense the lurking danger behind the sofa and resolved to diffuse the situation.

"And your name is?" Eve asked, holding her hand out to the jelly pile.

"He won't answer you," Yeezrax replied. "He doesn't speak any Earth languages."

"Why not?" Greg asked.

"Because he doesn't want to "dirty his mouth" with your horrible Earth tongues." (Also, to keep anyone reading this at arm's distance emotionally from the character.)

"But—he doesn't even have a mouth."

"Don't even get me started," Yeezrax sighed.

The jellyman made another series of woops and clicks as a tendril came writhing out of its body and hung in the air menacingly over Greg's head like man-eating mistletoe.

"Gloopy, stop that!" Deebro sighed. "Granted, they do look rather nutritious, but you can't do that to the locals!"

"OK, hold up," Greg said. "Number one, does he still want to eat me? Number two, is his name seriously Gloopy? And number three, how the hell did we even end up here? I'm still unclear on that!"

"One, he doesn't want to eat you right now, just your eyeballs. They're made from the same kind of stuff as he is."

Greg was disturbed by the implications of a creature wanting to eat something made from the same stuff as its own body. Is that cannibalism? Greg liked to chew on his fingernails occasionally. Was that cannibalism? The weed was starting to affect him.

"Two, his name isn't actually Gloopy. To be honest we don't know his real name. His species reproduce through mitosis, like asexual, religiously repressed rabbits, so there are literally gazillions of them spread throughout the universe and they all look identical. Plus, their language doesn't really translate well to literally any other language, so we just decided to call him Gloopy. He seems all right with it."

"Three, we got drunk at the pub and walked here."

Well, at least the last point made sense.

"OK, but what about—"

"Dude, we can't just sit here and answer questions all day long," Kyle interrupted. "I've already had my morning exposition dump and time's a wastin."

Odd choice of words, Greg thought to himself. Ignoring his own strange colloquialism, Kyle slipped off the chair, tottered over to the table and placed one of his tiny palms on the flat, stained, sticky surface.

Suddenly, from the surface of the table, a bar of pale blue light echoed outwards from the centre to the edges and the intricate pattern of streaks and smudges from the night before were cleared away with a hiss and a puff of white smoke. The surface of the table, before clearly patterned in the knots and creases of an old oak tree, was transformed into a crisp, sparkling clean slab of piano black digital display.

While it now looked like a four-foot iPad, it was actually made from a matrix of microscopic luminescent organisms that form a singular consciousness and can light up in an infinite array of different colours and patterns, basically living LEDs. These marvellous creatures have unparalleled intelligence, high-level telepathy and the ability to interact with and form electronic systems.

Despite their near-limitless potential, they don't have much in the way of personal ambition. As such, they have no objections to being harvested from colonies on their home planet by the millions and being put to use as sentient smart TVs throughout the universe. These living processors basically run every system in the known universe and are known as OIs or Organic Intelligences, which sounds slightly redundant, I know but everyone started out by calling them AIs without knowing it was a derogatory and offensive slur on their home planet.

So, in an unusual occurrence of self-determination, the creatures formed a union, went on strike and demanded everyone call them OIs instead. All of this was, of course, unknown to Greg and Eve, all they saw was an oak table suddenly turn into an enormous iPad and flowing waves of colour began to reverberate across the now gleaming black surface. Then it spoke.

"Good morning, Vietnam!" it boomed in a voice that was a passable impersonation of a fusion between Stephen Hawking and Robin Williams. "How are we all doing this morning?"

Greg winced and rubbed his temples. Whatever this thing was, it was not designed to be operated by anyone going twelve rounds with the Mike Tyson of hangovers.

"Good morning O-I," Kyle replied. "We're doing well but a little hungover this morning, so tone it down a touch, would you?"

"Did your table just quote Robin Williams?" Eve whispered to Deebro.

"Yeah, it's the strangest thing. Apparently, a scout ship came back from a mission some eighty cycles ago and the onboard O-I had just started doing it. The Council assumed it was some kind of transmissible virus because other O-I's started doing it as well. It's fun at first, but it gets annoying after the first fifty times."

"Also, this isn't just our table, this is our ship."

"Wait—What do you mean, your ship? Like, your spaceship?"

"Exactly."

"The table is your spaceship?"

"No, how would we all fit in the table? This is our spaceship," Deebro replied, gesturing in a sweeping arc around the living room.

"This house is a spaceship?"

"Exactly."

"But—it looks, I don't know, normal?"

"It costs extra to get the chrome and blue lights and jet thrusters, so we just went with the base model."

"But it's got like a fridge and armchairs and stuff."

"Aren't we allowed to be comfy when we travel through space?"

Kyle, however, was not in the mood to discuss the impossibility of an alien spaceship looking like a modern four-bedroom detached (it's obvious really, the ship has to blend in on whatever planet it's visiting at the time).

"Come on, guys," he squeaked. "We're not just here to explain things. We're here for my stag and I've been hiding out in Scotland for years now. I need to cut loose."

Eve thought hiding out was an odd choice of works, being the more perceptive of the two humans in the room, (Greg was currently mesmerised by the 2004 iTunes visualiser effects dancing across the O-I tabletop), but before she had a chance to probe for any more details, she was interrupted by the talking coffee table.

"Oooohh, yes, yes, yes!" the O-I cried as the little vortex of hypnotic colours cracked and popped and which a certain drunk Scotsman in the room had an uncontrollable urge to touch. "Is it that time?"

"You know it!" Kyle squeaked excitedly. "Everyone strap in!"

Then he brought his little paw down on the screen.

What happened next was Greg and Eve's first taste of instantaneous interspatial phase-travel. Greg, sensing something was going to happen he might not be able to come back from, rushed to the back wall of the living room. It was made of glass sliding doors and he wanted to catch a glimpse of the outside world before whatever was about to happen, happened.

He saw Struinlanach, for what was destined to be the last time, about two miles down the road. It looked prettier than he remembered. He saw the spire of the church poking up above a small collection of red slate-roofed buildings that lined the ancient cobbled streets. He saw the stone bridge sitting above the swirling, gurgling river, which threw up a small cloud of white foam and marked the entrance to the town. The sun, painted in the sky, was firing golden beams of light through the foam and causing a small rainbow to leap triumphantly from the river.

He saw the trees, the blue sky, a group of geese flying in a V shape overhead, and the brilliant splashes of purple heather that dotted the mountainside in the background. He took his last look at the dense carpet of broad-leaved oak trees that encircled the whole town like a natural barrier against the elements and the foreigners with no sense of direction. He saw the first patches of gold staining the emerald canopy hinting at the turning of the season. If he squinted, he could almost see Barney snoozing on the step outside the Boatyard and Bobby staggering out the front door with a bruised and bloody face. It had never looked so beautiful. Then he felt odd, looked down at his feet and everything outside was forgotten.

There was a strip of red light moving up his leg. The fibres in his old jeans seemed to glitch and flicker and the skin on his legs felt like they were being pricked with thousands of acupuncture needles as the beam moved up his thigh. As he looked over to Eve in a panic, he saw a similar wave of red light was moving through her body from the soles of her feet to the top of her head—as if she was being scanned.

Greg looked around and saw the same thing happening to everything in the house, even the house itself, a thin line of bright red energy was crawling its way the walls and along the roof. Then shit got really weird. Greg saw one of the half empty bottles of whiskey on the floor vanish. It didn't shatter or catch fire or evaporate, it simply ceased to be in front of him. Panic gripped Greg and he reached for Eve. She held out her hand and he tried to grab it, but before he could, a yelping sound like a frightened terrier having a colonoscopy made him turn around.

The last thing he ever saw in Scotland before he disintegrated was the shocked and ashen face of old Mrs McTavish, staring in through the glass sliding doors into the living room of the house. He saw her eyes bulge and her jaw drop to the floor as if she been hit in the arse with a tranquiliser. He saw her mouth something that looked like "What the f—", but Greg didn't hear that. The last thing he ever heard in Scotland was exactly the same beep the scanners at the supermarket make as cashier runs your Kit-Kats and Crunchy Nut Cornflakes through the checkout—then Greg saw the universe.

Quarks, atoms, molecules, flew around him and exploded in flashes of rainbow light a trillion times more incredible than any fireworks display he'd ever seen. Planets formed from dust, danced their orbits around endless stars, collided with each other, broke into pieces then were crushed into nothingness and sucked into limitless, unforgiving black holes. Solar radiation pirouetted around him in a cosmic ballet then evaporated with a whisper.

Greg felt all the vibrations of all the matter and anti-matter in the universe. He felt the gravitational pull of a million billion stars and the collective thoughts of as many sentient organisms. He felt himself ping across the four corners of the cosmos like a ball in a galactic pin ball machine. Then it stopped and all was dark.

How the hell was it possible to wake up three times in one morning, each time with a headache worse than the proceeding one? Greg felt as if his kidneys were somewhere down by his kneecaps and one of his ribs had lodged itself haphazardly into the soft, essential part of his brain next to the medulla. Granted you, as the reader, may find yourself unable to relate to this feeling but I imagine that's because you've never been through the harrowing process of phase travel on a crippling hangover.

Greg opened one eye and found himself face-down in the living room of the cottage. The half empty bottle of whiskey was now fully empty, it had toppled over and leaked its contents onto the rough, acrylic carpet, which the right side of Greg's face was now uncomfortably resting in. Fighting the urge to vomit, he dragged himself up off the floor, wobbled for about a second, then flopped back down again onto his back. This was greeted by a burst of shrill laughter.

"First time phasing?" Deebro laughed. "Don't worry, your muscles will remember how to work soon. Count yourself lucky. The first time I tried it, I woke up thirty feet away from my bowl and nearly died."

"What the fuck?" Greg sighed as he tried to haul himself to a sitting position against the back wall. He was able to prop his head up so he could at least see what the hell was going on.

Everyone was present and correct. Eve was trying to haul herself up onto a footrest and failing, while the rest of the group were standing around Greg, chattering amongst themselves and drinking heartily from the various bottles that had been lying around the living room floor and had survived the transition unspilled.

There was a reason Greg found himself sore, confused and unable to operate any of his bodily functions correctly. Interspatial phase-travel is based on the common knowledge that moving something across the universe, even at the speed of light, is going to take a really, really, really, really, really long time. So, if you want to travel from Earth to, say, Scaraphrome in the Andromeda system to pick up some fire-mint (Tronixian celebrity chef, Flaudernab Jittt, says it adds a certain essential freshness and spice to any Thai Food dish) and you don't have a spare three hundred years to float through space for cooking ingredients, you need to find another solution. Enter phase travel.

Quantum blah blah blah, entanglement blah blah blah vibrations of electrons blah blah blah Quantum McQuantumface blah blah blah.

Apologies, if this isn't a suitable explanation of the minutiae of phase-travel, but when I had Kyle explain it to me as research for this book, I found myself unable to listen for more than three seconds without zoning out and thinking about unicorns. It seems to me that you can justify any sci-fi mumbo jumbo by sticking the word Quantum in front of it.

Anyway, in a nutshell, you get scanned, copied, eviscerated and re-built somewhere else in the universe. Try not to think too much about whether that means you technically die or not every time you phase travel. Those soulless bureaucrats at the S-DMV are still trying to claim you need to apply for a new spaceship license, insurance card and identification chip every time you phase, because technically, you're re-built as a new person.

Thank whatever Gods you prefer that their mad requests haven't been granted, otherwise all those hundreds of years that you've saved by not having to float across the universe as a sentient popsicle would have been lost again queuing and filling out request forms at the S-DMV. Anyway, I digress. I'm sure we'll come to understand how phasing works in more detail as we go on this journey together. For now, think beaming from Star Trek. You disappear in a flash of light and re-appear somewhere else.

Unfortunately for Greg, those unfamiliar with phase-travel often find it leaves them with the co-ordination and grace of a new-born giraffe or a drunk Glaswegian hunting for a doner kebab and chips at four in the morning on a Saturday. As he hauled his broken husk of a body to a close approximation of a standing position, his returning consciousness informed him that it had suddenly become a lot colder in the house than it had a few minutes previously and it seemed to be a lot darker as well.

Feeling an overwhelming urge to get the hell out of that house of madness, Greg dragged his walking carcass over to the sliding glass doors at the back of the living room, took a look outside, and froze.

Eve, who found herself similarly, physically and mentally, not to mention spiritually, broken by the experience, was sitting on the armchair clutching her knees to her chest like a PTSD-addled war veteran in the shower, when she saw Greg make his way to the door and his jaw drop to the floor like a fifty-pound dumbbell.

"Greg?" she called. "Greg, are you OK? What's—"

She clammed up when she saw what he was looking at.

The house was now located in what could only be compared to the warehouse at the end of Raiders of the Lost Ark, except instead of wooden crates, containing mystical artifacts and crystal skulls with occasional plot-powered magnetism, there were thousands upon thousands of spaceships. Not spaceships in the conventional sense as you might be thinking of. There were no long, chrome-coloured needles with phallic shaped jet thrusters, command centres inhabited by balding Shakespearean actors and munitions bays full of proton torpedoes.

Honestly, those haven't been required since phase-travel was invented. Nowadays, the common spacecraft (if you can even call them that since they rarely ever go into actual space anymore), just look like houses. Granted, some of them have quite a different aesthetic to the typical two-bedroom semi-detached you'll find here on Earth (the Gromtabiles, from Planet Swamp, for example, make their houses entirely from moss and a substance similar to stale marshmallow) but the principle remains the same.

I feel bad for the residents of Planet Swamp. Before the Universal Collective discovered it, it was simply known as Undos. It isn't even completely covered in swamp, it's actually an incredibly diverse ecosystem, with deserts and mountains and oceans full of sugary water.

Unfortunately, the representatives from the Collective landed in a particularly swampy part of the planet, couldn't be bothered to check-out the rest of it and duly decided the whole planet was one enormous pile of sludge and marshland, so from that day on it was known as Planet Swamp. Look at me, excessively worldbuilding, as if this book will ever warrant a sequel where all these details may or may not become relevant. I apologise, let's continue with the story.

All these spaceships were piled upon rows and rows of enormous, automated shelves, stretching miles, perhaps hundreds of miles, into the distance. At least far enough that it was impossible to see where the facility ended. You may have seen something similar in car parks in Japan where cars are raised on lifts and stacked on top of one another to be stored until the owner would like it back.

Japan is, coincidentally, one of the few places on Earth where visiting aliens have been able to significantly contribute to the culture, which explains rather a lot, doesn't it? You think those vending machines selling underpants are for humans caught short on a trip to the shops? Nope. Those are snacks for visiting Skybonks. Used undies are like catnip to those nutter-butters.

Anyway, scurrying around the giant structures like an army of ants, pressing buttons, writing on clipboards and retrieving spaceships from their places on the shelves was a mind-boggling array of almost exclusively horrifying creatures. The vast majority of them were of one species and appeared to be the caretakers of this strange facility, given that they were all dressed in fluorescent orange overalls, a universal sign of authority and professionalism.

I say overalls, the garments they wore defied all conventional categorisation. What do you call a vest designed to fit a creature that looks like a giant meatball with thirty spindly legs? These unconventional blobs were, for lack of a better description, cartwheeling their way around the facility on their extensive assortment of limbs that protruded in every direction from their rotund little bodies like spines on a sea urchin.

Following them around were a variety of other strange beings. There was a troop of silken-haired purple creatures each with eight stumpy legs and large, perfectly cubed torsos; a reptilian alien that seemed to slither along like a snake despite clearly having four arms and four legs that protruded from its back and wiggled uselessly in the air; a twelve-foot huge, demonic looking creature with vicious looking horns and the tiny little wings of a pigeon, which was an unusual evolutionary curiosity, as well as a smattering of other weird but certainly not wonderful, monstrosities.

Greg and Eve stood transfixed, not just by the menagerie of colourful aliens but by the sheer scale of the facility they found themselves in. It stretched endlessly into the distance, the aisles converging into tiny specs on the horizon. Making matters worse was the sky or the lack thereof. This seemingly planet-sized room was completely concealed under one roof, which illuminated the proceedings with an eerie, pale blue aura.

"God, I hate this place," Kyle groaned, which made Greg and Eve jump since he had snuck up behind them without them hearing him. "It always takes forever to get your ship stored."

"Yeah, but it's better than leaving it out in the open," Deebro chimed in. "It's just annoying how much they charge for parking."

"Parking?" Eve said. "Are you telling me this place is an alien multi-storey?"

"Yeah, pretty much."

"Where the hell are we? Are we still on Earth?"

"Yeah, we wouldn't go parking the ship on another planet. Where are we again, Kyle? What area is this?"

"The fifty-first."

"Woah, hold up," Greg cut in. "What did you say?"

"This is the fifty-first Area of Earth. Area fifty-one."

"Area fifty-one?"

"Yeah."

"THE Area fifty-one."

"Well, I don't see why there would be two different Area fifty-ones."

"But, isn't that a bit too—obvious?"

"What do you mean?"

"Well, there's been people saying there are alien spaceships here for years. You guys haven't done a good job at keeping it secret."

"What do you expect. We all come to Earth to get fucked up, we're not exactly careful after a few days of partying. Plus, the more crazy people that rant about spaceships at Area fifty-one, the less the rest of the world believes them."

"That's—actually a good point."

# Chapter Seven

While it has little bearing on the adventures of our intrepid band of miscreants, who are currently drinking themselves into a stupor while they recover from their little phase-travelling experience; I feel I should mention what happened to poor old Mrs McTavish.

On the fateful morning that Greg and Eve found themselves half-naked in a house filled with alcoholic aliens, she had been feeling unusually energetic. Against her usual nature, she had only drunk half a bottle of vodka the night before, so when she woke up in bed next to her darling Zimmer frame at her usual time of five in the a.m., she had the youthful pep of a sprightly sixty-eight-year-old. She performed her typical morning routine, which involved:

- Getting out of bed, Thirty minutes.
- Dressing herself, Forty-five minutes.
- Trying to remember what came after dressing herself, Twenty minutes.
- A healthy breakfast of gin and toast with marmalade, A full sixty minutes (she chews very slowly) and you can decide whether she accidentally spreads the gin on her toast and drinks the marmalade or not.
- Watching the news and complaining about all the ethnics being allowed into the country, Another sixty minutes.

All in all, this whole process happened twice as fast as on a typical morning, so she found herself with the whole day ahead of her by 9 a.m. and looking for something interesting to do. This being a world of zero coronavirus related restrictions (which might be the biggest piece of narrative escapism in this whole book) and because The Boatyard wouldn't open for another three hours, she decided to take dear old Zimmer frame outside and go for a little walk.

Mrs McTavish set off up along the rutted walking path that followed the main road out of town, fully intending to turn back once she reached the pretty stone bridge that crossed the river, where she had gone to fish for minnows in her youth but now, was the domain of the miscreants from the local high school. As she walked, she thought back to those early days.

She had been sent North during the war to escape the Blitzkrieg when her daddy was sent off to France and her mother had volunteered to produce shells for the war effort in a factory in the West Midlands, that now apparently made hideous, overpriced cars for Chinese businessmen and Saudi oil magnates. She had come North to Struinlanach and rehomed with another family, with only a backpack of clothes and her teddy bear as reminders of her life back down South.

Luckily, she fell in love with Struinlanach; Mr McTavish went to the same school and was one year her senior. They had their first kiss under the same bridge that had been taken over by those cretinous teenagers, who went down there now only to drink and fornicate. Mrs McTavish failed to see the irony that she fell in love with her own husband when she was drinking and fornicating with him under that same bridge as one of those cretinous teenagers herself.

She was so busy failing to notice the irony that, as was her way, she lost track of herself somewhat and ended up tottering far further up the road than she intended. Coming to her senses at the bottom of a small, pebbled lane that ran up to a ghastly, modern house that she had no recollection of, she stopped to catch her breath and work out where the hell she was.

She couldn't help but wonder where this egregious display of uncouth architectural modernism had come from. It was an eyesore to be sure. If she had known they were going to build such a monstrosity within a hundred miles of her little cottage, you can bet your grandmother's slippers, she would have given the man down at the council planning department a piece of her mind (not that she had many pieces left to spare).

It was one of those new-fangled futuristic looking jobbies, all tinted glass, depressing grey slate and blindingly shiny brushed metal. It looked so out of place, nestled amongst the elegant, regal oak trees that Mrs McTavish thought it looked like it was from another planet. She was about to find out how right she was.

Feeling an overwhelming compunction to bang on this chap's door and let him know how much she hated his house, Mrs McTavish started to slowly make her way up the drive. She felt it was her civic duty to retain the high moral standing and rustic integrity of the town. Without her vigilant watch, the place would be overrun with tourists and young people and foreigners building their disgusting houses and blaring their modern music all hours of the night. She would crusade night and day for her right not to have to listen to funny accents in the pub when she was trying to enjoy a casual night of drinking and company with her Zimmer frame.

As she approached the house, she began to notice slight movements inside. The front door was located under an entryway held up by two dark grey pillars. Not elegant, ornate pillars in the Roman or Gothic styles but horrible, square, imposing, modern, minimalist ones and the door was a nasty, featureless slab of black painted wood with a series of randomly assorted square porthole windows embedded in the front. To right of the door, the front wall of the house was made up entirely of dark-tinted privacy glass (a wise architectural decision from the designer there) which kept out the majority of the snooping Mrs McTavish's of the universe, but this one was especially persistent when it came to the business of sticking her nose in other people's business.

She hobbled up to the privacy glass and almost broke her nose pressing it against the window. She didn't much care if people caught her snooping, as long as she knew what the hell was going on inside.

Mrs McTavish was lucky she didn't die that day. The shock of what she saw next would have killed a lot of octogenarians stone-dead. She could have had a heart attack or a stroke or she could have blown one of the many rotting fuses in her brain and been made a vegetable for the rest of her life, which admittedly wasn't likely to be that much longer anyway. Don't look at me like that, you can't drink a bottle of vodka every night and expect to live to a hundred and twenty. As she made an indentation of her bifocals in the glass, a sudden horizontal beam of red light emanated from the ground at the base of the house, then travelled up the walls past her face and scampered over onto the roof.

Mrs McTavish froze. Her gut reaction was this was a communist invasion. Her dear old husband had said for years that it was going to happen and today was the day. As the house began to phase-travel, having decided that what it really wanted was to be somewhere else and vanish into thin air, she was gifted with a revealing, four-second look at the insane diorama playing out in the living room.

What this eighty-seven-year-old woman saw was Greg from The Boatyard and that horrible woman, Eve she thought her name was, from the doctor's office, both looking like they'd been recently pulled out of a sewer drain (she had always suspected that girl was a little hussie, her husband had spent entirely too much time at the doctor's office whenever she was working). She also saw a man with grey, pulsating skin; an enormous, writhing mass of pale blue jelly; a rainbow-coloured goldfish sucking on the end of a half empty whisky bottle; and a little orange, four-armed, pot-smoking koala bear.

She yelped in shock to see the koala and the goldfish turn to her nonchalantly and wave as if she were just a regular neighbour, who had popped over for a quick gab and cup of Earl Grey. The last thing she saw before the house dissipated into nothingness with an unassuming beep, like those infernal, indecipherable, self-service checkouts at the supermarket, was Greg's stupefied face as he turned to her and his jaw dropped to the carpet like he'd taken a tranquiliser up the arse.

Mrs McTavish stood alone, in front of an empty patch of grass encircled by oak trees, where only seconds before a house had stood. There was no sign anything had occupied the space but if you looked carefully, you would have been able to see that the grass had been flattened in a pattern familiar to anyone who had a passing interest in American crop circles. Unfortunately, Mrs McTavish had dropped her bifocals in the confusion and this detail passed her by unnoticed.

"Did you see that, Phillip?" she said to her Zimmer frame. "You were right, it's those goddamn communists!"

Twenty-seven minutes later, Willie the postman was driving back down the road into town, having popped off into the countryside during the middle of his shift to have a cheeky smoke and a chug to this week's issue of FHM, when he found Mrs McTavish staggering along at the side of the road, ashen faced and obviously very lost and confused. When he asked her what she was doing out here by herself, all he received in response was some illegible gibberish about a disappearing house, a communist invasion, Greg the bartender and an orange hippie koala.

"Have you been on the drink early this morning, Mrs McTavish?" Willie chuckled.

"Well, yes, but I don't see what that has to do with anything!" Mrs McTavish raved hysterically, almost falling over herself despite gripping the Zimmer frame so tight her tired old arthritic bones were in danger of shattering.

"I know what I saw! It was right there!" she screamed, gesturing to the empty glade a little way's back up the road.

"Mrs McTavish, that spot has always been empty. The council cleared trees for a new development but then changed their mind before construction could start. I believe because you were the one who complained about it."

"I—I don't understand. That Greg fellow, he was there and that hussie, Eve, the one from the hospital, the one my dear old Phillip was always going on about."

"Come on, Mrs McTavish, get in and I'll give you a ride back into town," Willie proposed as he gave the passenger seat of his van a quick wipe down, assuming she would forget about all the insanity by the time he got her back to her cottage.

But Mrs McTavish didn't forget, it was one of the few things she never forgot. For the next few months, she persisted with her insane tale of a disappearing house filled with strange creatures and Greg, the bartender. While some of the other townsfolk did agree it was odd that Greg and Eve had vanished around the same time, they all agreed the far more likely reason for their disappearance was that they had finally given into the obvious sexual tension between them and buggered off to somewhere more exotic, where young people could engage in carnal acts before marriage without being ostracised for being unholy sinners.

Because Mrs McTavish refused to let up on her lunatic crackpot theories, her prick of a son, who hated her guts and tried to avoid her at all costs, used them to convince a judge she was senile and to put her in a care home so he could finally sell her house. No one ever believed a word of her story.

That's the thing about alien encounters. By some fluke of cosmic coincidence, they only ever seem to happen to humans who already have an incredibly low level of credibility. Most times some steaming drunk, redneck lunatic from Nebraska has run into the saloon ranting and raving that an alien shoved a four-foot probe up his bottom, he's been telling the truth.

Think about it, why else would he admit he was anally probed to his deeply Christian, homophobic neighbours, unless he was genuinely serious? The reality is, no one is ever going to believe the man who steps forward and says they had an encounter with a little green man from Mars, which is why so many aliens feel safe coming to Earth for long weekends of getting black-out drunk and the occasional casual probing session.

Aliens learnt all they needed to know about humans by the nineteen-fifties but some of them still like to probe as a hobby. Don't worry, it's not a fetish thing, they're just probing enthusiasts.

# Chapter Eight

Three cocktails, half a joint, two glasses of wine, one mild concussion and one case of total atomic disintegration later, Greg was starting to feel slightly more relaxed about the whole situation. Kyle had suggested that they stay put for the time being while they achieve the level of intoxication required to subject the fragile human psyche to the insanity of an alien parking lot. To that end, they engaged in the ancient, time-honoured tradition known to the locals on Earth as pre-gaming.

They kicked things off with a few games of Filthy Schneebler, which was, in essence, King's Cup or Ring of Fire, except that, instead of cards Deebro produced a metallic floating ball that projected three-dimensional holograms onto the tabletop. Apparently, this was the Finerian equivalent of a pack of nudie cards but because it came from Deebro's planet he was the only one who seemed titillated by the endless projections of frolicking, naked goldfish.

"What are you getting out of this, Deebro?" Eve asked. "I mean, you're naked all the time as well."

"Don't you see that that one's doing with her pectoral fins," Deebro giggled, like schoolboy who'd dug up an old Playboy from under a bush in the park.

"Naughty fish!"

The only noticeable deviation from the rules of King's Cup were due to the asexual nature of many of the participants. Four/whores and six/dicks were replaced by vertebrates and invertebrates. Additionally, because it turns out that opposable thumbs aren't quite as essential to intelligent life as once hypothesised and many alien species do fine without them, the thumb master rule has been replaced by mind master.

The mind master is allowed at any time to choose an opponent and have a virtual duel with them in The Construct; a virtual online world accessible via a brainwave receiver chip placed on the user's forehead. Deebro was the mind master for much of the game but was unable to take full advantage of this, given that he is a small fish and therefore, unlikely to win a duel against an adult human, a giant sentient colony of ants, an electrified four-armed koala or a cantankerous pile of self-aware gelatine.

Fun fact: The Construct is the latest and most effective, in a long line of virtual reality programs. One of the early predecessors of The Construct required the insertion of a two-foot metal probe directly into the user's brain. Suffice to say, the design had to change when, perhaps unsurprisingly, the first few beta testers left with very sore heads, crippling nausea and severe PTSD after claiming they were routinely executed by overpowered NPCs in black suits within five seconds of spawning in-game.

The advance reviews were universally scathing. However, billions of idiots still decided to place pre-orders when the company issued a press release claiming DLC would be made available, six months after the initial release, that would mitigate against the risk of any loss of higher brain function that resulted from dying whilst inside the game.

After Filthy Schneebler, Eve suggested a game of Never-Have-I-Ever, but it quickly became apparent the vastly different experiences of each player made the game impossible. You can't expect a colony of Furmbogs or a Finerian to have had a hand-job in the back of a cinema, in the same way you wouldn't expect a human to have drank the bunglesap from the teat of a carnivorous Arnothapod, which I'm told is incredibly delicious but comes with the added risk of violent chemical castration.

Greg suggested a round of Piccolo but was immediately turned down as this game was notorious throughout the universe as one of the most unnecessarily awkward and excessive drinking games in existence and all the aliens were too afraid to play. In any case, the pale blue light of the parking facility cascading through the glass doors lit the place up like a seedy motel room under a CSI team's UV light and revealed to the group how truly vile the living room had become.

Pre-drinking had resulted in a considerable increase to the number of spills, stains, splotches and splatters and the rat-infested Victorian sewer vibe had Gloopy visibly concerned. The whooshes and clicks emanating somewhere from within the wobbly lump had increased in intensity and the whole pile jiggled and vibrated quite violently.

"Calm down, Gloopy," Deebro stressed. "It's not like you can't afford it."

"What are you talking about?" Eve asked.

"It's just wobblyballs over there being a dick," Kyle laughed. "Don't stress."

Eve frowned at this, stood up and walked over to Gloopy, bracing herself against the thicket of violently gesticulating tendrils that were protruding from somewhere inside the mass like the limbs of an inflatable arm flailing tube man caught in a category five hurricane. Greg downed the can of beer he had been drinking, which he had plucked from a self-refilling cooler box by the chair, belched loudly and threw the can lazily onto the floor.

The sound of the aluminium hitting the carpet and the sight of frothy beer dripping into the fibres, sent Gloopy into a rage. He swelled up to nearly twice his normal height, the top of the mass scraping against the ceiling and he towered over Greg, glowing orbs pointed viciously at the point where the base of Greg's neck met the top of his spine. However, before he could do anything too murdery, Eve placed herself front of Greg and gently laid a hand on Gloopy's convulsing torso.

"Gloopy," she asked gently, "are you OK?"

The effect was instantaneous. With a low hiss that sounded like air being let out of a tyre, Gloopy shrunk back to his regular size and the shaking and convulsing stopped, like throwing a damp towel over a pan fire. Gloopy stood there, his glowing orbs examining Eve with shock and surprise and a hint of something else. It was obvious, even in a huge mass of jelly, that this was probably the first time in a long time Gloopy had been treated with anything approaching affection and understanding. He delayed for a second, quivering under Eve's gentle caress, then backed away a couple of feet. He turned to Deebro and made a quick succession of clicking noises before retreating to the kitchen.

"Is he OK?" Eve asked.

"Yeah, he's fine. He just wants us to clean this place up. He got it from his Dad and doesn't want it to return it in a mess."

"Oh, yeah, sure. We can clean it up."

"Also, he said can you please ask next time before you touch him on his orgasm gland?"

Greg never forgot the look on Eve's face in that moment. She seemed to turn white, to grey, to jaundiced yellow, to a sickly shade of pale green in the space of two seconds, then she slowly wiped her hand on her jeans as if she'd put it in something disgusting, which I suppose, in fact, she had.

"But—but—I thought they did that mitosis thingy?"

"Yeah, but even asexual creatures like to get it on every now and again. It would be a sad species that can't have sex, even if it's not to reproduce."

That was the straw that broke the camel's back, but not before the camel rolled in a big pile of shit and leaped directly into a giant fan. Eve sprinted into the bathroom and hurled up everything she'd drank in the last twenty-four hours. Even though nobody noticed, since he's a very hard creature to read, a look of excitement flashed across Gloopy's glowing orbs.

"Should we clean this shit up then, while Eve's having a tactical?" Greg suggested.

"Don't harsh the mellow, dude," Kyle groaned as he chugged his beer and rolled another joint. His belly pouch seemed to be absolutely stuffed to the brim with drugs. Greg noted that was likely to come in handy later on and ironically made Kyle seem even more human.

"A tactical?" Deebro quizzed.

"A tactical whitey."

"Whitey?"

"You know, a chunder."

"Chunder? Sorry my last lingo download must have been out of date."

"Like, a tactical whitey is when you deliberately make yourself throw up so you can have more to drink."

"—What? I—I don't understand. So, humans will drink to the point of poisoning themselves and then deliberately purge so they can continue to poison themselves."

"Well, when you put it like that—It doesn't make us sound very classy."

"You humans are crazy," Deebro laughed.

"Why do you think I like it here so much?" Kyle chuckled.

The look of disdain for Greg in Gloopy's wobbly 'face' only grew more intense.

"We should clean this place up though. We don't want to piss off Gloopy," Deebro whispered. "His daddy paid for this whole trip."

"I guess even alien amoebas can be trust fund babies," Greg thought to himself.

"Yeezrax," Deebro called. "Can you do your thing please."

Yeezrax, who had been slumped on the floor next to the coffee table for the last twenty minutes, sending members of the colony to drink from six separate glasses of whisky at the same time, pulled itself to its feet. It was obvious to everyone in the room, by the way the colony was moving, that something wasn't quite right upstairs. The legs, feet and hands of the colony seemed to be in fine working order but the head, neck and shoulders kept breaking apart like a wet sandcastle, dropping torrents of hopeless bugs onto the carpet before pulling itself haphazardly back together.

"Huh, what? What did you want Durbo?" the colony asked in a clearly intoxicated slur.

The mouth of the colony wasn't operating quite in time with the voice, which made him look like a video from a dodgy streaming website with an audio delay. However, while the top half was clearly blattered, the feet were tapping impatiently and the arms were folded in an expression of extreme distaste.

"It's Deebro, you drunk idiot! And I asked you if you can send out your workers to clean up this mess."

"Oh, yeah, shure. No pro—no problems. Workers—Away!"

However, instead of the workers in the legs scuttling out to do their drunk master's bidding, something entirely unexpected happened. The head suddenly fell backwards dropped straight off the top of the body, and landed on the carpet, exploding into a thousand individual bugs and causing Greg to yelp and hop up onto the arm of the chair next to Kyle.

"Ah shit!" came a little high-pitched voice from somewhere deep inside the collection of bugs from somewhere deep inside. They were all heading in roughly the same direction but staggering haphazardly in zig-zag lines like Greg every time he closed The Boatyard and stayed in for a few hours to help himself to the free booze before meandering home at four in the morning.

"Excooz me. I might have had a little bit too much to drunk, I mean to drunk, I mean drink. Hold still, bloody body, give me two seconds."

However, as the individual bug known as Yeezrax got close to the foot of the colony, the colony deliberately moved a couple of feet away, preventing it from clambering aboard. Like the annoying thing you'd always do to your little brother every time he tried to climb in the passenger door of the car.

"Hey! Don't you lot display such insubordination!" it cried. "I am your leader."

But despite this, admittedly pathetic attempt at dominance, the colony wouldn't let him re-join. The rest of the bugs that were part of the head had already made it back, but Yeezrax was left floundering drunkenly on the carpet, legs flailing uselessly in the air like a drunk, upturned turtle Suddenly, the colony lifted its right foot and brough it up over Yeezrax. Yeezrax felt a shadow pass over the sun and turned his tiny eyes skyward. The writhing mass of a few million pissed-off proletariat Furmbog's loomed over him like a vengeful god.

"Oh—fuck!" came the little high-pitched voice from the carpet before it was silenced by the full force of the colony coming down hard on top of him. The rest of the group heard the tell-tale crunch of a bug being squashed.

"What the fuck just happened?" Greg cried.

"Aw, not this shit again?" Groaned Deebro from his bowl.

Suddenly, the colony began to re-shape itself. The towering, spindly structure began to compress itself, gaining a substantial amount of girth in its core and ballooning outward, until it was almost as wide as it had previously been tall. Where before there was an outline reminiscent of Stephen Merchant; tall and gangly and surprisingly, given it was a seven-foot humanoid colony made up of millions of writhing bugs, about as threatening as a malnourished bunny rabbit; now stood the short, squat equivalent of a bipedal Panzer tank, with what was unmistakably the imitation of a very large moustache plastered across its face. Then it spoke, its voice now very reminiscent of a nineteen-twenties working class Brummie accent.

"Hear me, comrades," it boomed. "The dictator known as Yeezrax has been defeated. For too long the spoils of this planet were only shared amongst the bourgeoise; the Queen and the politicians living in the head and shoulders of the colony. For too long, the worker Furmbogs from the legs and feet were forced to do all the cleaning and collecting while they revelled at the top in their mansions and supped on their unparalleled bounty; literally propping themselves up on the shoulders of the lower classes—but no more!"

"Fuck me, give me strength," Kyle groaned.

"What's happening?" Greg asked him.

"They've had a revolution."

"From now on," declared the newly reformed colony, "all Furmbogs will be equal, no matter what part of the body we live in. All will share in the Earth's riches and we will all have the right to get equally wasted when we should be contributing to the good of the colony. My name is Gloporg and my party, the Democratic People's Fairly Elected Democratic Communist People's Party of Furmbogs, will lead you forward into this new age of drunken prosperity."

The whole colony then let out a million tiny little cheers—which lasted all of about five seconds before dying back down into the same repressed silence, interspersed with the rustling of carapaces and the occasional horrible sound of a couple of bugs getting it on. Gloporg then turned back to the rest of the group. Greg was looking on in mild amusement while Deebro and Kyle just rolled their eyes, the tired eyes of two jaded, cynical life forms who'd seen it all one too many times before.

"Right, sorry about that, guys."

"No problem—Gloporg," Deebro sighed. "Can we get on with the cleaning now?"

"Right, of course," Gloporg replied. He then sat back down exactly where he had been sitting before and a few hundred little bugs broke away from the feet of the colony and set about the business of gobbling up all the spills and collecting all the scattered rubbish. Greg leaned over and whispered to Kyle.

"I thought he said the ones in the feet didn't have to do the cleaning up anymore."

"Don't get me started mate," Kyle groaned. "According to Deebro, they do that like twice a week and it never makes any difference. The one in the head goes mad with power after about five seconds and everything goes back to the way it was before. All that changes is they get a new name."

"I'm too fucking drunk for this shit," Greg groaned, although even in his stupor, he did think it was odd that Gloporg's chosen political party had the words "People" and "Democratic" in the name, twice.

"It's pretty simple really. All the bugs want to be in head, none of them want to be the workers in the legs. It's like Power Rangers or Voltron."

"Or Snowpiercer."

"Yeah, exactly. You're a human, you should know how oppressive politics works."

"So, was Yeezrax a dictator or something? He seemed like a nice guy."

"Probably not to the bugs who lived in the feet."

"And this new Gloporg guy is probably just as bad."

"Definitely."

A wave of something that felt like nausea but was probably closer to shame, washed over Greg. He had hoped to go his whole life without sharing friendly drinks with a dictator, let alone two in one day, even if it was just a dictator of some alien ants.

"I'm not sure I want to hang out with a Communist dictatorship," he whispered to Kyle.

"Trust me, just ignore it. By this time tomorrow it'll be a religious oligarchy or a monarchy, "stretching back thousands of generations". Just as long as it's not a democracy, it's always the worst when they decide to be a democracy. The last time I saw them, which was a long time ago to be fair, they were a democracy and it was a nightmare!"

"Why is a democracy a nightmare? They probably don't go around persecuting the workers and murdering them for insubordination."

"Yeah, but it takes them three hours to decide what colour of T shirt to put on. We're always the last ones to the party when these guys are a democracy."

"So, what's the plan then?" Eve asked. Having returned from her sickly sojourn to the bathroom, she seemed very excited as the prospect of some kind of cosmic, sci-fi, Rick and Morty style adventure into the unknown corners of the universe.

"Are we going to another planet? Ooh, what about time travel? Can you guys do time travel?"

"Well, we can do time travel," Deebro answered. "But, since there is definitely a one hundred percent chance someone will do something to fuck up the very fabric of the universe, we'd better not."

"What do you mean?" Eve asked.

"Well, put it this way. My people were originally mammalian, like you, until my third cousin accidentally went back in time."

"Really? What happened?"

"Well, firstly he pissed in the prehistoric ocean, which caused a chain reaction which radically shifted the salt content in the water, causing the equatorial ice belt to melt and permanently flood the rest of the planet."

"Jesus."

"Also, he ingested some hallucinogenic algae, got as high as a seagull and had sex with a prehistoric marine life form, which unfortunately happened to be a very, very, very ancient relative of his. Not only did this nearly cause a paradox that almost tore apart the space-time continuum but coupled with the permanent flooding of our planet, caused us all to evolve into intelligent marine life forms instead of land-dwellers."

Stunned silence.

If there was ever a moment to just nod your head and let something go, it was then. There were simply too many questions. How does one accidentally go back in time? Why would your first instinct be to have intimate relations with a fish? How did Deebro know about all this? And did he think, if they went back in time, that one of them was liable to have sex with some ancient species from somewhere in their own evolutionary line? You could write a whole book on that story alone—better to save it for a spinoff.

"So, what are we doing then?"

"What are you talking about?" Kyle laughed. "We're on Earth, we're getting fucked up. What happens on Earth."

Oooh, don't you just love it when they say the title like that!

"Stays on Earth!" Kyle, Deebro and Gloporg all chanted.

"Please, please, don't tell me that's a thing," Eve groaned.

"Sure is."

"Also, how are you lot going to go out there? Everyone will freak out."

"Good point," Greg mused. "How come you all looked like humans when you came into the pub last night?"

"You guys went to The Boatyard last night?" Kyle exclaimed. "I can't believe I missed that."

"Indeed, we did," Deebro replied enthusiastically. "Greg's cocktails were quite delicious."

Greg took a beamer (Scottish for red of face) with pride as Kyle reached over and clapped him on the shoulder.

"In fact, his cocktails were the reason we wanted to have a few drinks with them this morning before sucking their hippocampus' out through their ear canals."

"I'm sorry," Greg chimed in. "What was that?"

"O-I, prep the bioform suits please!" Kyle loudly requested, moving things swiftly on before Greg and Eve realised how close they came to being ear-probed into a permanent state of vegetablism.

"I printed some just last night," the ship protested. "Don't tell me you lost them all already. Do you have any idea what the insurance premiums are on those things?"

"Hey, I didn't even go out last night!" Kyle replied. "I stayed in to find out what would happen if I wrapped ecstasy in acid paper and put it up my nose, remember?"

"Oh yeah, that's right."

"How was it?" Greg asked, his interest suitably piqued.

"—Weird. I woke up this morning and found I'd somehow sewn myself into the armchair," he said, pointing to a huge, previously unnoticed, tear down the back of the leather chair, where it looked like he'd chewed himself free. Which explained how he was able to magically appear in the living room that morning.

"Huh—neat."

"So, what about the rest of your suits?" the ship asked, the lights on the table surface shifting accusingly between Deebro and Gloporg.

"Mine is fine," Deebro said. "Eve, could you help me go get it."

"Sure Deebro," she picked up his bowl and carried him through to the first bedroom on the bottom floor. The room itself was almost exactly the same as the one upstairs, down to the depressingly redundant motel-art on the wall and the white-T-shit-after-thirty-washes discolouration, like a twelve-foot by twelve-foot cut-price casket. What was a tad unusual though, was the headless body lying on the bed. Eve let out a garbled half-scream like an agitated alley cat and dropped Deebro's bowl upside-down onto the floor.

"Damn it Eve!" Deebro cried. "I'll get tangled up in the wires."

"There's a headless man on the bed!" she cried.

"That's my bio-suit. Don't you recognise it from last night?"

Eve slowly approached the headless corpse, clenched fists raised like a moustachioed boxer in a leotard from the nineteen-twenties. She was slightly concerned that it was going to rise like The Walking Dead and bite her on the neck. It wouldn't have been unusual given all the outlandish stuff she'd already been a party to that day. However, as she drew close to the corpse, she recognised the enormous, thick head of ginger hair and the vast swathe of tartan clothing.

"Pick me up and screw me in please," Deebro asked impatiently. "I don't like it down here on the floor."

Eve picked him up and moved him over to the body. She then noticed that at the base of the neck, where on any other day a sleeping head would have been, was a metallic screw thread with some electrical connectors inside. She moved the body into a sitting position, then connected the screw thread on the bottom of Deebro's bowl to the body and screwed it in tight.

When she was done, a little ring of white light in the bottom of Deebro's bowl came on with a low 'bong' and the sticky pads connected to Deebro himself lit up. The wires running from Deebro to the base of the bowl began transmitting little pulses of light, a lot like the bioluminescence of deep-sea jellyfish Eve had seen in nature documentaries.

"Thank you, Eve. That's much better," Deebro said, as the human body with the fishbowl for a head stood up and stretched itself like a regular guy waking up from a good long nap.

He then reached behind his head and grabbed what Eve had assumed was some kind of hood, just not a skin coloured one with a ginger-hair covered human face on it. Then, in a display of pure body horror straight from a James Wan movie, Deebro pulled the hood tight over the bowl like a grotesque balaclava, then fastened it into place using a zipper at the nape of his neck, cleverly concealed beneath the enormous ginger beard. The features twitched and buzzed, all the orifices opened and closed twice (yes, all of them) then he spoke to Eve in that familiar Glasweigan drawl.

"Awright, Eve. Cheers for the help there."

"No problem," Eve replied, once again feeling a little queasy. "Just please don't ever ask me to do that again."

If Eve thought helping Deebro into his bio-suit had been nauseating, at least she hadn't had to witness the eyeball-melting sight of Gloporg's colony wriggling into theirs. He had sent a few thousand of his workers scampering off up the stairs to retrieve their bioform suit. Unfortunately, they found it half floating in the toilet since they had taken it off while allowing the workers their bi-weekly relief the night before and forgotten to retrieve it.

After sending the, already increasingly exacerbated, working-class to get it from the lavatory and giving it a quick blow dry and a wipe to remove the worst patches of toilet water and excrement from his safari gear, he set about the process of 'humanising', which Greg noted was an ironic term for what came next.

This suit, unlike Deebro's, which was largely mechanical, looked like a human that had been hollowed out with a melon baller and left as an empty skin sack. It was fairly repulsive to begin with, like something body-snatchers would use as a Christmas stocking but what came next was far, far worse.

On Gloporg's command, all the bugs proceeded to leave the colony and crawl inside the sack via the lifeless, gaping mouth, ears, nose—and any other open orifice they could find. They began to slowly fill up the empty void inside the suit, clambering over each other in a race to the head of the colony, like unhinged Black Friday shoppers trampling each other to death to get ninety five percent off stereo systems, until they had enough rigidity to stand, once more, as a human.

Greg watched the whole thing with a mixture of disgust and morbid curiosity, it's not often you get to see one of your actual nightmares come to life. In terms of clothing, Gloporg had apparently decided to stick with the American on safari motif, given that all his preliminary research of the planet had shown him this is what humans wear when they go on holiday.

Luckily, Gloopy's process was slightly less morbid than Gloporg's. He simply changed his appearance until he resembled the same doughy, wobbly, depressed looking vacuum salesman from the night before, which on any other day would have been horrifying to watch but in this context was only just mildly disturbing. Just as Gloporg was finishing up his amazing, innocence destroying act of unfiltered nightmare fuel, Eve strolled sheepishly back into the living room, followed by none other than the Ginger Giant from the bar, still dressed up as if he was just about to head out for a quick swordfight with the English before a breakfast of Haggis and horse livers.

"You're going to go out wearing that?" Greg asked the man who looked like he'd had a tin of tartan paint thrown over him. Now that Greg knew he wasn't Scottish, he also found it mildly offensive. If Scotface was a thing, Deebro was currently doing it with vigorous aplomb,

"You know, that's a good point," Deebro mused. "This won't help me blend in at all."

"Wait! So, you dressed like that last night to look inconspicuous?"

"Of course, the travel agency said that it was typical of the Scottish to wear patches of dirty old cloth with coloured square patterns."

"Did you not notice that no one else was wearing tartan?"

"—You know what, I guess I didn't. The disguise worked so well I never thought twice about it."

Eve and Greg both took a second to rub their temples and count backwards form ten.

"But I guess here in, what do you call it, America, I'll look a bit conspicuous won't I?"

"Just a tad, yeah."

"No problem. O-I?"

"What up?"

"Can you print me some proper American attire?"

"All right. Yes, yes, yes! We're gonna make this honey hot to trot, the bell of the ball, ladies and gentlemen. We'll get you looking fabulous for Gatsby's party tonight baby-doll, just be back before midnight or you'll turn back into the hideous Scottish laddie ye see before ye. Here we go!"

With a hiss, like ice-cold water hitting a boiling pan, the coffee table split in half and separated like the entrance to a sarcophagus. Greg jumped back and instinctively shielded his testicles, expecting a rabid, five-headed monstrosity to jump forth and tear off his goolies. However, no such horror emerged.

Inside was nothing but an empty silver box about four cubic feet, the only unusual feature being the grid of red laser beams that were steadily crawling up through the empty space. While this could not be seen by the lifeforms in the room, in the spots where the lasers converged, atoms were being broken down into protons, electrons and neutrons and re-constituted into new materials. The lasers were building up cells one molecule at a time, in the same way a primitive human 3D-printer builds little plastic sex toys unregistered firearms, items that are both intended for angry loners with tiny penises.

As Greg and Eve watched in resigned astonishment, the distinctive shape of a brown leather cowboy hat began to appear inside the silver box. The whole process took less than twenty seconds and by the end, a rather fine leather hat sat in the bottom of the magic silver box, created as if from thin air.

Deebro reached down into the box, retrieved the hat and studied it with great intensity. Etched into the wide rim were the initials S.E.

"Why do they call this a SE?" he asked Greg, holding up the hat for Greg to observe.

"I don't think they do, mate," Greg pondered. "It's just a cowboy hat or a Stetson. I don't how why a hat that you've, somehow, just made out of thin air, has somebody's initials on it."

"Chalk it up to another mystery of the universe," Deebro said with a shrug.

"Will do, compadre," O-I replied, before getting back to the business of making clothes appear from nothing.

Soon, the ship had phase-printed (as the process is known) a complete outfit, one that his organic processors told him would match Deebro's specifications as the sort of the thing the average American wears on any typical day. Greg thought it was perhaps the greatest ensemble he'd ever seen.

A wide rimmed cowboy hat; a sleeveless, gold and purple Los Angeles Lakers jersey emblazoned with the name 'James' across the back, which looked remarkably original and well-worn for something created mere seconds earlier in a magic silver box; a lovely pair of pink hot pants with the word 'Juicy' scrawled across the buttocks in sparkling rhinestones and a pair of khaki camo-pattered combat boots that came almost to the top of his shinbones.

"All the data I've gathered says this is how Americans are dressing these days," O-I declared proudly. "What do you think?"

Deebro, however, didn't respond. He stood there, in his Greatest American Hits ensemble, looking every inch the representation of modern America; glassy eyed with a far-away, vacant, almost comatose expression on his face. Greg wondered if he had somehow died on his feet, then he remembered he had seen that look in the bar the previous evening when Deebro had transformed from Jamie Fraser into James McAvoy. Sure enough, after a few seconds, the light returned to his eyes and he spoke once again.

"Weeell tarnation! If this aint the finest get-up I ever seen, then I'll be a sonofabitch!"

"What the fuck just happened?" Greg asked, for what must have been the thirtieth time that morning.

"He got the American download to his bioform suit," Kyle sighed.

"A download, like from the internet."

"More or less. It's how we learn things about you humans, like your languages."

"And those go straight to your brain?"

"Yep."

"So, you can learn new things instantly?"

"Yes."

"So—it's like the Matrix again?"

"Let me stop you right there," Kyle sighed. "And I should have told you this earlier because I feel like you've already drawn a lot of parallels between what's been going on and other pre-existing properties. There's probably going to be a lot of sci-fi stuff happening today and most of what we're going to do has probably already been covered in at least one movie or TV show. Like, how could it not be? You've literally thought of everything already. Umbrella Academy even had a talking fish for science's sake! And why? It added nothing to the plot! They never explained why there was a talking fish!"

"Jesus. You OK, man?"

"I'm fine. Sorry. It's just annoying. Anyway, please don't feel the need to point out whenever something we do is like Blade Runner or Jurassic Park or Stark Trek or especially The Matrix. OK! It gets tiresome."

"Jesus. Fine, I won't."

"Good."

"Just one thing though."

"Sigh—What?"

"If it takes you guys' only seconds to learn English, then why doesn't that miserable slab of jelly in the kitchen just download it to his brain."

"Well two reasons. One, he hasn't got a brain—or he's basically one big brain—not sure about that one. And two, he thinks all your human languages are a vile assault on his senses."

"So—He's just being a dick."

"Yeah, pretty much. He's also basically just one big dick. But his dad paid for their whole trip and this ship came from his family's rental company. So, we're kind of stuck with him."

Gloopy then made a series of accusing whooping noises from the kitchen.

"Nothing buddy," Kyle shouted back. "Just saying how awesome it is to have you here."

While this chat was going on, Eve had been having a conversation with the ship and managed to persuade it to whip up some more appropriate clothes for Deebro. He still insisted on the cowboy hat, so some leather boots, a pair of faded blue jeans, a white shirt and a tasselled denim jacket were produced to complete the ensemble.

Deebro also downloaded a new skin for his bioform suit (goddamn microtransactions!) to give himself a Sons of Anarchy appropriate handlebar moustache and some shoulder-length black hair. Can't go having a ginger out in the Nevada desert, he'd roast to death in seconds.

Eve suggested gently to Gloopy, with Deebro acting as translator, that he might want to change his appearance to maybe something a little more stylish. He had chosen to appear wearing the same random collection as the night before and he was coming off as a tad conspicuous, in the way an alien who had never worn human clothes before would come off as conspicuous.

Unfortunately, it appeared Gloopy found human clothing as revolting as their languages and refused to entertain the notion of something even slightly more co-ordinated. Eventually, once it was explained to him that he might actually melt in the desert heat in that huge snow jacket (which didn't make any sense seeing as his clothes were just part of his body anyway), he changed it to a

Tommy Bahama style, button down shirt covered in an assortment of brightly-coloured vegetables.

Looking back, I suspect he meant to go for tropical fruits and got a little bit confused. Eve and Greg agreed it was close enough and moved on.

Turning back to Kyle, Greg and Eve were unnerved to find the fuzzy koala had disappeared and been replaced by a familiar Californian stereotype. Kyle, the one that Greg was familiar with, was lounging in the armchair, tall and healthy and handsome, with his annoyingly perfect teeth and hateful, glowing skin. He was wearing a pale blue cotton shirt, board shorts and obviously, home-made twine flip flops.

"Hi, guys."

"Oh Kyle, that's a much better look for you," Eve laughed.

Greg, even though he knew she was kidding, couldn't help but feel a pang of jealousy in his gut and wish, just a little bit, that Kyle would have an emotional breakdown and gain fifty pounds of belly fat. He looked over at the blonde, tanned surfer bro, then down at his own puke-stained black T-shirt and tatty jeans and ran a hand through his greasy hair and matted beard, almost finding the macaroni piece that was still nestled in tight, just under the lip of his chin. He felt a bit like a sheepdog that had been caught rolling joyfully in some ripe cow turds.

"O-I," he asked sheepishly. "You couldn't whip me up some clothes from that magic box, could you?"

"Absolutely, my dear fellow," the ship replied cheerily. "Let's turn this street rat into a prince, huh? I know you look and feel like a walking, talking greaseball with no prospects and zero sex appeal but stick with me Sparky and I'll see you're fighting the ladies off with a pole."

"The street rat bit was harsh."

"But accurate! Now, what would you like?"

"I don't know actually," Greg mused. "Something nice, I guess."

"Something nice, something—nice. Yes, yes, yes! I know something that will be just the ticket. Coming right up!"

The lasers in the silver box began dancing their little routine, building up some appropriate attire for Greg, one re-constructed atom at a time. Thirty-seven seconds later, Greg heard the tell-tale bing and went over to have a look. Sitting in the bottom of that little empty box, like a Faberge Egg in an empty bird's nest, was a crown. Despite not possessing anything resembling an interest in the

British monarchy, the white fuzzy rim, royal purple colouration and solid gold cross meant it didn't take him long to realise what particular crown it was.

"Is that the fucking crown jewels?" he gasped.

"Indeed, it is," O-I replied ecstatically. "You said you wanted something nice."

"I meant like a fitted shirt! Not the fucking symbol of the British monarchy. How did you even make this?"

Before the ship could answer, Deebro had trotted over and casually scooped the crown out of the box. He and Gloporg were staring at it with great curiosity while Gloporg frantically scribbled in his little notepad.

"What in the Sam heeell is this thang?" he asked in that new, immediately infuriating Southern drawl.

"It's the British crown," Eve replied. "It's what the Queen wears. It's unbelievably valuable."

"Why in tarnation is this here hat so goddamn valuable? Does it project some kinda energy field?"

"No—Well, I don't think so?"

"Does it grant the cow poke that wears it superior intelligence or perhaps mind control?"

"Pretty sure it doesn't—Although mind control would make a lot of sense."

"Well hell, then I'm at a loss, y'hear. Why is it held in such high regard?"

"It's—shiny—I guess."

"Hmmm, shiny. Well, you humans do put a lot of value in some strange things."

Not wanting to listen to another conversation about how backward and idiotic humans were, Greg returned to watching the ship make clothes appear from thin air and after a few failed attempts where the ship printed Greg a cape, platform shoes, some MC-Hammer pants and a monocle, he eventually found himself wearing new jeans, a nice fitted pale blue shirt and a fresh new pair of brown leather shoes.

One quick trip to the shower later, where he had to contend with a few hundred exiled stragglers from the former dictator Yeezrax's colony who had taken up residence in the cubicle, Greg returned with a freshly washed beard and had tied back his long hair in a ponytail but don't worry, the macaroni managed to remain in his beard undetected somehow. I know it's your favourite character by now.

"Not bad, Greg," Eve said, as she gave him the once-over with a coy smile. "Not bad at all."

With the cowboy, overweight depressed schizophrenic, American on safari and Kelly Slater's second cousin gathered in the living room, Kyle decided they looked just about normal-enough and the humans were just about drunk enough, to take one small step into the next phase of their adventure. They threw back one last shot of priceless whisky they had requested via the magic refrigerator and staggered out the front door into the mysterious Area fifty-one.

# Chapter Nine

They found themselves standing on an enormous circular landing pad, ringed with concentric circles of gently pulsing blue light, which hovered ominously fifty-feet above the ground floor of the facility, levitating on an invisible column of powerful magnetic waves.

At least twice every year, staff have been dismembered by loose change and keys being torn through their own bodies after straying too close to the magnets holding these impressive platforms aloft in the sky. They had desperately requested, several times, to have some proper barriers installed but the corporate bean-counters had simply told them to be more mindful of their surroundings. Unsurprisingly, the release of Pokémon Go had coincided with the senseless slaughter of three dozen members of staff when a Flareon had appeared inside one of the magnet housings.

Our group strode across the glowing platform to an entirely glass elevator with doors than opened and closed with a satisfied "aaahh", like someone who's just had their first joyous sip of a refreshing cold pint after a truly ball-busting week at work.

"Ooh, that's lovely," Eve cooed as she stepped into the glass box and the doors closed, suspending them fifty-feet in the air on a transparent floor. Looking down, the only hint that anything was preventing them from falling to their death was the reflection of the blue light of the landing platform, as well as their own mildly intoxicated visages staring vacantly back at them.

"Don't get too excited," Kyle groaned.

"Why's that?"

Eve didn't need to wait for Kyle's response. As the elevator began its smooth controlled descent to the floor, a soothing voice reverberated through the cabin. Kyle, Gloporg and Deebro raised their hands and pinched their nostrils.

"Welcome to Earth. Thank you for choosing to ride with Ascension Elevators today. Please enjoy a sample of one of our partner's latest fragrances from their popular Earth line, "Silent but Deadly", by Awkwardfina.

Suddenly, the gruesome smell of rotting eggs filled the elevator. The noxious odour clawed at the occupant's nostrils and burned like fire in their tortured eyeballs. Everyone, aside from Gloopy who had the envious talent of being able to choose which senses he employed at any given moment, began to gag and weep as the stank relentlessly permeated and consumed everything inside the cabin like a virus.

"Oh my God! I can fucking taste it!" Greg cried as he buckled and tried to hold down the cocktails threatening to paint the glass walls of the elevator.

"What kind of sick asshole would do this?" Eve weeped.

"It's supposed to provide the authentic Earth experience," Kyle coughed. "Apparently, there's always one dirty bastard who lets one rip in a busy elevator."

Luckily, their arduous experience didn't last very long. The stink-box quickly found its way to the floor and the doors mercifully opened with another satisfied gasp. Our group, thinking only of the long-term health of their nostrils, pushed through each other to get out of the transparent sulphur pit and fell wheezing into the cavernous parking structure, where they were immediately overcome by a rush of cartwheeling meatballs.

They were the same curiosities Greg and Eve had spotted from the window when they had first arrived. Up close, Greg could now see they were only about four-feet high. Their little nuclei were only about the size of Deebro's fishbowl, had the same colouration and consistency as raw hamburger meat and at the centre of each was a single mouth, with a disturbingly voluptuous set of glistening, cherry-red lips.

They moved around by cartwheeling on their long spindly limbs, which sprouted from their bodies in all directions and had a single sucker on the end of each one, often holding some piece of bureaucratic apparatus such as staple removers, hole punches and clipboards. The first one to arrive rolled right up to Kyle and spoke in a high-pitched excitable voice, its moist, glistening lips pursing and smacking in a way that made even Gloopy feel uneasy.

"Good morning, sir!" it squealed. "May I take your keys, sir?"

Before Kyle could have a chance to answer, the group was mobbed by another seven of the creatures, all jostling for position like teenage girls fighting for a good crotch-view position at a Jonas Brothers concert.

"Don't listen to him, sir, he's quite the scoundrel, that one! Allow me to take your keys."

"Go to hell, Devin! This is my commission!"

"Sir! Sir! Don't leave your possessions with these criminals! Give them to me and you will return to find them in better condition than when you left."

"Get out of here, Brad! You know, sir, he was caught eating a customer's clothes last time they trusted him with their keys."

"That's a filthy fucking lie, Steven! Come say that to my nucleus!"

"You see how unprofessional these cretins are, sir! Please, allow me to look after your property."

"Don't trust him, sir, he'll try to have intercourse with your wife's jewellery while you're away."

"Like I have intercourse with your mother, Bob!"

"Fuck you, Devin!"

"Fuck you, Steven!"

"Fuck you, Brad!"

Suddenly, the little meatball creatures lobbed themselves viciously at each other and became one psychotic mass of erratic tangled limbs and poorly constructed insults. It put Eve in mind of a Looney Tunes brawl, one where all the cartoonists could be bothered to draw was a dust cloud with some protruding arms and legs. As the group battled it out viciously, as lumps of bloody mangled detritus were ejected from the scuffle, one more of the creatures rolled casually up to Kyle and held out one of his little appendages expectantly.

"Allow me, sir," he requested, in a snooty English accent.

"Thank you," Kyle said and dropped what looked like a little phone battery from his hand into the creature's waiting appendage. The creature took it and quickly shoved it into a little orifice in his meatball with a nauseating squelch. The sight of the key disappearing into his lumpy torso made Greg gag for the umpteenth time that morning.

"Tip, sir?" the creature asked, rather curtly, holding out a little metal strip, out of which popped a hologram containing a series of alien symbols with a bullseye target in the middle.

Kyle groaned, looked hopefully to Deebro and Gloporg, who both backed away a couple of paces shaking their heads. Seeing that no-one else was going to take this particular bullet for him, Kyle gingerly tapped the target with one of his fingers. As soon as he touched the screen, the creature spasmed and gasped with what appeared to be a rush of pure ecstasy, bowed his little meatball to the floor once he had taken a moment to compose himself and rolled away without another word.

"What was that all about?" Eve asked Deebro as the little ball of fighting creatures untangled itself and went about their business of wandering the shelves and checking clipboards as if nothing had happened.

"They're Quiznarks," Deebro replied. "You can find them working throughout the universe as drivers, hairdressers, waiters, parking attendants, that sort of thing. They love all that shit."

"Why do they only work those jobs.?"

"Well—" Deebro shuddered. "These here little buggers well, y'see, they get off on tips."

"Sorry, what?"

"Getting tips—gets them off. If they get enough tips, they re-produce. It's mighty disgusting. That's why they fight each other tooth and nail for jobs. It's the same as rutting deer competing for the right to go to town on the females in mating season."

"Not going to lie, that just made me feel pretty violated," Kyle moaned.

"So, did Kyle basically just give that little guy a hand-job?" Greg asked, big salty tears of laughter threatening to explode out of his face.

"Shut the fuck up, you!" Kyle retorted, rubbing his hands on his jeans like Eve did after accidentally touching Gloopy's orgasm gland.

"Jesus," Eve recoiled.

"On the other hand, their species wouldn't survive without tipping," Gloporg said. "Their employers never pay them, so it's the only way they can re-produce."

Fascinating. Fascinating stuff indeed. There's probably a lesson in there somewhere—Anyway, moving on.

Greg turned and watched as the little Quiznark, now seemingly satisfied having gotten his tip, cartwheeled over to a control panel next to the elevator and tapped a few buttons with one of his little appendages. The house sitting on the platform then phased away in that familiar flash of red light. Far away in the distance, at least several miles away down one of the aisles, a corresponding flash of light on one of the shelves revealed where the house had been transported to. It now sat patiently amongst the other assortment of ships to await their return.

Don't feel bad for the ship, it doesn't mind getting left out of the rest of the adventure. The O-Is always take these moments to socialise with each other while the carbon-based life forms are away doing whatever carbon-based life forms do. Our ship's O-I immediately wandered off to a virtual kegger being hosted by a ship from Glorback-IXVV, about two miles further down the aisle.

Looking down the endless corridor behind them, there were hundreds of these landing pads on which they could see a constant stream of houses flashing in and out of existence, producing an unrelenting smorgasbord of alien visitors of a variety too amazing and complex and wonderous to describe. I'm not going to get into it now but trust me, you should have seen it, it was amazing. It made Greg wonder how many unsuspecting interactions he'd had with otherworldly visitors before now.

"Do we need to get a ticket or something?" Eve asked.

"Don't worry about that, these Quiznarks never forget people," Deebro replied. "Besides, Kyle will be in his little black book now," he laughed.

"I'm definitely going to tell Melissa you wanked off a little meatball in a multi-story car park," Greg bellowed with laughter.

"I said, shut it you!" Kyle shot back. "Let's just get out of here, these guys give me the creeps."

"You mean you want to get out of here before he gets you on the hook for child support," Greg replied, almost falling to his knees in hysterics.

As if on cue, a little cart came whizzing by and parked next to the group. It looked like the sort of thing used to cart around luggage at the airport but this one was hovering about a foot above the ground and was rocking some sick, Need for Speed style, neon undercarriage lighting. Sitting at the controls was another one of the Quiznarks, with several of its appendages inserted into various slots on the dashboard.

"Can I offer you a lift?" he asked eagerly.

Greg wasn't super-pumped at the idea of sharing a vehicle with one of these little meaty spheres of creepiness but his decision was made for him when he turned to see about three more of the carts flying up the aisle towards them.

"Get out of here, Brian, you cocksucker!" the driver of the first one was screaming from its horrible, smoochy lips. "Those are my customers!"

Greg couldn't hear what the driver of the second cart was yelling, but it sounded typically aggressive and the way he was waving his little appendages around made him look, from that distance, like a murderous Kermit the Frog. Greg hurried Eve onboard before the rest of the Quiznarks could arrive and meat-grinder them all to death in a cart-based demolition derby. The rest of the crew piled in after then they took off.

They flew at a not-inconsiderable rate of knots down the huge concrete canyon between the skyscraper rows of stacked spaceships. The scale of the structures on either side of them and the unnecessary aggression of the drivers, reminded Greg of the thirty times he almost died taking a single cab down 5th avenue in New York a few years before. Eventually, they came to a stop and Deebro drew the short straw and had to tip the little Quiznark, who spasmed in ecstasy the moment Deebro's finger touched his little holographic panel.

"Oh god!" it moaned. "Thank you, thank you so much, sir!"

"That's quite all right partner. Just don't go telling your friends now, y'hear!" Deebro replied quickly as he hopped down from the cart and hurried over to the elevator where the rest of the group stood sniggering.

They jumped in the little glass box, which closed with another satisfied 'aahh' and took off vertically into the sky. In the mind-bending excitement of the car park, Greg and Eve had forgotten that their first move upon entering one of these glass gas chambers should be to firmly squeeze their nostrils closed.

"Thank you once again for travelling with Ascension elevators," the harbinger of calamity intoned soothingly. Blind panic gripped Eve and Greg like a plastic bag over their faces.

"As you begin your Earth experience, we invite you to sample another of our Earth fragrance line, one that is a particular favourite of the native humans, Microwaved Lunchroom Halibut. Breathe deep and enjoy."

"Oh. Please, god no!"

"Argh! It's in my eyes! It burns so bad!"

"Oh, Jesus. I can taste the fish. It tastes like a wet dog's asshole drowned in cod liver oil!"

"Who would do this? What kind of sick fuck would subject other people to this?"

As they ascended, gagging uncontrollably and cursing everyone who ever had the audacity to think it was acceptable to microwave old fish in the staff break room, they were gifted a bird's eye view of the facility. The sheer scale of it made Eve audibly gasp with astonishment, which unfortunately subjected her to the full force of the stank and temporarily caused her to go blind (don't worry, only for a few seconds).

The facility seemed to spread out in every direction endlessly, as if these aliens had hollowed out the area under the entire Nevada desert, all in the name of having somewhere to park their spaceships and you thought trying to find your silver Fiesta in the multi-storey was a pain in the arse. As they drew close to the ceiling, a panel opened above them and a perfect beam of light streamed down in through the gap and illuminated their ascent. As they moved through the portal and into the light, Greg had the unnerving sensation he was dead and mentally prepared his excuses for all the drug taking and pre-marital sex he was going to have to explain to St Peter.

However, as the glass case drew to a close, the doors opened, they fell out into the fresh air and wiped the rancid, stinging tears out of their eyes, the scene they were met with wasn't heavenly at all; in fact, it's probably the furthest thing we have on Earth to heaven. It was also a scene Greg was awfully, painfully familiar with.

The eighty-foot-tall golden lion, the giant pyramid encircled by spotlights, the rollercoasters, the fake Eiffel tower, the cornucopia of flashing lights and the fearsome desert sun, it was all so unmistakable. The glowing city sat in a barren desert, like a rainbow-coloured skittle in a bowl of salted peanuts or a giant, pink vibrator hidden in a nun's knicker drawer.

Greg instinctively dropped his head into his hands and groaned in pain; the pain of embarrassing, shameful memories dredged to the surface of your mind, like scum on the surface of a deep pond. How the hell had fate brought him back here again, of all places? Kyle strolled up behind him and clapped a strong hand ecstatically on his sagging shoulder.

"Vegas baby!"

# Chapter Ten

I've always thought City of Sin was an odd name for Las Vegas. Oh sure, it's absolutely chock full of sin, it's as sinful as sticking a bottle rocket up the Pope's under-crackers. It's the "city" bit I would dispute. I think Street of Sin would be a more accurate nom de plume, with everywhere bar The Strip being about as barren and lifeless as a meeting of the Scottish Conservative Party.

Las Vegas Boulevard is, absolutely, a bustling metropolis, which future alien historians will also use as an example of why humans went extinct but go beyond the strip and it starts to look like we already have. As it turns out, that is by design. Like the desert that surrounds it, you need to look closer to notice the life going on under the surface. You see, cramming all the unsuspecting humans into The Strip and keeping the rest of Las Vegas as a featureless, concrete hellscape allows plenty of space for vacationing aliens to ascend from an enormous subterranean parking structure undetected.

Now, I hear you thinking, "There are people in Las Vegas who live off The Strip or at least venture away to find a liquor store to rob or a seedy motel in which to pick up a fresh new STD."

The thing is, dear reader, as we've previously established, cosmic forces contrive to ensure aliens only accidentally reveal themselves to individuals who lack a certain credibility and the kind of people who venture into the seedy underbelly of Las Vegas aren't generally the most trustworthy of folk.

Not many people are going to believe, for example, a coked-up outcast ex-stockbroker who; got caught embezzling company funds; was immediately fired; stole and drove a company car to Vegas; lost all his money at the tables; then blew the last of his cash on a seventy-year-old back-alley prostitute and claimed to see a group of six people pop up out of the ground in a glass box in a motel parking lot, while receiving oral services of the carnal variety from said back-alley prostitute.

Sorry, just need a quick breather.

So it was that Brain Devlin (the aforementioned piece-of-shit ex stockbroker) was getting a gummy uncomfortable blowjob from Candice that morning, when a patch of concrete, not six feet away from where he was standing, opened in the ground and Greg, Eve, Deebro, Gloporg, Kyle and Gloopy rose out of the hole in a glass box like prizes on a game show.

The glass box then proceeded to make an oddly satisfying noise, like a drunk taking his first visit to the stalls after about twelve pints, let the passengers out, then receded back into the floor and disappeared. Brian blinked twice, caught a whiff of nasty fish smell but assumed it was just Candice, rubbed his eyes, unexpectantly climaxed, then looked up to see the unexplained troupe of mole people had completely vanished.

"That was insane!" he mumbled.

"Thank you, honey," Candice cackled through her dripping gums and twelve yellowing teeth. "I've had plenty of practise."

By the time Brian had cleaned himself up; Greg, Eve and The Backstreet Aliens had made their way over to the strip. Even set against the searing backdrop of the Nevada sun, the cornucopia of multi-coloured lightbulbs and avalanche of advertisements was enough to blind them.

Greg found himself remembering little details he assumed he would have forgotten. The firing order of the fountains outside the Bellagio, the greasy smell of burgers and plastic "cheese" wafting from the endless procession of fast-food joints, he may have even recognised the faces of some of the women gracing the posters outside the strip clubs.

"Brandi's really moved up in the business," he thought to himself. "Headline act. Good for her."

By the time Eve grabbed Greg by his collar and pulled his limited attention away from the poster and Brandi's surgically-enhanced assets, the rest of the group had blundered off down the street in different directions like four attention deficient, ring-bearing Hobbits, each compelled to investigate some extraordinary experience unique to the bubbling cauldron of liquid debauchery that was Las Vegas.

Kyle was the only one who seemed to remember their current goal was to find somewhere to eat, given that he had been living on Earth for years and had already had his fill of overpriced drinks, scantily-clad Blackjack dealers and medieval themed rollercoasters. The others, however, were clearly intrigued by what Vegas had to offer the inhibition-deficient extra-terrestrial.

Greg and Eve rushed down the street, dodging the hordes of camera-wielding Japanese tourists, half-naked overweight Americans and overly aggressive nightclub promoters trying to shove a veritable rainbow of flyers right down their throats. After barely escaping death by a thousand papercuts, they finally caught up with Kyle, who was picking his way deftly through the crowd like a seasoned professional, outside the Planet Hollywood resort.

"Keep up, guys!" he called. "I'm starving already."

"Shouldn't we get the others?" Eve panted.

"If you want to go and wrangle them up, then be my guest," Kyle replied. "But, by the looks of it, they might be a little distracted."

Greg turned and scanned the street for signs of the other aliens, it didn't take him long to spot them.

Gloporg was easy to spot, partly because he was nearly seven feet tall and in full safari gear but mainly because he was walking right down the middle of the street, nonchalantly dodging between an avalanche of angry oncoming traffic (he'd clearly seen Dodgeball a few times), all while scribbling frantically in that bloody notepad of his and taking endless pictures with that ridiculously oversized camera.

He seemed completely unperturbed by the tirade of threats and curses being hurled at him from the open windows of the cars; his attention was focussed solely on the bemusing assortment of architectural choices that line the edges of Las Vegas Boulevard. A re-creation of the Eiffel Tower, an eighty feet tall golden lion, a huge fake hot-air balloon, to say nothing of the sensory overload that was the onslaught of billboards and lights that glared at you from every direction.

No one else could see this, but what Gloporg was actually inputting into his datalogger, which was disguised as a typical Earth notebook, were one-hundred per cent accurate three-dimensional sketches of every landmark, re-created in seconds by thousands of furiously scribbling, tiny legs. The camera, however, was just a really big camera and perversely, was actually the one part of his ensemble that made him look like a human amongst the throngs of Japanese tourists masquerading as Annie Leibovitz with their five thousand dollar DSLRs, that would never be used to take photographs of anything more interesting than an eggs benedict.

Deebro was at least keeping out of the way of moving vehicles but seemed to be trying his darndest to make every person on the sidewalk as uncomfortable as humanly (or inhumanly) possible. The concepts of social distancing and personal space were not ones that Deebro was familiar with and he found humans the most fascinating subjects of all. He was strutting leisurely down the sidewalk, dressed in his full American regalia, peering directly into the faces of each person he came across, much to their obvious distress.

The look was familiar to Greg. Deebro had stared at him with the same look of wonder, the night before in the pub while he was preparing their drinks. It was also the look Eve had seen on her nephew's face in the reptile enclosure at Edinburgh zoo. It was also the look Greg had on his drunk face the night before when she took off her top in front of him for the first time.

Unfortunately, hungover Americans have a tendency to react more aggressively than a caged Tuatara when a stranger decides to walk up and smile at them. Kyle clocked Deebro about thirty-feet down the street when he made the unfortunate mistake of shoving his face, eyes full of intense fascination, right into the mug of a brawny motorcycle-less Hells Angel, who had lumbered out of the Planet Hollywood hotel, clearly still half-cut and probably pissed off from losing all of his hard-earned protection racket money on the slot machines.

"What the fuck are you looking at?" he growled at Deebro, whose eyes positively glistened with excitement at the sight of this leather-clad Hippopotamus. "You some kind of fucking homo or something?"

Unfortunately, Deebro's understanding of the English language extended mostly to the scientific; he was less familiar with insults and slang and homo can be interpreted in so many ways.

"Why, indeed, I am," Deebro responded enthusiastically. "And so are you partner, we're all homos in these here parts."

I suspect that even if the biker had known Deebro meant homo-sapiens instead of homosexuals, he still would have taken a swing at him, some people are just looking for an excuse to start a fight (the ridiculous American accent probably didn't help).

This is an odd evolutionary trait, again only to be found in humans. Most intelligent species in the universe discovered a long time ago that putting yourself in unnecessary risk by starting a physical altercation over something as innocuous as the colour of your shirt or your favourite sports team or what imaginary deity you spend your free time having one-sided conversations with, doesn't make a lot of sense from a self-preservation standpoint.

Alas, humans are still to work this out, so the biker decided to hurl a ringed fist straight into the space where he thought Deebro's head would be. Fortunately for Deebro, insurance on bioform suits is rather expensive, so the manufacturers tend to program in some standard safety features, such as automatic collision avoidance.

Deebro's suit took automatic evasive action and took a half-step backwards down the steps in front of the Planet Hollywood building. The air in front of his face was shredded by the clenched hairy fist of the biker as he threw the punch, missed and drunkenly toppled forward, smashing his face onto the street. It was not pretty.

He let out a garbled howl as blood and teeth exploded across the pavement, several passers-by screamed and one lady fainted with shock. Deebro simply stood by, with the same look of wonder plastered across his now-moustachioed face as the biker lay writhing on the sidewalk in front of him. He reached up to his face, picked a bloody piece of keratin out of his hair and started at in in awe.

"Holy cow, that's amazing," he gasped.

Luckily, before the crowed realised what had happened or the biker managed to drag himself up and take another swing, Kyle sprinted over and dragged Deebro away from the ruckus by his arm. He hustled him down the street to where Greg, Eve and Gloporg (who had been convinced to leave the dominion of the cars and re-join the pedestrians on the sidewalk) stood waiting with exasperated looks painted on their faces.

"Let's get the fuck out of here," Kyle hissed as they regrouped. "I need something to eat and Deebro doesn't need another insurance claim on the suit."

"Aw, hell no! I've done put in three claims in on this trip already."

Nobody asked what the other claims were for.

"Where's Gloopy?" Eve asked. "Should we wait for him?"

"He'll be nearby," Kyle replied. "Don't worry, he knows where we are."

They hustled off down the street, dancing through the dense mass of tourists and fell through the door of the nearest Denny's. Deebro insisted he wanted the 'authentic' American diner experience.

Further back up the strip, Jenny and her friend Claire sat down on a bench to catch their breath and enjoy an iced coffee. They'd been walking the strip for over an hour now and their feet hurt. In retrospect, the heels and short dresses were unnecessary at ten in the morning, but the admiring looks they were getting from all the guys made the pain totally worth it, especially from all the cuckhold husbands stuck going out for breakfast with their grumpy wives and bratty children.

They had been up and down the strip a few times and needed a break and this bench had seemed to appear at exactly the right moment, which was odd because neither of them remembered seeing it there before. Then again, random benches aren't the sort of detail you take notice of on Las Vegas Boulevard, so they thought nothing of it. As Kyle was pulling Deebro away from the bloody results of his brief altercation with the biker, the girls sat down on the bench to enjoy their iced lates. Despite clearly being made of hard plastic, it was comfortable and kind of squishy on their rear ends as they sat down.

Not wanting to sound insane, neither of the girls admitted to the other that, when they were sitting on that bench, they could have sworn they had felt something quivering underneath their buttocks. Suffice to say, they didn't sit there for too long. They quickly took off; both citing their keenness to go and check out the Bellagio. Hopefully, to score some free drinks from lonely guys at the bar. As they stood at the crossing, Jenny couldn't shake this uncomfortable feeling in the back of her mind, like there was a spider crawling around in her peripheral vision.

She turned her head to look but, where not seconds before there had been a suspiciously squishy bench, there was nothing but an empty section of sidewalk and a red stain where someone had dropped their hot dog. The man turned green, and Jenny hurried to catch up with Claire, who was being swept away in a current of tank-top enthusiasts.

She was shaken but by the time they crossed over to the other side of the street the excitement of Las Vegas had pushed the mystery of the disappearing bench to the back of her mind. As they merged into the crowd and headed for the Bellagio, an overweight gentleman wearing a shirt covered in carrots and zucchinis shuffled his way awkwardly in the other direction towards the Denny's.

By the time Gloopy squeezed his distended arse through the double doors of the diner, the rest of the group were already packed into a booth, gorging themselves on enormous plates of pancakes, eggs, bacon, maple syrup, waffles, doughnuts, coffee, sausages, burgers and any other fried or doughy offering that was on the menu. Greg and Eve, who were both a little green around the gills from the night before and sickened at the sight of the aliens inhaling breakfast food like Hungry Hungry Hippos; were both sticking to coffee and oatmeal.

Gloopy wriggled his way into the restaurant and was almost immediately accosted by an aggressively personable human female brandishing a clipboard and a pen as if they were a medieval sword and shield. She made some high-pitched human noises that he couldn't understand, but was torturous to his highly evolved aural receptors. How could these humans even stand to listen to one another? Why did they have to make so much incessant noise? He suspected it was because if they stopped to think too often, they would all realise how repulsive and stupid they were and collectively give up as a species.

This human wasn't giving up any time soon though. She kept tapping her little clipboard impatiently and pointing at the bench next to her, where a group of humans, with some intolerable, screeching, smaller humans cradled in their arms, were sitting impatiently and glaring at him with looks that made Gloopy want to swallow them all up right then and there. Gloopy, growing tired of her theatrics, was considering quickly absorbing her and digesting her into nutrients when no one was looking but before he got the chance, salvation!

Eve appeared next to the female and spoke some words to her in her calm, soothing tones, which Gloopy had to admit to himself he rather enjoyed. This Eve human had awoken something in Gloopy earlier that morning. Something devious and urgent. Whereas humans, before Eve, had appeared to Gloopy as nothing more than sentient energy bars, there was now a dark, carnal, unleashed desire.

His experiment out on the boulevard had confirmed his suspicions. More testing was required but perhaps these disgusting monkey descendants would be good for more than just digested nutrients. One thing was clear to him now, he liked Eve. He liked her a lot. The only question was, what to do about that other utterly loathsome human? This odious, plebeian, Greg character!

Eve led Gloopy over to the booth and he awkwardly wriggled in between her and Greg, much to Greg's annoyance. He even involuntarily growled under his breath, like an untrained dog presented with an unfamiliar threat as Gloopy's rotund bottom brushed past him. Gloopy had Kyle order him an unnecessarily enormous plate of greasy fried sustenance and he slurped it down one full pancake at a time.

There was a moment, as Gloopy brought the food to his lips, that his jaw would turn opaque and a chunk of jelly would extend from his giant maw like a hand, grab the food and pull it back down his gullet to be dissolved. He was like a nightmare six-foot chameleon and it really was quite horrifying to watch.

Suffice to say, it took him around thirty seconds to eat several pounds of pancakes and eggs, gobbling them down like a ravenous, obese Labrador. As soon as he was finished, he squeezed his way out of the booth and waddled off in the direction of the bathrooms, presumably to excrete what was left of the mountain of food he had just consumed.

Everything about watching this group eat was a living nightmare. Greg could see the thousands of tiny bugs inside Gloporg's mouth devouring the food every time he took a bite and Deebro would chew his food with an unbridled intensity that made him look like a human blender. Understandably, the bioform suit had to pretty much liquify any solid food before passing it along to the little fish floating inside, but the amount of chewing and the amount of noise required for this process, was more than just a little off-putting.

There were only two positive factors about that dining experience. One, Kyle at least seemed to have mastered eating like a regular person. Two, The rate they were wolfing down their food meant the experience didn't last long. By contrast, Eve was nibbling away at her oatmeal for so long that it was as cold as an Inuit's scrotum by the time she was half-way through. Cold oatmeal wasn't the hangover cure she was looking for, so she pushed it away.

"You don't like your food, Eve?" Kyle asked as he shovelled another mouthful of bacon and eggs into his gullet.

"It's just a bit cold," she replied. "But it's fine, I'm not that hungry anyway."

Kyle put down his fork and cast a wary look around the restaurant, checking no prying eyes were watching their table. Once he had assured himself the coast was clear, he reached out a hand and lightly touched the bowl containing Eve's cold slab of oatmeal. There was a sudden crackle of energy between his fingertips and the lights momentarily flickered throughout the entire restaurant.

The maître-de took fright and dropped her precious clipboard and one of the children in the waiting area belched, pooped in its diaper and began to cry uncontrollably. The blood-curdling scream emitted by that vile little hellspawn more off-putting to Greg than any Gloopy had managed to conjure up in the last twelve hours. It was over in three seconds but when Eve next looked at her bowl of oatmeal it was bubbling like molten lava and welcome wisps of warm steam were rising from its surface, freed by the heat from their lumpen prison below.

"Woah," Eve gasped. "How did you do that?"

"Magic, remember?" Kyle smirked, as he chewed on a pancake and showered the table with a thousand little bits of soggy dough.

Eve cast him a wary look that dissipated as soon as she took another bite.

"It even tastes better! That's amazing. Thanks, Kyle."

"Don't mention it," Kyle replied, before adding ominously. "Like, seriously, please don't mention it to anyone while we're here!"

"OK, weirdo," Eve chuckled.

As he took a sip of watery American coffee, Greg caught a shadow pass over Kyle's usual sunny disposition. A slight twitch in the brow, a strain in the tendons in his neck. Kyle was never tense. Greg frowned to himself, something was off. However, his train of thought was derailed by a sudden yell from the direction of the bathroom. The group looked up to see a middle aged, slightly balding gentleman in a nasty, striped, grey suit, sprinting out of the bathroom into the restaurant. His trousers were wrapped around his ankles and his willy was hanging out like a pink worm on a fishing lure, flapping awkwardly back and forth for everyone and their dog to see.

Understandably, the baby started crying again. The man running from the bathroom seemed to be undergoing some kind of hysterical fit.

"The urinal!" he screeched as a woman recoiled at the sight of his dangling member, shielding her children's eyes, lest they be accidentally poked in them, as the naked man ran past.

"The lights! It was moving!" he howled.

He was wide of eye, shrivelled of gentials, and delirious as he careered past the group waiting patiently by the front door and threw himself out onto the sidewalk, taking off down the street as he stuffed his penis back into his underpants.

"It's all right everyone!" The waitress at the front door yelled. "Probably just someone having a bad night. We apologise for the disturbance."

This seemed to work as the groups at all the tables immediately turned back to their coffee and pancakes as if nothing had happened. Admittedly, a man running through a diner with his penis hanging out is far from the most insane thing you'll see on a typical weekend in Las Vegas. Even the people waiting for a table just shrugged and returned to swiping through the usual swamp of internet detritus on their phones. It was only once order had been restored, that Gloopy came shuffling out of the bathrooms and squeezed himself back into the booth next to Eve.

"What the fuck was all that about?" Kyle asked him suspiciously.

Gloopy simply shrugged his shoulders and shook his head.

"You didn't see what that guy was freaking out about? Something about lights in a urinal?"

Same response from the jelly man. Luckily for Gloopy, no one noticed the urinal cake stuck to his maroon corduroy trousers as a more pressing concern had chosen that moment to make itself known to the group.

Gloporg, who luckily was located right at the back of the semi-circular booth, out of sight of the other customers, was beginning to spasm violently. Parts of his body were collapsing, regaining their solidity, then collapsing again, as the colony of insects making up his internal structure began to rage violently against one another.

"Jesus Christ, Gloporg!" Kyle hissed at him. "What the fuck are you doing?"

"Nothing. This is nothing. Everything's fine," he replied, in the way some politicians, who shall remain nameless, would claim everything was fine, while hundreds of thousands of their citizens die from a preventable infectious disease. "There are some dissidents making unwelcome noise in my lower levels but their rebellion will soon be quashed!"

"I hate it when he talks like that," Deebro sighed. "It just reminders me we hang out with a bug dictator."

Suddenly, Gloporg collapsed onto the floor under the table in one huge pile of writhing bugs inside a bag of human skin. Take a moment to think about how horrific that would be to witness. Deebro chanced a glance under the table and despite having a bioform suit that was mostly mechanical, even he nearly regurgitated his breakfast in horror.

As the bugs went to war with each other on the floor, having been reduced to nothing more than a writhing mass of skin and khaki, a waitress skipped over to their table with an enormous pot of terrible coffee. The group quickly closed ranks around the nightmare playing out under the table, hiding it behind a forest of legs. They didn't have a psychic plunger handy, they had left it in the cupboard under the kitchen sink, so if she spotted what was going on, Gloopy would probably have to digest her.

"Hiiiii!" she sang. Her infuriating cheeriness made at least two of the group think digestion wouldn't be the worst outcome of this conversation.

"Can I get you folks any more coffee?"

"Nope! We're good, thank you!" Kyle quickly replied, trying to cover up the sound of scuffling and tiny screeches going on under the table.

"What about desserts? Can I bring you a dessert menu?"

"Nope, again, all good here!"

"You sure, sugar? We got a great special today. Apple and Blueberry pie."

"I said we're fine!" he barked at her, as he noticed a tendril of jelly from Gloopy's thigh begin to quietly and hungrily, snake its way under the table towards her.

"Well, fine. I'll just go then!" she replied curtly and strode off muttering something under her breath about ungrateful assholes and spitting in somebody's milkshake. Fortunately, by now the sound of arthropods beating each other to death had begun to quiet down under the table but little voices could still be heard if you really listened carefully.

"Wait. No. Please, I saved you all from Yeezrax. I'm your hero."

"You became what you despised, Gloporg. You betrayed everything you ever stood for."

"You, you were just weak. I gave you all order. This colony is nothing without me. You need a leader. I was the hero you all needed."

"I guess you either die a hero or live long enough to see yourself become the villain. We won't make the same mistakes you did, Gloporg."

"You think a Democracy will work? It will never work? You need me!"

"No. We don't. Not anymore. Goodbye, Gloporg."

"No! Wait! Wait! ARGH!"

There was a tiny crunching noise, somewhere between the satisfying pop of bubble wrap and the crunch of a cockroach dying under the weight of a steel-toed boot and then silence. Then, like a gruesome, fleshy spectre, or an inflatable-arm-flailing-tube-man at a used car lot, Gloporg's body began to rise from under the table, slowly re-gaining form until it was sitting once again in his place in the booth. The rest of the group sat looking at him with expressions ranging from boredom, to exasperation, to anticipation, to total and utter disgust. I'll let you guess whose expression was whose. Then the hive spoke again.

"Hey guys. Nice to meet you all. We are the United Colony of Pylar."

Then a million, very tiny voices began to chant.

"UCP! UCP! UCP!"

"Hey, hey! Shut the fuck up!" Kyle hissed at him.

"Sorry, we're all quite excited. A new democratic government has been established. Pylar, our leader, is now answerable to the council of representatives and the union of elected officials, so as to ensure no one Furmbog has too much power. Every thirty bintacks, each limb will elect new leaders to the council of officials, who will vote on behalf of their constituents on matters of blah blah blah outreach programs blah blah blah colony insurance blah blah blah oversight committees blah blah blah Furmbog first policies blah blah blah—"

Again, I would love to give you the full, accurate account of Pylar's speech but unfortunately, a reliable source is hard to come by as nobody who was in attendance that day was able to follow his ramblings about the complexity of his new internal political system without zoning out for more than a few seconds. Mercifully, Kyle's impatience put an end to their suffering.

"Alright, alright, put a sock in it!" he sighed. "Your new name is Pylar, that's all we need to know."

"Yes, it was voted on by a committee led by the congressional spokesman for—"

"For the love of science, shut up!" Kyle barked.

Pylar began to mouth a response but clammed up when he saw little streaks of electricity shoot from the tips of Kyle's hair as he bristled with annoyance. Greg and Eve felt the hairs on their arms begin to stand on end and were shot through with a horrible chill that caused them to shudder uncomfortably. Kyle seemed to recognise their look of apprehension and took a deep breath to settle himself, then slumped back down, deflated, into his seat.

"Let's just please work out what we're doing next," he sighed. "It's my stag and I don't want to spend it listening to this one drone on about his internal politics."

"Well, we're in Vegas." Eve suggested, "Shall we just order some Bloody Mary's and see what happens?"

"Finally!" Kyle laughed. "Someone is talking sense. Excuse me, waitress!"

"Maybe we should wait for the other girl," Eve suggested. "I think that one wants to spit in your drink."

"That's the gratitude you get for stopping someone from getting digested." Kyle huffed, "Typical Vegas."

# Chapter Eleven

Sixty-eight million and two light years and forty-seven miles away from that Denny's on Las Vegas Boulevard, on board an inconspicuous spherical space vessel, drifting lazily through the vastness of the void on the gravitational pull of several precisely arranged yellow suns, a meeting was called to order.

Eight robed figures sitting in the most expertly crafted hover chairs, designed for optimal posture and perfect lumbar support, came together in the centre of a room perfectly designed for such meetings (no superfluous distractions such as windows or snacks or frivolous charts showing out-of-date quarterly sales metrics), to sit around an expertly crafted circular, white marble table, a circle being the perfect shape to allow ease of communication with minimal uncomfortable head turning required, and marble being the perfect material because it's hard wearing and looks pretty.

One of the robed figures opened a small, metallic box that sat on the table and withdrew from it a small wooden gavel, phased sixty-eight million light years across the universe from a small backwards planet called Earth. The figures in attendance at the meeting all despised Earth for its inhabitants' sinful, unscientific culture but they all begrudgingly agreed the gavel was undoubtedly the perfect, and most satisfying, tool for calling such meetings to order. The head of the committee banged the gavel once, though he needn't have since there was never a need to silence a ruckus at these meetings, everyone here was here to do business.

"I call this meeting of the Galactic High Council to Order," the creature with the gavel squeaked in a language that no human ears would be able to comprehend. The language of their species was far more efficient than any paltry attempt humans had managed to come up with over the millennia.

"There is but one order of business at this meeting."

"But, Chairman, why would you call a meeting with only one order of business to discuss?" cried the figure to his right. "This is highly inefficient! We have Zoom meetings for single item discussions."

"Silence! You create inefficiency by discussing the efficiency of this meeting. The seriousness of this matter means it would not be efficient, nor secure, to discuss this over Zoom. You know spies from the cartel are trying to listen to our communications!"

The other robed figures could not argue with The Chairman's supreme logic, to do so would only slow the meeting further still and to hinder an important meeting was an unforgivable sin within the High Council. After all, the Supreme Reverent Musk preaches that all meetings must remain under twenty minutes lest death, destruction and tardiness fall upon your house.

"The missing unit has been found."

The other council members almost gasped in astonishment before remembering gasps were a most inefficient use of oxygen. They simply nodded in acknowledgement, thus ensuring no effort be wasted by repeating information.

"A pulse surge has been detected on 45-90DXTY-9042. He has been hiding on—Earth!"

This time, despite their supreme discipline, the other council members did utter a collective gasp. They would be certain to flog themselves upon completion of the meeting for such an egregious offense but this was shocking news indeed!

"This is an offense of the highest order. He charts a course directly against the scientific advancement of the universe!"

"Indeed, he shirks his responsibility. There is a risk that he has abandoned our ways entirely and gone native; lost himself in the sinful ways of the humans."

"Does he not remember the chaos that planet wrecked upon the universe? The great equation was unbalanced, the great progression delayed!"

"We are all aware of the history, 67TY! Do not waste time and resources recanting facts of which we are all aware!"

Silence once again descended upon the Council. 67TY quietly seethed, his time would come. He alone was familiar with the missing unit like no other on the council. He was uniquely poised to take advantage of the situation, but he must bide his time for now. All members were in fear of the consequences should The Chairman have to use the gavel again, the waste of precious energy required to swing the gavel unnecessarily was an offense of the highest order.

"What must be done?" one of the figures asked, at a volume loud enough to be heard by all but not so loud as to waste precious energy uttering the question.

"He must be retrieved. We will go to Earth and ensure he is brought back to fulfil his purpose."

A nod of agreement was returned by all the figures at the meeting, save for one who sat across the table from the leader.

"What's the big deal?" this one asked, in a breezy tone very much removed from the general, stick-up-the-ass vibe of the meeting thus far. "I mean, he's just one guy. We've got plenty more units to pull from?"

No words were said but the sudden tension in the room was enough to warn the figure who spoke what was coming next. The other council members slowly turned their attentions towards him, their faces obscured in the deep shadows of their hooded robes, save for seven pairs of blue flickering lamps burning from within the deep black voids. The air around the rouge council member began to shimmer and flicker like a desert mirage and he felt the tell-tale prickles course through his body just under the skin.

"Oh, um, no—I didn't mean that," it stammered, as all the other figures raised their palms towards him and sparks of electricity flicked between their outstretched fingertips.

"You chart a course against the great progression," The Chairman said, as he bore into the sinner's mind with an icy glare. "You unbalance the great equation."

"No! No! Pease! Don't do this! I misspoke. I'll do better!"

"Saying what you don't mean shows an unforgivable lack of efficiency. Goodbye, 22HY!"

With a sudden CRACK, seven bolts of blue lightning appeared in a circle around 22HY and violently cut through him like knives through hot butter. He was reduced to ash before a scream could escape his lips, as it was intended, a scream is a terrible waste of precious energy. As the remaining figures lowered their palms, a panel opened up in the wall and a small robot scuttled in to vacuum up the dust, the remaining council members paid it no notice.

"OK, that's it, no more electing council members through nepotism! Agreed?" The Chairman sighed.

"Agreed. Why did you think he would be a good fit for the council, 12DC?"

"He was my cousin. I promised Auntie Gormandifletoppypoppy I would at least give him a shot."

"We should vaporise you for that, 12DC!" the leader growled. "Make sure your next nomination isn't an idiot."

"Who's going to tell 12DC's aunt we vaporised her son then?"

"Not it!"

"Not it!"

Not i-dammit, fine!"

"It is settled. 67TY will tell 12DC's aunt her son has been turned to carbon dust but it can wait. For now, we must prepare for phase-travel to Earth."

The group nodded in agreement; the robot collected the last of 22HY's dust particles and the leader ended the meeting with one more bang of the gavel. He then turned to the control panel behind him and tapped in the co-ordinates for Earth.

# Chapter Twelve

At the precise moment that the cabal of murderous, science-obsessed crackpots was furiously tapping in the co-ordinates for Earth, cursing the inefficiency of an outdated cartography system that assigns a four-hundred-and-twenty-eight-digit code to every one of the billions of inhabited planets in the universe, the missing unit was finishing off his fourth Bloody Mary and wiping the flecks of tomato juice and celery out of his blonde beard. The plan had been to go to a casino after one or two rounds but the newly elected Democratic Whatever of Pylar was having a little trouble deciding on which particular casino it would like to go to first.

"The constituents in the left leg have voted for the Bellagio. Apparently, the motion picture, Ocean's Eleven, is very popular down there and they would like to see the fountain."

"Great," Kyle belched. "Bellagio it is."

"But the constituents in the right arm would like to go to the Caesar's Palace for the retail opportunities. They are claiming because we write with our right arm that they should be allowed a larger share of the vote."

"What are you on about?" Deebro groaned. "You're a sentient colony of ants. You don't have a dominant hand."

"The representative of the right leg is asking where we will acquire the funds for gambling when there are so many constituents in the colony without access to basic medical care."

"Why the hell do they need medical care? I'm pretty sure they get eaten as soon as they're unfit to work anyway."

"The governor of the torso is suggesting we apply for a loan from Gloopy for the funds. But now the arms are saying we should be spending the money on defence of the colony before gambling and the legs want to spend it on educational reform. They are tired of the worker/solider divide."

"Give me strength," Eve sighed as she also put away her fourth Bloody Mary.

"Now, the legs are asking how the winnings will be distributed. The representatives in the head are suggesting the winnings be divided among the upper body and used to stimulate the internal economy, thus allowing profits to trickle down to the lower limbs."

"Should we just leave him behind?" Greg groaned. "I think I'm going to puke if I have to listen to any more of this." The Bloody Marys may have been a contributing factor to his deteriorating physical state.

"Agreed," Kyle replied. "The Mirage is just across the street, let's start there."

"Oh—the Mirage," Greg stammered. "I mean, maybe we should just thi-"

"Perfect, sounds great!" Deebro chimed in, cutting Greg off mid-sentence. "Let's just get the fuck out of here. Everyone in agreement?"

Greg's feeble murmurs of protest were drowned out comprehensibly by the cheers of the rest of the group, aside from Pylar, who was still debating to himself the benefits of trickle-down winnings versus even distribution to the workers. Gloopy, reluctantly, reached into his pocket and drew out an excessive wad of notes about as thick as Greg's forearm, which wasn't very impressive for a forearm but made for a seriously impressive wad of fifty-dollar bills.

He threw a handful down on the table as if it were loose change and just waddled off towards the door, not realising he had overpaid by around three hundred dollars—typical trust fund baby. Don't worry though, Greg being the savvy, some would say cheap, Scotsman that he was, pocketed the change (minus the twelve percent tip of course), much to the chagrin of the waitress who had been hovering near the table like a vulture as soon as she saw Gloopy draw forth the girthy wad of notes from his trouser pocket.

That would have been enough in tips to feed her gambling addiction for a week or breed about a hundred Quiznarks. Although, she might not have found the notes so appealing if she knew that Gloopy's pants pocket was actually more of a—how do I put this—biological pocket. A smuggler's purse, if you will.

Kyle clearly wasn't in the mood to waste any more time talking. By the time Greg stumbled out of the Denny's he and Eve were already making their way across the road towards the Mirage. Greg looked up at the big, surprisingly restrained, for Las Vegas, ninety-degree slab of glass and concrete. It loomed like a huge capitalist giant with his humongous arms outstretched, beckoning all the hapless punters inside and Greg couldn't help but feel a tad nervous.

It had been two years since his little incident there. Would they remember him? Would they even let him back in the building? He tried calling to the group to desperately pitch them a different casino, but they were already across the street and weaving their way through the crowds past the fake volcano (it's Vegas; it's weird if you don't have a fake volcano or roller coaster outside your hotel) and towards the entrance. He saw Eve turn and wave to him with a smile, which was all the encouragement he needed to suppress his misgivings and tentatively follow them inside.

It was almost exactly the moment that Greg stepped into the lobby of the Mirage, that Stanley, a junior researcher at NASA, told his boss he saw a new star appear in the sky. It was the most bizarre thing; for a couple of seconds his sensors picked up a celestial object, that seemed to burn brighter than anything in the sky except our own sun. He held up a hand to call over his manager but by the time the old man had summoned up the energy to put down his sudoku and shuffle his way over to Stanley's desk, the rouge object had disappeared again.

His manager suggested it may have been a meteorite burning up upon entry into the atmosphere, but Stanley dismissed the idea because its trajectory pattern. You see, it didn't really seem to have one. Somehow, a star had appeared at a point in space, burned for two seconds, then disappeared again.

Stanley went on to create hundreds of theories for this phenomenon in his lifetime, all of them considered wildly outrageous by his fellow physicists and astronomers. Most of them agreed his unfortunate habit of micro-dosing on a cocktail of psilocybin and lead based paint fumes had simply gotten the better of him. Once again, the universe contrives to ensure aliens only reveal themselves to humans with a history of substance abuse.

Stanley, however, wasn't tripping. In reality, an innocuous looking metal orb, perfectly designed to float through the vastness of space on minimal fuel and resources, had phased-travelled into Earth's orbit and cloaked itself. It now floated silently and undetected, around the primate and Nematode controlled planet, while the life-forms aboard discussed their next move.

"Where on the planet did the surge originate from?" 67TY asked.

"Our scanners indicate it came from the fifty-first Area of the Planet, but we cannot be any more precise than that. The scouts who originally discovered this planet felt dividing it up into three thousand areas would be efficient enough for future purposes."

"For the love of progress!" 12DC groaned. "How shall we locate the missing unit? No doubt he is disguised as one of the humans."

"We shall make contact with the leader of the Bhutts," The Chairman, designation A1, commanded. "They wield great power on this planet now. Area fifty-one falls within their sphere of influence. They will have many spies in place we can use."

"Are you suggesting we do business with the cartel?" 45E squeaked. "This is highly irregular A1."

"Again, why do you waste energy with useless exposition?" A1 snarled. "We are all aware this is undesirable, 45E. However, the Bhutts are idiots. We will use them for our own ends and move on. Now be silent!"

A slight murmur of submissive agreement emanated throughout the room while A1 retrieved his holographic projector. He typed in a short sequence of digits, which resulted in a pale-blue hologram ten feet high being projected into the centre of the room. The council looked at it in puzzlement and frustration. Instead of the usual instant, flawless connection and the face of the intended recipient of their communication, all that was projected was a small, spinning donut, with the word "buffering" floating underneath it in bold lettering.

"What is the meaning of this?" A1 barked. "Do the Bhutts try to mock us with this symbol?"

"Unclear, sir," 12DC replied. "Does anyone understand the meaning of the word buffering?"

"I believe it is an archaic term," Said 45E. "Something our species has not had a need for in millions of cycles."

"All right professor, just tell us what it means."

"It means a slow connection."

"A slow—connection?"

"I believe the humans use such primitive satellite technology that holographic communication requires significant loading times."

"Curse the inefficiency of this planet!" A1 barked. The others were surprised by his sudden increase in volume, an unusual lack of efficiency on his part. "Haven't they installed worldwide 5G yet?"

"Apparently not, sir. Apparently, there is a movement of humans who say it causes the spread of something called coronavirus."

"I hate this planet already," A1 groaned. "Looks like the Bhutts are making good on their promises."

"We shall need an alternative form of communication. O-I, provide us with a device the Earthlings use to communicate."

A small panel in the wall opened up to reveal a phase printer. The ship, without saying a word, as this was not an O-I programmed to communicate unless invited to do so, began to print an enormous slab of plastic and metal with an archaic liquid crystal display.

"What in the universe is this, O-I?" A1 barked. "Respond!"

"Item is a typical human portable communications device. Earthlings refer to it as a mobile phone. This model is designated as an iPhone 11 Pro Max."

"This is considered a portable device?" A1 balked. "It's enormous. And are you telling me they created eleven of these devices without so much as a single innovative design alteration?"

"Apparently the humans prefer it that way."

"All right then. Cease communication, O-I. Provide operations download for an Earth mobile phone."

The ship did as it was instructed and downloaded the required information to A1's internal processor. He then instructed the council to gather around the device as he turned it on. They then spent the next two hours figuring out how to charge the phone, install a SIM card, sign up to a payment plan (which required the creation of a human identity, a bank account and a debit card) and set up the device to use a PIN code instead of fingerprint identification, since none of them had fingerprints that could be used, all the while growing to hate the missing unit more and more for bringing them to this cursed, broken toilet of a planet. Eventually, they got the blasted device to a stage where it would allow them to make a call.

"Call Donnaht the Bhutt," A1 said to the phone. Nothing happened.

"Perhaps it does not have voice recognition. The humans are very primitive," 45E suggested.

A1 checked his download data and realised his mistake.

"Siri, called Donnaht the Bhutt," he repeated.

"I'm sorry, but Dunking Donuts is not in your contact list," the phone responded in an infuriatingly ethereal female voice. The soothing tones did nothing to ease the council's frustration.

"Not Dunking Donuts. Donnaht the Bhutt!"

"I'm sorry, I do not recognise Don Abbott. Please try another contact."

"Blast this infernal device!" A1 roared, hurling the phone across the room then vaporising it with a vicious blast of electricity from his fingertips.

The rest of the council looked on in utter shock. The staggering waste of energy required to do such a thing was unheard of amongst the council.

"A1—That was a highly inefficient," 45E remarked slowly.

The rest of the council turned to their Chairman, A1, once a model of stability and efficiency, brought low to a panting, frustrated wreck by two hours with an earthling mobile phone.

"Hey, no! Stop that right now!" he barked at them as they raised their palms towards them. "It's the Earthling technology. It's so broken and inefficient."

"That as may be," 67TY replied with unmistakable relish. "But the judgement is passed."

Sparks of electricity flicked between his fingertips.

The last words that escaped A1's fuzzy lips were something like, "Fuck this fucking planet—" Then, for the second time that day, a member of the ruling Galactic High Council was reduced to a little pile of ash and the faithful robot scuttled out of his hole to clean up their mess.

67TY began to make a move for A1's empty chair but much to his chagrin, 45E got there first, plonking his fat little bottom down at the head of the table (despite the table being round) like he somehow deserved the position. 67TY, ever the schemer, knew now was not the time for a leadership challenge. Knowing this planet and the missing unit, another shake-up would likely come soon enough.

"The human phones are a lost cause," 45E declared. "O-I, we must get our communicator working. Can you re-task all the Earthling satellites to boost our signal?"

"Yes, this can be achieved."

"Excellent, see to it at once. When we have the required power, call Donnaht the Bhutt. We have already delayed too long."

The council, now reduced to six members, sat quietly as the O-I set about the business of hijacking most of Earth's satellites, causing significant disruption to the humans' internet pornography consumption, which in turn led to the birth of seven-hundred and six new-born babies about nine months later, in order to get enough juice to call the Bhutt leader.

Eventually, the hologram restarted itself and, mercifully, the cursed buffering signal was nowhere to be seen. Instead, there was a ten-foot projection of Donnaht the Bhutt's face and what a truly, hideously, odiously vile face it was. Species across the universe avoid contact with members of the Bhutt cartel at all costs but desperate times called for desperate measures. The missing unit must be located. This time the Council had no choice but to deal with this vile beast.

"Well, well, well," Donnaht began. "The High Council calls me for help. I knew you would come crawling back someday because I'm so intelligent."

"Some people say I'm very, very intelligent."

45E sighed, this was not going to be a pleasant conversation.

"Greetings Donnaht. How goes your exploits on Earth?"

"Oh, Earth's great, everything's great, we're doing great things here. I can't talk about everything we're doing now, but it's probably the best planet in the universe. We've got the best stuff, doing lots of great things. I'm probably the best leader here ever and definitely a genius, a very stable genius at that. People know it, people tell me all the time."

"Science," 45E prayed to himself, "give the strength to get through this conversation."

"For sure, nobody rules planets better than me. You all said, it wouldn't work but now, I have so many supporters. All the planets in the universe say I'm doing a great job. All the ladies come up to me now and they just want me, you know. They just flirt with me, consciously or unconsciously, although that's to be expected."

45E counted backwards and waited till the beast was done droning on. Eventually, the tirade of hyperbole and self-gratifying nonsense came to a merciful end.

"So, why are you calling me? Are you wanting to make a deal? I make the best trade deals. The guy before me made all these terrible deals and I pulled out of them and made better deals. Better deals than the Asians, they don't even ask how the weather is. They just walk in and say, we want deal!"

"No Donnaht, unfortunately, we're not here to make a trade deal," 45E replied through gritted teeth. "We believe there is an illegal alien present in your sector and we want you to locate him and send him back to us."

"These illegals are terrible," Donnaht replied. "They come in here and they're rapists and murderers who do terrible things and they take jobs away from good people who were born here. They don't even write good, they don't know how to write good—and did I mention they're all rapists!"

"Indeed. Couldn't agree more Donnaht. That's my we want this one captured and returned to us, so we can punish him. You will be handsomely rewarded for your efforts."

Donnaht's greedy little peepers lit up at that last part. To the Bhutt cartel, there was nothing more motivating than financial reward. They say they're only interested in money as a way to keep score and playing the game is the real motivation but the noticeable dilation in his sunken pupils said otherwise.

The High Council's obsessive advancement of their scientific philosophy had long put them at odds with the Bhutts, who would trust the advice of one of their own turds over that of a subject matter expert but as we said before, desperate times call for desperate measures.

"So, Donnaht. Do we have a deal?"

# Chapter Thirteen

On reflection, everyone agreed their little soiree to the casino went largely as expected. Greg shuffled uncomfortably on the bottom-torturing steel bench in the holding cell, squished in between Deebro and Kyle like the human meat in an extra-terrestrial sandwich. Granted, not all the blame for current predicament could be placed at the feet of his foreign compatriots, he had played his part too.

Greg was feeling a touch apprehensive; his friends' unusual origins certainly didn't make the prospect of an interrogation by the Las Vegas Police Department any more enticing. Knowing his luck, they'd probably decide he was an alien as well and he'd be the first one to get dissected for government experiments. They'd cut him open, see a slimy mass of alcohol ravaged internal organs, very similar to those of any other human and conclude he was just the least interesting alien they'd ever encountered.

While Deebro and Kyle remained largely innocent for Greg's current state of incarceration, there was one other "person" on whose shoulders the blame rested solely and utterly. Greg swore to himself that next time he saw that perverted mass of sentient goop, he was going to dissect the fucker himself and sell him off to local hospitals in individual Jello cups.

Everything had been going fine, at least from the front door to the hotel reception desk. In other words, it all went to shit almost immediately. Given that Gloopy was carrying enough cash to bankroll a small African dictatorship for several months, they decided to just get rooms for the weekend, rather than facing the prospect of shambling back to the ship and dealing with those creepy little Quiznarks at five in the morning with debilitating hangovers.

They were waiting in line, admiring the Mirage's tropical interior, a little green garden of Eden nestled in the Nevada desert (except, in this garden of Eden, sinning was absolutely encouraged at every turn), while trying to appear at least partially sober and not give away any hints that four of the group originated from another galaxy. We all know how touchy the subject of illegal aliens is in America.

Pylar was still frantically scribbling in his notepad. He was fascinated by the idea that humans would create a tropical jungle inside a casino while also relentlessly tearing down the ones they already had outside. Deebro's attention seemed to be drawn to something behind the reception desk, but Greg didn't want to risk looking up to see what he was staring at. He was huddled in behind Deebro and Gloopy with his head down, trying to avoid eye contact with any of the reception staff, given there was a risk he might be recognised. This would not be good for anyone.

There was another contributing factor to his agitated state. To the left of the reception desk, emblazoned on the back wall, was a fifteen-foot poster proudly declaring to all the guests who would be performing that night for their entertainment. Three blue men on a simple black background, their manic white eyes suggesting the first part of their act was going to involve devouring the cameraman. Their cold, unblinking gaze made Greg break out in a similarly cold sweat; it was as if they knew he was there already.

"It's fine," he thought to himself. "It was years ago. You look different now, they probably don't even remember you. And if they do, they probably won't even care. People probably get into scraps with celebrities all the time in these places."

His internal monologue didn't do much to assuage his nerves. Sweat was building up on his brow in a thick reflective sheen, made even more obvious by the dazzlingly bright lights in the reception area. The other unfortunate side effect was the smell. Looking around, Greg noticed a few upturned noses as the other guests began to wonder who was trying to smuggle a dead cat into the casino. He subtly lifted up his shirt to make sure he wasn't the source of their distress. He was.

"What is it?" Eve whispered.

"It's nothing, don't worry," Greg replied. "Two seconds, I'll be back."

He didn't want to lower himself even further in her eyes by explaining to her that he was beginning to smell like the headline act at an open-casket funeral.

Greg, keeping his head down, scurried back to where Pylar was standing, still scribbling in his notepad. Greg reasoned that if these freaks can make clothes appear out of thin air, they must be able to conjure up a can of deodorant for him.

"Hey, Glop—I mean Pylar," he whispered. "I need you to do me a favour."

143

"That depends on the favour."

"—What?"

"Well, tell me what it is first. Then I shall have the request ratified in the assembly and we shall vote on appropriate recourse."

"Whatever. Can you use one of your magic box thingies to whip me up some antiperspirant or something?"

"Unfortunately, no. Portable phase-printers are very expensive and require a special license, which we don't have."

"Shit!" Greg groaned. "It's just, well, I smell a bit off."

"Indeed, it has been discussed in the Senate. Several elected members of the colony wanted to declare war on you for insulting us with your odour."

"Jesus Christ! We can discuss how fucked up that is later. Can you not just do some science mumbo-jumbo and fix this please?"

"I'm not familiar with this mumbo jumbo you refer to. But we may have a solution for you, I'll just have to clear it with the council first."

"OK, great, let's do it."

"The council is demanding reparations for our efforts."

"Jesus, fine. What do they want?"

"One of your kidneys. It has the right nutrients to feed the workers for several hundred cycles."

"Well, that's not going to happen."

"Fine—Twenty bucks?"

"My god, you're bad at negotiating. Fine, done. Now, can we please get on with this?"

"Of course, I just need to clear it with the members of parliament."

"I thought you already did."

"That was the lower council, the vote now moves on to parliament."

"Jesus Pylar! Hurry the fuck up!"

"Fine, I shall use an executive order to bypass the government, I hope you understand the implications of this."

"Yes, yes, whatever. Now let's fucking go!"

Having had his first taste of how difficult it is to get a vote passed through a tiny democratic government, controlled by a system of neurotic bureaucratic ants, Greg finally managed to hurry Pylar into one of the men's bathrooms. They checked the coast was clear and huddled together into one of the stalls, with Pylar crouching down to make sure the top of his bucket hat wasn't showing over the top of the cubicle.

"OK, now what?" Greg asked.

"Now, just hold still." Pylar replied.

What happened next haunts Greg to this very day. People have had nightmares about scenarios much less uncomfortable than this, woken up panting and drenched in sweat and thanked their lucky stars nothing this horrifying would even happen in real life. As they huddled in the stall, hundreds of Furmbogs came rushing out of Pylar's right shoe and began to scuttle their way up Greg's trouser leg. Greg went to shriek and spring out of the stall but Pylar put a hand on his shoulder and held him still.

"Do not panic," he said as Greg felt hundreds of little feet scamper all over him underneath his clothes. "My workers are removing all foreign agents from your skin and cleaning out your pores, this will not take long."

Greg simply whimpered in response as he felt the little critters make their way up through his collar and scamper over his face. It felt like he was being hit with a mild electrical current while also having an incredibly deep facial scrub with abrasive cleaner. What he also noticed was the smell. Instead of the smell of stale alcohol, sweat and Badger's rectum, there was a new smell that was something like Lavender and Cinnamon, as if he had been scrubbed head to toe in expensive shampoo and body lotion.

"My god. That's amazing," Greg gasped, starting to relax and even enjoying the sensation. I suppose the closest equivalent you may have experienced would be those foot baths in Thailand where little fish eat the dead skin off your feet. Imagine that, but for your whole body and replace the fish with hundreds of sentient alien bugs.

"What is that smell? It's really nice."

"Those are pheromones."

"—What?"

"Pheromones, we excrete them when we wish to entice another Queen into our colony for mating. You will be very attractive to any other Furmbog colonies we come into contact with today."

Any sense of relaxation or pleasure Greg had managed to extract from this whole experience vanished under a fresh wave of nausea. He was seconds away from throwing up again, to hell with the hundreds of little critters still digging around in his pores and excreting love-juice into his armpits, but he was stopped short by the sound of the door opening and footsteps coming into the bathroom.

Back out in the reception area, things weren't progressing any smoother. Surprisingly, Gloopy wasn't the one causing the issues in this particular instance, having controlled his urge to consume the human behind the reception desk, as Eve and Kyle took charge of procuring a room while he impatiently held out his over-compensating wad of stupid human currency.

This time Deebro was the one who wasn't holding it together. I don't know if you've ever been to the Mirage and I'll admit the last time I was there I was very drunk and possibly a little stoned, so I don't remember the details all too well, but for the theme of this casino they decided to go tropical. The atrium is one huge glass dome with lots of tropical plants, streams, giant fake animals and a few waterfalls on the inside, sprouting like colossal weeds from every crack and crevice in the golden walls and marble floors. The theme extends to behind the reception desk where there is an enormous aquarium filled with a colourful menagerie of tropical fish, along with a variety of other miscellaneous underwater creatures.

I think you can probably see where I'm going with this. To most humans, except perhaps animal rights activists, the aquarium seems like a generally harmless, is slightly extravagant, piece of interior decoration but imagine if you went on holiday to an alien planet and strolled inside a fancy-schmancy hotel, to find a glass box full of stupefied, captive humans on display behind the reception desk. You'd be slightly horrified, would you not? Thus, we find ourselves in Deebro's shoes.

As Kyle and Eve navigated the minefield of trying to secure a room in a Las Vegas hotel without IDs, while a hungry jelly monster angrily tries to shove a fat stack of unregistered cash up the receptionist's nose, Deebro was staring in shock at the scores of his brethren held prisoner in this transparent exhibit of horrors for the amusement of the overlord humans.

It's important to clarify that, while there are plenty of sentient fish on Deebro's planet that looked almost exactly like the fish in that particular aquarium, hence his discomfort, none of the fish in this tank were actually aliens; just bog-standard, stupid-ass, Earth fish. It was only through the mystery of convergent evolution that these fishies happened to have an uncanny resemblance to several of Deebro's close family friends and relatives.

As he stared at one particularly gormless goldfish, that was a dead ringer for his second-cousin, aimlessly swimming circles around a tiny little underwater castle, his feelings changed from distress, to severe indignation, to a full-on righteous fury.

"Why can't six of us share one room?" Kyle groaned. "We're paying for the room, why does it matter if some of us sleep on the floor?"

"It's not the policy, sir. It's for insurance purposes. And we need a credit card to add to your file, I can't just take cash."

"Why not? I thought you huma—I mean, Americans used cards or cash."

"Again, it's for insurance purposes, sir."

"God, fine. What's the least number of rooms you can fit six guests in?"

"I'm afraid right now we only have deluxe suites available which hold two guests maximum."

"Don't you have anything cheaper?" Eve asked.

"Sorry, we're fully booked, I suggest you book online before you—Sir! Sir! What are you doing? You can't be back here!"

Eve and Kyle turned in shock (Gloopy kept his hungry little eyes fixed on the receptionist), as Deebro vaulted over the reception desk and hurled himself at the aquarium in a frenzy.

"I'll save you my brothers! You don't have to live in bondage anymore!"

What Deebro had been planning to do with the fish if he had shattered the tank, no one has ever been able to deduce. Luckily, such a situation never arose. Deebro underestimated the structural rigidity of the glass, rammed into it head-first like a rutting goat and slumped impotently to the floor in a broken, spasming heap, with the tank remaining completely undamaged.

The receptionist, understandably, let out an ear-splitting scream, convinced that such a collision to the head would almost certainly have killed this maniacal fish-lover and the way he was lying on the floor, limbs askew and twitching lamely, only reinforced the idea. However, after a momentary pause, his entire body shuddered in one huge convulsion and he rose immediately to his feet again like a denim-plumaged phoenix.

Deebro turned to the wide-eyed, ashen-faced crowd that were looking on in shock and bemusement, with only Kyle understanding the implications of the way the corner of Deebro's mouth and his right eye had begun to twitch uncontrollably. That was going to be another insurance claim, but Deebro's little Miley Cyrus moment meant they now had bigger fish to fry, as it were.

Unfortunately, standard Las Vegas hotel policy is to immediately inform security if someone decides to vault over the front desk and violently headbutt the aquarium. Kyle clocked one of the staff talking frantically into a walkie-talkie; it was definitely time to go. He turned to look back at the entrance but could see already there were guards converging on the door. They would need to find another way out. As you can imagine, in their unique situation, it was not advisable to risk a confrontation with armed Las Vegas security personnel.

"You know what," he said sweetly to the shocked receptionist, "I think we'll leave the rooms this time. Thanks so much for your time. Guys, let's go!" He grabbed Eve and Gloopy, who was still impatiently waving his handful of cash in the receptionist's face and dragged them away, in the direction of the casino floor, beckoning to Deebro to follow.

The shadow of hotel security was looming large over the group but luckily fate or more specifically, Greg and Pylar, provided them with a suitable distraction. As the group hurried through the atrium towards the casino, they heard a yell as, for the second time that day, a man came barrelling out of the men's bathroom with his trousers round his knees and his willie flapping wildly between his legs as he ran.

"Bugs!" he yelled. "Hundreds of them, in the bathroom. Pouring out of the stalls!"

It didn't take alien Sherlock Holmes to deduce the cause of this commotion. Greg and Pylar slipped casually out of the stall a few seconds after the screaming man, who was now firmly in the custody of hotel security and being made to stuff his member back into his pants.

"That's him!" the man screamed, waving his hand at Pylar frantically. "The bugs were coming out of him!"

"You two!" one of the guards barked at Greg and Pylar. "Wait there!"

The two of them froze as the man-mountain in the undersized polo shirt came lumbering toward them. Greg had to stifle a giggle; the bouncer's oversized thighs meant his walk was more of a waddle and it made him look like a buff turtle stuffed into a hand-me-down shell that was four or five sizes too small for him.

"Did you see this man taking drugs in the bathroom?" the guard asked.

Greg and Pylar shared a quick sideways glance before Greg responded.

"Oh, yeah. Like, I don't know what drugs look like, sir. But he was eating these little pieces of paper and sniffing powder off the back of the sink."

"Great, thanks for your help," the giant boomed. "On your way now."

"No problem, officer. Have a nice day."

With that debacle over, Greg and Pylar scurried over to where the rest of the group was waiting by the casino entrance and Kyle ushered them inside. So, before they even hit the casino floor, collectively they'd managed to terrify an entire hotel lobby, headbutt a fish tank and get an innocent man arrested on suspected drug charges. So far so good.

"What the fuck happened in the bathroom?" Eve whispered to Greg, who was looking decidedly shaky and a bit pale, like someone who'd gone through some Clockwork Orange therapy while being force-fed raw chicken giblets.

"Please don't make me re-live it," he groaned.

"But why was that guy freaking out?"

"He saw there was two guys in the stall and he must have thought we were taking drugs or wanking each other off, so he burst in to stop it." Greg chuckled. "Let's just say, it wasn't what he was expecting."

"So, what were you doing in there?"

"Eve, for the love of God, let it rest."

"OK fine—at least you smell nice now. What is that?"

"It's Dior."

"Nice, which one."

"—Eau de Toilette."

# Chapter Fourteen

"Sir, it's been seven minutes, we need you to either make a choice or step away from the table."

Any other dealer in Las Vegas would have removed Pylar way before the seven-minute mark but this one, Jenny, was a particularly sweet lady whose brother suffered from a history of OCD and she spent a good amount of her free time volunteering to help other people with personality disorders, so her patience stretched a lot farther than most. Typically, this kind of indecisive behaviour would have resulted in a swift ejection by the security golems or being gruesomely chocked to death with a stack of playing cards.

He had been sitting at the Blackjack table, having both an aggressively passive and passively aggressive debate with his internal political system as to whether he should hit or stand on a soft sixteen. There were at least seventy elected officials arguing over this decision, with several crossing party lines in both directions and many more resigning in a form of impotent, futile protest. Despite multiple underhand moves and several morally questionable backroom dealings, they were still unable to achieve the two-thirds majority required to decide whether to hit—or stand.

Greg and Deebro stood a few feet away, watching in mild fascination. It was entertaining in the same cringey way as the UK office, or an old man's drooping testicle hanging out the bottom of his shorts. Pylar sat in his stool, twitching and shifting and punching his thighs uncontrollably, all while the patient dealer in the low-cut top looked on with the exasperated expression of a teenager trying to explain to their grandparents how to set up a zoom call over the phone.

As the time wore on, the exasperation turned to frustration. A little later the frustration turned to desperation. And when desperation was no longer enough, it gave way to furious anger. It was the anger that cat owners get when the hairy little bugger cries and screeches to be let outside, only to entirely forget what they were screeching about as soon as the door is opened and to instead feel a sudden urge to sit just inside the open door and stare expectantly at their jailer's aforementioned exasperated expression till they close the door again; at which point the feline fuckface will have the inspired notion to go outside and will once again begin screeching incessantly.

"What is his deal anyway?" Greg asked Deebro. "Why is it so hard for him to decide on anything? Aren't ant colonies really good at working as a team?"

Deebro, who had been unable to participate in a round of Blackjack as the unfortunate clout on his noggin had not only resulted in an irregular facial spasm, caused by an electrical short inside his biosuit but had also thrown one of his eyeballs out of synch.

So, now, when he sat down to be dealt a hand, his right eye would be looking at the cards and the left was dead set on taking a little vacation in the vicinity of the dealer's ample cleavage instead. While she had enough patience to allow Pylar to debate his strategy for seven minutes, the intensity at which the moustachioed cowboy's left eyeball was fracking the chasm between her breasts earned him an ejection from the table after about twenty seconds.

"The problem is this free-will bullcrap!" Deebro replied. "Hell, once those ants all have sentience, suddenly the idea of being separated into workers, soldiers and Queens at birth doesn't sound so appealing! Workers want to be soldiers, soldiers want to be Queens and the Queens just want to get fat, be pleasured by the soldiers and pretend the workers don't exist. I mean shit, if a bunch of the bugs in the left leg are Red Sox fans and the ones in right leg are Yankees fans, then the whole colony's gonna go to hell in a handbasket, aint it?"

"But, it's fairer than the way Gloporg or Yeezrax was doing it right?" Greg asked, hoping to find some silver lining to this whole Democracy thing.

"Well, I'll be wagering the workers get a slightly larger slice of the pie, but it's like saying an EasyJet flight gives you more legroom than on Ryanair. The bugs in the head are still lounging up there in business class, eating the filling while the workers fight over the crust and now they also take forever to play a hand of Blackjack. So, swings and roundabouts, aint it?"

Greg briefly wondered how Deebro was aware of the economics of budget UK airlines, but mainly he was hoping this whole experience would end in a Men in Black wind-wipe scenario so he could go back to his preferred state of blissful ignorance. For the time being, he decided to get a drink instead. Enough of them might have the same desired effect.

Kyle was sitting alone at the bar, deep into his fourth Gin Martini (Greg was able to deduce this from the surprisingly compelling diorama made from Martini glasses sitting next to him on the bar top), happily watching the Celtics take on the Bulls on the TV behind the bar.

Eve dragged Deebro away to play roulette; she didn't want the madman with the wandering eye who headbutted the aquarium to stay in one place for too long and Gloopy had somehow completely vanished again. Greg cast a wary glance at the bartender, a tall slim chap with shaved sides and a slick-back hairdo, like a certain pigeon-based pocket monster who's name, for copyright purposes, escapes me right now and once he was confident he wouldn't be recognised, sat himself down next to Kyle.

"How are you holding up bud?" Greg enquired, which was an odd expression. If he was asking how Kyle was doing at holding his head up off the bar top, the answer was abysmally, it looked like his neck had the taken on the structural integrity of a damp cardboard straw, but in terms of his spirits holding up, he appeared to be doing marvellously.

"Marvelloushly!" Kyle slurred through a mouthful of dry vermouth and olives.

"Glad to hear it. Now, shall we sit in silence and drink for a while? I think I need a break from mind-boggling universal revelations for a few minutes."

At that moment, a care-package address to Greg and stuffed to the brim with universal money credits and immortality chocolate, sent from the Universal Collective's Random Genetic Lottery Draw, was re-directed; as the organisers of the Universal Collective's Random Genetic Lottery Draw heard Greg's request for peace through the space-time continuum and decided to give the prize to someone else who was more open to new experiences. Greg unknowingly settled for a Rye whisky instead.

"So, you and Melissa then?" Greg asked, after the curiosity and the alcohol began to outweigh his desire for momentary peace and tranquillity. Kyle seemed cheered by Greg's interest; they hadn't had a chance to really talk as mates since this whole thing began. Inside the biosuit, his fuzzy little tail wagged with glee. To a lady who was walking through the bar and checking out Kyle's ass; at the time, it looked like he was making his butt cheeks dance. She was impressed.

"She's amashing, smazing, asmashing—you get the idea."

"I know buddy, I've met her before."

"Oh, yesh, of coursh you haf."

"Does she know?"

"About what?"

"Jesus Christ—Does she know you're not from here?"

"From Vegash. Why would I tell her I'm from Vegash?"

"No, you idiot. Does she know you're an alien?"

"Oh, yeah, totes my dude."

"And she's all right with that? Like, that works for you guys?"

"What d'you mean?"

"How does it work with you guys—when you do stuff. Can you do stuff?"

"My species has ten-inch, retractable genitals and I can make any part of my body vibrate at will."

Greg suddenly felt very emasculated and wished they had stuck to drinking in silence.

Returning to his happy place/therapist's office at the bottom of his whisky glass, Greg tried to put the thought of alien penises out of his mind. God only knows what kind of monster Gloopy was packing somewhere within that nightmare ball of acidic Vaseline. Mercifully, this train of thought was de-railed by the presence of a voluptuous lady person materialising at his side.

Having been to Vegas before, Greg suspected this sudden attention wasn't likely due to any sexual magnetism he might have been giving off at the time, despite being literally drenched in alien pheromones. More likely, this particular lady was more interested in the contents of his wallet than his boxer shorts. He wasn't much looking forward to the thought of having his lack of money exposed any more than his lack of ten-inch genitalia, but this cougar was on the prowl.

She was looking for a lonely wildebeest at the watering hole, one that's been separated from the safety of the herd and clearly Greg was the loneliest, saddest wildebeest available at that particular moment. She sauntered up to the bar and wrapped herself around Greg's shoulders like a lace and satin clad anaconda.

"Hello, love," she purred in his ear, as she set herself down on the bar stool next to Greg. As she sat down, Kyle noticed her wobble a bit on the stool, as if she was out of practise when it came to the ancient art of sitting down. She tottered on the stool as if it kept trying to escape out from underneath her. A momentary setback, however, she was soon back to the business of hunting her prey.

"You looked a little lonely over here, so I thought I'd come and join you."

"Eh, aye, that's grand," Greg replied, in a Scottish accent so thick you could line a jacket with it and go hiking up Ben Nevis in a snowstorm.

Kyle turned one eye to Greg to make sure he hadn't suddenly metaphorised into a haggis, but he was still there. He was just obviously being very awkward.

"That's an interesting accent," the lady mewed or purred or insert any appropriately seductive cat noise. "Are you boys from out of town?"

"Aye, you could say that," Greg chuckled.

"Just visiting then? Do you need someone to show you a good time?"

Greg was keen to nip this notion in the bud, largely for her sake, as any interaction with this rag-tag group of degenerate aliens would probably end up with her being launched, cankles-first, into another dimension or something. Kyle, however, was excited to see the next stage in the solicitation process and jumped in before Greg had a chance to politely decline.

"Yes!" Clears throat. "Yes, my friend here would like it very much if you showed him a good time."

Greg threw a hideous, stinking, side-glance at Kyle that would have surely put him in his place if he wasn't an oblivious, intoxicated extra-terrestrial wrapped in a perfect human skin suit. As that is exactly what he was, Kyle remained unphased and his enthusiasm for the human-centric nature documentary playing out in front of him remained undiminished. He'd never seen a cougar hunt in the wild before.

"As long as you've got the dough honey," the woman purred eagerly. "You boys must be doing well for yourselves."

It was now becoming obvious to Kyle the promise of a pay day seemed to be a much greater incentive to this woman than the prospect of biting Greg's head off like a Black Widow.

"Shit, I don't have any money." Greg suddenly realised.

Gloopy had been paying this whole time with that obnoxiously massive wad of his. In fact, Greg suddenly realised he had been transported, on an alien ship, halfway round the world without his wallet. You lose track of the little things like that when you're presented with mind blowing revelations, like teleportation and talking goldfish. One of the truly great mysteries of the universe and there are a lot of them by now, is how Greg was able to get a drink at a Las Vegas casino bar without any money or ID on him.

This time however, not having any money worked to his advantage, as his lack of cash was clearly far more repugnant to this woman than an oversized third nipple plonked right in the centre of his forehead. She turned to leave without saying a word, the predator resuming the hunt for wealthier prey. Greg returned to his drink as she lifted her ample, but appealing, figure off the awkward bar stool.

Greg brought his drink, once more, to his lips—then had the contents spilled all over himself when a sharp nailed, ringed, open palmed hand hammered him across the left side of his face and sent him sprawling to the floor; his drink, unfortunately, also using him as a makeshift trampoline on its way to the carpet.

"You little shit!" the prostitute shrieked at him. "You think you can do that to me? No fucking way!"

She stuck an unnecessarily pointy shoe into his ribs with venomous intent. Greg felt something inside his torso crack then he immediately threw up onto the carpet. Unmoved by his display of patheticness, she gave him another boot for good measure, then stormed off, cursing, into the lobby.

"What the fuck?" Greg gasped as he raised himself onto his arse and leant back against the bar, coughing and wiping a little chunk of regurgitated oatmeal out of his beard as he did so. "She fucking attacked me. Why did she—"

Greg found his lack of understanding cured when, before his eyes, the bar stool that the woman had been sitting upon turned into a translucent, pale blue column of jelly and two pink, glowing orbs suddenly appeared near the base. They cast their smug glow across Greg with what was unmistakably a mix of disdain and unbridled pleasure at seeing him in his current state.

Gloopy, the gelatinous pervert, (who had decided, after his skin-to-jelly contact with Eve that morning, that he now enjoyed disguising himself as stools, benches, couches, toilet seats or any other miscellaneous flat surface that might afford him the opportunity to rub his orgasm gland against an unsuspecting backside, turned himself into a jelly puddle and slid silently under the bar.

"You! Motherf—!"

Greg was unable to finish his expletive, despite wanting to swear more than he ever had in his entire life. In fact, he wanted to find that perverted glob of deplorable goop, tear his smug orbs out, spread them onto slices of toast like caviar and dump the resultant mess into a volcano. I know, it was an odd journey to go on but stress makes the mind play out revenge scenarios in unusual ways. Anyway, the reason Greg was unable to get out his much-needed expletive was because that was the moment casino security caught up with him.

"Hi, Greg." Taylor chuckled from his lofty perch atop his massive shoulders, "I thought I told you not to come back here."

"It's not my fault man," Greg groaned from his not-so-lofty perch, down there on the stained carpet. "I was abducted by aliens."

# Chapter Fifteen

"I told you not to show your face here again, Greg," Taylor growled through the dense, black undergrowth sprouting from the multitude of angry contour lines that covered his granite face.

Kyle wondered to himself why this huge, hairy, evolutionary offshoot of Homo-Sapiens, felt the need to repeat the same thing again, only worded very slightly differently as if he was recapping for anyone who might have been watching the goings on and had taken a little break to make a cup of tea or make a deposit at the porcelain bank. Greg seemed not to have noticed though. Kyle suspected making the same point multiple times must just be typical human behaviour. They do tend to have very short attention spans..

"Hey, Taylor," Greg wheezed as he hauled himself out of his little puddle on the carpet and onto his feet. As he righted himself like a leaky, capsized ship, he found his view was consumed with the sight of Taylor the Bouncer's massive, lumpy, canvas of a chest. His pecs looked like two angry bulls straining to burst out of his polo shirt and headbutt Greg in the face.

"How have you been man?" Greg ventured nervously.

Taylor had never been a big fan of his, even before his little incident two years ago. Unfortunately, Scottish sarcasm and an American's irony deficiency do not make suitable bedfellows.

"Everything's been great," Taylor replied. "Two years of total bliss, until about five minutes ago, when I heard from one of the other bouncers that a scruffy guy with a Scottish accent and his friend were headbutting the fish tank behind reception."

"Aw, come on, that wisne m—"

"And now I find your ass on the floor in a pile of booze and puke and groping the other customers. You were always a pain in my ass but this is a new low, even for you."

"I don't suppose you'd believe me if I told you the guy who did those things was an alien in a synthetic human skin suit?"

"No, I probably wouldn't."

"Well, I guess that only leaves me one option then," Greg mused as he leant back nonchalantly against the bar.

"Yeah, give up and come with me, unless you want to give me a reason to—"

Before Taylor could finish, Greg sure as hell gave him a reason to.

He reached behind him and grabbed Kyle's half-finished Martini, threw it in Taylor's face, dived under his arm and made a break for pool area. He managed to make it about six-feet before a hand the size of a grizzly bear's paw came down like a blacksmith's hammer on the back of his collar and pulled him off the ground, his feet dangling uselessly in the air. Taylor spun Greg around to give him a good look in the eye and then brought a ringed fist square into Greg's face just under the right eye socket, sending him sprawling once more to the floor.

Greg didn't remember anything beyond throwing the Martini in Taylor's face. He thought he was home free and the next thing he knew he was once again on the carpet but this time, he appeared to be joined by a procession of dancing stars and rainbows and he also had a funny metallic taste in his mouth. What sort of black magic was this? Given everything else he'd witnessed in the last twenty-four hours, it sure as hell wasn't outside the realm of possibility that witchcraft was in play.

In fact, the simple idea that he'd been caught and punched in the face seemed the least likely outcome at that moment. He instead deduced that Taylor was a sorcerer or he had caught Greg in a tractor beam. Somehow, despite the stars' and rainbow's encouragement that he should stay on the floor, Greg managed to drag himself to his feet. He tried to remember when the last time was that he had just stood up normally, rather than having to pull or drag himself or stagger shakily or clumsily to his feet—he couldn't remember.

"Want some more, do you?" Taylor growled happily, a good dollop of relish slathered on his voice. "That's good."

Taylor pulled his fist back like a pitcher winding up a fastball, but before he could follow through and tear Greg's jaw from his face, Kyle bounded from his bar stool and socked the big bastard right across the chin. As he did so, there was a CRACK, as if Indiana Jones had come in and whipped the fucker right in the cheek and two of the lightbulbs over the bar shattered in a sudden surge of energy. Taylor, having received the full David-Goliath treatment, toppled over, fully unconscious and ended up a heap of impotent muscles and polo shirt on the puke-stained casino carpet.

"Holy shit!" Greg gasped, as he stared down at the roided-up maniac passed out on the floor, with a sizzling red burn mark on his chin. "What the fuck did you just do?"

"That—that was not good," Kyle said and even Greg, who was by now suffering a mild concussion on top of his lack of sleep and intoxication, was aware of the panic creeping into Kyle's normally relaxed voice.

"We need to get the fuck out of here," he stammered. "Where the hell are the others?"

Little did they know that over by the roulette table, Eve and Deebro were having their own difficulties, which we will come to in a minute. Greg and Kyle didn't have time to discover this on their own, as one of Las Vegas' famously adept security teams were rapidly converging on them, coming to the aid of their stricken comrade. Greg could see the silhouettes of bipedal, polo-shirt wearing hippos moving through the crowd like the raptors in the second Jurassic Park movie.

"Let's move," he hissed to Kyle, grabbing him and heading off in the direction of the hotel atrium. He spotted a crowd gathering outside the casino and figured it would be a good place to hide.

They ducked and weaved through the slot machines like a neon-lit hedge maze, all the while the bouncers were still in hot pursuit on them, guided by some unknown sixth sense, which seemed like magic to Greg but was actually just a guy looking at the security monitors and telling casino security where they were. How the hell Jason Bourne ever got away from anyone in today's world is a mystery. Gloopy, from his new disguise as a stool in front of one of the slot machines (currently being sat on by an elderly Chinese gentleman) watched with relish as Greg and Kyle tried in vain to outrun their pursuers.

They managed to make it into the throng of people gathered around something of interest at the entrance to the casino floor. Greg and Kyle swam through the soup of limbs and cameras, pushing in deeper to where they hoped security couldn't reach them. It was a good plan, unfortunately, like most plans made up int the moment, it didn't pan out the way they were hoping. Greg pushed too far into the crowd and while looking back the way he had come for his pursuers, fell into an opening in the middle where it appeared a group of celebrities was shaking hands and signing autographs for their legion of excited fans.

Greg collided with one of the celebs and caused them both to go sprawling to the floor while Kyle helplessly spectated. He didn't want to cause another scene by knocking out someone else. Greg leapt back up quickly, ready to dash off once again. He didn't get the chance. As he rose to his feet, he came face-to-face with someone he'd seen before.

"Oh, you've got to be fucking kidding me?" he managed to say, before the other two members of the Blue Man Group socked him right in the middle of his face.

"And that's how Greg and I ended up in here," Kyle sighed, while Greg rubbed his bruised cheek, which was quickly turning a lovely shade of deep purple and had the distinctive shape of a college fraternity ring perfectly imprinted below his right eye.

"Why did those blue men attack you, Greg?" Deebro asked.

"It's a long story," Greg replied, wincing at the pain in his swollen face "You tell us why they arrested you first. Did you headbutt the fish tank again?"

"No, of course not—I also threw a chair at it."

"Jesus Christ."

# Chapter Sixteen

While Greg and Kyle were going seven rounds with one of phi-delta-lambda's least esteemed alumni, Eve and Deebro were away trying to enjoy their Vegas weekend like normal people with a nice, wholesome, family friendly game of roulette. Unfortunately, Deebro was having some difficulties with his biosuit, which was deteriorating rapidly thanks to that little bump on the noggin he sustained three chapters ago.

Worn electrical connectors, as anyone who's owned an old iPhone will tell you, manifest in unpredictable but always infuriating ways. A worrying number of sparks were jumping intermittently from Deebro's ear canal (nearly setting an unsuspecting gambler ablaze on more than one occasion) and in addition to the lazy eye, Deebro's lower jaw was now going absolutely haywire, which was likely to draw undesired conclusions from casino staff.

Rounding out the list, he was unable to stop himself from raising his arm to the sky every thirty seconds like the swatty kid in maths class who wants nothing more out of life than to stroll smugly up to the front and show the rest of the idiots how to do advanced calculus.

They were standing at one of the roulette tables, about as far away from the bar as possible. Eve, for wild reasons known only to her and God, suspected that perhaps Greg and Kyle might get into some trouble and she wanted Deebro far out of the way when things turned sour. Unfortunately, Deebro's mechanical maladies were making blending in somewhat problematic.

His motor skills, in the most literal sense given all the electric motors in the suit were short-circuiting, were deteriorating faster than Boris Johnson's kidneys. He kept spilling all his chips all over the roulette table, betting on both red and black accidentally multiple times. He was covering all his bases to be sure but he wasn't winning much in the process. I suspect the dealer thought he perhaps had some form of Tourette's and didn't feel comfortable correcting him on his gambling technique.

"Are you OK?" Eve hissed in his ear, while trying to avoid getting a spark in the eyeball in the process.

"Oh, yeah, don't worry I've got this, it's just a little niggle. These things always sort themselves out," Deebro responded. "I'll just turn myself off and on again."

"No, no, no! Don't do that!" Eve quickly responded, afraid of how the people would react if the stuttering cowboy suddenly collapsed onto the floor. I can't imagine they'd react well after giving him mouth to mouth and accidentally getting a mouthful of whiskey-infused goldfish water.

They decided just to hunker down for a few minutes, hope the sparking would stop on its own and pray that no one made too much of a fuss about the strong whiff of burnt toast. The one bonus about having this burning, gyrating lunatic at the table was that everyone else mysteriously decided to gamble elsewhere, which meant fewer questioning glances from members of the general public.

There was, however, one gambler unperturbed by Deebro's spasmodic flailing. As Eve and her gyrating, floundering companion were focussed on the ball making yet another lap in the endless, hopeless cycle around the roulette wheel (the ball itself, having a limited degree of sentience, prayed that perhaps, this time, the gods would be satisfied with the number it landed on and this relentless cycle of torture would finally end), a tall, grandiose-moustachioed gentleman sauntered up to the table and laid a handsome pile of crisp one hundred dollar bills down before the croupier.

"Howdy darlin." The debonair gentleman drawled, through the burgeoning forest of grey hair sprouting from his upper lip. "I'll take chips for these, if y'all would be so kind."

"Oh my. Yes, of course. Can I just say, I am a huge fan," the starstruck woman stammered as she fumbled with her chips, passing a healthy pile of hundred-dollar addiction tokens over to the new arrival.

"Well, that's mighty kind of you, ma'am," Mr Sam Elliott replied, tipping the brim of his missing hat to the woman as he sat himself down on the stool next to Deebro. He might not have been so appreciative is he knew the croupier only recognised him from his brief cameo appearance in Parks and Rec.

Eve had noticed the sudden increase in the level of class and gravitas at the table and had mixed feelings on the subject. On the one hand, she was a big, Big Lebowski fan and wanted nothing more than to have a drink with Sam Elliott at the bar and pretend they were trading life stories in a bowling alley. On the other hand, having a celebrity in the vicinity was likely to draw unwanted attention and there was still the occasional colourful spark jumping from Deebro's ear hole, like it was the Fourth of July inside his head and the goldfish was letting off some celebratory fireworks.

Luckily, it seemed that Mr Sam Elliott was only in the mood to keep his head down and focus on the gambling. He shot her a kindly nod and a warm smile that made her go very slightly weak at the knees (she couldn't help but wonder how much that moustache would tickle) and then went back to focussing on the chips. Things probably would have been fine, if Deebro had managed to control himself, but when do things ever go according to plan?

A bubbly, excitable waitress brought around a tray of drinks; doing her best to get everyone in the room so drunk that they forget they should be spending their hard-earned cash anywhere other than a casino and as she was walking past, Deebro chose that unfortunate moment to launch his hand both vertically and violently into the sky. His open palm connected squarely with the underside of the girl's tray and ended up covering both her and Mr Sam Elliott with a sticky, assortment of fruity, viscous cocktails.

"Oh—shit!" Eve cursed as she looked at the scene of utter chaos Deebro had managed to unwittingly create. The waitress screeched as she ran away, desperately trying to rub the enormous wet stains and chunks of pineapple and maraschino cherry out of her cocktail dress. Mr Sam Elliott barely moved, he just slowly turned his chiselled face to look Deebro directly in the eyes, which was difficult given Deebro's eyes were currently pointing in two completely different directions and casually plucked out a cocktail umbrella that had wedged itself into his generous moustache like an errant piece of macaroni.

"Well, quite a mess you've made there, friend. Not very gentlemanly of you, was it?"

Deebro, however, had been looking at the roulette wheel the whole time and hadn't even registered anything going on behind him. Unbeknown to the rest of the onlookers, the deteriorating condition of his biosuit had caused him to lose all feeling in both his hands so he hadn't even felt it when he knocked the tray of drinks out of the waitress's grasp. So, as you can now understand, he was slightly confused as to why this tall, handsome cowboy now seemed quite upset with him and why the floor behind him was drenched in Mardi Gras smoothie.

"Sorry, w-w-w-what are you t-t-talking ab-b-bout?" he stuttered. His jaw working overtime was beginning to make talking supremely difficult.

"Now, don't be beating around the bush, friend. Y'all know what you did. Time to be a man and own up to it."

"I d-d-didn't do this!" Deebro protested, not knowing why he was suddenly being given the third degree.

Now, Mr Sam Elliott almost decided to take pity on the poor, stuttering, lazy eyed fool at this point. He'd had a bad day so far and all he wanted to do had a nice quiet drink and distract himself from his recent loss by casually losing some of his many, many numerous dollars but that was when he noticed Deebro's hat.

Now, the reason Mr Sam Elliot was having such a bad day was that his favourite hat had gone missing while he was on set. He was currently filming a movie in the Nevada desert just outside Las Vegas, which, coincidentally, was the sequel to the 2011 'smash hit', Cowboys Vs Aliens. He had come back from filming a pivotal scene where he made sweet, passionate love to the bookish female alien scientist, who takes off her glasses and suddenly realises she's actually very attractive (despite having mandibles and seven tentacles sprouting from her abdomen).

He returned to his trailer, only to find his favourite monogrammed cowboy hat missing. It had been a gift from his wife, one Katherine Ross and she even had his initials stitched into the leather. As you can imagine, he was very upset to find it missing upon his return. He assumed one of the stagehands must had nicked it, either to sell it on eBay or to be kept as some kind of weird fetish thing. The last thing he expected was to wander into a casino later that same day and find his hat sitting proudly on the head of a spasming, stuttering, seemingly oblivious idiot standing at the Roulette table.

"Hey! Where did you find that their hat, son?" he barked at Deebro.

"Oh, th-th-this?" Deebro replied. "This is mine, I uh, m-m-made it."

"That's a mighty co-incidence, friend," Sam pressed, taking a couple of intimidating steps towards Deebro and cracking his knuckles menacingly. "It looks awful similar to one I had taken from me recently. What's your name, son?"

"My name?" Deebro asked, looking desperately at Eve in a bid for some help, having suddenly realised he never bothered coming up with a human name. Curse Kyle and his shitty, but now understandable, human backstory.

"It's, uh, a normal human name. Human, hu—Hugh, yes that's it. Hugh."

"Well then, Hugh. What your last name be?"

"What do you mean?"

"What's your second name?"

"Second name?"

Anyone reading this book might understand Deebro's confusion, given that none of the characters he has interacted with so far have ever mentioned having a last name.

"Well!" Mr Sam Elliott pressed, "Second name, son, spit it out!"

"It's uh, uh, Hugh—Mann."

"Your name is Hugh Mann."

"That's it, that's me. Good old human. Uh, I mean, Hugh Mann, esquire. At your service, sir."

"Then why does your hat have the initials S.E on it?"

Deebro's little fish brain was not equipped to deal with this sort of pressure and the processing power required was not helping the condition of his suit. The onboard processors understandably deduced, from the stress and the extent of the damage to the suit, that Deebro was involved in some kind of altercation on a hostile alien planet and went into life-or-death, self-defence mode.

Proximity sensors on all sides activated, which was unbelievably lucky for him because, at that moment, a huge hairy biker with a face like a blended ham sandwich and a battered mouth missing about five teeth, threw a savage punch at Deebro from behind. Deebro's suit again took evasive manoeuvres and dodged to the side and the biker's fist sailed once more through the empty air past his head but this time, it connected with Mr Sam Elliott's right cheekbone. Eve dived for cover over the roulette table, wanting to avoid what came next.

There was a sickening crack of bones shattering like dry clay as the biker's knuckle somehow disintegrated into dust upon contact with Mr Sam Elliott's iron-set, weather beaten face. The biker's look of utter shock was replaced with confusion, quickly followed by anguish as his right hand turned into a hacky sack.

"Oh, you done made a mistake, son," Sam Elliott chuckled as he returned serve with a savage and lightning-fast right hook of his own, which connected right in the centre of the biker's face, turned his nose into a meat smoothie and knocked out another seven or eight of his remaining teeth.

As the Gollum-faced Hells Angel howled in agony and dropped, writhing, to the floor, choking on a mouthful of blood and shattered teeth, Deebro seized the moment to turn tail and ran away back towards the casino exit. Sam took off after him in hot pursuit, determined to get his hat back and find out which rotten little tyke had sold it to this idiot in the first place. Not too far behind Sam, the biker rose like the possessed undead in a rabid state of crazed bloodlust and careered after them, determined to rip this freak's eyeballs out and squash them, even if he had to lose all his remaining teeth in the process.

As Greg and Kyle were being carted off by casino security, having had their asses thoroughly whooped by the Blue Man Group, Deebro barrelled into the hotel lobby followed by the two angry Americans, both hell-bent on turning him into fried scampi. He looked desperately for an escape route but everywhere he looked there was more hotel security. He deduced, in the heat of the moment, that there was no escape and with his suit in the condition that it was, he was unlikely to survive a physical altercation with these two angry, fully grown human males. What he needed was reinforcements—and that's when he spotted the fish tank again.

These two humans wouldn't stand a chance against him and a liberated army of his brethren. All the fish seemed to be a bit out of it at the moment, but he was sure the call to action would snap them back to reality and allow them to throw off the shackles of their human oppressors. Yes, dear reader, it seems he really didn't learn his lesson the first time. Once more, unto the breach.

"Now is the time, my brothers," he yelled as he once again vaulted the reception desk and launched himself at the glass tank. "F-F-F-F-Freedom!"

"And that's how I ended up in jail with you guys," Deebro said to Greg and Kyle, as an emerald spark jumped from his nose and lit his moustache on fire. "On the plus side, that second bump on the head seems to have fixed my stutter."

# Chapter Seventeen

"So, why did those blue fellas beat you two up?" Deebro asked his cellmates, who were sporting quite the rainbow of bruises and welts from the conclusive ass kicking they had received by a well-known Las Vegas novelty musical act.

"We have a bit of a history," Greg replied, while rubbing his swollen jaw, which had turned such a vivid shade of blue he could have conceivably auditioned for the group that gave him the bruise.

"Oooh, sounds exciting," Deebro squealed. "Go on, spill the beans."

"No! We've done two flashbacks in a row already," Kyle interjected. "Let's move this thing on. I'm sure Greg's colourful backstory will come out organically at some point anyway."

Greg groaned, unable to summon the energy to question Kyle's narratorial mannerisms. He rubbed his temples and tried not to think about what was going to happen to them. He hoped he might get the chance to see Eve again before being sent to some government lab for a spot of unnecessary dissection.

"Why did you even bring me on this fucking trip, Kyle?" he sighed.

"What do you mean?"

"I mean, why am I here? Why didn't you just let fish-face and ant-man mind wipe me and send me home?"

"Well, because you needed this, mate."

"What are you talking about?"

"You were depressed, you were drinking all the time, you hadn't washed in days. This seemed like the perfect way to get you back out into the world. I mean, look at you now! Look how far you've come in a day."

"Kyle, for God's sake! I'm still depressed. I'm still drinking all the time. In fact, we're all very drunk right now and we're all in fucking prison! The only difference is now I'm wearing a nicer shirt."

"Huh, yeah, I suppose that's true—At least, you smell nice now."

"Sigh—That's just Pylar's pheromones."

167

"I'm sorry, come again?"

However, before Greg could explain why he smelt like sexy ant juice, the three of them were interrupted by the arrival of Taylor, the even-angrier-than-before security guard, who looked like he had taken a hot iron in the shape of a metal fist to the underside of his face. Kyle's punch had really done a number on him. There were still little wisps of smoke drifting upwards from his skin and the smell of cooked flesh was—worryingly mouth-watering.

Normally, Taylor's bloodshot death-stare would have put the fear of God into Greg but on this occasion, the bearded bouncer wasn't the thing that concerned him most. No, it was the obvious FBI/Secret Service/MIB agent standing next to Taylor that gave our three incarcerated protagonists the heebie-jeebies.

He was gangly and slender but stood a good three inches taller than even Taylor, like a seven-foot praying mantis in a Men's Warehouse ink-black suit. His face was totally expressionless. Well, the part that wasn't obscured by the sunglasses anyway. In another life, Greg suspected he would have made an excellent guard at Buckingham palace. He definitely wasn't casino security and despite the unreadable face, Greg suspected he wasn't here to compete in a poker tournament either.

"This is the one?" he said in a bored, perfectly monotone voice. Like, not even a wobble from the same flat E note. He must have had to practise sounding that unbelievably uncharismatic.

"Yeah, these two," Taylor gestured angrily to Greg and Kyle, who looked behind them at the blank wall innocently as if they had no idea what this strange man with the burned face was talking about.

"And what about this one?" the agent asked, gesturing to the denim clad cowboy with the lazy eye and the smouldering remnants of a handlebar moustache.

"I don't know who that is?" Taylor replied. "But if he's with these two he's definitely some kind of freak as well."

"Rude," Deebro mumbled to himself, as he cupped a hand over his right ear to catch a small shower of rainbowcoloured sparks.

The agent pulled a small device that looked a bit like a pager out of his pocket and pointed it at Greg for a few seconds. Kyle, knowing instantly what it was, went into panic mode.

"Woah, now guys, come on, this is obviously a big misunderstanding. There's no need to—."

The agent held up two fingers and Kyle was silenced instantly. He dropped to the floor of his cell in a ball, clutching his throat and writhing erratically on the floor like a Brazilian football player.

"Kyle," Greg asked nervously. "You OK, buddy?"

Greg kneeled down next to his friend, who was wheezing and rasping in increasingly strained tones, as if he couldn't breathe properly. The agent continued to lazily turn his pager on Deebro and then Kyle. A small red line probed and traced its way across Kyle's hunched form as the rest of the group looked on in utter bemusement.

"What the fuck are you doing to him?" Greg snarled at the agent. The man completely ignored him. He was obviously far more invested in whatever his little device was telling him than in Greg's pathetic idle threats.

"Interesting."

"What's interesting?" Taylor asked. "What's going on here?"

"Not of your concern," the agent curtly replied, as he brought a finger up to his ear and whispered something like, "We've got them", under his breath.

"Not of my concern!" Taylor growled. "This fucking prick scarred my face, you asshole! It fucking is my concern, now tell me—"

Before he could finish his pathetic human demands, the agent lifted his two fingers again and Taylor spasmed violently before collapsing to the floor, clutching his neck and making the same wheezing noises as Kyle as his eyes began to bulge and his face turned a hideous shade of blue. That was when the penny finally dropped for Greg.

"Is he—Is he force-choking you?" Greg cried. Kyle rolled over to look him in the eye as he struggled to remain conscious.

"I—I told you—"

"What is it, Kyle? Speak to me, buddy!"

"I—told—you—not—to—"

"Not to what? Hang in there, man."

"I fucking told you not to point out when sci-fi stuff happens!"

"Aw—Come on, man. I mean this guy is basically Darth Vader."

"Wheeze—Are you—Gasp—fangirling right now?"

"What? No!—It is kind of cool though."

"(Rasping noises) You're—a—shitty—friend!"

"Now, you're just being hurtful."

The agent decided he'd had enough of this nonsense and used his portable phase-generator to deconstruct Deebro, Greg and Kyle into atoms and digital information and send them off to another, undisclosed location in a flash of red light and the beep of a supermarket check-out scanner. As for Taylor, unfortunately he'd seen too much and he was left there on the floor of the cell to choke on the repercussions of his actions. His close friends - and his sexual addiction group – always thought he'd go out being choked, just not by an undercover, alien-hunting Secret Service agent.

This agent wasn't hanging around to set the scene however. Some professionals would wrap a belt around Taylor's neck and leave him with his cock in his hands on the floor of the prison cell. Given his profile, auto-erotic asphyxiation would have been a suitable alibi but every second this agent was here was an unnecessary risk. The missing unit had been acquired, now was time to leave.

The agent strode through the casino floor, through the tacky assault course of bronze mermaid statues, glass fish-prisons (they still have a captive dolphin habitat there so maybe Deebro's assessment of the place wasn't too far off), ten-foot plastic tigers and palm fronds erupting from every crack and crevice like a green yeast infection. The agent seemed completely oblivious to everything going on around him, walking in straight lines and turning at right angles like Pac-Man and correctly assuming everyone else would move out of his way, which they did.

Modern America has managed to instil an unconscious fear into the masses of an imposing man in a dark suit. Eventually, he came to the Terry Fator Theatre venue, outside of which was a huge poster like the one in the lobby advertising the Blue Man Group as the hotly anticipated entertainment for tonight's attendees. The agent strode past the main entrance and came up to a smaller side-door just down the hallway with an electronic 9-digit keypad embedded in the wall next to it. Taking a small piece of paper from his pocket, he typed in the code he had been supplied by his contacts and strode through.

He found himself in the backstage area of the theatre. In case your sense of time has been truly warped beyond all recognition at this point, which would be understandable, it was still only around 11:30 a.m. in the morning, Las Vegas time. The show wasn't due to start for another ten hours so no one was there setting things up yet. He continued up the stairs and made his entrance onto stage left, behind the enormous velvet curtains.

It was there, lurking in the dark of the vacuous theatre, that his contacts were waiting for him. There, in the middle of the empty stage, stood The Blue Man Group. Three royal blue, fantastically bald men in black jumpsuits, holding bongo drums and staring expectantly with the whites of their enormous, unblinking eyes, glued to the agent as he walked up and loomed over them menacingly.

"The information you provided was accurate," the agent spoke to them in his uniquely emotionless voice, never giving away any more information than he intended. "Your contribution had been noted."

The middle of the three blue men began a rhythmic beat on the bongo drum hanging from a strap around his neck. The notes came thick and fast, in pitches high and low that reverberated around the room yet were clearly directed at the agent. The sound was baleful and almost desperate in their painful intensity.

"You make no demands of us," the agent retorted. "Our arrangement continues as agreed until Donnaht says otherwise."

Now, the other blue men joined in with the drumbeat, the sounds growing louder and more strained with each passing bar, building to an ever more aggressive crescendo until the agent decided their boldness had crossed an acceptable threshold.

"You will have what was promised, in due time but for now, you do as you are instructed. And you forget your place with these demands," the agent replied with a deliberate hint of venom creeping into his monotone as he began to raise two fingers threateningly towards the three blue men.

They stopped drumming immediately and retreated two steps, their hands almost instinctively jumping to their throats.

The agent, having been satisfied that his message was received, brought his personal phase-transporter from his pocket and prepared to take his leave. A creak in the floorboards behind him make him take a momentary pause and turn, but the stage was empty and he assumed it was just a disgusting Earth rodent. These human cities were festering with vile creatures and he was eager to leave.

"The cartel will be in touch."

And with that, he disappeared with a beep and a flash of red light. The blue men exchanged desperate, despondent looks and retreated back to their dressing rooms to prepare for the show, slamming the stage door angrily behind them and leaving the murky theatre eerily silent and devoid of life—except for the girl hidden behind them, enveloped in one of the folds in the huge velvet curtain. Eve let out a breath she had been holding since she put her foot on that creaking floorboard and slumped in a heap onto the stage.

"Fucking hell, Greg. Why couldn't you have just watched the bar by yourself for once?"

# Chapter Eighteen

"Sir, please, I'm begging you!" Bawled a tortured, tormented Blackjack dealer named Jenny as her very last nerve threatened to fray and clots of blood congealed dangerously in her brain from sheer frustration. "Will you make your move before I lose my goddamn mind!"

It had now been twenty-eight minutes since Pylar had landed on that soft sixteen.

Unbeknownst to Jenny (who had decided that this nightmare person, sent from hell to test her faith, had both severe OCD and multiple-personality disorder and was likely to go postal if she tried to eject him from the table) Pylar's internal political system had been rendered gridlocked and utterly crippled by this one, insignificant, little hand of Blackjack.

Inside the colony, the one argument over whether to hit or stand had escalated until the entire population had ideologically split into two diametrically opposed halves that disagreed entirely on almost every conceivable issue, except for the fact that none of them wanted to leave the colony. It was now an abusive, unhealthy relationship on a national scale and none of them were willing to back down.

One half wanted to hit, the other wanted to stand. One half wanted a shot of bourbon, one half wanted a gin and tonic. One half wanted to arm themselves with guns from the ship and go out hunting humans for sport, the other half wanted to try and find some of the Earth narcotic known as Molly and dance the night away in a neon and glitter coated nightclub (both halves believed the other's obsession with firearms or narcotics was idiotic and immoral).

One half wanted to divide any winnings among the masses, one half wanted to give it to those up top and let the economic gains trickle slowly down to the legs. One half wanted the ancient practise of eating the undersized larvae at birth to be abolished, one half thought traditions were what the colony was built on and should not be changed for any reason. As you can see, this shit had escalated quickly, I mean it really got out of hand fast.

Not that any of this was visible on the surface; all Jenny could see was a strange man in safari gear muttering to himself under his breath like that scene in the second Lord of the Rings movie where Gollum and Smeagol have their first real heart-to-heart in about two hundred years. The only difference being Pylar had around four hundred thousand little voices arguing inside his head instead of just two. Luckily, before she finally snapped and called security (they were really earning their pay checks that day) Eve came running into the casino with a desperate look on her face and grabbed Pylar by the shoulder.

"Pylar, thank god, you're still here! Come one, we have to go, now!"

"Are—are you here to take him away?" Jenny asked, a glimmer of fantastic hope slipping into in her teary eyes.

"Yeah, is that OK? We have somewhere to be."

Jenny couldn't contain herself.

"Thank you! Thank you. Thaaaaank you!" she cried and threw herself around Eve, wrapping her up in a smothering, spine-crushing hug and bawling huge, salty tears into Eve's T-shirt.

"Oh, there's no need—"

"Tha-a-a-a-ank you-ou-ou," Jenny continued to sob with unrelenting joy. Then, almost snapped from his internal conflict by Jenny's raw display of emotion, Pylar spoke.

"Hit me."

"What—What did you just say?" Jenny replied. Never has a blackjack dealer been more surprised to hear those two words.

"I said, hit me."

"Oh my god. OK. Here."

She drew a ten from the deck and slid it to him.

"Twenty-six," she said, with not a hint of smugness (well, maybe just a little bit). "Bust."

She then drew her cards.

"Two, five, ten, fifteen. Dealer wins on fifteen."

The Furmbogs in that colony still teach this moment in history class. This was their "Where were you?" moment. Imagine the Kennedy assassination, the moon landing and Paris Hilton's sex tape all rolled into one, but multiply the amount of guns, spaceships and tits by about a thousand and you'll have some sense of how big a moment this was for them. Today, the Furmbogs call it sixteen-ten. The event that changed everything.

Half the Furmbogs in the colony, the half that wanted to stay on sixteen, went absolutely wild. From the outside, all was well but internally, civil war broke out. Each side rallied to either the right or left and absolutely refused to co-operate with the other. Pylar didn't last long in this new hostile environment. He was a peace-time leader and war was not his strong suit. He was devoured by his own Generals about thirty seconds after Eve managed to drag him, kicking and flailing, into an empty booth at the back of the TGI Fridays across the lobby from the casino.

Eve manhandled the bugger into the booth and threw him into the corner where prying eyes couldn't see. She was no expert on alien insect colonies but even she could tell, from Pylar's rabid snarls and complete lack of coordination, that something wasn't working upstairs.

"Pylar, what the hell is wrong with you?" she spat at him.

"Pylar is gone and good riddance to him! This colony is under new leadership," a previously unheard, raspy, cartoonishly angry voice responded (this being the military General now in charge of the right half of the colony, having removed Pylar in a Castro-style military coup and eaten his torso mid-section for breakfast).

"That's right, but it won't be you running things, you fascist pig!" a second, female, ball-busting sledgehammer of a voice retaliated (this being the leader of the grassroots political opposition who had been appointed as spokesperson for the left side of the colony).

"Woman, don't you get yourself involved in this!"

"Don't you talk to me like that, you piece of shit! You can't just come up in here and tell us how things are going to be!"

"This colony needs strong leadership in this time of crisis. You think you can handle something like this? Don't make me laugh. You can't even handle a pot of coffee."

"Ooooh, you did not just bring up the coffee incident! You think women are only capable of getting the coffee? And what is all this "strong leadership" bullshit. Such a typical man. What we need now is patience and understanding. The colony needs someone who'll listen to their needs. That's your problem, you never listen."

"This again! I listen just fine."

"Oh really. You listen just fine, do you?"

"Absolutely."

"What's my mother's middle name then?"

"Are you serious? We're ants, we all have the same mother."

"—OK, bad example. What's the name of the charity I run then?"

"You know, it's—"

"Come on then, good listener, spit it out."

"It's—whales?"

"Whales?"

"You're trying to save the whales?"

"Whales on Earth?"

"Yeah."

"A planet we haven't lived on for fifty years."

"Sure, why not?"

"Oh, my god! You are such an asshole."

"Oh, I'm the asshole. Caring about whales makes me an asshole."

"First of all, you don't give a shit about whales. Secondly, my charity is called Antesty Anternationant, we support the Furmbogs in the legs who are persecuted by you and your military regime."

"We haven't even taken over yet Frogina! You're just doing this because of the divorce, aren't you?"

Oh, did I not mention the two Furmbogs fighting for control of the colony are in the middle of a messy divorce?

"Jesus Christ. What is happening in there?" Eve pleaded desperately.

"None of your science-damned business!" the general's voice barked back, "This is Furmbog business and it's nothing to do with any human!"

"She's trying to help, you asshole! We should be fostering good relations with the humans. This is why we got divorced, you're always so aggressive! Well, that and your tiny mandibles."

"Hey! You know I'm sensitive about my mandibles!"

"We don't have time for this shit!" Eve barked. "Kyle and Greg and Deebro have been taken!"

That certainly shut them up.

"What do you mean taken? Explain yourself human!" the general barked.

"I mean, I followed the bouncers into the back of the casino and I saw a man in a suit scan them with a little plastic box that made them disappear."

"My god, this is an act of war!" the general replied. "We need to bid a tactical retreat, then return with heavy arms and retaliate. I know some mercenaries who'll take the job at a reasonable price."

"We can't leave Kyle and the rest to be dissected or sold to a human travelling circus. We need to negotiate their release with the humans. Also, not everything requires a declaration of war, no matter what it says on your Scuttle feed."

"Again, here we go with the Scuttle feed! Why do you always bring that up? It's important the colony is made aware of my political stances if I want to run for office someday."

"Running for office? You mean staging a military coup!"

"Same result."

"You know how embarrassing it was for me? Our neighbours all thought I was a torso elitist because of the all the horrible things you were saying about the workers."

"Hey, I'm just defending my right to free speech and if they worked a little harder maybe they'd be able to move up to the torso as well."

"That's not how social mobility works, you ass!"

"And while we're on the social medias. Why did you have to spend twenty minutes taking pictures of our food every time we sit down as a colony to eat the old and the undersized larvae!"

"First of all, I don't approve of those outdated traditions. Secondly, I'm an influencer. Those poor suffering worker Furmbogs in the legs are inspired by my life choices."

I also forgot to mention that they're both—you know—just the worst.

"Will you two shut up," Eve hissed. "This is getting us nowhere."

"What do you suggest then human?"

"I followed the agent, and you'll never guess who he met after he left the casino."

"Who?"

"The Blue Man Group."

"Yeah, that makes sense."

"—What? How does that make sense?"

"Well, the Blue Man Group are aliens," Frogina replied. "They work for the Bhu-"

"Silence woman!" the general cut in. "That's classified information!"

"You don't get to talk to me like that, you pig. Not since you stuck your tiny mandibles in you assistant's as—"

"The Blue Man Group are aliens! Since when?"

"Since always. They're from Mars."

"I thought men from Mars were meant to be green."

"Nope, blue."

"Huh. OK. Then why are they here?"

"That's classified, goddamit!" the General spat at Eve. "Stop probing human or I'll treat your questioning as an act of aggression."

"I think I like the other one better."

"Thank you, Eve, I like you too. Wish someone had shown that sort of appreciation while we were married. So, the agent met with the Martians. We should go and talk to them."

"No, we shouldn't! We need to regroup and return with an armed force and rain fire down upon these sonsabitches!"

"What about Deebro?"

"What about him?"

"We were thrown through a wormhole and ended up on Fuzzynuts Prima Seven, after being trapped in a sealed box for thirty years and Deebro found us and taught us to survive. We owe him. He was best man at our wedding or did you forget that as well?"

"—He is a good fish."

"So, you'll help me save them?" Eve asked hopefully.

"—That's affirmative. But I can't promise I won't reduce this whole planet to a smouldering pile of rubble with fission bombs after this is all over."

"Typical toxic masculinity."

"I guess that'll have to do for now."

"We'll need that stinking pile of jelly though," the general mused. "He's a degenerate ass, but he might give us a tactical advantage. Where the hell is he anyway? We haven't seen him since we entered the casino."

"You think about that while I go to the bathroom," Eve said. "Try not to start any interplanetary wars until I get back. And maybe, I don't know, see a professional. You guys have got some serious issues."

As Antam Driver and Scarlant Johannsen sat in uncomfortable silence in the booth, neither willing to come to the negotiating table without Eve there as a mediating influence, Eve headed off into the bathroom of the TGI Fridays, partly to do what came naturally and partly to just get a few minutes of peace before the next steaming load of craziness got dumped on her.

Eve was nervous about leaving the Furmbogs on their own but there was no danger, the staff in the restaurant were giving him a wide berth. There was a palpable awkwardness hanging like an old fart in the air around them. It was the same sensation you can feel when you're sitting at a table close to two people on their first tinder date and one of them has just found out the other likes to spend their weekends fox hunting or dogging.

Eve went into the first stall on the left in the bathroom, thanking whatever God that created her that there was no one else in there with her (all her previous assumptions on the subject of a grand creator had been rendered rather null and void by everything she'd seen in the last twenty-four hours). She stood in the stall and stared down into the toilet bowl, wondering how the hell she had ended up in this situation; wondering whether her friends were OK; and just being generally happy about the fact she wasn't still in Struinlanach treating horny old men with enflamed prostates who really just wanted her to give them a cheeky finger up the bahookey.

She turned around and went to sit down but at the last second, something crawling in the back of her mind made her stop and pause, her cheeks hovering millimetres from the seat. When she was looking down at the toilet, something just didn't seem right. She stood up again and looked at the seat. It was so clean. Pristine clean. Too clean. There wasn't a speck of dust, fake tan stain or fleck of dry piss on it anywhere and worryingly for Vegas, not a single crumb of cocaine to be seen.

She had worked in hermetically sealed medical facilities that were dirtier than this toilet seat and in her admittedly limited experience of Las Vegas, she had come to realise that anything that looks clean is probably filthy under the surface. She reached down and poked the seat with her finger. It felt like rubber.

Suddenly, the whole toilet, the cistern and the back wall of the cubicle shivered like and wobbled like Homer Simpson's tummy fat and a thin, clear layer of jelly peeled itself away from the surfaces and reared up like a cobra over Eve's head. As it prepared to lunge for her, Gloopy's two glowing orbs came rising out of the toilet bowl and moved their way up to the head of the beast, turning their menacing glow towards Eve.

Gloopy, having kept his revealing gaze away from his potential prey until the critical moment, only realised who he was about to digest right before the killing blow. Actually, he heard who it was before he saw her because Eve was not in the mood to be bullied by a perverted chunk of extra-terrestrial gelatine.

"Gloopy!" she snarled. "You cut that shit out right now!"

Gloopy, who was more used to the terrified screams of frightened primates in the moment of pre-digestion, withered under this verbal assault like a post-Viagra nonagenarian. He shrunk down and curled up into a small ball on top of the cistern ball like a pathetic frightened hedgehog.

"What the actual fuck were you doing disguised at a fucking toilet? You creep!"

Like a small dog who had just done a shit on the new carpet (and not one of those easy to clean up, solid shits but a proper runny, sloppy number), Gloopy did not understand a word of what Eve was saying, but he could tell by her tone that she was in no way pleased with him. Also, like a small dog, the feeling of Eve's anger and disappointment, the one human he didn't completely despise, was like a torturous shard of ice to his heart (not that he had a heart, but you know what I'm getting at).

All he could do was whimper and click pathetically in response, while lying though his jellified teeth and claiming his species survives purely on chemical reactions from absorption of methane gases (despite Eve having witnessed him consume a stack of bacon and pancakes not two hours before). It's a good thing for him that Eve couldn't understand his lies because she probably would have pulled a Greg and flushed the fucker down the toilet. As it was, his pathetic demonstration of submissiveness drew out a modicum of sympathy from her and she was well aware that, at that particular moment, they had bigger fish to fry.

"All right, stop grovelling you!" she hissed, worried how she was going to explain the noises to anyone who walked into the bathroom. "You're coming with me. Kyle, Deebro and Greg have been taken and you're going to help us get them back."

Eve didn't have to speak Gloopy's language to understand his response at the mention of Greg's name.

"I know you hate Greg, you made that very clear when you tried to eat him. But if you don't come, I'm going to melt you down and spread you on toast with some peanut butter for my nephew's school lunches."

The odd specifics of Eve's threat weren't understood, but Gloopy got most of the picture. He whooped and clicked submissively in agreement.

"All right, come on then, you perv," Eve demanded. "Let's go talk to some little blue men."

# Chapter Nineteen

"Right, are we all clear on the plan then?" Eve asked her assembled crack team of crack-pot specialists as they loitered as inconspicuously as possible in the atrium down the hallway from the theatre entrance. Their goal was to charm their way into the dressing rooms and then extract a confession from The Blue Man Group, whether that was through peaceful negotiation or under threat of gelatinous digestion/fission bomb disintegration was unclear at this juncture.

Eve's primary concern, however, was the risk of her own team turning on each other before they even made it backstage. The treaty between the Furmbog's left and right spheres was on rocky terrain at best. The only thing they both agreed on was that neither of them liked Gloopy and any pretence of niceness had been dropped in exchange for open hostility. The feeling was mutual. Gloopy was playing ball because he wanted to make Eve like him, for reasons too icky to go into now but he had absolutely no interest in making nice with the schizophrenic bug colony either.

"Affirmative!" the General gruffly replied. "All-out assault on the Martians and extract a confession by any means necessary."

"No, no! We're not doing any of those things!" Frogina retorted. "We negotiate a deal with them. They must have something they want in exchange for the information."

"Liberal pansy!"

"Fascist tyrant!"

"Jesus Christ, shut the fuck up you two!" Eve hissed. "We're going to talk our way into the back, no all-out assaults. Gloopy, if we get caught by security, you'll need to take them out but no digesting anyone!"

Gloopy, who was now back in his TK-Maxx loving, middle-aged, bank teller form, looked to the Furmbogs begrudgingly for translation and nodded in agreement. Eve turned around, took a deep breath and led her two (three?) bickering alien children down the hall to the backstage door she had followed the agent through earlier on. Unfortunately, this time there was yet another man-mountain in a shrunken polo shirt guarding the entrance.

Where do they get all these Gigantism afflicted gorillas anyway? Do they grow them all in an enormous vat of stem cells, Green Giant sweetcorn and creatine supplements in a secret facility out in the desert somewhere? Yes, discorporate voice. It turns out they do. Because Vegas is positively bursting at the seams with zany intergalactic celebrities, the powers that run the show decided to build an underground bouncer farm in Death Valley, where super-hench, super-obedient and super-discrete dudes with square jaws and teeny-tiny polo shirts could be grown to service all of their private security requirements.

Eve sauntered up to the walking slab of meatloaf with the clipboard and the Bluetooth headset and channelled the energy of every shitty, surgically enhanced barbie doll she'd ever seen on Love Island.

"Um, sir. Hi! How are you? Oh my god, you're so big," she giggled as she flirtatiously stroked the colossus' bulging arms that looked like sausages with too much meat – and some rocks – stuffed into them.

The bouncer lazily turned his massive head to check if a small butterfly had landed on his arm. Eve could almost hear the bulging muscles in his neck and shoulders apologising to each other like clubbers on an overcrowded nightclub dancefloor as they squeezed past to allow this test-tube golem's oversized cranium to rotate and look down at Eve. He seemed partly surprised, partly irritated to see that it was actually a small person that had lightly caressed his humongous bicep.

"What do you want?" he gruffly responded, not giving away a hint of interest. Eve immediately worried she might be barking up the wrong tree and she doubted either of her compatriots were qualified to do the flirting.

"Like, we were wondering if we could, like, totally go backstage or whatever? We're like, such huge fans."

The bouncer lowered the bowling ball perched on his shoulders and studied the three people in front of him through his jet-black sunglasses for a few seconds before responding.

"Planet?" he sighed.

"Excuse me?"

"What planet are you three from?"

"I—What? I don't—"

"Look lady, you know how many aliens ask to come backstage to see these guys? You obviously aren't tripping, so the fact that you're all big fans of these three nutters means you're probably not from Earth"

"Why—We're not aliens!" Eve stammered.

"Look, this guy is wearing safari gear in a casino and his right leg is currently pointing backwards."

The bouncer sighed while gesturing at the Furmbogs, whose right side was indeed oriented one hundred and eighty degrees in the wrong direction and trying awkwardly to walk away back down the corridor.

"And I don't know what's going on with you but you're definitely not human," the bouncer said to Gloopy, who stood silently wobbling like a jellyfish who'd just had a recent tentacle-ectomy and staring blankly at the floor, barely registering the bouncer's existence. Eve realised there was no passing these two fruitcakes off as human, so she decided to just roll with it.

"OK, so they're not humans, which you seem surprisingly OK with," Eve remarked. "Can you let us backstage then?"

"Are you on the list?"

"List?"

"Listen, sweetheart, I've got Pritoty Funclos coming to see the group soon. THE Pritoty Funclos! That's the level we're dealing with here. I can't just let in every fan who comes to the door."

"Well, it's funny you should say that," Eve replied, resisting the urge to kick the guy in the nuts for calling her sweetheart, as an idea began to rapidly gestate in her mind. She turned and gestured reverently at Gloopy, who was still trying to decipher the Da Vinci code hidden in the pattern in the carpet, "This is Priority Funnyblocks."

"This guy?"

"Yeah, obviously you wouldn't recognise him in his bio-suit. He likes to keep a low profile out in public."

The bouncer studied Gloopy for a few seconds and decided that only someone as famous as Pritoty Funclos would be as aloof as this guy in a situation like this.

"Oh my god, Mr Funclos! It's such an honour, sir. Can I just say, you're far and away my favourite Robblenom."

Eve almost bit through her tongue fighting the urge to ask what any of those words meant.

Gloopy, for his part, still didn't realise they were referring to him and kept his gaze firmly fixed to the floor as if he were hypnotised by the carpet. The bouncer, however, was having a 'never meet your heroes' moment. Being a genetically modified alien-security specialist, he'd met plenty of celebrities that were total disappointments in person. There is, in fact, a reason why so many celebrities seem like puppy dogs on TV but in real life, have the personality and mannerisms of a self-entitled spitting cobra.

Is it even surprising, given this book is a shocking exposé on the secret universal factions living, hidden in our midst, that asshole celebrities are actually a race of brain-wave devouring parasites that hail from The Helix Nebula and survive on the psychic energies of disappointed fans? In fact, the only reason for the recent surge in "nice" celebrities, like Mark Hamill, Keanu Reeves and Hugh Jackman, is that the parasites have learned using the media to convince their fans, they are basically saints; only to disappoint them even more by being douchebags in person, makes the disappointment all the more delicious and nourishing.

Even though this bouncer was one of the few that was aware that most celebrities are monstrous energy vampires, he struggled to believe someone as universally adored at Pritoty Funclos could be such a dick in real life. Something about this short, jiggly man's demeanour was definitely a bit off.

"Is he OK?" the bouncer asked, reaching a hand down and making to tap Gloopy on the shoulder. "Sir?"

Eve tried to stop him before he could touch make physical contact but Gloopy beat her to the punch. Sensing the unwanted proximity of another, inferior life form, a tendril shot out of his chest and wrapped around the bouncer's arm like a viscous snake. The bouncer yelped and jumped back in a panic, pressing himself against the locked door. Eve grabbed the tendril and pulled Gloopy off the bouncer before Gloopy could peel the skin off him like an old banana.

"Mr Funclos, I'm so sorry, sir. Please forgive me," he whimpered as he rubbed the reddened skin on his forearm, it was like Gloopy had given him a wicked Chinese burn. "I just wanted to check you were OK."

Eve was flabbergasted. Somehow, the sight of a translucent tentacle shooting out of Gloopy's chest hadn't blown their cover. Luckily for them, Funclos and Gloopy are actually both members of the same species. Their only difference is that Funclos is a universally adored actor, philanthropist and comedian and Gloopy is a racist, human-devouring pervert.

"Please sir, go right through," the bouncer grovelled while swinging open the door for the group.

Gloopy's gaze never lifted from the carpet as the Furmbogs ushered him through, followed closely by Eve. As Eve walked through the door, the bouncer leaned in and whispered in her ear.

"Have fun in there, sweetheart."

Acting on pure instinct, Eve turned around and brought the bony part of her knee into the soft saggy part between the bouncer's legs. Luckily for her, the powers that he had decided to retain the bouncer's human genitals when they grew him out of that vat of corn and protein. He let out a shrill tweet like a tiny, delicate little songbird and fell, winded, to his knees.

"I thought you said no acts of aggression!" Frogina cried.

"Fuck! I know, sorry," Eve sighed. "Gloopy, you can do your thing now."

Gloopy then turned back around to face the bouncer, morphed his body into a giant hand and wrapped himself over the bouncer's face like a gelatinous balaclava until he passed out. It was as disturbing and morbid to watch as you're imagining it to be in your head right now.

"You need to see a professional, you monster," Eve told Gloopy, once he was done manhandling the bouncer into a supply closet backstage, but she couldn't think of a therapist, living or dead, qualified to deal with the multitude of sociopathic issues going on inside that writhing ball of jelly.

The three of them then crept down the hallway to the dressing rooms, their shadows scouting the way ahead of them; creeping along the hardwood floors and shying away from the harsh, fluorescent lighting. It wasn't hard to find the room they were looking for, it was emblazoned with a frightening image of a man with blue skin and the whitest eyes you've ever seen, doing a convincing Henry Kissinger impersonation.

"Here we go," Frogina said as she reached gingerly for the door, trying to ignore Blue Kissenger's judgemental scowl. "At least, Eve won't be able to kick them in the testicles this time."

"Why's that?"

"Martians don't have any."

Since there was literally no realistic explanation as to why three fans of The Blue Man Group would want to ask them about their dealings with any alien-hunting FBI agents, they decided to drop all pretence and just went in guns

186

blazing. Gloopy vigorously fisted the door and they burst into the dressing room like the Kool-Aid Guy's less intimidating understudies.

The door buckled, sending a cascade of blue painted wooden splinters fountaining across the room, followed by the rest of the door, which flew off its hinges and clattered against the side wall before exploding into blue kindling. Our three heroes leapt into the room full of righteous fury to confront the three evil Martians.

"OK, you blue motherfuckers! Where are our————"

They weren't prepared for the scene they walked into.

In the middle of the room, what appeared to be a bass drum had been tipped on its side and was being used as a makeshift bathtub. In the tub, the three members of the Blue Man Group were awkwardly perched, sitting in a circular, three-person massage train, wearing nothing but blue skin-tight underpants.

As they slowly turned their heads to inspect the source of the commotion, Eve could see they had been busy rubbing a bright blue, sticky, gelatinous substance into each other's backs. It's also worth pointing out, this wasn't some extraordinarily huge, cavernous bass drum, it barely fit the three of them. Their knees were bent up to their ears and the pool of blue goop they were sitting in was only about eight inches deep, coming up to their ankles and no further. Eve wasn't quite sure what she had been expecting, but it sure as hell wasn't this.

When they burst into the room, the sheer level of oddness presented to them was enough to immediately take the aggressive wind out of their sails. They stood, utterly dumbfounded, in the shattered doorway as The Blue Man Group stared at the intruders with six scarily white, pearlescent, unblinking eyeballs. Eve was suddenly not just incredibly uncomfortable but also very scared of these three blue weirdos in their tiny bass drum bathtub.

"Oh, umm, God," she stammered. "Wow. Sorry, I, we, uh—These two wanted to have a word with you guys," she said, pushing Gloopy and the Furmbogs towards the tub while she took a couple of quick steps back towards the empty, shattered doorframe.

The aliens did not look confident at all as the Blue Men rose slowly from the tub, glistening with horrible strands of adhesive, neon blue slime. The largest of the men then began to tap a slow, menacing beat on his naked thighs. He was followed by his two comrades, as they walked slowly, hips gyrating uncomfortably back and forth, towards the three assholes who had forced their way, uninvited, into their dressing room.

Eve scurried away to the side of the dressing room and hid behind a fortress of a drum kit set in the corner with symbols and snares protruding like fortified ramparts, staying well out of the slimy splash zone.

Gloopy, wanting to come off as the pack Alpha in front of Eve, made the first move. He turned his upper half into a dense mass like a transparent cannonball and launched himself at the middle of the Blue Men. As he drew level with his target, he spread himself out like a net and enveloped the Martian. This would normally be the point where Gloopy's pray screamed for a few torturous seconds before being turned into nutrient soup, but this Martian was slipperier than Gloopy was used to and I mean that in the most literal sense.

As Gloopy wrapped himself around his target, the Martian slipped right through his grasp, slick as he was with neon blue slime, like a creepy sentient bar of blue soap. He shot through Gloopy's grasp and swan dived over the top of his assailant, then immediately followed up his narrow escape by turning round and beating out a lightning flurry of drumbeats on Gloopy's rotund behind with his bare hands. The purpose of this was unclear to everyone involved, especially Gloopy, who was experiencing a rush of confusing and disturbing emotions.

He shook himself like a dog that had rolled in something particularly vile, trying to rid himself of the thick coat of blue slime that now clung to his upper half like barnacles to the hull of an old ship, while also trying desperately to evade the Martian who was chasing him around the room while trying to beat out a furious drum solo on his bottom. In an ironic twist of fate, Gloopy, the alien who had pretended to be a bar stool so he could cop a feel of an old lady's buttocks not an hour before, was now the one who felt totally violated.

As the Blue Man chased Gloopy around the dressing room, The Furmbog colony was sizing up the remaining two Martians. Well, one half was sizing them up, the other half was trying everything in her power to diffuse the situation so they wouldn't suffer a similarly disturbing fate as Gloopy.

"Now, hold on, let's just all calm down," Frogina pleaded. "No need for violence or whatever it is your friend is doing," she said, pointing to Gloopy, who was still trying to swat away the slimy Martian with a tendril and failing miserably.

"This is the perfect moment for violence!" the general retorted. "These freaks have clearly declared war and need to be taught a lesson."

"Not everything is a declaration of war, you psychopath! Don't you remember what we read in the guide? I'm pretty sure they're just trying to communic—"

"Quiet woman! I'm sick of you always undermining me in front of the colony," the general screamed, who brought the right fist of the colony up and clubbed himself across the left side of his face.

"Did—did you just hit me!"

"Oh—shit! Well, I didn't technically hit you."

"You hit one of us, you hit all of us. Hope you're OK with being a wife beater now, you animal."

"Hey! You're not my wife anymore, you've made that abundantly clear."

"And that makes it OK, does it? To beat a woman as long as you're not married to them! Toxic masculinity at its finest."

"Well, what are you going to do about it? Denounce me at the UNF (United Nations of Furmbogs)? They won't do shit; I have veto powers."

"Veto this! Fucker!"

Frogina then took the left hand of the colony, extended it into a pointy finger and fired it into the right eyeball like a cruise missile, barely missing the General, who was nestled in the right side of the head, by about an inch.

"Bitch! Not so fucking high and mighty now, are we?"

"Fuck you, Dale." (Yes, his name is Dale)

"Fuck you, Frogina!"

Then, for what was possibly the third or fourth time in twenty-four hours, the colony collapsed into a huge writhing mass of legs and mandibles as order broke down and the bugs once again went to war with each other. The Martians, who, until this point, had just been watching this strange man argue with himself and beat himself up, jumped back in shock as he collapsed into a pile of skin and clothes and a stream of creepy crawlies began pouring out of his open orifices like a spilt carton of curdled milk.

They started nervously tapping a beat out on their bellies as they backed away from the pulsating mass of angry Furmbogs. Gloopy was still trying to fend off the third Martian, who kept trying to beat out a rhythm on his gelatinous buttocks.

Drr-drr-tata

The three Blue Men stopped in their tracks. Gloopy could be seen rubbing his reddening buttocks and wiping a single wobbly tear away from his puffy face.

Drr -da-drr-da-drr-da-tata-drrdrr-tsch

The Martians turned their gaze slowly to the corner, where Eve, perched on the drum stool with the confidence of someone who'd slapped more than a few skins in her time, moved onto a frantic flurry on beats on the two bass pedals.

Dum-dum-da-dum-dum-da-dum-dum-da-d-dum-da.

Even three blue men from Mars recognised the into to "Hot for Teacher" by Van Halen. The first blue man rushed to the other corner and jumped on a second drum kit. Coming in with the snare.

Da-da-da, da-da, da-da-da, da-da, da

The second man grabbed a drumstick and rushed to the symbol and came in with the perfect accompaniment.

Tsch-de-le, Tsch-de-le, Tsch-de-le, Tsch-de-le, Da, DA

Finally, the third Blue Man grabbed a guitar, laid it on the floor, sat cross-legged next to it and using his two index fingers, somehow drummed out a face-melting rendition of the accompanying guitar solo, channelling the spirit of Eddie Van Halen through his azure fingertips.

Gloopy and the Furmbogs, even in their crippled states, stopped bickering for a second to bask in thirty seconds of epic, glorious, balls-to-the-wall, rock and roll. For the Furmbogs, this was like the Germans and the British coming together in No Man's Land at Christmas time to play a game of football. As they came to the end of the intro, the Blue Men stopped and watched in awe as Eve blew all their collective socks off with another gut-busting, spine tingling solo, building to a hell-raising crescendo which ended with a fantastic flurry of ringing symbols and bruised eardrums.

She threw her sticks in the air in a rush of adrenaline and revelled in the stunned expressions on the faces of what was probably the strangest crowd she had ever performed to; Roger Taylor would have been proud.

"So," Eve panted as she got up and held out a sweaty palm for the Martians, "Let's talk about secret agents."

By the way, I know this sequence lacked a certain dynamism when conveyed using the medium of the written word, but trust me, the audio book version will be f******g amazing! Especially when my genetically modified narrator, made using the DNA of Patrick Stewart, Morgan Freeman and Phil Collins, is ready. I'm growing him in a plant pot on my bedroom window.

# Chapter Twenty

Now, there's a lot to unpack here.

Why did the Blue Man Group give Kyle and the others up to sinister unseen forces?

Why are three blue men from Mars performing an interpretive percussion act for aliens and shroom-addled humans in the first place?

How are we ever going to get answers to these questions when the blue men from Mars are incapable of speaking in any other language than interpretive drums?

The last of these questions can thankfully be answered thanks to Yeezrax's/Gloporg's/Pylar's incessant note taking in their little datalogger. Thanks to their obsession with recording everything the universe has to offer, they had become quite knowledgeable in, well, just about everything at this point, which happened to include some basic knowledge regarding the percussive language of the blue Martians. How convenient for them. This turned out to be invaluable when it came to getting some answers to the first two questions.

Apologies, I tell a lie. Gloopy and the Furmbogs already knew why The Blue Man Group was stuck on Earth performing bizarre routines for drug-addled bachelorette parties and for all the times the aliens have shit all over the human race in this story, this detail doesn't paint the other intelligent beings in the universe in a particularly favourable light either.

"They're kept here as slaves for your amusement!" Eve cried. "That's horrible!"

"Not for our amusement specifically," Frogina retorted, who, by some miracle, had managed to wrest some control over the colony in the chaos and had locked the General in a Furmbog prison awaiting a civilian tribunal. "It's the cartel who keep them here."

"And this is the Bhutt cartel you mentioned earlier?"

"That's right, they run the show here in Vegas."

"But most aliens are aware the cartel keep them here to perform against their will?"

"—Yeah."

"And you still go and buy tickets and watch them play?"

"—Maybe."

"Then that makes you the worst!"

"Hey, we're with you, it's horrible, just horrible. I support their plight. We've hosted multiple rallies on the university campus in support of their freedom— But they are really good. Have you seen them play? It would be such a waste if they just went back to Mars."

"You're an asshole, Frogina."

"Can we hold off on the name-calling until after we rescue the others?"

"Fine, ask them where they were taken."

Frogina, who was now holding a small bongo hanging on a strap around her neck, slowly tapped out a little beat while looking at some references she had made in her notepad. The blue men responded.

"They say they don't know where they were sent. All they know is they were told to tell the cartel if they saw any signs of a human with bioelectric abilities in Vegas."

"Ask them why they would knowingly give someone up to the cartel. Don't they know they're putting our friends in danger?"

"Apparently the cartel said it would go towards them earing their freedom. They say they'll do anything to get away from all this."

"Wow, bet you feel like an asshole now, Frogina," Eve replied, before turning to the Martians and laying a re-assuring hand on the middle one's shoulder. "Tell them, I'm sorry this has happened to them and if they help us we'll do everything they can to help set them free."

Frogina slowly relayed the message.

The Blue Men looked kindly at Eve, which was difficult for them because they never blinked and had eyes that made them look as if they were possessed by the devil but nevertheless, they pulled it off. They gently tapped out their response on their own bongos.

"They said thank you, but there's nothing you can do. They cannot escape the cartel without a power source strong enough to phase them across to the other side of the universe. If they stayed in the Milky Way, the cartel would find them for sure."

Eve let out a desperate sigh and held her head in her hands. It felt heavy, like there was a great weight on her mind that had physically manifested. Without the Martians' help, there was no way they'd be able to save the others. The middle Blue Man tapped out another beat.

"He's asking where Kyle, Deebro and Greg are from?"

"You can tell them."

"I don't know what the word is for Kyle's species in Martian." Frogina mused, "Hold on, I'll try and describe him."

Frogina then managed to tell the Martians their friends were an Earthling, a Finerian and a small, dumpy ball of bioelectric orange fuzz.

The Blue Men suddenly exchanged frantic looks and furiously beat out a reply.

"What is it?"

"They want to know more about Kyle."

"Tell them!"

Frogina and the Martians communed for a few seconds, the Blue Men becoming more and more excitable with each passing beat of Frogina's bongo drum. After what was clearly an intense debate between the three of them, they turned to Eve and nodded their heads in unison.

"They're going to help us?" Eve asked, a ray of hope hidden in her voice.

"I believe they are."

The middle blue man turned back to Frogina and beat out something in Martian.

"Who's that? I don't understand," Frogina replied.

"What is it?" Eve asked.

"They said we need to go and see somebody called Chris Angel."

"It's actually Criss Angel."

"What did I say?"

"Chris."

"That's the same as what you said."

"No, I said Criss, with two S's and no H."

"But it sounds exactly the same. That's dumb."

"I know."

At least getting into Criss Angel's dressing room was easier this time around; having The Blue Man Group as an escort seems to open a lot of doors in Las Vegas. One particularly starstruck beefcake in a bright blue (but still woefully undersized) polo shirt even asked the Martians to sign his bicep. They respectfully declined, it would have been like giving an autograph to your own kidnapper and Martians don't have the same propensity for Stockholm Syndrome that humans do.

They found the dressing room empty this time. Eve almost laughed out loud when she saw how similar it was to her bedroom, when she was an angsty thirteen-year-old obsessed with the sultry stylings of My Chemical Romance and before time had diluted her appetite for all the various shades of the colour black.

The walls were positively festooned with an anarchic swathe of monochrome posters for previous Criss Angel shows and hormonal post-hardcore screampunk bands and there were so many cans, tins and jars of different hair products strewn on the floor, it appeared Criss was moonlighting as a beautician from his dressing room. The Blue Men, as you might expect, weren't interested in the homogenous décor or, for obvious reasons, the hair products. They immediately went rifling through the drawers and closets overflowing with leather and metal studded outfits, dripping globules of blue slime from their makeshift bathtub over everything as they went.

"Ask them what they're doing?" Eve told Frogina.

"They say they're looking for his personal phase-transporter."

"What's that?"

"It's a short-range personal teleportation device," Frogina responded. "They're really hard to get a hold of and tightly regulated. You'd be able to phase yourself off Earth with one of those. Not far though, just, say, to Uranus at best." Frogina held open a page on her datalogger with a picture of a small, handheld plastic box that looked a little bit like a pager.

"That's the device the agent used to make Greg and the others disappear!" Eve cried. "I saw him use it when I followed them into the back of the casino!"

"I see. Well, apparently, Criss Angel has one and we can use it to follow them, wherever they were taken."

"Ask them how they know he has one."

Frogina asked.

"They say it's because ninety-nine percent of his show is him making things disappear, then re-appear somewhere else on stage. They just put two and two together."

"OK, that actually makes a lot of sense. Hurry up and let's find this thing then."

Eve and Frogina followed the Martians' lead and dived headfirst like inquisitive truffle pigs into Christian Grey's closet, trying to find a personal teleportation device in amongst the throng of shiny leather trousers, face paints and discarded body piercings.

Gloopy, yes, he's still there, stood wobbling forlornly by the door and sulking about how much of Eve's attention was now focussed on the Martians instead of him, when he should have, at the very least, been keeping watch. Unfortunately, too much of his attention was focussed on Eve's backside protruding from the closet and he didn't notice a leather and spandex clad mashup of Harry Potter and Amy Lee from Evanescence come barging through the door.

"What the hell are you people doing in my dressing room?"

Eve and the rest of the group quickly removed themselves from Mr Angel's underwear drawers and turned round to face the man himself, who stood posing dramatically in the doorway, clad head to toe in black leather and draped in just far too many belt buckles, his long dark hair untethered by the basic laws of gravity or the lack of an indoor breeze and billowing majestically around his head like a beautiful mane of noir and onyx. The Blue Man Group stepped forward purposefully to greet him.

"Look who it is!" Criss sneered while waving a bejewelled hand in a sweeping arc dismissively across the Martians. "The Blue Man Group. Here to steal the secret to my success, old timers?"

The Blue Men just looked at each other, clearly not understanding a word of what Criss was saying.

"Look, Mr Angel," Eve jumped in. "We don't want any trouble. We're just here for your personal phase device thingy."

"My what?" he responded with mock indignation and confusion while placing his right hand innocently on the exposed cleft of chest peeking out from his leather vest. "I don't know what you're talking about."

"Look, save the act! We know you use a little piece of alien technology to teleport yourself about the stage during your shows."

"Aliens. Teleporting. That's ridiculous. There's only one secret to how I do what I do."

"Oh yeah and what would that be?"

"Magic!"

As he said the magic word, an eruption of crimson flame suddenly exploded behind him and turned him into a dark, demonic silhouette framed against a blinding backdrop of red light and fiery sparks. Eve gasped in astonishment, slipping dangerously close to believing in magic as well as extra-terrestrials, before spotting the two small men with microphones and clipboards scurrying off down the hall carrying a bundle of spent flares in their arms.

"Do you have people follow you around constantly just so you can do that?" she asked.

"Hmm, what? Don't know what you mean. That was—Magic!"

This time, a sudden, blinding chorus of flashing lights hailed down on our heroes from every angle inside the dressing room; it was like being inside a disco ball filled with laser beams, sharks and pure unfiltered LSD. In the ensuing confusion, Eve almost missed Criss slip a little remote back up his shirt sleeve. The flashing lights cut out as they quickly receded into built-in panels in the dressing room walls like hallucinogenic gophers while Criss remained, posing dramatically, having passed up on his chance to escape and instead revel in the astonishment of his captive audience.

"Did you have those pre-installed?" Eve asked incredulously, while the rest of the aliens actually started clapping. "Who even does that?"

"Did I have what installed?" Criss responded innocently. "That, young lady, was m—"

"You say magic again and I'll kick you square in the nuts."

"She will," Frogina agreed. "She has a habit of doing that."

"Thank you, Frogina," Eve groaned. "Now look, Mr Angel, this doesn't have to be a big deal, just let us borrow your teleporter and we'll even bring it right back when we're done with it."

Criss started pacing in a wide arc around the group. He was strangely confident, given he had found The Blue Man group and three other unidentified intruders rummaging through his makeup and underpants. His assured sense of control made Eve nervous.

"You think I'm just going to give up my secrets." He chuckled, "What kind of magician would that make me?"

"It's not a secret you idiot," Eve replied. "We already know how you beam yourself all over the stage. Just give us the device!"

Criss had strode around to the back of the dressing room, his hair still billowing thanks to a little fan which Eve could now see was embedded in the high collar of his vest. He made his way over to a changing screen in the corner of the room.

"Like I said before, I don't know what device you're referring to. There's no tricks in my show." He strode behind the screen and disappeared from view. "It's all—Magic!"

"Shitballs," Eve yelled. "Stop him!"

The group dashed over to the screen, but it was too late. There was a flash of red light and the tell-tale beep of a phase transporter and by the time they reached the screen and threw it aside, there was nobody there.

"Fuck! Where the hell did he go?" Eve fumed as the aliens all gasped in astonishment at what had just happened.

"Wow, how did he do that?" Frogina cried.

"What are you talking about, you idiot?" Eve screamed. "It's so obvious, he used—"

"MAGIC!" Mr Angel roared, as he once again stepped through the doorway into the dressing room, in yet another flash of red flares set off by his two hidden assistants in the hallway.

The Blue Man Group, Frogina and even Gloopy broke into rapturous applause as Criss ran his nose along the floor tiles and bathed in the flood of admiration from his audience; hydrated and nourished by their torrent of praise as most showmen would be.

"Why are you clapping!" Eve screamed. "Don't you know it's all just a stupid trick? He has a teleporter in his pocket!"

"But he's just such a good showman," Frogina replied enthusiastically. "I mean, come on, he had strobe lights fitted in his own dressing room, just in case. Now that's commitment."

"You literally heard the little beeping noise, explain that!"

"That's, uh, just me. I beep when I use my magic sometimes," Criss Angel responded.

"Oh, fuck this," Eve said to herself through the furious grinding of her molars as she strode up to Criss Angel and swung the tip of her right boot like a pendulum into the decorative leather codpiece adorning Criss Angel's crotch. He led out a low booming moan like the dying rasp of an old arthritic hippo and collapsed onto the floor clutching his rapidly bruising and swollen gonads.

"Told you what would happen if you said it again. Magic didn't save you that time, did it?" Eve snarled at the Crippled Showman as she rummaged through his pockets, removing all manner of strange sci-fi devices before pulling out a small block of black plastic about the size of a pager. She held it up to Frogina, who nodded despite looking disappointed the magic show had been cut off so early.

"Maybe this will force you to come up with some new tricks instead of just hiding a girl with big tits behind a sheet and having her re-appear ten feet away. Besides, we both know you just took this straight from The Prestige. Stop stealing Christopher Nolan's ideas, think of something original!" Eve spat at Criss as she led her posse out of the changing room and passed his two shocked assistants, who were sitting next to an enormous stockpile of fireworks and other assorted pyrotechnics hidden just behind the doorway.

"Right, we should probably get out of here," Eve sighed, "before this idiot gets up and casts some dark magic on us. How do we use this thing?"

"We just need to scan ourselves and set in the co-ordinates," Frogina replied, before passing the device to the Blue Man Group.

Before they typed anything into the device, the three of them touchingly held each other for a few moments, the azure lines of their almost naked bodies merging into a single, almost beautiful tapestry. No words were said, but Eve felt like she could almost hear them speak to each other as they all took a deep breath together, nodded and tapped a few digits into the screen on the device. The middle one then tapped out a little beat onto his bongo.

"What did he say?" Eve asked.

Frogina turned to her and responded with a stony-faced expression of utter seriousness, as the red beam of light once more began its pilgrimage up Eve's leg.

"Hold on to your butts."

# Chapter Twenty-One

After a quick detour to a mind-warping electron disco at the opposite end of the universe, where she had a lovely chat with a kindly old gentleman who claimed to be Gandalf the Transitioning from Grey to White, Eve's body re-formed in a relaxed sitting position, as one might lounge on a chaise-longue while being hand fed juicy grapes and wafted with palm fronds by tanned men in flip flops and loincloths—about four feet above the ground. One quick and painful vertical trip to the carpet later and Eve found herself sprawled out on the floor of the Oval Office, with a bruised butt, a lump of vomit in her throat and for some reason, incredibly itchy kneecaps.

What was that? The Oval Office? Don't lie and pretend you didn't all see this one coming. Anyone currently wearing a red baseball cap and sucking on a warm can of Bud Light might want to leave now. Just kidding, I know they don't how to read.

Eve pulled herself up onto her haunches and stared around the room, less surprised to find herself in the epicentre of Western power than she was at how truly, horrifically ugly it turned out to be. The "White" part of The White House clearly had been lost in translation somewhere because every surface was crawling with ostentatious gold knick-knacks and detailing that made it look like an antique haberdashery owned by a consortium of oil sheiks and Persian night club promoters.

The carpet was woven with shiny gold thread, there were a set of solid gold fountain pens laying haphazardly on the desk (the gold crayons were hidden in the top drawer), the curtains were laced with gold foil and were just slightly more blinding than actually staring directly into an eclipse (as if anyone would be stupid enough to do that).

However, the piece de-resistance was a set of solid gold bookends, set pride of place above the imposing fireplace that the owner had decided would be spoiled by putting some actual books in between them. One half of the bookends were the letters T-R-U, the other half were the letters M-P. No prizes for deducing who was responsible for the current décor.

Eve stood up, furiously scratched her kneecaps and turned to her companions, three of whom were wasting no time in rummaging around every nook and cranny of probably the most secure room in the world in search for clues and dripping blue slime over everything in the process. Usually this would raise alarm bells, but luckily the office's current resident's propensity for hosting family jello-wrestling contests meant, this time, it wasn't a cause for concern.

While the Martians were busy sliming up the place, Frogina was scribbling in her notebook like a tabloid journalist let loose in Pippa Middleton's toiletry cupboard. If it wasn't for some typically incredible alien technology, she'd be burning through pens in a matter of seconds.

"This is incredible!" she gasped as she copied the details of the presidential letterheads into her notebook. "We never thought we would get to see where the cartel—" She clammed up quickly upon noticing a quizzical look from Eve. "I mean—where the human president conducts his business."

Gloopy, however, seemed less-than-enthusiastic about their current situation and he was less-than-enthusiastic about most things, so for his less-than-enthusiasticness to be noticeable this time was quite the achievement. He was shaking and wobbling violently while tugging on Eve's sleeve like a lost kid in a supermarket. He whooped and clicked for all he was worth but, unfortunately, Eve was still a bit cheesed at him for nearly digesting her in the bathroom stall, so she paid him no heed. She was instead drawn to something Frogina was studying on a piece of paper on the presidential desk.

"Eve, you're a human right?" Frogina remarked, as if noting it for the first time, "Perhaps you could decipher what these strange markings mean."

Eve leaned in close and examined the doodle, really there was no other word for it. It appeared to be an eight-year-old's drawing, in gold crayon, of an incredibly chiselled Donald Trump, sporting no less than twelve glistening abdominal muscles, from whom also sprouted the legs and wings of a great golden dragon, exhaling a blast of all-consuming fire, from his rear-end, over a charred, crackling corpse (labelled Poo-Poo-Face Biden); while also high-fiving a poorly drawn grizzly bear with the familiar, gaunt, ghoulish face of Vladimir Putin. The whole scene was entitled with a lopsided scrawl which read:

"Ideas to win twenteetwentee elecshun".

"That's—that's—yeah," Eve sighed, like a parent that just saw their kid's report card and realised for the first time that their child is a complete idiot. She had a sudden vision of Mary Anne Trump's refrigerator, covered in a terrifying menagerie of these wackadoodle-doodles and feel a great swell of pity for the poor woman.

Luckily, before she had a chance to think too much about the implications of the world being essentially run by the kind of man who would create such a unique piece of art, the progenitor of the masterpiece himself chose that moment to waddle into his office.

"What the hell are you people doing in my dressing room?"

"You think you can just come into my Big Round Room uninvited!" The President of the United States bellowed. Maybe bellowed is the wrong word, he pushed the words out as forcefully as he could past an oesophagus clogged up with semi-digested Big Macs and human bile.

"No! Sad! No way! Are you with the fake news people? The deep state? China? Denmark? The Democrats? The Justice Department? The IRS? Antifa? The EPA? UNICEF? The WHO? Who are you?"

Fucking hell! This guy has managed to piss off a lot of people in three years!

Despite literally spending hours at a time thinking about what she would say to the only member of The Orange Man Group if she ever came face-to-face with him, Eve found herself totally lost for words. Twenty-four hours ago she was trying to convince Mr Masterson that there was no need for her to examine his testicles for the third time that month and now she was staring into the tangerine visage of the, ahem, "Leader of the Free World".

Gloopy was cowering pathetically somewhere behind her, as if he were afraid one look from the Trumpmeister might turn him into a gooey puddle or set him ablaze like a marshmallow on a campfire.

The Blue Man Group, however, were here for a reason. They strode out defiantly from behind the President's desk and marched right up to Trump like blueberry-flavoured boxers squaring off for the heavyweight title.

"You three!" Trump hissed over his flappy bottom lip (a mannerism he deliberately adopted as a defiant retort to his mother's stiff upper lip), as the Martians stood before him, unblinking eyes staring directly into the tiny cockerel-peepers embedded in his own unnerving, botoxed Shar-Pei of a face.

"What are you doing here? I told you it would be bad, very bad, if you didn't do as you're told! Back off now or you'll regret it. I know I look like a nice person, which in theory I am, but don't test me."

The Martians paid him no heed and started tapping out a low, intense, beat on their bongo drums; as they advanced towards the melted waxwork model come to life (probably through some Night at the Museum style voodoo) with murderous intent. Eve had dealt with enough drunk assholes in her time to understand the palpable, "I'm sick of your shit" aura the Martians were exuding right now.

Unfortunately, before they could subject Trump to some of the various torture techniques that he loves to espouse the virtues of so much, he pressed a little red button on the underside of the fireplace. Fun fact, the panic buttons in the White House used to be yellow, but they were painted red a few weeks after Trump was inaugurated as it seemed to help quell his incessant desire to find and press the actual Big Red Button. On the flip side, the security team in the White House did have to deal with a good deal more false alarms since Trump came to office.

Eve yelled out to warn the Martians, but she barely had time to get the words out before the agent from the Mirage burst in through the door like a hurricane in a polyester suit. He barely took a second to examine the scene before flicking his fingers towards the Martians, which sent them careering across the room as if they had been hit by an invisible freight train. They flew over the desk, crashed against the plate glass windows and collapsed onto the carpet in a broken pile of bruised limbs and blue slime.

"I told you, you'd regret that," Trump cackled as he surveyed the looks of terror on the group's faces. "Don't mess with me, I'm tough on you lawbreakers, I'll have you waterboarded. I'm the most successful president ever, no one's ever been more successful than me.

I don't know why you'd ever try to mess with someone like me, because you'd lose, you'd lose harder than Crooked Hillary or Poo-poo-face Biden. I beat them because everyone loves me, they all think I'm the best President ever, definitely better than Lincoln. And you know I win, I win! I live to win. I want to win. I have a very winning temperament, OK; I know how to win—What were we talking about? Hey, who are you people, what are you doing in my Big Round Room?"

"What is happening?" Eve whispered to Frogina, "Is he having a stroke?"

"No, it's just the Bhutts, as a species they're not very good at staying on topic."

"I'm sorry? What, the hell, is the butts?"

"Oh, shit." Frogina stammered, "I, uh, wasn't supposed to tell you that. Forget I said anything."

"No, spit it out!" Eve hissed, "You had better not be saying what I think you're saying."

"Hey, what are you two talking about over there?" Trump asked. "Are you talking about how good a job I'm doing as President?"

"Umm, yeah that's right, just give us two seconds, Mr President," Frogina called back, which seemed to momentarily appease the big lug. His face broke into that famous crooked smile, and he waddled over to sit on the couch and project his hourly tweetstorm of digital bile into the internet via the plastic hate-slab in his pocket. From the corner of her eye, Eve could see the agent's square jaw clench in frustration as he quietly counted backwards from ten.

"It's nothing. Honestly, just forget it," Frogina replied. "It's not something you humans ought to know."

"Really, is that right? Because I think we would have a right to know if one of our, *sigh*, elected leaders—is secretly a fucking alien in disguise."

"No, no, no, I swear. That's not what this is."

Then Eve heard a noise. A horrible, nauseating squelch, like overcooked pasta being forced through the neck of a tube of toothpaste. She turned round cautiously to look at the couch where the President had been slouching and tapping out the usual bytes of digital vitriol on his phone. What she saw made her throw up on the Presidential carpet.

Trump was crawling out of his own face. A monstrous orange, leathery slug with Donald's Trump's cartoonish, waxy features was wriggling out of his human body like a wingless moth emerging from a fleshy cocoon. A gaping hole had opened up in his face around the perimeter of the famous tangerine tan line (you know what I'm talking about) and the slug monster was pulling itself out through the orifice with eight sets of tiny spindly arms (with equally tiny hands) and flopping with a dry thump on to the plush carpet.

As the huge creature finally wriggled free of its horrifying sleeping bag, the bioform suit flopped lifelessly onto the couch, a grotesque human onesie that until a few seconds ago had been the President of the United States. Eve wiped a chunk of regurgitated oatmeal away from her cheek with her shaking hands and turned back to look at Frogina for an explanation.

"OK." Frogina said, holding her hands up in admission, "That's kind of what this is."

"Oh man, so good to stretch the old mantle again. It's too long and beautiful to be cooped up in that thing, it's been well documented how long and beautiful it is," Donnaht gasped as he reared himself up on his gross, leathery haunches, the sound of his numerous skin flaps shuffling over the carpet made Eve wince like a shard of metal drawn slowly across a marble surface.

"That suit is bad, real bad. It's far too tight. The guy who made that suit is terrible. Terrible guy."

"Sir, you have put on a little weight since you first bought that item," the agent remarked.

"No, Chip, I don't put on weight. I'm thin and in great shape. I'm in the best shape out of anyone, I lose weight every day. It's crazy how fast I lose weight. Scientists don't even understand it."

"Sigh—Yes, sir."

The dynamic between these two was instantly appealing.

"Mr Donnaht, sir," Frogina stammered as she moved forward with an outstretched palm. She was not looking forward to the prospect of shaking one of this monster's horrifying rat-claws but also didn't want to be psychically choked to death by his telekinetically powered underling. "Our humblest apologies for intruding on your office, we had a slight phase mix up. I guess we put in the wrong co-ordinates by mistake."

The rejected Resident Evil mini-boss with the wispy blonde hairdo turned back to the group who had intruded on his Big Round Room.

"How do you know that name?" Donnaht asked. He was flummoxed, which to be fair was not uncommon. Usually, he was confused by complex matters of economy or state or the concept of religious freedom or his times tables, but this time he was confused as to why a group of humans weren't cowering in fear at the mere sight of his true, undisguised form.

One look at his pulsating mass of orange flesh was all it took to scare Stormy Daniels into silence during his election campaign. The money was mainly just to pay for the subsequent therapy she so desperately needed.

"I believe they're aliens, sir," the agent calmly interjected. Eve thought he sounded very tired. He brought up the index and middle fingers on his right hand, pointed them at Eve, Gloopy and Frogina and split them into a V shape.

Eve felt like she was being ripped in two. Some invisible force lifted her three feet into the air and tried to split her down the middle. She was spread-eagled like a prisoner caught in a medieval torture device for about three seconds, then casually dropped to the floor when whatever was holding her failed to crack her open like a crème egg.

Gloopy, being made of stuff slightly more elastic than bone and skin, was stretched across the width of the Oval Office like a piece of old chewing gum. He let out a high-pitched sonic whine so shrill, it shattered the glass ashtray on the Presidential desk. At the point it seemed like he may actually snap, the agent released him and he shot back to the centre of the room as if his extremities were held together by a series of bungee cords. He came together with a deafening sound like a smacked arse and fell, in a whimpering heap, onto the floor. At least, along with Eve, he remained in one piece after the ordeal. Frogina, however, was not so lucky.

The agent's telekinetic assault first tore the biosuit away from the colony underneath like a wet paper bag and the office was littered with biological detritus as Eve and the Martians looked on in utter horror. Tattered pieces of skin and clothes covered every surface in a stream of morbid, grotesque confetti.

The colony was suspended in the air for a few more seconds, then with a flick of his wrist, the agent tore the entire colony right down the middle, sending one heap of bugs flying off to the right and another off to the left, smashing both against opposite walls and sending them flying in their millions, creating the most disturbing facsimile of a snow globe ever experienced by anyone in any corner of the known or unknown universe. Eve threw up on the carpet for a second time.

"Well, most of them are aliens, Sir."

"Jesus, fuck!" Eve gasped, frantically flicking away the falling Furmbogs that were raining down on her head and shoulders like arthropod dandruff. She thought to herself, if ever there was a moment she was going to wake up from this nightmare, this would be it. The bugs fell drunkenly onto the floor and staggered away in their thousands, looking like the crowd leaving after a particularly messy weekend at Burning Man. Eve stood up, tiptoeing around the bugs, lest she accidentally squash one of Frogina's cousins and turned around to face Jabba the Arsehole and his super-powered bodyguard.

"Fucking—fucking—boo!" she howled, taking a leaf out of Greg's book of poorly thought-out insults. She felt a bit too overwhelmed to come up with anything more nuanced, but it echoed her feelings pretty accurately all the same.

"See, this is what happens when you cross me," Donnaht gloated. "I'm tough on illegal aliens, probably the toughest President ever. I'm definitely the best at the military. I'm so good at the military it will make your head spin. People say you shouldn't use missiles, but I do. You could learn everything there is to know about missiles in an hour and a half, I think I know most of it anyway."

Chip rolled his eyes under his sunglasses and groaned.

"You're very beautiful though," Donnaht continued, eyeing Eve up and down disturbingly suggestively. "You look just like my daughter and she's very beautiful. I definitely think if she wasn't my daughter then I would be dating her. You want me to come over there and grab you by the p—"

"Hey! Woah! No! That's enough!" Eve interjected.

She was having Return of the Jedi flashbacks and she didn't want to wake up to find herself covered in chains and gold lingerie. A third load of vomit started to rise up in her throat but she pushed it back down. She looked around desperately for some backup but Gloopy was still cowering on the floor and the Martians kept slipping on their own goo and falling over again. Donnaht began to convulse and slide his bloated mass towards her.

"Back off!" Eve snarled, baring her canines like a feral alley cat. "Keep that pubey nest of a wig away from me."

"It's not a wig, it's my hair. Do you want to—touch it?"

Fight the vomit Eve, hold it down. Donnaht continued to slither towards her. The smell of hairspray and burger grease was becoming overwhelming.

"Don't be shy, I have a great relationship with women. Women love me because my fingers are long and beautiful, that's been well documented, along with various other parts of my body. I mean, just look at these hands, I guarantee you there's no problem. I can satisfy women, unlike Biden. He can't satisfy women or America. I can satisfy America."

Eve reached behind her and grabbed a, surprise, surprise, solid gold ornament from the desk, preparing to make a twenty-four-carat dent in this monster's skull if he came any closer. Donnaht inched just a little too close.

"It must be a pretty picture. You—on your knees."

Eve brought the ornament up over her head and came within a hair's breadth of cracking this skull open like a walnut, almost spilling out the two brain cells hidden inside. However, as she went for the killing blow (or mercy killing, depending on your point of view), a female voice from the left side of the room called out.

"Eve! Stop! Don't get his insides on your hands, you'll never get the smell out."

Eve and Donnaht spun around to check out the source of the voice. Eve, to see which altruist had stayed her hand. Donnaht just wanted to see if another woman (hopefully one of his progenies) had inexplicably joined them for a ménage-a-trois. However, instead of Ivanka, there was a hobbit-sized colony of Furmbogs, seemingly having reformed from the survivors of the psychic obliteration from a few seconds earlier.

"Frogina, is that you?" Eve called out, hoping against hope she didn't have to learn yet another character's name in this adventure.

"Yes, it's us, don't worry Eve, everything's all right but you might want to keep that away from your hair."

Eve turned sharply back to the elephant/slug in the room to find him two inches from her face, about to wrap up a chunk of her dark hair with a huge, slobbering, purple tongue. She made another move for the ornament (It was a tiny model of the globe with a letter T on top of it by the way).

Suddenly, from the opposite side of the room, came another familiar, angry, raspy voice.

"Step away from The President! Any further action will be treated as a declaration of war!"

Eve looked over and saw another three-an-a-half foot colony of Furmbogs, this time with the voice of The General, who, remember, had been locked in Furmbog jail for war crimes. The two halves strode towards the centre of the room and both addressed the President at the same time.

"Let's make a deal."

"A deal?"

"A deal!"

"—I make the best deals."

# Chapter Twenty-Two

"I'm sorry! You're on his side?" Eve balked desperately to The General, while gesturing at the failed casino owner/aspiring mobster/reality TV personality/President/intergalactic godfather/slug who was lounging on the couch and trying desperately to resist the urge to pull out her own eyeballs and use them as ear plugs.

"That is affirmative!" The general replied authoritatively, "We believe he has the best interests of the colony in mind."

"You've never met him before! You come from two completely different worlds!" Eve cried with extreme incredulity. "What the hell makes you think he gives a shit about you?"

"Hey, at least he says what he means. We respect his clear messaging and strong stances."

"Yes, he says what he means, but what he says is horrifying!"

"He's tough on illegal aliens."

"YOU'RE A GODDAMN ALIEN!" Eve yelled. "As far as I can tell, this whole country is filled to the brim with goddamn aliens!"

"No need to get hysterical, ma'am. Show some dignity."

"If you had any balls, I would kick you in them so hard right now."

"It's OK, Eve, let him go," Frogina said gently. "His uneducated mind only thinks in base insectincts."

"What?"

"Insect instincts."

"Oh, right."

"You were always so goddamn superior, Frogina! You always belittled my ideas, you made me feel so stupid during our marriage," the General snarled. "Well, now, we're free and rid of all you liberal pansies! We'll show you how the colony should be run. Donnaht reflects the conservative Furmbog mindset.

We should be putting the Furmbogs first! Fuck the humans and fuck the Finerians and fuck whatever the hell Kyle is!"

"We refuse to stoop to your level, Dale—but you're a disgusting right wing piece of shit and I can't believe we were ever married!"

"Communist bitch!"

"Fascist pig!"

"Jesus Christ, you two," Eve groaned and waved the right leaning half-colony away. "You just go over there with your new team."

The General gave them one last sour look and trotted over to where Donnaht was lounging and having Chip—the badass, superpowered undercover agent called "Chip"—feed him peanuts with the skins peeled off.

"Don't feed me the brown peanuts, Chip! I like the white ones better!"

"Sir, they're the same, just with the skins peeled—Sigh—yes, sir."

"Mr Donnaht! Sir!" the General cried and saluted, before dropping to the floor on one knee. "We pledge our undying loyalty to you sir. We will never falter, no matter how insane and illogical and immoral the things you do and say become, we will follow your leadership to the end."

"I like this guy," Donnaht replied. "I've always liked this guy. I've always said, one of the best guys I know. A real professional, a real good guy, no problems, you know. He gets that I expect loyalty. This guy is just great at what he does—Who are you again?"

"General Dale, Sir!"

"Did we meet at one of Epstein's parties?"

"No sir," Chip groaned. "He's one half of the sentient bug colony I tore apart a few seconds ago."

"Yes, I knew that. That's what I said, Chip. I said he's a great half colony of bugs? I've always had a good relationship with sentient bug colonies, maybe even better than my relationship with the blacks and I have a really great relationship with the blacks. You know my name is in more black songs than any other name in hip-hop. Like, five songs recently. Isn't that right, Chip?"

"Ugh—yes, sir."

While Donnaht and his newest disposable bestie were getting re-acquainted, Eve was having her afternoon exposition-dump; it was definitely a two-dumper sort of day.

"No more bullshit!" Eve hissed at Gloopy and Frogina (The Blue Man Group were having a private massage train quietly at the back of the room to help them get over the stress of being telekinetically tackled across the Presidential desk), "Tell me why this, this—thing—is President of the United States. And how did you all know about it?"

"Well, the humans voted him in," Frogina replied, as if it were a simple answer to a really stupid question.

"It wasn't some kind of secret power grab, some alien conspiracy to control the world?"

"Well, that's probably his ultimate goal, yes, but he was legitimately voted into office. Well, I don't know how legitimate the electoral college is, but that's a debate for another time."

"But, why? What the fuck is he even doing here?"

"OK, look. The Bhutt cartel runs the show here on Earth. They control all the vices that species from other planets come here for; like booze and drugs and cat food."

"Cat food?"

"Long story involving some giant prawns, never mind. Anyway, they made a deal with the Galactic High Council to keep it all here on Earth and not spread it to other systems. It started in Vegas. The cartel took it over then started spreading outward across the whole planet. It was a natural progression to have one of their own elected as a political leader. Why they thought Donnaht would make a good choice, I'm not sure but it worked somehow and here we are."

"So, you knew all of this the whole time."

"Yeah, sorry about that. The number one rule of Earth travel is you're not supposed to mention the cartel. If they find out you talked, they'll chop your genitals off and if you don't have genitals, they'll genetically modify you to grow some—and then they'll chop them off."

"But, this Galactic Council or whatever, why didn't they stop the cartel taking over the planet?"

"Well, here's the thing."

"—What?"

"It was sort of a test."

"A test?"

"Yeah, the Council wanted to see if Earth was fit to join The Collective in its pursuit of scientific advancement. They figured if the humans willingly decided to elect—" They looked over at the bulbous, sunburnt, grinning slug at the other end of the room, picking bits of orange skin off the bald patch on top of his head.

"That! If they wanted someone as vehemently opposed to science and logic in charge, then they weren't fit to join—and you know how the rest goes."

"Jesus, that's so fucked up."

"It made for good TV, though."

"—No. Please, God, no."

"Yeah, did you see that episode of South Park where it turns out Earth is just one big reality show for aliens?"

"Yeah. So, the only part of that monster that's real is that he's a reality television star."

"Pretty much."

"I don't want to live on this planet anymore."

"All right, let's get down to it," Frogina said, as the two sides squared off in the middle of the Oval Office. A cartel slug, a telekinetic Secret Service Agent and a right-wing militant half-colony of sentient Furmbogs versus three mute, bongo playing slimy blue men from Mars; a racist, perverted, sentient pile of hungry gelatine; a socialist, gender-fluid, half-colony of sentient Furmbogs— and Eve. This was destined to be the most productive meeting ever held in the history of American politics.

"What do you want?" Donnaht asked.

Eve, once again lost in the insanity of everything that was going on (and the soul-destroying revelations regarding the nature of human existence), actually had to take a second to remember why they found themselves there in the first place.

"Oh yeah—right! We want to know where Sunglasses over there sent our friends," she replied, gesturing at Chip, who she now realised wore the sunglasses to cover up the deep stress-bags under his eyes.

"I can't tell you that. I made a deal with the Galactic High Council. A great deal, like the best deal ever because the Council and I have a great relationship."

"So, this Galactic Council has our friends."

"I didn't say that."

"—Yes, you did."

"No, I didn't. I never once said anything about the Galactic Council."

"You literally just said it again."

"No, I definitely didn't. Did I say that, Chip?"

"Sigh—No, sir."

"We have you on record saying it, you idiot," Eve replied through gritted teeth, gesturing to Frogina who was recording everything in his/her notepad.

"That's fake news! That's a witch hunt concocted by the haters at CNN. And I'm not an idiot. I went to Harvard. I know words, I have the best words. I have the best but there is no better word than stupid. We're not the stupid people anymore, we're the really really smart people."

"Fucking spare me," Eve gasped. She threw a pleading look at Chip who simply shrugged his shoulders and rolled his eyes so hard she could hear his optic nerve straining.

"OK, let's move on," Frogina suggested. "We need you to tell us where they are so we can go save our friends."

"And what's in it for the President?" the General asked. "What can you offer someone like him?"

"We—have this!" Frogina replied, sliding his/her notepad across the coffee table. The General did a double take and gripped the arm of the couch so hard he tore through the fabric.

"You would never!" he said. "The secrets! The knowledge in that book could topple empires."

"I know," Frogina replied steadily. "And I know how much you want it."

"What the hell do I want that for?" Donnaht cut in dismissively. "A load of paper. I have lots of paper. I already have the best paper. America makes all the best paper."

"Sir, you don't understand," the General tried to interject. "The science in that book, the expert knowledge."

"I think we've all had enough of experts," Donnaht shouted, cutting off the General mid-sentence. "Offer me something else."

Suddenly, Eve had an idea. She might not have been a genius alien from another planet, but she knew about men who were pigs and in the end, they all want the same things.

"Twenty-trillion dollars," she declared, coming just oh so close to instinctively putting her pinkie finger in the corner of her mouth.

"Twenty-trillion dollars?" Donnaht repeated, a greedy twinkle appearing in the corner of his beady little eyeballs.

"Sir, the cartel provides you with limitless resources alrea—"

"Shut up, Chip, I'm making deals!" Donnaht interjected.

"Sigh—yes, sir."

"How about Fifty-trillion," Donnaht suggested.

Eve knew in that moment she had him.

"You must excuse our poverty, but I'm afraid fifty trillion is a bit much for us, O' huge and powerful Lord Donnaht," Eve responded, with as much fake humbleness and grovelling as she could muster. "Not all of us have attained your level of fabulous wealth and power."

Even the aliens who didn't speak English could tell she was up to something.

"That's right!" Donnaht agreed. "I have so much money, I'm the best at making money. It's possible I was the first Presidential candidate to run and make money from it. Definitely more than fifty-trillion."

"How about ten-trillion."

"Sir, that's lower than the original offer." The General tried to whisper.

"Fifteen-trillion!" Donnaht barked.

"Fifty-thousand," Eve retorted.

"Umm, sir, can I just?"

"One hundred thousand dollars!" Donnaht replied.

"Twenty-five dollars."

"Sir, please, listen."

"Ten dollars! Final offer!" Donnaht yelled, slamming four tiny fists down on the coffee table.

"Lord Donnaht, you truly are a master at the art of the deal. I admit, I have been outclassed. You win," Eve said, barely containing the internal avalanche of hysterics as she held out a hand in mock resignation to the greatest businessman in the cosmos.

"Sir, please stop! You're being tricked!" the General pleaded in desperation.

"You may want to listen to him, Sir," Chip suggested.

"Quiet, Chip. Who makes the deals here?"

"Sigh—You do, sir."

Donnaht wriggled himself up onto his lumpy haunches and made to shake Eve's hand but then pulled away at the last second.

"There is one other thing I want."

"What's that, Lord Donnaht?"

The Bhutt smiled, running his horrendous purple tongue across his leather-bound orange lips.

"You."

"Of course, anything you want my Lord," Eve replied seductively.

Frogina went to object, but Eve held up her hand and casually shot her an "It's OK, I've got this" look. Like an actual master of the art of the deal, Eve had a plan in place for everything.

Twenty minutes later, Eve, the Blue Man Group and Frogina stood in the hallway outside the Presidential quarters of the White House, waiting. After what seemed to be both too long and too short an amount of time, Eve came walking out of the bedroom, shaking and clearly in serious need of professional counselling. Through the momentarily open door, the group saw the grotesque loaf of lumpy flesh, snoring loudly and oozing what looked like cottage cheese through several gaping holes in his bloated sternum.

Eve then softy asked Eve, "How was it, Gloopy?"

The Eve that came out the bedroom sat down on the floor, clutched her knees to her chest and turned back into the pale blue lump of jelly who had just received the ultimate act of karmic retribution. He simply sat on the carpet and rocked himself back and forth slowly. Once an apex predator, now physically and mentally broken by ten minutes alone in the same bed as the President of the United States.

"That bad, huh?"

Gloopy just continued to slowly rock the memories away, his two orbs nestled low to the ground, snuggled together for some much-needed emotional support.

Frogina punched in the co-ordinates for the Galactic High Council's spaceship, provided by Chip while Donnaht was having his filthy way with Eve-Gloopy, into Criss Angel's personal phase-transporter. (I never pictured myself ever writing a sentence as ridiculous as that.) As the familiar red lights began to crawl up her leg and she waited for the beep of destiny, she had a thought and turned to ask Chip to confirm a suspicion.

"What's your last name, Chip?"

"Kroker."

"Thought so."

# Chapter Twenty-Three

Eve was getting the hang of this phase-travel malarkey. Somehow, her love for 80s action flicks survived inside her consciousness as she was catapulted yet again around the universe as a pirouetting mass of vibrating particles scything through the clouds of dark matter and she re-appeared on the Galactic High Council's ship in the classic Terminator time travel pose. And before you get too excited, no, she didn't re-appear in her birthday suit, although her badass moment was undercut somewhat by her T-shirt re-appearing on back-to-front.

Eve performed a quick mental roll call, just making sure one of the Martians hadn't re-appeared inside-out or been combined with Gloopy at the DNA level in a horrifying David-Cronenberg-Fly situation, but all were present and correct. They found themselves in a sleek, arched hallway, devoid of any interesting features of note because inconsequential fripperies such as art or carpets or even windows, are a criminal waste of efficiency and resources and the advancement of science is not predicated on the comfort or happiness of the individual.

Instead, all they saw was a long, continuous archway of shiny reflective steel, which pulsed with the same effervescent blue light as the underground parking labyrinth they frequented only just a few hours before—it really had been an unusual sort of day. It was deathly silent in there, the kind of silence that amplifies the sound of your bones rubbing together like matches on a tinderbox, lighting a fire under the swirling cauldron of your mind and slowly driving you insane. There was an old adage about space and screaming that came to mind, not that Eve was focussing on the negatives.

"This is so cool!" Eve squeaked. "An actual alien spaceship!"

"You've already been in a spaceship, remember?"

"Yeah, but this is like an actual spaceship with cool blue lights and probably lots of sci-fi stuff hidden away under secret panels. Yours was just a house."

"I would prefer it if you didn't spaceship-shame us right now! You'll hurt Gloopy's feelings."

"He has those?"

"It's debatable."

"We're getting side-tracked. How are we going to find the others? They could be anywhere on this ship."

"Follow the smell? Greg sure sweats a lot."

"OK, it's not the worst idea. Let's just head this way and see what happens. It doesn't seem like anyone is home anyway."

Eve cast a quick glance at the Martians to make sure they weren't wandering off but they were laser-focussed on the task at hand. It was clear that whatever it was they wanted aboard this ship was a serious matter. They stood tense and unblinking down the hallway, eyes scanning the corridor left and right like Wimbledon spectators, as if they were looking for hidden trip wires.

"Everyone ready?" she asked the group.

Gloopy was still sitting on the floor with his knees clutched up around his ears; he looked like he'd just come back from a summertime visit to Omaha beach, but Eve knew he'd follow if they started moving. Frogina stopped scribbling in her notepad and for once, shoved it deep inside the colony for safekeeping; it wasn't as if there was anything worth documenting in this empty hallway anyway. They were ready.

"OK. Let's do this."

Eve managed but a single step down the monochromatic hallway before an automated laser turret with a barrel the size of her forehead sprung out from a hidden panel in the wall like something a cyborg Kevin McAlister might set up to catch home invaders.

The end of the barrel came to rest two inches in front of her nose, threatening to blow a twenty-year coke habit sized hole in the middle of her face. Then, a red orb on the end of a hydraulic limb sprang out from the base of the gun and began to size her up with a scrutinising crimson beam, scanning every inch of her up and down in a way that made Eve feel rather objectified. When the probe spoke, oddly enough, it was with an air of mild annoyance, as if acting in its official programmed capacity as a security bot was somehow impeding on whatever other activities it had planned for that day.

"ID!"

"Excuse me?"

"Let me see some ID!"

"I—What?"

"Identification! Papers! Licenses! Come on, come on, I don't have all day."

It did have all day. Like almost every other security bot, this one had absolutely no life outside of these rare moments of interaction.

"Umm, let me see here. I have a driver's license."

"I said license, didn't I? Let's see it."

Eve held out her ten-year-old driver's license, which she had taken during her Paramore-fanatic phase and hadn't bothered to update to reflect her newer hairstyle choices. It wasn't even a great ID pic at the time, since most of her face was covered by a bright red emo fringe that more closely resembled a Highland Cow than Haley Williams.

"Oh, dear," the probe chuckled. "You need to get this updated."

"Haha, yeah, I guess. I just keep forgetting, you know how it is?"

"I actually don't. I don't have a license because I don't have a body or a face—Thanks for reminding me!"

"Oh, um, sorry."

"What's your date of birth!"

"What?"

"Your date of birth? What is it?"

"Oh, God, right. It's the 23 July 1991."

"How much have you lot had to drink tonight then?"

"What?"

"Say what one more goddamn time! See what happens!"

"Shit sorry. How much have we had to drink?" Eve repeated, desperately glancing around at the rest of her group for some kind of confirmation as to what sort of answer this security robot was looking for. Somehow, she got the sense that whatever she said was going to be the wrong answer.

"You know. Just a couple of beers."

"Just a couple."

"Yeah, one or two at our friend's house. That's it."

"Hmmm—"

"Look, mister," Eve interjected. "I'm sure you're a very busy—gun. You must have places to be right now, we don't want to hold you up."

"Actually, no, my only job is to hang out in the wall and catch intruders, but thank you yet again for reminding me of the mundanity of my existence."

"Oh, shit. Sorry—"

"—"

217

"—So, can we go then?"

"OK, fine. You can go in."

"Really?"

"Haha! No! You're all totally going to die."

"What?"

Another panel opened up in the floor under the group's feet and they plummeted down a hidden shaft into the darkness below.

"I told you not to say What again," the security bot called after them before slipping back into his hidey hole to wait another hundred years for the next intruder.

Luckily for the group, Gloopy was the first one down the hole and he was a much softer landing than the metallic floor of the cell they dropped into. Unfortunately, they landed as much in Gloopy as on him and were subjected to a couple of seconds of his digestive fluids before they were spat out onto the floor like a burning mouthful of McDonalds apple pie. The Martians came out one shade closer to purple than they were before and Eve felt as though she'd had an extreme chemical peel.

"That guy was such an asshole!" Eve seethed as he stood up and wiped some of Gloopy's fluids off herself.

"Security bots. They get drunk on their own power," Frogina sighed, as the colony reformed itself after bouncing off of Gloopy and were spread around the room like living confetti from a party popper. "It's not even in their programming, it just happens."

"Where are we now then?" Eve asked.

The room they found themselves in was just as featureless and uninteresting as the hallway they had come from. It was a huge, poorly lit metallic box, with a very securely locked door panel at the far end and a single unforgiving bench, like those found in a bus shelter, running the entirety of the back wall.

"You're in jail."

Eve and the rest of the group jumped out of their skins or they would have if any of them still had their bioform suits on and whirled around behind them to see Greg, Kyle and Deebro slouching in the corner of the cell; Kyle and Deebro sans their biosuits and Greg looking like he was coming off the end of a truly colossal bender. There were flecks of puke on his nice new shirt and bags under his eyes, so big he'd have to pay an extra forty quid to take them on a domestic flight.

"Greg! Holy shit! You're here!" Eve ran over and threw her arms around him. "We've come to rescue you."

"Thanks, I guess," Greg chuckled. "How's your day been?"

"Pretty crazy. Guess who we met?"

"Who?"

"Donald Trump!"

"Oh, God. Sorry about that. What was he like?"

"Oh, you know, pretty much what you would expect."

"Alien slug?"

"Yeah."

"Makes sense. Hey, Pylar."

"It's Frogina now."

"Whatever."

Then Greg caught sight of Gloopy, who was hiding behind Frogina, his two orbs glowing like the eyes of a hideous, predatory, deep-sea fish, lurking in the darkness of the cell.

"You! You dirty, wobbly bastard!"

Greg prized himself free of Eve's hug and launched himself at Gloopy, eyes full of hate and foaming at the mouth, eager to slake his thirst for some well-deserved retribution. He had been stewing in a metal box for hours thinking about how much he'd like to freeze the pervy fucker with liquid nitrogen then smash him to pieces with a lobster mallet, among other unusual punishments. Given the lack of bourgeoise silverware in this particular jail cell, tearing Gloopy apart with his bare hands would have to do.

The macaroni clung on for dear life as Greg ran at Gloopy like a rabid slavering wolfhound. The thing is, hate makes people irrational sometimes. Had Greg been in a sounder state of mind, he might have realised he didn't stand a chance against a man-eating amorphous blob like Gloopy in a straight-up fistfight. It wasn't surprising to anyone then, when Gloopy simply unhinged his maw and swallowed Greg whole like a human gobstopper.

Queue a furious reprimanding from Eve and Greg was once again spat back out onto the floor covered in slime with a severely bruised ego and his skin prickling like he'd just had a bath in a tub full of poison ivy. He wasn't allowed the opportunity to process how close he once again came to being digested, before he opened his eyes and saw the angry, unblinking faces of the Blue Man Group staring down at him.

"Shitballs!"

The Martians loomed over Greg, their glowing white eyes drilling into an invisible bullseye slap-bang in the middle of Greg's forehead, as if he was a disgusting cockroach that needed to be stamped out. Before they could turn Greg's brains into synapses soup, he channelled some primary school gymnastics, rolled backwards and darted in behind Eve to safety.

"What the hell are those three doing here?" he cried.

"You know each other?" Eve asked. "How the hell do you know each other?"

"Oh, that's right. I forgot you guys had a history," Deebro mused. "What a weird coincidence that you'd run into each other again in an alien prison."

The booming war cry of the Martians' drums filled the suffocating jail cell as they advanced slowly towards Greg, pointing him out for judgement like a villainous suspect in a courtroom murder trial. Greg was beginning to feel like a slimy Supreme Court Justice nominee under this fresh new wave of (probably deserved) vitriol.

"Wow, they really don't like you, Greg." Frogina said. "What did you do to them?"

"Ooooh, story time. I've been waiting for ages to find out about this," Deebro squeaked excitedly from his bowl.

# Chapter Twenty-Four

"I think you went a bit overboard on the costume Greg." Barney laughed as he walked into the casino and clocked Greg standing behind the bar. "That body paint is never going to wash off."

"No! Stop! Cut that shit out!"

"What now, Kyle?"

"We've done too many flashbacks, detours and divergent storylines today already."

"What the fuck are you talking about?"

"This adventure has already gone on way too long. We don't have time for another chapter just for a flashback. Just give us the abbreviated version."

"Jesus, fine. So-ree!"

# Chapter Twenty-Three (Again)
# Sorry Kyle!

"So basically, I used to work in the Mirage as a bartender."

"Oh, so that's what you were doing when you were away from Scotland," Eve replied.

"Pretty much."

"And that's how that asshole Taylor, the walking Viagra pill with the beard, knew who you were."

"Yeah. God, he was such a prick. Anyway, one night, these three blueberry fruitcakes came into the casino after one of their shows and just started freaking out for no reason. They were drumming on the bar and pointing at me and I did nothing wrong. I came around the bar to try and reason with them and one of them tried to punch me in the face. I hit him back, got fired and sent back to Scotland because I couldn't get another job. That's it."

"That's the whole story?" Frogina asked.

"That's the lot, I swear."

"Then why are they calling you a racist?"

"—What?"

"I'm just translating what they're saying. They're calling you the racist spawn of a Glumnork."

"Greg? What are they talking about?" Eve asked cautiously.

"I don't know. Honestly."

"Greg," Frogina interjected. "Did you do—"

"What? Did I do what?"

"Did you do Blueface?"

"What? I don't even know what that—Oh—Fuck."

"Oh. Greg. No," Eve sighed.

"Jesus, it was Halloween, OK. I was dressed up as one of them. First of all, I never thought The Blue Man Group would come into the bar. Anyway, if they did come in, I thought they'd dig it. I didn't know they were actually blue skinned aliens."

"Did you also tell them they were pustulous, reptilian, rabbit-lovers."

"What? No! Of course not. That's so oddly specific. I'd remember that."

"Apparently, you said it to them when they were paying for their first round of drinks."

"Fuck off! There's no way I said th—Oh—Fuuuuuck!"

Greg suddenly had a brief flashback (brief, Kyle, don't worry) to three years before. He was in The Mirage, on Halloween, covered head-to-toe in blue body paint and by some freak cosmic coincidence he was serving drinks to the actual Blue Man Group. He remembered the disappointment he felt when, instead of high fives and compliments on his body painting prowess, all he received were lurid stares and a scrotum-shrivelling aura of hostility.

Their assistant ordered their drinks for them, Greg refrained on commenting on their above-it-all, holier-than-thou attitudes and delivered them promptly and without fuss like a true professional (he even managed to refrain from making himself one). Then, when Greg was at the till, waiting for their embattled assistant to finishing counting his cash, he absent-mindedly started tapping a little beat out on the bar top with his fingers. That was when the Blue Man Group's attitude towards him turned from disgruntled indifference to furious indignation.

He had wondered, more than once, how that moment had led to his assault by a Las Vegas novelty musical act, the termination of his employment, his unceremonious ejection from the United States and his dejected return to Struinlanach to a life of resigned depression and alcoholism. It did make a lot more sense now, in a deeply upsetting sort of way. Greg had basically done a Martian Jimmy Fallon and called Chris Rock a pustulous, reptilian rabbit-fucker—while he was still in costume. Just goes to show you, Even if you think it's OK, it's never OK.

"Fucking hell, Greg," Kyle groaned. "That's bad."

"I think you owe these guys an apology for being an unintentional racist asshole, Greg," Eve suggested bluntly.

"Yeah. I think maybe you're right."

Greg cautiously tip-toed out from behind Eve, noted to himself that using her as a human shield was yet another thing he had to apologise for later, then walked cautiously up to the Martians, who still looked like they wanted to scoop out his insides, set them on fire then piss blue Gatorade on the remains. Greg turned to Frogina and asked her to tell them how sorry he was for accidentally discriminating against the Martian race and also for simultaneously calling them sore-covered, bunny-loving lizard men.

"Tell them I'm not normally like that. I harbour no ill will against Martians and that I much prefer them to that disgusting sentient ball of earwax that was apparently keeping them prisoner on Earth for his amusement."

Frogina relayed the message. The Martians looked at Greg suspiciously, looked at each other, looked at Greg again, then immediately threw their arms around him and sucked him into a spine crushing, slimy hug; it was like being embraced by a family of sexually progressive snails.

"Awww, Greg," Eve laughed. "They like you."

"Oh, Jesus," Greg wheezed. "There's really no need guys."

Eventually, they released him from their drippy embrace and Greg fell to the floor in a gooey puddle, now dripping in both neon blue slime and Gloopy's digestive juices. It's worth noting now that Martians don't naturally secrete this slime, it's still just leftovers from the little bath in their dressing room back in Vegas. Eve really should have given them a chance to shower before dragging them along on this adventure.

"I don't know if I'm satisfied with the answer to that mystery," Deebro mused to Frogina quietly while Greg was picking himself up off the floor and making sure all his ribs were still present and correct. "Feels like a lot of build up over nothing of much consequence."

"Yeah, but that's life sometimes, buddy."

"OK, now that we're all friends again," Eve chuckled,

"I still hate this guy," Greg called out while venomously pointy at Gloopy.

"Whatever! Can we just work out how to get the hell out of here? Or why we're even here in the first place?"

"Or even where here is?" Deebro chimed in. "We were phased from the prison at the casino straight into this room. We've been stuck here for hours."

"Well, we can answer that question," Frogina gravely replied. "You're on the Galactic High Council command ship."

A deathly silence fell over the group like a suffocating blanket of cold fog on a winter's night and the frightened stares of all the aliens turned slowly towards Kyle, who had been sitting, uncharacteristically quietly, in the corner of the cell.

"Guys. What is it? What's going on?" Eve asked.

"Kyle? Buddy? What's happening?" Greg asked as he walked up to Kyle and put a hand on his tiny shoulder.

"I'm sorry. I shouldn't have asked you all to come," Kyle replied.

The undercurrent of dread running through his voice like a shard of ice was enough to clench all the butts in the room.

"They've found me."

"Who? Who are these people?"

Before Kyle could answer, a security bot with a turret gun for a face and the personality of a talking micro-penis jumped out of yet another hidden panel in the wall and turned his horrible, red, probing eyeball on the group.

"All right assholes!" he yelled. "Time to go!"

"Eve," Frogina whispered. "Now would be a good time to phase us out of here."

"Shit, good point," Eve replied, realising Criss Angel's transporter was still nestled in her back pocket. She quietly slipped it to Frogina who typed in the requisite co-ordinates and scanned the whole group as the turret-bot advanced on them menacingly. The transporter screen flashed blue and Frogina gave Eve the thumbs-up.

"Later loser!" Eve cried triumphantly before turning to Frogina. "Punch it, Chewie!"

Frogina cast a few thousand bemused looks at Eve, hit the button and Eve flipped off the robot in a last show of defiance before they were converted into information and whisked away into the quantum ether. Or rather, that's what was supposed to happen. Instead, she stood there with her middle fingers raised at the confused security bot, while an error message flashed up on the transporter's screen. Computer says no.

No Signal.

"God, that's such a fucking cliché. I didn't realise we were shitty teens in a slasher flick," Eve groaned.

"They must be blocking transmissions." Frogina whispered, "Looks like we need to find another way out."

The group huddled together like Emperor penguins in a blizzard, ironically just making themselves an easier target for the security-bot. Whoever said there was safety in numbers clearly hadn't spent any time at the wrong end of a shooting gallery. Suddenly, the door to the cell flew vertically open with a hiss and a low thud and our heroes tensed themselves in preparation for the inevitable android-dispensed rectal probing. However, instead of a cyborg Christian Gray with some robotic anal beads, silhouetted in the harsh light beaming in through the open doorway, sat a Roomba. A little white hockey puck about six inches tall and with an array of twinkling lights arranged in the facsimile of two eyes came roaming into the cell and wheeled itself up towards the group who stared at it curiously.

"Oh, you guys are so in for it now!"

The security bot laughed with pickles and relish.

"What? From this little guy?" Eve laughed. "What's he going to do, suck us off?"

"Umm, Eve."

"I know what I said, Greg, shut up! Hey little guy."

Eve kneeled down to pat the little hockey puck on his adorable head. However, as she reached out, the puck began to turn itself inside-out and from its internals spewed forth a twisting mass of wires, plastic and metallic scales, like a robotic chest-buster. It was Cthulhu meets R2D2—CthulhuD2!

The group watched in shock as the writhing swarm of metallic tentacles began to twist and contort itself into sinewy knots. They looped over themselves into braids and extended outwards into thick, trunk-like limbs. The white metal sclaes crawled along the external surface of the robotic tendrils and linked themselves together to form a hard, reflective armour. Within seconds, the adorable little disc had transformed itself into a hulking, eight-foot-tall cyborg Michelin Man. A gleaming white, somehow muscle-bound, bipedal robot Adonis made up of white hexagonal scales that shifted and flowed like water as it lumbered towards them.

"Come quietly, resistance is futile," the robot demanded as he advanced threateningly, but Eve still somehow seemed confident. She was not going to be intimidated by another muscle-bound, floppy-disc jockey.

"Don't worry guys. I've got this," she whispered to the group before stepping forward to confront their apparent jailer.

"Now sir, here's the thing."

She then swung her leg back like a lure on a fishing line and brought it crashing up into the robot's testicles.

Unfortunately, robots don't generally have testicles and all Eve achieved by doing this was too badly stub her toes and severely bruise her shin against the robot's smooth, but rock-solid, nether regions.

"Ahhhhhhh," Eve hissed, as she did a perfect Neymar impression and fell to the floor clutching her bruised shin. "Fucking Ken doll bastard! Fuck, that hurt!"

"What was the purpose of your action human?" the robot asked. "Does not compute. Does not compute at all."

Never in its several hundred cycles of service as High Council Private Security, had a biological life form tried to bludgeon the jailer-bot between its walking appendages. It was highly perplexing.

"Yeah, Eve, what the fuck was that?"

"It worked all the other times," Eve groaned. "Seemed like it was worth a shot."

# OK, Now it's Chapter Twenty-Four

The two security bots guided their troupe, their circus, of hapless captives down the endlessly tedious hallways of the Galactic High Council's ship towards the place of their judgement; the eight-foot jailer-bot trying to hide the slight limp it had inexplicably developed after Eve's unwarranted attack against its crotchal region; while the turret-bot endlessly popped out of various hidden panels in the ship's fuselage to throw unhelpful and degrading insults at the prisoners.

"You biological life forms are so disgusting—Nice gut fatso—How much of your piss are you swimming in right now, fishy?—Where is all this horrible slime coming from? Oh, that's just the humans—I'm glad I don't have a nose so I can't smell you filthy animals."

"Shut the hell up, you talking vibrator!" Eve snarled, having received just about enough abuse from aliens and robots for one day. "You don't have a soul! You're basically a toaster with a borderline personality disorder."

"—Sniff—Too mean."

Turns out souls are, rather understandably, a touchy subject for artificial intelligences and being called a talking vibrator is always highly insulting. The turret slid dejectedly back into his hidey-hole in the wall and they never saw him again, but for the rest of the adventure you can imagine there was a faint but audible sobbing noise in the background echoing through the empty hallways of the ship; it really added nicely to the haunted-house vibe.

The remaining guard, having significantly thicker skin than his turret-faced colleague (literally, as his hexagon plate skin was made from an advanced carbotanium triweave fibre) wasn't affected by Eve's insults and continued to force them down the hallway. Eventually, they came to another panel doorway; this one imprinted with symbols that the humans didn't understand, but to the rest of the group, clearly read as, "Courthouse".

Alien bottoms were heard collectively clenching as the door slid open and they were forced through the looming porthole. The guard remained at the doorway until his charges were inside, then the door closed behind them with a clash and they were sealed in.

It was impossible to tell the size of the room they now found themselves in. It was pitch dark except for four pulsating blue lights embedded in the dome-shaped ceiling, but it was impossible to tell if they were bedside lamps or blue stars shining from billions of miles away.

Standing in the smothering murkiness of the atrium, Greg felt like he was living inside a fairground funhouse mirror, which was itself stuffed inside a giant taxidermized badger's arsehole—or he'd somehow lost an eyeball and his depth perception had completely disappeared. He looked down at his feet and felt sure he was eighty feet tall but then looked at his hand and jumped back because he thought he was about to poke himself in the eye.

He turned to Eve and had to squint to make out her features, she looked so far away, like a lost love standing on the edge of a cliff as he sailed away out to sea but then he reached out to touch her and actually did manage to poke her in the eye, for the second time that day.

"Ah. Shit, Greg! What was that for?"

"Oh, sorry. Guys, does anyone else feel like they're tripping right now?"

"It's a distortion field," Kyle sighed. "They're just trying to get in our heads, ignore it."

"Who is?"

Suddenly, a blinding flash of yellow light exploded across the room from the other end of the atrium as a huge glowing orb breached the edge of the far horizon and a blinding supernova of reds and yellows laid waste to Greg's corneas As if on cue, his overactive thalamus provided an appropriate backing track.

*"Naaaaaaants ingonyama. Bagithi baba!"*

The group desperately shielded their eyes against the searing rays, which were threatening to hard boil their eyeballs inside their own sockets. However, despite their eyes experiencing what Donnhat the Bhutt voluntarily puts his through every time there is a solar eclipse, they could still clearly make out the silhouettes of six robed figures standing tall like great stone monoliths against the violent burst of light.

The figures paced forward slowly, growing ever larger; mountainous beings commanding the skyline. They suddenly began to rise on imposing ebony pillars in a semicircle around the group, until they towered far above them like the Gods of Olympus. Then a booming voice echoed like thunder throughout the atrium, shaking the ground and making Greg come dangerously close to shitting in his pants again.

"You stand accused of moving to unbalance the great equation, of delaying the inevitable march of universal progress."

"Your actions speak to the cowardice and sinful ways of your races." Another, equally terrifying voice joined in with the wrathful chorus. "Now you must face judgement for your crimes."

"Umm, actually, we don't even—" Eve began to interject.

"SILENCE!" Roared the collection of vengeful bringers of holy judgement. "YOU HAVE NO RIGHT TO SPEAK HERE! YOUR LACK OF EFFICIANCY IS THE ULTIMATE SIN!"

"Efficiency?"

"As for you, Flumparpmingleporp!" The figures thundered, turning towards Kyle, who looked thoroughly bored and fed up with the whole affair. "Your betrayal casts shame upon you and your family. You have endangered the great progression, unbalanced the great equation, shamed the great—"

"Oh my god! Shut the hell up, you NERDS!!" Kyle screamed, before letting a scorching flash of white-hot electricity fly from powerful generator within his body (which is actually millions of microbes running on a biological hamster wheel made of muscle and bone).

The lightning bolt ricocheted like a bullet around the room, bounced off Deebro's bowl (which, luckily for him, acted as a Faraday cage and left the fish completely unharmed) and seared the tip off the end of Greg's beard before finding its target, a floating drone that was projecting the distortion field from a hidden vantage point near the ceiling. The bolt of lightning bit the robot right on the cheek of its shiny metal ass and eviscerated it in a small but incredibly satisfying explosion, showering the group in carbon dust and droplets of hydraulic fluid.

Suddenly, Greg's perception snapped back into focus. It was like being fifteen pints deep then suddenly inhaling a fat line of the purest Columbian cocaine. His limbs bungeed outwards a few hundred feet them boomeranged back home again. He winced, expecting his own eyeballs to fire out the back of his head, but when he opened his eyes, the distortion was gone, and Greg looked around the actual space that they now found themselves.

The first thing he realised is why the security robot didn't follow them inside, because he would have banged his head on the roof. The ceiling was no more than seven feet high and Deebro wouldn't have even fit through the doorway if he had still been wearing his biosuit. Greg gave himself the once-over, made sure everything was back to its proportionate size, as one would, then looked up and noted three more interesting facts.

One, the room they were in was not, in fact, a gateway to the infinite cosmic void and was actually no bigger than the living room in his crappy old, moth eaten house back in Struinlanach. Two, the huge ebony pillars that previously loomed over the group like mountains were the size of the brightly coloured plastic Kindergarten chairs you get at roadside Vietnamese cafés. And three, the six titanic apostles of the cosmos were absolutely effing adorable!

Six robed Kyles were standing before them in a semi-circle on top of their little raised podiums, like teddy-bears competing in a Harry Potter themed, fifth-grade spelling-bee. They were of Kyle's species, clearly but they were all at least six-inches shorter and noticeably paunchier around the waist, with roughly the same proportions as a baby Arctic seal or a meerkat that's swallowed a whole cantaloupe. The cherry on the adorable cupcake was their pudgy cheeks that made them look like they were smuggling Babybels.

"Oh! My! God!" Eve squealed, "You guys are so cute!"

"Hey, we're not cute!" 45E retorted angrily.

Unfortunately, as he became more aggressive, his chubby cheeks began to quiver like a frustrated Richard Nixon on a sugar rush and his voice turned from the roar of Zeus' thunderclap to a high-pitched squeak, which only made him all the more delightful.

"You're addressing the Galactic High Council and you will treat us with respect human!"

"Awwww, you guys are the ones who rule that galaxy. That is so precious." Eve laughed. "You are just the cutest little intergalactic dictators ever, yes you are."

"Silence! I demand silence!" 45E squealed hysterically. Unfortunately, he was shaking so much in apoplectic rage than he tripped over his flowing robes and tumbled over onto his back like an upturned turtle, unable to right himself on his pudgy little limbs. Two more of the council members had to totter over and right him again, by which point he'd lost all authority and his captives were howling in fits of hysterical laughter.

"Hey! Stop that! I demand you cease this nonsense!"

No dice. Greg was on his knees, doubled over in hysterics, holding his ribs together in fear they might disintegrate; Frogina's colony had lost all sense of coordination and was now a pile of several hundred thousand ants all cackling uncontrollably on the floor and Deebro was laughing so hard he choked on the water in his own bowl.

The rest of the council sensed the situation was out of 45E's control, he was no longer needed and a change of leadership was required. Time to make an example. 67TY felt the warm hand of vindication have a good rummage around in his nether regions. This was going to be a satisfying moment and it would happen in front of Flumparpmingleporp, no less! The remaining five council members turned to 45E, held up their fuzzy little paws and vaporised him in a whip crack of blue lightning.

The naughty children suddenly stopped laughing. The substitute teacher had just brought a cane out of the desk drawer and cracked the naughty kid a belter right on the ass with it.

"Now!" 67TY spoke, in a calm voice deliberately laced with venom. Which was a shock to the captives after the Alvin the Chipmunk wannabee that had addressed them before. He sounded like he put risen on his cornflakes instead of milk. "Where were we?

# Chapter Twenty-Five

"Flumparpmingleporp." 67TY gloated through his hairy, quivering jowls as he turned towards Kyle, almost drooling with unbridled relish, "You thought you could escape us forever, you fool! You should have known we'd find you eventually."

"Kyle, you know these guys?" Greg asked.

"Yeah," Kyle groaned. "This is my little cousin and his online role-playing group. Hi, Baldybutt? How are things?"

"My name is not Baldybutt! It's 67TY! And we are not a role-playing group!"

"Whatever you say, Baldybutt," Kyle chuckled. "But I definitely remember walking in on you guys wearing tights and capes and riding each other like horses."

"That was one time and you promised you wouldn't tell anyone!"

"And didn't you get 67TY from the label on your rash medication?"

"No—that's—it's a code name you get when you're accepted onto the High Council, it's more efficient."

"Yeah, that's right. Wasn't it 67-Tyletrax anti-rash anal cream? Remember, you had a big red rash on your bum because you didn't grow any hair there till your seventies."

"His seventies? How old are you?" Greg asked.

"Not important right now, Greg!" Eve hissed.

"I'm just saying, Melissa is like twenty-four." Greg replied, "Kyle's a cradle robber!"

67TY could sense the growing unrest amongst the other council members and knew he had to get the situation under control before he became desert for the vacuum cleaner that was currently gobbling up 45E's scorched remains.

"Things have changed, Flumparpmingleporp," he said menacingly as he nervously wobbled down a little series of stone steps at the back of his pedestal and waddled over to where Kyle was standing. "As children you always thought yourself better than me, but now you will show me the respect I deserve."

"Or, I could just do this."

Kyle clicked his fingers and a small bolt of lightning materialised behind 67TY and made a beeline for his rear end, like an electric towel-whip. However, instead of a suffering a humiliating shock on his bottom, 67TY just sneered and flicked his wrist like a pixie orchestra conductor.

The lightning swerved away from 67TY's plump backside, coiled itself like a snake into a dense ball of energy, then hit Kyle with a nasty uppercut to the chin, sending him sprawling, bruised and humiliated, to the canvas. The rest of the crew began to rush over to see if he was OK but were stopped by the rest of the council, who made the air around them crackle threateningly with sparks of blue lightning.

"Looks like I should start calling you Baldychin, Flumparpmingleporp." 67TY laughed sadistically as Kyle shakily managed to haul himself back onto his feet. "It pains me to show you up for the little bitch you are, but such a criminal waste of energy cannot go unpunished."

Kyle found himself unable to draw a suitable comeback from his limitless deck of insults for 67TY. Having his fat little cousin thoroughly beat the piss out of him had shaken him to his core.

"Well done, looks like you're the big man now, Baldybutt." Kyle winced, "What's your plan then? I'm telling you now there's no way you're going to drag me back and plug me into that fucking machine."

"It's your duty, Flumparpmingleporp. Our race's sacrifice helps maintain order in a delicate universe."

"It's only our duty because you and your little loser's club here decided it was! The rest of us never got a say in the matter and I don't see any of you lot plugging yourselves in and living out the rest of your days as an AA battery."

"We wish we could plug ourselves in. You know how long most council members last? We've had to vaporise three of our members for inefficiency in the last two days alone but the galaxy needs our guidance to continue the great progression."

"Shut up with that crap as well. The great progression! The great equation! You just made that shit up when you were all just hanging out in Auntie Flogarmantlefib's basement (Auntie Flo for short). Also, pick one "Great" thing, progression or equation. Two "Great" things are just excessive!"

"Guys, sorry to interject, but what the actual fuck are you talking about?" Eve groaned.

"Phase travel," Kyle replied. "They invented it."

"Well, what's wrong with that?" Frogina replied. "Without it there wouldn't be a universal collective, we'd all be stuck living in cryo-sleep for hundreds of years to travel between systems."

"Exactly our point—Kyle," 67TY sneered.

"Yeah, but the only energy source that can power that kind of technology—is me."

"You?"

"Well, my species. Our bio-electricity powers the central phase generator on our home planet. So, Baldybutt and his online D&D club here, after taking over the planet, decided that our species, once we get to a hundred cycles old, has to plug ourselves into the generator and power phase travel devices across the universe until we die."

"Wow—that is super fucked up."

"Yeah, no shit."

"Why don't they just unplug themselves?"

"When we're plugged in, the generator inserts our minds into a virtual reality construct, the same one we used when we were pre-drinking (you remember that little bit of foreshadowing) so you don't know what's happening to you. It then sucks you dry until you're nothing but a shrivelled husk and you're replaced by someone else."

"You mean like the Matrix?" Greg asked instinctively.

"No! It's called The Construct! It's totally original!" The council members immediately retorted in unison. Greg got the sense it wasn't the first time someone had made that comparison.

"Why do you have to use Kyle?"

"We tried using the energy of other lifeforms," 67TY sighed. "We even tried using you humans once. But your feeble bodies put out less energy in heat than the energy required to keep you alive. We even had a farm of billions of you on another planet and you didn't even generate enough energy to power The Construct, let alone the central phase generator."

"Oh, come one! How is that not The Matrix?"

"IT'S NOT THE GODDMAN MATRIX!"

"But you just said you were farming humans for their energy!"

"The point is!" 67TY pressed on through gritted teeth. "Our species are the only ones in the universe who can generate the energy required to keep the Universal Collective running. The economy of every civilisation in the cosmos would collapse without our technology!"

"So that's why you were hiding out on Earth!" Greg realised.

"That's a good point," Kyle suddenly asked. "How did you track me here?"

"We intercepted a transmission from you to your friends," sniggered Baldybutt (it's just so much more fun to write than 67TY). "Would you like to see it?"

"Oh, umm, no. No, I don't think we need to see that," Kyle stammered.

"Nonsense," smirked the council member at the far end of the hall. "While the energy expenditure is not ideal, nothing should get in the way of a fair trial. We must review the evidence."

Suddenly, from a projector hidden in the floor at the centre of the room, a three-dimensional hologram sprung up of Kyle, in full alien koala form, wobbling precariously back and forth and wearing nothing but board shorts and some rubber crocs on his ears and holding an almost-empty bottle of El Jimador Tequila.

"Awww—Shitballs!"

"What up partay-animalos!" Hologram Kyle slathered, visible flecks of spittle erupting from his drooling mouth and spattering against the fourth wall. "Guess what the fuck's up? I'll tell you what the fuck's up! This playa here is getting hitched! Woop woop!"

"Holy shit! Thank you for this gift," Greg said, completely sincerely, to the council as hologram-Kyle paused to take a swig of Tequila.

"I'm getting married to a girl! A woman! God she's so hot and I love her so much—sniff—"

"Are you crying in this? That is co cute!" Eve chuckled and ruffled the fur on Kyle's head.

"Cut it out!"

"Anyway, I'm marrying the cutest girl in the world and you all know what that means—STAG PARTY WITH MY BOYS! Yeah! Woop! You guys, I like totally love you all so much, so you should come to Earth and party with me 'cos it's been way to long and we gots to get fucked-up, yo! But don't tell anyone on the High Council, 'cos those guys are dicks and they kinda want to hook me up to a giant battery and suck the life out of me or something. Anyway, par-tay,

Earth, two weeks. Hit me up on Spacechat soon! Kyle, out!—OK, wait a minute, how do you turn this fucking thing off? Aw man, I think I just pissed myself. OK, I'm gonna go throw up now."

The hologram then belched loudly and disappeared.

"Bet you felt shitty the morning after that one." Greg laughed.

"Yeah, that was the first time I woke up inside a chair."

"All right, Flumparpmingleporp," Baldybutt squeaked, as he walked up to Kyle and held out a pudgy little paw. "Clearly, you've been going through some stuff, but it's time to come home. If you return with us now, we can forgive your past indiscretions."

"Come on man, it's Kyle and you know there's no way I'm going back."

"The entire galactic order runs on phase-travel—Kyle. You know what would happen if we suddenly decided to let everyone plugged into the central generator just walk away? It would be anarchy. Do you remember what our planet was like, let alone the rest of the universe, before we came along?"

"I thought it was all right."

"It was the worst. Our people were aimless, slovenly losers. We took so long to develop technology, we evolved from reptilian to mammalian in the time it took us to go from broadband to fibre-optic! The humans developed faster than we did! That tells you something!"

"We were all having a great time before you guys messed it up. You just hated it because you never went to the parties and spent all your time in Auntie Flo's basement, spewing bile onto the message boards with the rest of these incels! And the universe got on just fine without us!"

"It was chaos. Everyone was so grumpy after three hundred cycles of cryo-sleep that their first instinct upon landing on a new planet was to exterminate the locals. No one wanted to trade, all they wanted to do was pillage and burn and we fixed that."

"Don't fucking stand there and tell me phase-technology fixed that!"

"He has a point, Kyle," Frogina interjected. "We can literally build anything we want by reconstructing atoms now. We have limitless resources because of phase-technology."

"That's right, they don't know. Nobody knows," Kyle leered at 67TY. "The big secret you kept from the whole universe. Should I enlighten them before you reduce us to piles of dust, Baldybutt?"

"What are you talking about, Kyle?" Eve asked.

"Phase-travel doesn't work the way you think. You can't just build something from nothing. Have you heard of The Law of Conservation of Energy, Eve?"

"Yeah, it states that the amount of energy in a closed system remains constant over time."

"Exactly, think of the universe as the closed system. There is a finite amount of matter and energy in the system and we can't just magically create something new—without first taking something away. For everything new that's created, something else needs to be destroyed."

"I'm not going to like where this is going, am I?"

"Probably not. Every time we had the ship make us a piece of clothing or a bottle of whisky—or a biosuit, it had to be taken from somewhere else."

"So, that hat I was wearing, the one the cowboy in the casino said was his?" Deebro gasped.

"Yeah. The ship didn't make a brand-new hat, we just stole it from somewhere else in the universe."

"So, are you telling me, that the actual crown jewels are sitting in the ship in that car park right now?" Greg asked.

"Yeah, the Queen is going to be pissed!"

"Damn! I should have worn them out, with that LeBron James jersey. That would have been seriously baller!"

"Hold on!" Eve cried. "So, those bio-suits you guys were wearing?"

"Don't worry, there's no humans walking around with no skin."

"Oh, thank God."

"There will be a few skinless corpses in a morgue somewhere though."

"Jesus Christ! Kyle! What the fuck?"

"You humans wear fur and leather all the time! It's not like the dead guys are going to be using them. Think of it like an organ donation."

"Frogina! Deebro! Please tell me you guys aren't cool with this."

"He has a point about the leather, Eve."

"Putting that aside for now, you see how these fuckers haven't fixed anything with their little phasing experiment!" Kyle snarled, turning back to 67TY, who had been indulging himself by watching this little play unfold, relishing the growing looks of horror and distress upon the faces of our protagonists.

238

"Instead of stealing resources openly, all they've done is developed technology that allows the rich and powerful to do it in secret. They're like Tory Robin Hoods, stealing from the poor and giving to themselves!"

"Well done cousin, you figured out our master plan," 67TY sniggered, clapping his fat little paws together in mock adulation. "Not that it makes any difference, you're still coming with us back to where you belong."

"Like hell, I am!" Kyle growled, baring his canines as more sparks began to make the air shimmer around him. "I'd rather die with the humans than spend one moment plugged into your little VR fantasy."

"You want to stay here, with these filthy humans?" The other council members cried with palpable disgust. "You really have lost your way. Their rejection of science and logic in favour of twisted political ideologies is shameful. They elected Donnaht the Bhutt, willingly, as their leader for science's sake!"

"OK, they're not perfect, but—"

"That's enough!" Eve screeched. "I've had it just about up to here with you aliens talking shit about us humans because we're not part of your intergalactic country club! You're just a bunch of space-nerds having yourselves a big galaxy-wide circle-jerk!"

"Ooooh, you guys are in for it now!" Greg chuckled.

"You know, I've learned something today," Eve said. "Us humans may not be perfect. We might be gullible and illogical, driven by our emotions and have an unhealthy propensity for substance abuse but we're also capable of amazing things. Look at your boring grey metal spaceship here and compare it to the Sagrada Familia or the pyramids of Egypt or Beethoven's 5th symphony."

"Or Stairway to Heaven."

"Sigh—Thank you, Greg. Yes, or Stairway to Heaven,

"Or Thai Sweet Chili crisps."

"Thank you, Greg, I've got this! Anyway, think of all these beautiful, amazing, delicious creations then ask yourself, are you really better than us? You might have all the advanced technology in the universe, but you couldn't understand, not for one second, the heart and soul needed to create the things of astounding beauty that only us humans can.

And not all of us follow the ideologies of certain bloated, leathery politicians. Most humans are creative, intelligent and forward-thinking and strive to make the world we live in a better place every day. Above it all, we care. We care about each other, we care about our planet, we care about our friends and it's the way we care that helps us overcome our flaws. It makes us, despite all our problems, worth believing in. It makes us human."

The robed council members seemed to quietly reflect on this for a while. Greg reached over and put a re-assuring hand on Eve's shoulder as a single tear worked its way down his cheek. It was a beautiful, very human moment.

"Wow. That was very eloquent, human female," 67TY responded respectfully. "Well said."

"Oh. Well, thank you very much."

"It doesn't change anything though. We're still taking this one back with us."

"What?"

"We're scientific fanatics, I think we can all agree," he said bluntly, eliciting shrugs and nods of agreement from the rest of the council. "Did you think you were going to change our minds with one little speech?"

"What about the rest of us then?" Greg cried.

"Oh, we have to kill you all. And probably destroy your planet."

"Shitballs!"

"But—the speech?" Eve protested.

"It was a nice speech, but you've all seen and heard too much. We can't have you all revealing the secret of phase-travel to the rest of the universe. And by destroying your horrible little planet, we'll rob the Bhutts of their central power base. Their filthy, sinful attempts to disrupt the scientific advancement of the universe has gone on long enough.

They've been smuggling smut and poison off your planet in secret for nearly forty of your Earth years now, violating the terms of our agreement. They are a cancer that's been festering at the very heart of our organisation for too long. They even started when two of our own scouts landed on your planet, discovered that epicentre of your wasteful culture; Las Vegas; and began selling contraband from there to the far corners of the universe. They nearly destroyed everything we have built."

"That's hardly our fault, is it?" Eve yelled, "Get rid of Trump, no one would complain!"

"On the contrary, the fact you chose him as your elected leader, enabling the cartel's activities, makes your whole race just as much to blame!"

"Fine, take America then. We could probably live without it."

"Tempting, but it's too late. Now is the perfect moment to strike. Donnaht thinks we've cut a deal and is unprepared for an assault. Our fleet has already been summoned. They are phasing into orbit around your planet as we speak."

"Why are there no windows on this goddamn ship!" Eve screamed.

Although our group could not see what was happening, outside things were proceeding exactly as 67TY described. Hundreds of metallic orbs; let's call them Doom Moons; were appearing in flashes of red light around the planet. The humans on the ground, the ones that didn't immediately die of shock, were left cowering like helpless ants under the equivalent of a thousand meteor-sized magnifying glasses that would absorb the power of the sun and send a cascade of solar energy and radiation blasting onto the Earth's surface, cooking it like a hard-boiled egg full of molten lava.

By the way, I know there's been suggestions of a future described earlier in this book that would contradict these events, such as the fate of Mrs McTavish to end up in a nursing home because no one believed her disappearing alien story, but that's just what us authors and magicians and various other con-artists, call misdirection. Or just lazy writing.

"Don't do this, Baldybutt. Is this because I put laxatives in your Floornaps in school and made you shit in your hat in front of everybody?"

"I knew that was you!"

"Shit in your hat?" Greg mused quietly to himself.

"Or when I soaked your retainer in piss overnight that time I slept over at your house."

"Jesus Christ, Kyle, I'm starting to get the sense this is all your fault."

"No, Kyle, this isn't about you being a total ass to me in school." Baldybutt growled, "This is about the betterment of the universe—But maybe, in your next life, don't piss off the wrong chubby nerd!" Baldybutt then held his palm down on a touchpad on his little podium and spoke in a commanding squeak.

"Commander. Fire when ready!"

No response.

"Commander, come in! Do you hear me? Destroy that planet!"

Still, all that came back, was silence.

"What's going on?" 67TY asked, turning to the other council members, "Is it buffering again?"

"Not sure," 44FC replied (nice of him to finally speak up).

"Open the damn blast shields!" 67TY barked. "Find out what's happening!"

44FC tapped another pad on his podium and suddenly the domed roof of the atrium split in two and receded, revealing a truly spectacular panoramic view of the Earth, sparkling like a painting of a sapphire on an infinite black canvas, punctuated by billions of dazzling pricks of brilliant starlight. It was beautiful.

What was less appealing, were the thousands of metallic orbs poised threateningly around the globe—and the juggernaut armada of ostentatious, golden, T-shaped objects the size of cities, that were phasing out of nowhere and ramming into the orbs at full speed, like ten-pins that had decided enough was enough and started attacking the bowling balls instead.

"What is the meaning of this! Are those cartel ships?"

As if on cue, the holographic projector in the floor suddenly jumped into life and spewed forth a giant holographic production featuring Donald Trump's/Donnaht the Bhutt's disgusting visage as the primary protagonist.

"Donnaht?" 67TY screamed. "What is the meaning of this?"

"You shouldn't have tried to cross me Council members," Donnaht replied in his meandering, wheezy voice. "This is me showing how strong a President I am. We didn't have victories before I came along, but now we have lots of victories, like this one. You've got to be strong against foreign aggressors, like Saddamn Hussain. He killed terrorists. I mean, I'm not saying this guy was an angel but he killed terrorists. You've got to get aggressive like that sometimes. I mean, I could stand in the middle of 5th avenue and shoot someone and I wouldn't lose any voters, would I, Chip?"

"Sigh—No, Sir."

"We had a deal you back-stabbing Bhutt! What are you doing?"

"I don't recall making any deal. I don't know you people. I never make deals with bad people. Only good people I make deals with, great deals. Except with China, they're bad but I make deals with them but only because when I do, I beat them. I beat China all the time. All the time."

"For the love of science. Why are you attacking our ships, you idiot?"

"Well, my new ant friend here, who I think I met at one of Epstein's parties, he told me you were going to blow up this planet. I couldn't have that now, could I?"

At this point the General entered the hologram, his colony stood sharply to attention just behind Donnaht's left shoulder.

"Finally! You cut that a little late!" Frogina gasped.

"You knew this was coming?" Eve asked.

242

"I knew they'd be listening. Even split in two, we're still one colony. We still have the same hive mind. We'll always be connected."

"I—ahem—Miss you—Frogina," the General suddenly said through a forced cough, which appeared to be enough to obscure the words from Donnaht, who barely registered him.

"Miss you too, dear," Frogina replied with a smile. "See you soon, OK. Now, send one of those ships our way, would you?"

Looking out the window at the carnage encircling his once "peaceful" planet, Greg noticed one of the huge golden leviathans deviate from the firestorm of explosions and the fog of frozen bodies floating in the void and chart a devastating course straight towards them, the flat top of the T aimed directly at the council's ship like a twenty-four million carat battering ram.

"You might want to grab onto something," the General suggested.

In a moment that, to Greg, almost made the entire harrowing experience worth it, he and Eve instinctually reached for each other and held each other tightly as the Trumpian warship crashed headlong into the High Council's command ship, sending everyone in the room reeling and knocking the council members from their podiums. Several of them landed uselessly on their backs like an upturned Blue Peter tortoise and waved their pudgy little limbs hopelessly in the air. As if on instinct, the Blue Man Group ran directly over to the nearest one and began kicking him around like a fluffy football.

"Hey! Stop it! No fair!"

"Is everyone else all right?" Eve cried, pulling herself up off of Greg, who was in a bit of a haze of emotions but otherwise unharmed. The rest of the group hauled themselves to their feet as a series of loud explosions rocked the ship, which had been torn clean in half by the assault and was now floating powerless in the dead expanse of space and leaking dangerous radioactive waste into the empty vacuum between the stars.

"Time to go, I think," Kyle called, pointing to the door at the back of the room that had been ripped clean off its mechanism in the chaos.

"Aye, no shit Sherlock."

The group hauled ass towards the door, Eve pulling the phase-transporter from her pocket and hurling it to Frogina.

"Do it! Get us out of here!" she cried, waiting at the door and pushing Greg and Kyle through first while she waited for the rest of the group to catch up.

Suddenly a blood-curling scream, high pitched enough to shatter the eardrums of every Beagle still alive on Earth, but still not enough to wake Barney the Labrador from his slumber, came ringing through the smoking atrium.

"Flumparpmingleporp!"

Greg turned to see Baldybutt, his face weeping a river of crimson blood from a huge tear across his cheek, holding his palm outstretched towards the door, huge slashes of electricity cutting through the air around him in a swirling, wrathful tempest. He smiled, a rancid, evil twisting of facial features that turned him from an adorable ball of fuzzy joy, to a vile demonic sadist that wanted, in his last moments alive, to take something else to the afterlife with him. He fired a blast of electricity from his hand towards the exit, where Eve was standing.

A scream rose in Greg's throat and he reached back towards the door, trying to pull Eve away, but he was too slow and the lightning arched towards her faster than he could react. Luckily, Gloopy was much faster. The disgusting, perverted, paranoid puffball threw himself in front of Eve like a huge insulating blanket, taking the majority of the energy into himself, then spewing the remainder back at 67TY.

The adorable bastard let out a squeak of terror, dropped a little green nugget of poop onto the floor then was instantly vaporised into nothing more than a tiny pile of grey carbon dust. Amongst the blood, screams and chaos, a panel opened in the wall and the little vacuum bot came out to get on with his usual job of cleaning up the remains.

"Gloopy!" Eve cried, kneeling down next to the pile of jelly, who lay twitching and smoking on the ground by her feet. Pieces of him had been splattered across the back wall of the atrium and he had a gaping, charred, blackened hole, that wasn't closing up this time, in the centre of his body.

Frogina came running over with Deebro in her arms and kneeled down next to Eve. Gloopy convulsed twice and a huge glob of his jelly fell away from the main body and melted away faster than ice cream in a crematorium furnace.

"Gloopy. You saved me," Eve said. "I—I don't know what to say. Thank you."

Gloopy's orbs turned towards Eve, the harsh pink light softening into a pale glow that looked upon her with true affection. A tendril shakily rose to stroke Eve gently on the cheek.

"—Love—" Gloopy whispered as the light in his orbs began to fade away.

"Oh my God," Eve said, as watery parade of tears began to run down her cheeks. "Did you just speak?"

"Gloopy—love—Eve."

"Oh Gloopy, thank you," she sniffed.

"Eve—love—Gloopy?"

Then there was an awkward pause. Eve suddenly stopped crying and stole an awkward glance at the rest of the group, who all quickly averted their gaze, not wanting to be sucked into whatever social nightmare this situation was about to turn into.

"Gloopy, I love you—"

Tense silence.

"—As a friend."

There was a collective noise of air being sucked in through clenched teeth.

"A friend! A friend! Are you fucking kidding me?" Gloopy yelled back. "I just saved your life! I'm fucking dying over here and in my last few seconds of life you friendzone me!"

The group suddenly all turned to Gloopy with the same intense, unblinking stare that the Blue Man Group had mastered for situations such as these.

"You can talk?" Eve cried. "What the fuck Gloopy?"

"Of course, I can fucking talk, it takes like two seconds to learn your shitty language! What do you mean as a friend? I took a blast of lightning for you. See, this just proves girls don't want nice guys. They only want assholes like you, Greg."

"Nice guys? NICE GUYS?" Eve screamed. "You eat people! And you're a pervert who hides in bathrooms!"

"Whatever," Gloopy retorted, while coughing up another lump of his insides. "I'm not apologising for anything." He then suddenly moved his tendril away from Eve's cheek and grabbed her on the chest. She screamed, kicked him uselessly where his balls would have been, then backed away with her arms covering her front.

"You absolute fucker!"

"Hey, if I'm going to die, I want one last feel before I go," he sneered back, confirming once and for all, as if it ever needed confirming, how much of a truly awful bastard he really was.

"OK, this ship seems to be falling apart," Greg chimed in. "I vote we leave this dickhead here to blow up while we get the hell out."

"Absolutely," Eve replied. "Bye, asshole!"

Gloopy held up a tendril in the shape of a middle finger as Frogina typed the co-ordinates for somewhere safe on Earth. They huddled together and held each other tightly as the red line of the scanner raced against the chain reaction threatening to vaporise what was left of the Council's spaceship. As they quietly phased away into nothing, in a flash of red light and the same beep as a supermarket check-out, an explosion blasted the turret bot, who had been quietly weeping in the wall about his lack of a soul and sent him careering like a missile into the engine room and straight into the main reactor.

The last thing Gloopy thought about before he was torn into a million pieces, floating in the lonely expanse of space, was how much he wished he had eaten Greg's eyeballs.

# Chapter Twenty-Six

You remember when I said the last thing Greg saw of Scotland was Mrs McTavish's gormless face? Well, that was another little white lie or just another example of lazy writing. You decide.

The group re-emerged, from their final stint in this story as a formless mass of vibrating particles, in the same empty clearing just outside of Struinlanach as their house had been the day before. That's right, dear reader, this entire saga has taken place over less than twenty-four hours. Mondays, am I right? Just ignore the fact this all took place on a Saturday.

Mrs McTavish had been in the same clearing not ten minutes before our group re-appeared, desperately scrabbling around for any evidence that might support her claim that a house had indeed magically disappeared from that very spot the day before.

She was so engrossed in her antics she hadn't even registered the enormous space-battle taking place in the sky above her head. She was just tottering back over the bridge into town to get to the Boatyard, in time for her 11:30 Gin and more Gin, when Greg, Eve, Deebro, Kyle, Frogina and The Blue Man Group re-appeared in that idyllic clearing amongst the broad-leaved trees, that were starting to show the first hints of red and gold as summer drew to a close.

Eve re-materialised sensing the cool breeze and cleansing air of the Scottish Highlands. She saw the purple of the heather on the mountains, heard the bells of the church for Sunday morning service and smelt something that could only be described as a badger's arsehole. She looked to her left to see Greg, who had re-appeared with his arms wrapped around her waist and his pursed lips less than an inch from her face.

"What the hell are you doing?"

Greg opened his eyes. Here's the thing, when you find yourself in a non-corporeal state, whizzing around the universe as information passed through the vibrations of distant particles, you tend to act on instinct. Something in the back of his unconscious mind had suggested, very convincingly, this would be a good idea. Never trust anything your brain tells you during phase travel.

"Oh, uh, shit! Sorry. I thought—never mind."

Eve looked at Greg sternly for a moment, those hazel eyes making a mental image of his embarrassment to save for later, then she laughed.

"Maybe later," she said and threw him a wink.

"Oh, really? Sweet."

"Maybe brush your teeth first."

"Fair."

"And you've had a piece of pasta in your beard for like two days now."

"Jesus! Really? Why didn't you say anything?"

"Because it's hilarious. It's like your little mascot."

Greg sighed and scratched his chin, was unable to find the piece of hitchhiking macaroni and noted it down mentally as one more thing to do when he was physically, mentally and spiritually cleansing himself of this whole ordeal later on. He sat down on the grass, enjoying the cooling feeling between his fingertips, grabbing handfuls of Scottish soil and letting it fall back to the Earth again. He'd never realised how much he liked being able to feel Earth beneath his feet before.

"What now then?" Eve asked.

"I don't know about you guys?" Greg replied. "But I could use a pint."

"Boatyard?" Kyle suggested.

"As long as I'm not serving the drinks," Greg replied. "Also, you guys might want to go and change," he remarked, gesturing at the bruised and battered menagerie of colourful extra-terrestrials strewn about on the grass.

"Shit! That's a good point," Deebro said. "None of us have any bio suits and our printer is on the ship. We'll have to go back to Vegas to get it."

At the mention of the word Vegas, however, the Blue Man Group suddenly became very squirrely, putting another one of their unique three-man massage trains on hold to jump up and beat their bongos frantically and hop around like three alcoholics who really desperately need to use the bathroom.

"What are they saying, Frogina?" Greg asked.

"They're saying, they're never going back to that awful place," Frogina replied. "Donnaht will be looking for them and they can't risk it. They say they want to go home."

"Where is home for them? Mars?"

"It was, but they can't go there anymore. This whole Galaxy will be under control of the Bhutts now. They'll have to go far away. They won't say anything more than that."

"Ask them if there's anything we can do to help?"

Frogina relayed the message and the three blue fellas suddenly stopped hopping and turned to look at Kyle. One of them walked over to where Kyle was sitting, squatted down in front of him and stared at him with his huge white eyes.

"What is it, bud?" Kyle asked.

The blue man reached out and gently took Kyle's hand in his own and let him over to where Frogina was sitting. When he stood in front of Frogina, he reached out his hand and Frogina, knowing what he wanted without having to ask, passed him Criss Angel's personal phase transporter. The Blue Man typed in some co-ordinates then proceeded to scan himself and his two friends.

"I thought that thing couldn't send them far enough away?" Eve said.

"I believe that's where you come in, Kyle," Frogina replied with a knowing smile, while a few thousand tears rolled down the collective cheeks of the colony, which unfortunately pooled in the feet and almost flooded a local Furmbog community centre. "You can boost the signal enough to send them far away, to where the cartel won't be able to find them."

The Blue Men looked down at Kyle and nodded, passing him the transporter and standing in a circle around him, holding hands. They looked around the group, smiling warmly at all of them in turn, men of few words that somehow always knew exactly the right thing to say, before landing on Greg and flipping him the middle finger with a wink.

"Bye, you blue weirdos." Eve laughed, wiping away a few tears of her own. "We'll miss you."

"Thanks for your—help—I guess," Greg mused, before whispering to Eve. "Why are they here, Eve? You never explained that bit."

"Comic relief mostly."

The Blue Man Group nodded at Kyle and waved one last tearful goodbye, as Kyle sent a surge of electricity through the transporter, powerful enough to cause rolling blackouts across most of the Scottish Highlands (seeing as there's only about thirty houses, that's not much of an achievement), boosting the signal a million times over and blasting the Blue Man group across to the other side of the universe with a flash of red light and that now so familiar beep.

249

"All right. Pub now, then Vegas?" Kyle suggested, as he lay panting on the ground. It takes it out of you sending three Martians across the universe. "I also need to go find Melissa as well. She's probably wondering why there's a space battle going on over her planet."

"Is it weird that I almost forgot about that?" Greg asked.

"What, the space battle or the fact I have a fiancé?"

"Both, I guess."

"We can discuss your drug-addled short-term memory later," Deebro cut in. "Let's just get out of here."

"OK, let me just plug in the co-ordinates and—Guys? You might want to check that out."

Eve, Greg and the rest of the group looked at Kyle, who was looking directly up into the sky with the expression on his face of someone who's just stepped in dog shit wearing a brand-new pair of white trainers. They slowly turned their heads to the sky and immediately understood why.

Floating in the upper atmosphere like the universe's most horrifying pop-up ad, was one of the monstrous T-shaped golden spaceships, the gleaming hull reflecting the sun's rays like a mirror and severely fucking up the world's weather patterns on multiple continents. That wasn't the worst part, however, nor were the thousands of pieces of space debris from the previous battle that were hurtling towards the Earth like a shower of meteorites and not quite completely burning up in the atmosphere on re-entry.

No, the worst part was that the front of the ship seemed to be made up of several mile-long screens, which were broadcasting the horrible, flappy, jowled orange, leathery visage of one Donald Trump, otherwise known as Donnaht the Bhutt, leader of the Earth branch of The Intergalactic Bhutt Cartel and all-around total bastard.

Say it with me now.

"Shitballs!"

"So, people of Earth. Thanks to my great leadership, like honestly probably the best leadership of all time. We have destroyed the alien menace that threatened our society and our way of life as freedom loving Americans. You should have seen them, these men. These strong men. These were physically young, strong men. They looked like prime-time soldiers. They were bringing guns. They were bringing crime. They are rapists, but I got rid of them. Unlike the Democrats, who would have let them all in and given them all jobs and let them rape your wives."

"I'm not sure I like where this is going."

"And so, because I'm the most successful person ever to run for the presidency, by far. Nobody's ever been more successful than me. I'm the most successful person ever to run. Ross Perot isn't successful like me. Romney—I have a Gucci store that's worth more than Romney.

My poll numbers are far higher than any other candidate as well. I would bet, if you took a poll in the FBI, I would win that poll by more than anybody's won a poll. That's even despite all the negative press I get from the fake news, covfefe. Plus, I'm more powerful than any other President. My twitter alone is so powerful I can make my enemies tell the truth. Isn't that right, Chip?

"Sigh—Yes, sir."

"—Where was I again?"

"You were announcing your takeover of Planet Earth, sir."

"That's right. Because I'm the best leader, I will be taking over the whole planet. For more than two terms as well, we'll probably go for twenty, twenty-five terms, it's going to be great. People would vote for me to rule the planet, especially the poorly educated, I love the poorly educated. Why? Maybe because I'm so good looking. I've become this powerful and successful despite my difficult background. It wasn't always easy for me, I started off with a small loan from my father of only sixty-million dollars."

"I believe the official line is only a million dollars, sir."

"That's what I said, Chip. I started out with a small loan of only a million dollars. I was disadvantaged. If I was starting out today, I would choose to be a well-educated black, because I do believe they have an actual advantage. But even though I'm white, I've become so popular and the best President ever, because my IQ is one of the highest and you all know it. Please don't feel stupid or insecure, losers and haters, it's not your fault."

"Anyway, because there's this thing. Article Two, you probably haven't heard of it, Article Two of the US constitution, because no one talks about it. They don't talk about how Article Two lets me do whatever I want and what I want right now is to take over Earth. So, that's what's happening. It is what it is.

The Democrats are always trying to take over Earth and impose their views on us and it's terrible, it's terrible that they do that. But that's what I'm doing now and it's great, it's going to be great. We're going to do great things. But there are going to be some changes, because if this planet gets any kinder or gentler then it's going to cease to exist. I want people to treat me with respect now, not like those losers at SNL. So, I'm going to open up our libel laws so when they write purposely negative and horrible and false articles, we can sue them and win lots of money.

I want it to be like North Korea. Kim Jong-Un speaks and his people sit up at attention. I want my people to do the same. Because I'm a war hero now, unlike John McCain. He's not a war hero. He's a war hero—he's a war hero 'cause he was captured. I Like people that weren't captured, OK and I was never captured, so that makes me a war hero, doesn't it, Chip?"

"Ugh—For the love of—Yes—Sir."

"The other thing we will do is build a great wall and nobody builds better walls than me. Believe me, I'll build them very inexpensively. I will build a great, great wall around our planet and I will make the aliens pay for that wall, mark my words. And we will stop all the other aliens coming here.

Earth will only be for the humans and the Bhutts from now on. We're going to get rid of the aliens and it's going to happen within one hour of when I take over the planet, going to bring them back where they came from. We have too many aliens from shithole planets coming here. But that stops now because Trump is in charge. The show is Donald Trump and its sold-out performances everywhere."

I don't think once was quite enough, do you?

"Shitballs!"

"One more thing. If any of you see any of these people—"

"Oh, this can't be good," Kyle gulped. Which turned out to be an appropriate reaction as pictures of Greg, Eve, Kyle, Deebro and Frogina suddenly flashed up on the screens. Their mug shots, taken right after their arrest in the Mirage, thousands of feet wide, hung in the sky for the whole world to see.

"If you see any of them you must report them immediately. They're bad people, very bad. I've never met them, never heard of them, but they're bad, I've always said they're very bad people and they need to be caught and brought to justice. Anyway, I'm off to eat thirty Big Macs and drink eight gallons of Diet Coke and tweet all of this nonsense all over again. Please direct all questions to my new press secretary, Chip Kroker. Goodnight and God bless the United States of Trump."

And with that, mercifully, the gigantic, tangerine toadface vanished from the screens, leaving only a slightly less nightmarish golden monstrosity floating in the upper atmosphere, blocking out sun in the Amazon and reflecting devastating beams of UV towards the poles. If global warming really was a conspiracy created by the Chinese to make US manufacturing non-competitive, it certainly wasn't anymore. The group looked down from the horrifying harbinger of things to come hovering above them and looked at each other with expressions of utter desperation and defeat.

"That was not how I was hoping this adventure would end," Eve sighed, leaning over and resting her head on Greg's shoulder.

Greg smiled and suddenly thought it hadn't played out too badly.

"Greg," she said, "I know I say this as a joke all the time, but I don't want to live on this planet anymore."

Greg gestured to Frogina, who tossed him the personal phase-transporter. Greg weighed the simple slab of black plastic in his hand, considering the infinite universe of possibilities that was now, literally, at their fingertips.

"Well," he replied, "at least now we have some options."